PRAISE FOR
DOUGLAS A. VAN BELLE

"Rollicking high adventure in a scientifically plausible way!
With Van Belle's sure hand on the tiller, the clouds of Venus
are alive with excitement."

—ROBERT J. SAWYER, HUGO AWARD-WINNING
AUTHOR OF *THE OPPENHEIMER ALTERNATIVE*

A WORLD ADRIFT

A WORLD ADRIFT

DOUGLAS A. VAN BELLE

"Other than Earth itself, the most habitable place in the solar system lies fifty-five kilometers above the surface of Venus. At that altitude, the temperature, atmospheric pressure, and gravity are all earthlike.

And it would be easy to colonize. The atmosphere is so dense that breathable air acts as a lifting gas, turning every habitable space into an airship."

—DR. GEOFFREY A. LANDIS,
NASA, EARTH, CIRCA AD 2000

PRELUDE

A z wasn't sure if she wanted to survive the day.

It wasn't that she didn't care if she lived or died. She had embraced that indifference so long ago that she could scarcely remember what it was like to fear death. Something about that moment felt different, dangerous.

Ironically, a cavalier disregard for mortal peril was often the thing that kept you alive. When combined with a healthy survival instinct, the headlong rush at danger unleashed a plethora of physiological responses that often made the difference. Adrenaline and a whole host of other stress hormones boosted strength, reduced reaction times, and dulled pain. That gave you an edge, and the greater your willingness to risk losing your life, the sharper that edge became.

That was what made the fog of indifference so dangerous. As she stood there in the helm of the ridiculously but also appropriately named Drunken Monkey, she felt soft and dull. There was no simmering tension in her gut. There was no fury desperate to be unleashed. There was just a vague heaviness and a whisper of doubt asking if she wanted the life waiting on the other side of the gauntlet.

"There we go. I think that's the last one," Flint said, his face buried in one of the viewers at his odd hybrid of a navigation and rigging station.

"It's about time," Em grumbled.

"The regatta is always delayed by a straggler or two," Flint said. "Rich people like making other people wait for them."

Flint and Em were an odd pair. Flint seemed to exist in a moment just a few minutes clear of a long but fitful sleep. Indefinably not young, tall, heavy and soft, but not fat, his hair was untamable, and his entire person always looked just a bit ruffled. He exuded an unhurried, weary but pleasant calmness and his very presence was comforting. Em was pretty much his exact opposite. Young, short, lean, excitable, energetic, and abrasive, her accent and patterns of speech turned everything she said, no matter how innocuous or kind, into an accusation or a critique.

"Flint, I need more float," Em said. "I'm running out of the upward glide I need to hold this position relative to Lightcastle."

"There is no more float, Em," Flint said. "The lift cells in the wings are full, external floats are fully inflated, and we're going to need every bit of ballast we have for later. Unless you want to start dumping passengers, this is as floaty as we're going to get."

Em grumped and the Drunken Monkey shifted as she worked the flight controls.

"If that isn't the last yacht, we can porpoise a bit to hold station," Flint said. "I think we have enough nitrogen in the tanks for a few extra little dumps and refills."

The question was on Az's lips. She was forming the first word when she recognized that curiosity for what it was. She didn't need to know if porpoise was slang for a technical term that she already knew. It didn't matter if it was something that a junk runner did that military ships and larger transports did not. Her desire to know was nothing more than a distraction. It was her mind's way of distancing itself from the question of whether or not she wanted to live through the day.

There was too much activity around her, too much going on in her head. The edge was immediate. It was in the now, and if Az was going to find it, she needed to dig down to the essence of the moment.

Az initiated the process, taking a deep, slow breath. It took a second and then a third breath to calm the daemons in her head, and then a fourth to engage the process. She was out of practice. She hadn't needed to use the technique for ages.

The back-and-forth between Flint and Em continued, but the process diverted it. Now their words washed over her, leaving her untouched. The sounds of the ship, the humming of the air system, the creaks and groans of its structure responding to stresses; all those noises followed the voices, slipped past Az, and flowed into nothing. As the silence in her head grew, she pushed the sensations from the ship's movement away, leaving her instincts to handle the small shifts and shudders on their own. The ship went next. The helm stations, the well-worn levers, dials, and controls; it all slipped away. Even the deck beneath her feet faded as her vision drifted farther and farther into the distance. She edited out the window frames and all the rest of the structure that held the expansive array of windows of the helm in place, and with that she was alone, floating in the Drift.

She kept cutting away and discarding everything that was not part of her moment. She removed the impossibly distant. In her moment there were no stories of Earth. It did not matter if there was or was not a place with land, solid and unmoving under an endless sky. None of that history or myth was part of the now. The universe of her moment was entirely within the clear layer of the Venusian atmosphere that they called the Drift. All of her, everything was bounded by the thin, wispy white clouds above and the soupy yellow haze of the Deep, far below. She knew that the Drift was both bounded and infinite, it wrapped around the world to leave no edges. She dismissed all that knowledge. Those distant parts of the Drift only existed as the thought of a future journey or the memory of travels echoing from the past. Everything beyond what she could see was outside of her moment.

Having found the space of her moment, she focused on the moment. She started again with the stories of Earth and from there, cut away more and more of the past. It was easy now. She had found her place in the process. She had become the process. She pushed away the future. She shed plans, expectations, possibilities, and promises, letting them follow everything else into the nothing. That left only the now. The universe was nothing but the moment. A moment held no hopes or desires. It had no momentum or course. It simply was. She let the moment fill her until she possessed it in its entirety, and then she began rebuilding.

The city of Lightcastle dominated her moment. Like most of the habitats and other structures of the Drift, it was a wing-shaped airship, but its enormity was almost impossible to comprehend. It was at least twenty kilometers from end to end. Even when she focused on the dozens of high-rise buildings that were built up and through the transparent plastic skin that formed the top of the wing, her mind struggled to grasp the scale of the structure. From any vantage point distant enough to see the whole of the city, those towers looked tiny to the point of insignificance.

The city was surrounded by dozens of similar but smaller floating structures, some a mere twenty kilometers away. Towns, estates, farms, shipyards, industrial centers and all the rest, they all drifted along at the altitude where the pressure and temperature of the atmosphere offered an almost perfect match to the needs of the human animal. The wing and keel shape of all those nearby floating structures wasn't the only kind of habitat in the Drift. Breathable air was far lighter than the carbon dioxide that dominated the Venusian atmosphere, so any voluminous shape could work, but most of the structures that people had built over the centuries had converged on the wing and keel that was ideal for exploiting the physics of the Drift.

Altitude-driven differentials in wind speed, temperature, and pressure were extreme on Venus. At the surface, the atmosphere was all but stationary, hellishly hot, and under so much pressure that it was nearly a liquid, but at fifty-five kilometers, the hospitably thin and cool Drift circled the planet every few days. The gradient in wind speeds was so steep that it created exploitable differences across just a few hundred meters of altitude. It didn't take much for the keels of the wing-shaped cities, towns, and estates to descend far enough beneath the structures to drag big turbine arrays through slower, thicker air below. Those turbines not only extracted energy, they created the drag that slowed the habitats just enough to sustain a gentle but steady flow of the Drift over their aero structures. That airflow made it easy to control both their exact altitude and their positions relative to one another.

A flickering light caught Az's eye and she briefly slipped into thoughts about the signal arrays that transferred messages between those floating habitats. Seizing control of the signal nodes and telephone switching centers was a critical mission objective, but that was someone else's responsibility. It was their worry, not hers, and it would happen even if she failed. Her only worry in that moment was to get her girls, the most experienced of Kofi's Blades, into the city. The 213 women she was smuggling in on the Drunken Monkey had criminal convictions or were known in ways that made it too much of a risk to bring them in through the normal landing and customs system.

Az shifted her attention to the last yacht to leave the docks. As it unfurled its kite, she refocused her thoughts on the simple physics of the Drift to help her push the distraction of the signal lights aside.

Ships exploited the altitude-driven variations in wind speed to cut the Drift. They floated kites up into thinner, faster air above. Those big wing chutes were highly maneuverable and could pull at surprisingly sharp angles across the Drift, but their primary purpose was to provide pull down the Drift. The chutes the ships dropped into the deeper, slower air below were called plows. They were simpler and far less maneuverable. Their pull up the Drift was meant to serve primarily as an anchor so that the ship could act as the kite. Different angles of updrift or downdrift pull, combined with using the wings and fins on the bodies of the ships to create resistance to those pulls, could move a ship in any direction, sometimes quite fast. When momentum, glide, and buoyancy were added to the mix, ships could cut the Drift in remarkably complex ways.

"That is definitely the last yacht," Flint said. "Thirty seconds, Em."

Flint's words invaded Az's moment. The tiny part of her awareness that she had tasked to monitoring things beyond the moment had latched onto the words and demanded she notice them.

"Ladies and ... Flint." Hearing Em's voice both directly and through the intercom broke the sense of space around Az, pulling her mind back into the ship. Az fought it. It was too soon. Her moment was not yet complete.

"We're about to commence our approach to Lightcastle." Em spoke drolly, like the captain of a big liner or ferry. "Our docking plan is insane and we're probably going to die, so please buckle up. And for god's sake make sure nothing is rattling around loose back there. Thank you for choosing the Drunken Monkey. We do hope that the next time you want to try something ridiculously stupid, you'll think of us."

"Em ..." Flint grumbled.

"You really do want to buckle up," Em said, loudly, pointedly directing the words at Az.

Az nodded, but that nod as well as her step toward the half-disassembled rigger's station were automatic. She had not yet fully reintegrated her moment into the world around her.

"No, don't even think it!" Em snarled. "I need Kegley in that station."

That brought Az all the way back. She pulled her hands away from the buckles holding the beer keg in the rigger's seat. Her meditative sojourn was over. She had failed to fully embody the moment, but even in that failure, the effort had accomplished much of what she needed. The heaviness and sense of dullness were gone. There was still no hint of the edge she had sought, but she felt solid. She had found a better balance between momentum and intent as the moment carried her forward.

"Em ..." Flint said, soothingly. "Az is a passenger, and we play nice with passengers? Remember?"

"And Commonwealth regulations state that only crew members can occupy a helm station during docking, launching, or other close quarters maneuvers," Em spat back at him. "Kegley's crew; she's not."

"You're quoting Commonwealth regulations?" Az added a hint of menace with her tone, posture, and expression. "That's insane."

"Which is exactly why you hired us, right?" Flint asked. "You wanted the craziest pilot in the Drift."

"Insanely good," Az clarified, emphasizing the word "good." She was happy to leave the task of managing Em to Flint, but she also needed her authority to remain unchallenged. "So, this crazy little pilot of yours had better pull this off."

"Theoretically, Em's idea might work," Flint said.

"Theoretically?"

"Yeah, and you need to get your ass strapped into a seat." Flint gestured at the fold-down jump seats at the back of the helm. "As soon as that last yacht joins the others ..."

Em didn't give Az the chance to reach the jump seat. Despite the result of that action, Az knew that there probably wasn't any intention behind it. Em wasn't nasty, or vindictive, or even petty. She was the kind of person whose overly intense focus left her unaware of how her words and actions inflicted a toll upon those suffering the misfortune of sharing her moments. Az understood that. She knew the reason Em acted just then was because the countdown in her head had hit zero. Pulling the pair of red-handled emergency levers had nothing at all to do with Az. It was simply the next step in the intricate dance that Em had choreographed into the countless variations she had imagined for pulling off her insane maneuver.

In the long run, that understanding of Em would probably be the factor that led Az to decide against murdering the woman, but in that moment, it did nothing to make Em's actions any less infuriating.

"Dumping lift," Em said as the ship dropped out from under Az's feet.

The Drunken Monkey plummeted. That didn't quite leave Az weightless. Regardless of how heavy the ship might be, there was still a great deal of atmospheric friction on its hull as it fell. Logically that meant Az must have been falling just a touch faster than the ship, and therefore she should have had some sensation of weight, but as was often the case, reality had a habit of turning logic into a fickle bitch.

A desperate attempt to grab the jump seat spun her around as the floor dropped away. She covered her head and twisted just enough to avoid snapping her neck as she smashed into one of the big, thick plastic windows that made up most of the helm's ceiling and walls, but she still hit hard. Her shoulder and back slammed into the frame holding one of those windows in place, but before she could even wonder if any serious injury went with that flash of pain, another maneuver sent her flying in a different direction.

Em rolled the Drunken Monkey to starboard and pushed the nose even farther down, sending Az tumbling up to the ceiling and toward the stern.

The most apt, and perhaps the crudest, description of a junk runner was that it looked like a monstrous croissant with a sausage shoved up its ass. There were countless variations on the architecture that gave the little cargo ships their basic shape, but they all embodied the same utilitarian need to balance maneuverability and cargo capacity. They had to be nimble enough to manage all the unassisted landings on the makeshift docks they so often had to use, but that maneuverability was only useful in how it served the fundamental purpose of carrying cargo. The result of those conflicting necessities was an unusually robust structural core that was built to handle the stresses from difficult, frequent, and often rough landings, paired with thick, blunt wings designed to maximize the internal space available for cargo and gas cells. The thick, curved beams and the web of reinforcing cables that formed the structural core of the ship also defined its interior. The lower two-thirds of the sausage-shaped core housed all the engineering elements of the ship. That core extended beyond the trailing edge of the wing to form the aft control room and projected forward past the leading edge to form the helm. The top third or so of that core formed the arched corridor that served as the main deck.

The floor of the helm was down a half deck from the floor of the main deck, and in most junk runners there was a bulkhead between the helm and the main cabin. However, on the Drunken Monkey, the helm was open to the main deck, probably to make the ship easier for Flint and Em to fly it with just two crewmembers instead of the usual three or four. Whatever the reason, that open design meant that there was nothing but a railing and the difference in floor height separating the helm and the main deck. So, when Az tumbled along the ceiling and toward the stern, she was thrown over the railing and into the main cabin.

There was nothing more disorientating than the loss of down, and despite decades of intense physical training and all her experience implementing that training, Az was completely lost as she tumbled. Every little course correction had an outsized effect, tossing her around like a ragdoll. A nudge to the left threw her into the starboard wall. A twisting nudge to the right smashed her against the floor of the main deck and then the port wall. A hard nudge into a slightly inverted dive flipped her back to the ceiling, slamming her into the arched beams and reinforcing cables. The reinforcing cables offered plenty of handholds, but by the time she reacted enough to grab one, another movement of the ship had sent her spinning off into something else. Collision after collision, it was all a blur of black, grey, and bright blue. In the end, it was the bright blue that rescued her.

That bright blue was Kofi blue, the base color for the flag and uniforms of the Noble House of Kofi, which was the color that she and the rest of Colonel Kofi's Blades wore. The Blades almost always operated covertly, so they usually only wore the color as a decorative accent, but for this mission, they were decked out in the full kit; Kofi blue from their bootlaces to the ribbons holding back their hair. The short-skirted frock that Colonel Kofi made them wear over the skintight elastic bodysuits was a somewhat bizarre nod toward feminine modesty, but the cross-woven silky fabric did increase the cut resistance of the uniform and it didn't hamper the fight. And in that moment, it was a godsend.

Dodi, one of the Blades strapped into a jump seat in the main cabin, managed to grab Az's skirt. She held on just long enough for the Blade seated next to her to grab an ankle. A flurry of grabbing, failed grips, and more grabbing followed as the young women pulled Az into their laps. They held her for the additional moment it took for their commander to reclaim control. Az grabbed the harness that held one of her rescuers in her jump seat and with that the two women could visualize her next move. Shifting their grips, they pushed, pulled, and helped her shift around to get both hands on the jump seat and her feet on the deck.

The interior of the Drunken Monkey was designed for working and living with the sometimes-extreme tilts and random buffeting that a small ship endured while cutting the Drift. Handholds and railings everywhere. Even with Em subjecting them to a wild, twisting and turning plummet, those handholds made it relatively easy for Az to work her way back to the helm. She reached the railing just as they were about to pass through the fleet of yachts gathering for the start of the regatta, and she couldn't help but gasp. The yachts were right in front of them, bunched tightly, and they were plummeting toward them at a rate that Az struggled to comprehend.

"Em?" Flint shouted.

Em spun the Drunken Monkey to keep its port wing from cutting through the middle of one of the brightly painted, dragonfly-shaped yachts. In doing that, the crazy little pilot swung the helm around so close to one of the yachts that Az could see the terrified expression on the face of its rigger.

"Oh, relax you big baby." Em huffed. "It's the plows they're dropping that are the real worry. They don't paint them all gaudy and easy to spot like the yachts."

"Great," Az muttered.

Az considered hopping to the floor of the helm but decided that discretion was the better part of valor and proceeded carefully instead. Taking care to keep a secure handhold at all times, she climbed down the ladder.

"Hold on," Em called out.

For a moment Az was thankful that she had decided to be cautious. She had both feet on the last step down to the helm and both hands locked firmly on the ladder's railing when Em started to pull them out of their dive. Unfortunately, that caution didn't do her a damn bit of good. Despite being a stubby and bloated little ship, a junk runner's wings were designed to maximize the stall when a pilot pulled the nose up to stick a tight landing. The tips of its wings curved downward to cup the air when the angle of attack was raised, and when that was combined with the thickness of the atmosphere below the Drift, it turned the force generated by Em's pull out of the dive into something incredible. The ship groaned mightily, and Az's knees buckled. She managed to get an arm between her head and the deck, and that was probably the only thing that kept her conscious. The impact sent a flash across her vision and left points of light, swirling and dancing in front of her eyes.

A succession of quick course corrections rolled her around and left her lying on her back, staring up at Em as the pilot settled the ship into a straight, fast, and level glide under the city.

"And that was the easy part." Em grinned at Az, her eyes burning with the exact same fire that Az was used to seeing in the eyes of a Blade who was on her edge.

"Dammit Em, why do you always have to play games like that?" Flint loosened the harness holding him in his seat. That gave him the slack he needed to get his face against one of the viewers to start taking navigation readings.

"We needed to make sure they think that we're just some jackass show-off buzzing the regatta fleet. Then they'll assume we used this momentum to bugger off." Em sounded like a mischievous girl trying to sound innocent.

"Sure, I believe that," Flint muttered. "We're pretty close to course; fade to starboard, just a degree or two."

Az sat up, paused, and then paused again on one knee before she stood.

"Sorry about that," Flint said to Az, sincere.

Az accepted the apology with a shrug and a nod. She was bruised, but her head was clear, and she had avoided any serious injury that might impair her ability to fight. If anything, Em's stunt had helped. The crazy pilot had pushed Az out to her edge. Now all Az needed to do was to hold onto that edge and keep it simmering so she could bring it to a boil when she needed it.

CHAPTER 1

Officially, it was called the Lightcastle Yacht Club's Annual Cotillion. Everyone knew that, but that didn't stop people from calling it the regatta. In some ways that was fitting since it was the race that had turned the event into a holiday that was treasured by everyone in the Commonwealth. However, Willamette Lolofi also thought it was a shame that the nobles had all but abandoned the proper name of the social event that the yacht club held to celebrate that race. A cotillion was a formal dance characterized by complex but defined patterns of movement involving the frequent exchange of partners. Even though that meaning of the word had been all but lost to history, it was the perfect description of the social event.

For those with the status, legacy, or money it took to secure an invitation to celebrate the regatta on the yacht club grounds, the event truly was something of a cotillion. The glances, smiles, greetings, and conversations were all just steps through the choreography of the most complex and noble of dances. Every single one of the seemingly inconsequential interactions mattered. Who saw you? What did you show them? What did you let them see? Who heard you? What did you let them hear? A smile to one was a threat to another. A nod could seal a deal but add the slightest frown and it became a favor instead of an exchange. The regatta was the catalyst for all of the politics and most of the significant business transactions that would transpire over the coming year. Willamette's mother had been training her daughter in the artistry of that dance from birth, and it truly was an art. Detailed planning and preparation were essential, but the true soul of the cotillion was improvisation. The dance evolved with each step, and there were always surprises. Sometimes those surprises were huge, and when they were, they were usually timed to maximize their effect. A perfect example was her father's sudden and, for almost everyone in attendance, completely unexpected pronouncement.

"Niven?" Lady Susan Lister elbowed her bewildered son as she asked the gentle question. The woman was so excited that she looked like she was about to burst into girlish giggles.

"That's what you were doing all morning," Niven muttered to no one in particular. "Negotiating my betrothal ... to Willamette Lolofi?"

"We were sorting the last few details, yes," Niven's father, Lord Simon Lister, said, grinning.

"Isn't it wonderful?" his mother asked, fidgeting.

"Are you two out of your bloody minds?" Niven all but shouted. Now it was his parents' turn to be stunned, and horrified.

"He means no disrespect!" Lady Susan blurted out, making a pleading gesture at Willamette's parents, Grand Lord Morden Lolofi and the Grand Lady Jillian Lolofi. "Please. Please forgive him. He truly means no disrespect."

Niven realized the enormity of his ill-considered reaction and his stunned surprise gave way to terror. The color drained from his face, his eyes went wide, and his jaw dropped.

Receiving no hint of forgiveness in the icy glares of the grand lord and lady who ruled the Commonwealth, Lady Susan made a pitiful whimpering noise before turning to Willamette. "Grand Lady Willamette, he truly means no offence. He is overwhelmed by the honor."

Niven turned to Willamette, the look of terror giving way to an apologetic look that seemed quite sincere. However, before he could find the words to begin apologizing, she took his attention as her cue. Giving him a slight, smirking smile, she removed her feathered cloak.

Despite the impossible complexity of the social and political ballet that was the Lightcastle Yacht Club's Annual Cotillion, the instant Willamette shed that ornate feathered monstrosity, her steps became simple, and by any civilized measure they were also quite crude. The dress she wore under the cloak was not a bejeweled concoction studded with glass and metal baubles. Nor was there anything about the dress that was meant to symbolize their family's cultural heritage or represent their social status. She was a Lolofi. That name alone was more than enough to elevate her above and beyond any need to assert her power, wealth, or status. Instead, Willamette's dress served one and only one purpose. It advertised the young woman who wore it.

The dress was technically modest. The sleeves stretched to her wrists, the neckline hugged the base of her throat, and the hem brushed the tops of her toes, but that technicality had been twisted inside out by Willamette's magnificent seamstress. Mattie was scarcely older than Willamette, but she was truly an artist, and the dress would surely stand as her first masterpiece. The soft golden-white color of the thin silky fabric brought out the hints of lighter brown in Willamette's hair, accentuated the dark brown of her eyes, and it somehow seemed to add a glow to the color of her skin. The truly remarkable aspect of the dress's design was the way Mattie had combined three slightly different shades of color in the cloth. Those shades had been fit together and layered to subtly enhance the way the dress accentuated the slight but clearly feminine curves of Willamette's petite body. And that was but one out of the thousands of tiny details that served to elevate the dress into the realms of true artistry.

By dramatically revealing the dress from under the cloak, Willamette was also trying to shed all of the distractions of politics and the trappings of nobility that forever threatened to smother her. That touch of performance was meant to leave no doubt that she was no longer a child. She was a woman, an object of desire.

No, correct that, she was Niven's object of desire.

The dress told everyone that it was safe for men, and perhaps a few women, to desire her. In the politics of the Commonwealth, that had its own value, and one thing that she would probably have to do was teach Niven how to use his possession of her as a weapon. She pushed that thought aside. Regardless of how important that might become, at that moment it was secondary. The primary purpose of her dress and this passage through the dance that was the cotillion was to arouse the male animal within her new fiancé. His desire for her as a woman had to be his first and most enduring impression of her, and she wanted it to be overwhelming. Thrusting his lust to possess her all the way down into his soul would make all the rest of what she needed to do so much easier.

It turned out to be quite fortunate that she wanted to overwhelm Niven with desire, because at that moment the animal appeal of woman to man was probably the only thing that could have possibly cut through the tumult she could see churning behind his bright blue eyes. She had no idea why her father had decided to publicly ambush him with the announcement of their betrothal, but he had, and the poor young man's composure was shattered. The reveal of the dress had been meant to stir that chaos further, and judging by the look on his face, it had succeeded admirably. He seemed to have been stripped of his ability to think.

Willamette turned and handed the voluminous feathered cloak to her little servant girl, Ida. Even that simple act was choreographed for maximum effect. Facing slightly away from Niven, she set her feet with one just forward of the other so the slight crouch as she handed the cloak to Ida would accentuate the curves of her buttocks and hip. She pulled her shoulders back, clenched her stomach, turned a little farther, and lifted her chin as she stood to leave no doubt that she was a lean, strong, and graceful woman. Improvising, she took a few extra seconds to unnecessarily remind Ida to take care with the cloak, stretching that pointless conversation to a count of twenty before she glanced back at Niven.

The glance was to ensure that she still had his attention, but she also used it to offer him a smile. It was just enough of a smile to offer forgiveness and an acceptance of the very male reactions she was working so ruthlessly to provoke, but she added a touch of wry resignation to it in order to push him away, ever so slightly. Sustaining the impression that social norms of decorum kept her unobtainable, even if only temporarily, was nearly as important as inviting him to desire her. There was no force in the universe that was more powerful than the craving for something that was withheld.

Willamette understood she had obsessively overthought everything about that moment, but she also knew that she could not risk settling for anything less. As ironic as it might be, provoking

Niven's desire to possess her was the best opportunity she would ever have to take some control over her life. That offended her in countless ways, but it was the unpleasant reality for a woman of her station. As the husband of a Lolofi, Niven would be obligated to support her, and based upon her extensive investigation of the young man, she believed that he was more than smart enough to understand that following her lead was the best way to navigate the formidable challenges they would face, but what she needed was a partner. Enticing his lust may not have been the best way to achieve that end, but she was convinced it was a good place to start.

She clenched her buttocks slightly and shifted her weight onto her toes as she turned and walked away. That stroll toward the edge of the terrace was another passage through the dance that she had practiced, refined, and practiced again. Emphasizing the curve of her waist into her hip was critical. Throughout history and across every documented culture, in every serious discussion and artistic representation of feminine beauty, it was the transition from waist to hip that defined the desirable female body. It was so important that Willamette had not only instructed Mattie to design the entire dress around perfectly defining and accentuating that curve, she had made her seamstress sew her into the dress so the silky fabric would hug her belly and lower back perfectly but relax enough to slither over her hips rather than cling.

Raw, sexual attraction was all about the primal cues that evolution had honed over eons to help men identify a healthy and fertile mate. That made the walk critical. When the female body was set in motion, it was the buttocks that spoke to the deepest sexual instincts of men. They needed to be defined but not prominent, taut but not overly muscular. The movement of her hips as she walked was also where the man who Niven was, mattered. As the second son of an old but small estate, he had never enjoyed the luxury of being the heir to family titles or holdings. He was, first and foremost, a very young yet very successful businessman. He would have no use for a woman who was little more than an expensive trophy to decorate his arm at social events, and he was likely to prefer a partner over a plaything. She hoped that meant he would find the vitality indicated by the strength she demonstrated with her stride to be particularly appealing. Her hips needed to roll slightly, another indicator of sexual maturity and the ability to safely bear children, but she must not let her hips sway.

Swaying hips looked unbalanced, weak, tired, worn. As she walked, she focused on her balance. Balance was another powerful signal. She wanted to glide, not stride. She wanted to make it seem as if her balance was so sublime that she had transcended the need to walk.

Willamette was so focused on channeling years of ballet into that moment of seduction that she almost stepped up to the railing at the edge of the yacht club's expansive terrace. Fortunately, she caught herself. She had never shaken the habit of leaning on things, and, right then, to fall prey to that habit would have destroyed all of her hard work.

With her last step she turned slightly to the side. It was just enough to bring the curve of her bust into her profile. Slight as that might be, it would offer Niven the complete feminine figure. She punctuated that final movement by tucking the heel of one foot against the arch of the other. That stance provided a stable base to ensure that she looked balanced, poised. It also brought her feet together in a way that would further emphasize the youthful, athletic, and sexually desirable curves of her waist, hips, buttocks, and legs.

Relaxing her shoulders without relaxing her posture, she pretended to watch the activity around the automation in the park below. She had no interest in the huge clockwork mechanism or the race that it was tracking. She simply wanted to reassure Niven that she would not be looking back toward him without ample warning. She wanted him to feel like he could stare at her for as long as he wished. She wanted to burn that image of her figure deep into his very concept of who she was.

"So, Niven, what do think of that?" she whispered.

"What do I think of what, my lady?" Niven asked from just a few paces behind her.

It took every iota of self-control that Willamette possessed to hide her surprise. He could not be that ignorant, could he?

"Niven," she scolded him. "What do you think you are doing? Approaching me before I offer a gesture of invitation is horribly improper. It suggests a degree of familiarity that might lead people to think that we are already … acquainted."

"Ah yes, acquainted." Niven nodded thoughtfully, and then shrugged. "Well, perhaps your father should have considered the barbaric ways of the lesser nobles before selling his precious little princess to my father."

"My father did not sell me," Willamette snapped, offended as much by the crassness of the comment as the implication. "We have been betrothed."

"Semantic quibbles." This time a tilt of the head and roll of the eyes accompanied his casual shrug. "A contract was negotiated, and now I appear to own a child bride."

"I am not a child!" Willamette stomped her foot. It felt petulant and childish, but at that moment, she could not help it. "I am a grown woman who …"

Niven gave her a smirk, mischief stirring behind his blue eyes.

"Who appears to have been betrothed to a man who enjoys teasing."

"Indeed, it appears so, Your Highness."

"Please do not call me that," she grumbled, her mind racing. The foolishness of his uninvited approach was not a disaster, but it was certainly not something that she had anticipated. "Even if the Commonwealth was a kingdom, and even if I was a princess in title, 'Your Highness' would be far too formal for a husband to call his wife."

"Then what? It's not as if Grand Lady Willamette is any less formal."

"Perhaps you could select a pet name for me." The suggestion was offhand, a spur-of-the-moment thought meant to buy her a few more seconds to think, but her instincts told her that it could also serve as a segue back into something more comfortable and predictable.

"You, want me, to choose a pet name, for you?" he asked, disbelieving.

"Yes." She lifted her chin and adopted what she hoped was a comically exaggerated regal tone. "I do believe that it is customary for a noble husband to choose a pet name that is technically affectionate but can be uttered with extreme contempt and loathing."

It took Niven a moment to realize that she was teasing him, but when he did, he laughed heartily. His smile was warm and genuine. She could work with that.

"Technically affectionate, contempt and loathing," he said, feigning intense contemplation. "That sounds like a challenge."

"Indeed, it is." She returned his smile. The warmth she felt in it was unbidden, surprising her. She added a hint of impish. "Consider it to be the first of many."

Contrary to the mythology that Morden Lolofi had so generously, if unwittingly, helped construct, Colonel Landon Kofi found no pleasure in cruelty. When employed properly, it had tremendous utility, but it was a means to an end. It was a political tool that was not all that different from bribery, flattery, or the manipulation of the law. Cruelty was cheap, its effect could be powerful to the point of overwhelming, and it was immediate, but it was also quite limited in its utility. The information that was extracted through pain could never be trusted, and even though torture could reshape someone's mind, the risk was tremendous. Cruelty could break a person, crush their ego, shatter their humanity, and sever all the threads that tied their heart to the world, and the person that was rebuilt from that rubble could be incredibly useful. However, no matter how completely subservient that reconstructed person might seem, the memory of cruelty endured for a lifetime. If you left even the tiniest kernel of their soul intact, what you had created was a pathologically obsessed enemy that lurked patiently in the darkest corner of their mind, seething, and growing as it waited to be unleashed.

The fear of cruelty was by far its most useful effect and that was why the mythology that had been ~~largely~~ created by Morden Lolofi's propaganda was such a valuable gift. The fear of cruelty could constrain people in subtle and sustainable ways, integrating the effort to avoid punishments into their habits. But even in that, the actual infliction of cruelty was a risky proposition. An occasional demonstration of suffering reminded people that they should fear punishment. That tended to enhance the way people policed their own actions. However, it was also a risk, because if someone was willing to publicly defy that threat, an uncontrollable cascade of defiance could be created.

The proper use of cruelty also took effort. If all you wanted to do was punish someone or eliminate a problem, simple and mercifully quick was usually the best choice. That was why cruelty was the last thing on Colonel Kofi's mind when he spotted Ida running wildly into the lavish betting parlor that had been set up in the yacht club's main ballroom. His only thought was to finish cleaning up the stupid little girl's mess as quietly and as efficiently as possible. However, as was often the case, reality was utterly indifferent to his wishes. It turned out that there was something very special about Ida.

Servants lived as shadows in the light of those who mattered, but Willamette's pet serving girl was a ghost. Ida wasn't just ignored or dismissed; it was almost as if the nobles were afraid to notice her. Running was usually the first of the natural but improper behaviors that had to be beaten out of a child servant, but everyone in the betting parlor turned a blind eye to the girl sprinting in from the terrace. When Ida crashed into a patron, careened into another, and grabbed the dress of a third as she fell, it caused the facade of obliviousness to waver ever so slightly, but no more than that. A flicker of noble rage flashed across the face of the woman who had suffered the indignity of a stumbling child's unprovoked assault on her bejeweled frock, but that reaction was quickly buried with a backhand across the face of her own serving girl.

Servants wearing Lolofi uniforms were always given a degree of extra tolerance but the reaction to Ida was nothing short of stunning. Kofi couldn't even begin to imagine what might be driving such a concerted and complete effort to pretend they didn't notice such extreme transgressions of decorum. He could, however, imagine a plethora of possible things that harnessing her invisibility would achieve.

Playing the staid servant who was attending to whatever errand had been thrown upon his shoulders, Kofi followed Ida. The proper, stately pace required for his act meant that he reached the door to the Lolofi suite well after it swung shut, which perturbed him. The hall was crowded and there was a slight worry that someone might notice that someone who was not in a Lolofi uniform had a key to their suite. However, as was usually the case, no one noticed the actions of the servant, not even the other servants.

He found Ida in Grand Lady Willamette's dressing room, exactly where he expected. She was still struggling to catch her breath. Between gasps, she was muttering in the way that children often do.

"Do your responsibility all proper first," she said as she carefully hung the feathered cloak. "You're supposed to not get noticed, and Mum always says that doing your job all proper is the best way to not get noticed."

Once Willamette's feathered cloak was hung and covered with its drape, Ida retrieved her lady's travelling cloak and, oddly, checked its pockets before holding it out, frowning and scolding it. "Oh, you are going to stain so easy." A long moment passed, almost as if she was listening to the cloak's reply before she nodded at it. "Yes, you are pretty, but that's the problem. That color will show everything. I should hang you back up."

Hanging the cloak back up, Ida scuttled over to Mattie's big seamstress's trunk, worked the latch, and grunted as she flipped the big heavy lid open. She jumped when it slammed against the floor, but then she returned to her conversation with the cloak. "Don't worry, it's just for a bit. I'll just have to do all those other things first and come back for you. And I should probably wash my hands then too. I have to remember to wash my hands after I do all those other things they're making me do."

Kofi timed his interruption and chose his words carefully, waiting until Ida had removed the first of the two trays of buttons, needles, threads, and such from the top of the trunk.

"You know there was a point where someone should have just told me you were stupid all the way down to those little bones of yours." Kofi's words startled Ida so much that she yelped, but like a good servant, she didn't spill the tray. "Honestly, Ida. Running into the clubhouse like that? How many times were you told to be discreet? They told you what discreet means, didn't they?"

"I wasn't supposed to get noticed, but I had to run," Ida said, panicked, stammering. "They're making me do way too many things all at once. And Lady Willamette would kick up a fuss if I was gone too long. And it was hard to find an excuse to come back here to do all the stuff, but I made it here, and I promise I'll hurry as fast as I can."

"Ida, it's too late for promises and hurrying."

"I know they said there'd be lots of packages for me to move, but maybe I can carry everything down to the basement in one trip."

Being careful not to spill any of the futzy little bits of sewing supplies, Ida set the tray on the floor and removed the second. She was so intent on taking care with the trays that she didn't notice what those trays had been hiding.

"Ida," Kofi said. "Don't scream."

"What?"

"I said, 'Do, not, scream.'"

When she still didn't understand, he drew his big, black-bladed knife and pointed it at the trunk. It was a lousy knife. Laminated graphene didn't hold up, but it was the most intimidating thing that he could easily steal from the kitchen and, like cruelty, it was the appearance rather than the reality that mattered.

Nervously tearing her eyes away from the knife, Ida looked at what was in the trunk, and she almost screamed. She didn't. The volume of tears that erupted and rolled down her face seemed to be beyond the realms of physical possibility, and she collapsed like her bones had crumbled, but she didn't scream.

"Good girl, Ida," Kofi said, contemplating the implications of her reaction. "That's something, I guess."

Ida had known something would be hidden under the trays in Mattie's trunk, but she had been told it would be packages that she would need to carry down to the basement. The last thing she would have expected to find was the closest thing to a friend that she had ever known, bound and gagged, bleeding and struggling to breathe. And for her to be able to stifle the instinct to scream or cry out was impressive, especially for someone so young. Ida was at least two years younger than Kofi had expected.

Mattie had become a liability when she had decided to peek inside one of the packages that she had been coerced into smuggling into the yacht club. A quick flick of a knife across her throat was the obvious solution to that problem, but in the longer term, the things the seamstress knew about the Lolofis were far too valuable to throw away. So instead of killing her, Kofi had stuffed her in the trunk and shoved a small knife between her ribs, in her side, just under her arm. It was the perfect solution. Locking Mattie in the trunk eliminated any concern that she might do something stupid to upset his plans, and the knife set up two obvious possibilities going forward. If the day went as he expected, he could send a doctor for her. Then he'd have what the young woman knew, and the suffering would teach her an important lesson about obedience. And on the off chance that something went wrong, she'd almost certainly die before anyone found her and learned what she knew. What he saw in Ida, however, added an interesting variable to that equation.

"That's not what the stupid little serving girl was expecting to find in that trunk, is it?" Kofi asked Ida.

"The people who made me help … who made me help you, said the trunk would be full of lots and lots of packages for me to take down to the basement," Ida said, surprising Kofi with her realization that he was the one pulling the strings.

"And when were you supposed to take those packages down to the basement for me?" he asked.

"Before the choir finished singing," Ida said.

"Which was two hours ago."

"I couldn't find a good time," Ida protested. "They said to not make people notice me, and Lady Willamette notices if I wander off. She always notices when I wander off, and she makes a fuss, and yells, and everyone would notice that."

"That is a tragic story, and I feel bad for you, but I think the real problem here is that you don't seem to appreciate how important it was for you to do exactly what we told you to do and do it exactly how we told you to do it." Kofi gestured at the trunk with his knife. "Mattie didn't understand that either. She did something we told her not to do, but now she knows that there are always big consequences if you don't follow my instructions."

Kofi could see the light dawn in Ida's eyes. She had been scared, but now she was starting to understand just how much trouble she was in. The terror was raw, and she was just short of hysterical. Unable to decide if she should look at the knife shoved in her friend or the knife in Kofi's hand, her head whipped back and forth, but again, she managed to keep it all together.

"Please don't hurt me," Ida pleaded.

"Don't hurt you?" Kofi pretended he was puzzled by that and had to think about it before continuing. "Well, if you lift your chin and hold real still so I can get a nice clean cut on your throat, I can probably make it not hurt too much."

It took Ida a second to understand what he was saying. "You can't kill me. I was helping and trying. I really was."

He played with his knife, teasing her, waiting for the moment when the terror started to overwhelm her before he said, "Okay, the stupid little girl can have a second chance."

Ida sighed in relief and in that moment, she sold her soul to him.

"My people are stretched thinner than I expected, so I could have some use for a girl who can stand next to that Willamette bitch without being noticed too much," he said. "But if you disappoint me again, I won't be nice about killing you. I'll make you hurt so bad for so long that you'll beg me to cut your throat. You understand exactly what I mean when I say that?"

Ida nodded.

"Good girl. Now, the first thing you're going to do is reach down in that trunk and pull that knife out of your friend Mattie."

When Ida touched the knife, Mattie flinched, screamed into her gag, and kicked the side of the trunk. Ida yelped and jumped back.

"Go on. Grab hold of the handle and give it a good solid yank," Kofi said, acting as if it was a simple, everyday task. "Knives get kind of stuck when you leave them shoved between someone's ribs like that."

Ida reached in for the knife again and Mattie's eyes went wide. The seamstress shouted against her gag again, shaking her head with tiny, frantic shakes. Ida pulled her hand back. That was disappointing, but not unexpected. If Ida was as young as he suspected, she was at the in-between age where she was old enough to understand the consequences of her actions but too young to have all the compassion beaten out of her by the realities of her place in life.

"What did I say about disappointing me?" Kofi touched Ida's shoulder with the blade of his big black knife, making sure she could see the tip even as she kept her eyes fixed on Mattie.

Ida flinched.

"Too late to worry about my knife," he said, adding a bit of growl. "In fact, this knife isn't going to kill you, it's going to keep you alive." He traced her cheekbone with the tip of the blade. "You see, if you can't do what I need you to do, I'm going to take one of your fingers, and smash the end of it. I'm going crush the bone and everything and turn it into a bloody paste. Just that one finger and just that little bit of it. I'll leave it all smashed and ruined and let it just hurt, and hurt, and hurt for a day, and a night, and then maybe another day. And then, just when you think it can't possibly hurt any worse, I'll burn it a little, and stop, burn it a little, and stop, over and over and over. Can you imagine how much that will hurt?"

Ida nodded.

"No, you can't." He touched her ear with the knife. "No matter what you imagine, it will be far worse, and I'm going to make the hurting last for the rest of your life. After I'm done burning on that smashed bit of your finger, I'll let it sit for another day or two and let it start to rot, which hurts even worse than burning. That's when this knife is going to start keeping you alive. You see, I'll use this knife to cut off the smashed and burnt bit of your finger so it doesn't kill you with rot. Then I'll be nice to you for a day. I'll feed you a nice meal, and let you take a bath, and I'll let you sleep in a big comfortable bed, but that will only be because I want you to remember what it was like before I started hurting you. That will make it even worse when I smash the next part of that finger, then leave it, then burn it, then leave it, and then cut it off. And when that finger's gone, I'll move on to the next, and then the next. And when all your fingers are gone, I'll start on your toes. Then maybe your ears, and nose, and I've got something special I'll do with that middle part of your back that drives you mad when you can't reach an itch. Somewhere in there, I'll have to do your eyes. I'll save your eyes for when I think you've gotten used to me hurting you. Eyes are special and no matter how much I've already hurt you, just knowing I'm going to ruin your eyes will make you scream and cry and beg."

Ida was trembling so fiercely it looked like she was having a seizure.

"And just when you think you have nothing left, I'll start on your girl parts, but by then, they won't be girl parts anymore, will they? I'm going to take so long hurting the rest of you that you'll be grown up into a young woman by the time I start ruining those very, very tender parts of your body." He pushed the tip of the knife against a spot just in front of and above her temple, piercing the skin at the hairline. A tiny cut at that spot would be almost impossible for anyone to see, but it bled like mad, and he waited until he was sure she could feel the blood trickling down her cheek before he said, "Nothing but pain for the rest of a very long life. That is what you get if you don't do exactly what you are told to do and do it exactly like I tell you to do it. Got it?"

Ida nodded, cringing as the movement made the tip of his knife dig deeper into her head.

Kofi pointed into the trunk with his knife. "Then pull that damn knife out of Mattie!"

Gritting her teeth, Ida grabbed the knife that was stuck in the side of her friend's chest. It took two big tugs and some wiggling to get it out. Mattie screamed against the gag, kicking and sobbing, but Ida persisted until she finally pulled the knife free.

"Good," Kofi said. "Now put it back."

"Put it back?" Ida was confused.

"Yes, stab her, but not in the ribs, in the belly." Kofi spoke conversationally, using the shift in tone to keep the little girl off-balance. "That's a good first stabbing lesson. Unless you've got a lot of practice or are big and strong, you never stab people through the ribs. That's kind of what ribs are for, protecting you from stabbing. So, a beginner should always stab someone in the belly."

"I can't stab Mattie," Ida whispered.

"As far as the police will know, you already have." Kofi grinned wickedly as he closed the trap. "Mattie's blood is on your hands, and your dress, and your fingerprints are on that knife."

"But I didn't," Ida cried. "She's my friend and everyone knows I would never, ever hurt anyone."

"And that's another one of those tragic things," Kofi said. "But there's more than enough evidence here to convince everyone that you murdered Mattie. And she's pretty, and she's Lady Willamette's favorite, so that's the kind of murder where they don't just throw you into the Deep. I bet that Lolofi bitch makes them nail your hands to a cross and put you out on the dock, just like in the scary stories. Tell me you stupid little girl; do you want to find out what it feels like to have the acid out in the Drift burn on you until you die?"

Ida shook her head, sending tears and snot flying.

"So maybe you want to see if I can hurt you worse than that?" Kofi asked.

"It's not fair," Ida pleaded.

"No, it's not fair at all, but that doesn't change a damn thing. The only way you get yourself out of this alive and with all your parts still attached to your body is to do exactly what I tell you to, starting with you shoving that knife in Mattie's gut."

With a sudden spasm and a bit of a squeal, Ida all but dove into the trunk as she drove the knife into Mattie's side. It wasn't exactly in the belly, but it was halfway between the seamstress's ribs and hip.

"Good," Kofi said. "Now do it again."

Ida pulled out the knife and stabbed Mattie again.

"Again."

With the third thrust, Ida broke, consumed by a flailing, slashing hysteria.

Kofi was disappointed about losing what Mattie knew, but having a serving girl who could behave oddly without attracting attention was priceless. Regardless of how effective Ida might be at carrying out any of the tasks he might give her, placing her next to Willamette and setting her loose at the right moment should constrain the possibilities for one of the minor but annoying variables that he still had to contend with.

CHAPTER 2

The aft control room of the Drunken Monkey was designed for managing the loading and offloading of cargo. It projected out of the stern, but the windows wrapped all of the way around and into the cargo holds on both sides of the ship. That allowed the person working the ship's cargo winches to also monitor every aspect of moving the cargo around both inside and outside the ship. The view to the rear also covered the helm's blind spot, making it an ideal secondary helm station, so it also had controls that paralleled most of the rigger and navigator controls in the helm.

With his face buried in the viewer, Flint expertly worked the gimbal controls to move the navigation scopes. He brought the three lights on the underside of Lightcastle that he was using as navigational references together into one point of light. The instant they converged he pushed the button to lock the scopes in position, reading off the angles to determine precisely where the Drunken Monkey was in relation to the city above. He didn't need to calculate anything. He had the numbers for the next key point along their tricky, three-dimensional course etched into his mind, and they were on it.

"Can I go yet?" Em pestered him through the intercom.

"Give it thirty more seconds," Flint said, using the press-to-talk button on the microphone instead of just turning it on. Once Em got antsy, exposing her to any extraneous sounds just made things worse, and the last thing he needed was for her to be listening in on every breath, bump, and burp in the aft control room.

Roughly ten seconds early, just as he had expected, Em lifted the ship's nose, and he began dumping ballast to give her lift. He would have rather used the lift cells in the wings. Inflating the bladders with nitrogen to push the heavier carbon dioxide out of those cells was a bit slower than dumping ballast, but it was also a more flexible way to control their buoyancy. The nitrogen could be quickly sucked back out of those bladders or just vented, allowing him to adjust the Drunken Monkey's float quickly in either direction. In contrast getting ballast back on board was an agonizingly slow process. The same compressors that could suck the nitrogen out of the bladders in a couple of minutes had to labor for an hour or more to liquefy enough carbon dioxide to put a noticeable amount of weight in the ballast tanks. Unfortunately, the lift cells were no longer an option. He'd overlooked the impact of atmospheric pressure differentials when he'd helped Em transform her insanity into a plan, and that had caught them out just a bit. With the higher pressure down low in the Drift, it took more of the reserve lifting gas to reinflate the lifting cells. So, after the big dump for their dive through the race fleet, and then the refill to get back to neutral for the glide, they had used pretty much everything in the tanks. That made dumping ballast the only way to add the lift Em needed. Dumping ballast for the next part of their maneuver had always been part of the plan. It was one of the reasons they had limited the number of women they'd let Az bring, but none of that made Flint feel any better about overlooking the effect of the higher pressure and losing the margin of error he'd built into the plan.

"There is nothing in the world worse than the smell of vomit," Az grumped as she stepped out of the air lock connecting the rear control room to the cargo bay. Her conversational tone was a striking contrast to the terse and humorless attitude that Flint had come to expect from the woman. It also didn't fit at all with the latest evolution of her look. The way she had pranced around in her bright blue, stretchy dancing getup had been scary enough. Her every step, turn, and glance looked predatory. Now that she had strapped a dozen narrow-bladed organic crystal knives to her arms, hips, and thighs, she had upped scary straight past frightening and well into terrifying.

"You get used to it." Flint shrugged. "Em, passengers, and vomit are kind of a package deal."

"Flint, dump some ballast, I need more float," Em snarled at him over the intercom. He ignored her.

Az momentarily frowned at the float controls that he was ignoring, but she seemed to decide that it wasn't her concern. "And thank you for the idea of using the cargo bay decon system to clean it all up," she said. "I don't know how we would have gotten it all off the ceiling otherwise."

"No worries," Flint said. "Barf is basically just a chunky version of the atmospheric residue that the system was meant to clear out."

Without having touched any of the ballast controls, Flint leaned in over the control panel, held the microphone button, and spoke to Em over the intercom. "There you go, Em. More float. How's that?"

"Feels right. Well, good enough. Sort of. Might be way off. Yeah, it's way off."

"No worries, Em, I'll adjust." Flint let go of the button and turned away from the microphone. As he did, he spotted a woman in one of the cargo bays putting on one of the disposable deck suits they'd brought with them. Nodding at her, he said, "But that is a worry."

"What?" Az growled, with a hint of suspicion.

Flint flipped the microphone switch over to the cargo bay intercoms. "Uhm, ladies, don't put on the suits until just before you disembark. We've still got a few tough maneuvers in front of us and the last thing you want to do is to get vomit inside a hood or a breather mask."

"That is not a concern," Az said.

"Oh really?" Flint raised a skeptical eyebrow.

"Yes," Az said. "I told them not to vomit again."

Flint wanted to think that Az was joking, but she obviously believed that a simple command could stop every one of the two hundred or so women on the ship from succumbing to motion sickness.

Their passengers were a decidedly unsettling group of women, and that wasn't just because of their outfits and what was starting to look like a fetish for crystalline blue knives. Everything about them was a little off, and since picking them up, Flint had noticed countless little things that were unsettling. The strangest was that they had an incredible ability to synchronize their movements and interactions without exchanging words or gestures. Whether it was at mealtime or moving through the air lock connecting the ship proper to the cargo holds, or even the way they rotated through the toilets in the morning, he had never once seen them get in each other's way. They never had to pause or step to the side for one another, and they never even seemed to need to wait for one another.

"Flint! You gave me too much float!" Em shouted so loud that the intercom speaker buzzed.

Again, without touching any of the float controls, Flint pushed the button and spoke to Em over the intercom. "There. How's that?"

"Better," Em said.

Az gave Flint a frown, rolled her eyes, and shook her head at the intercom. He shrugged, and after she gave the speaker that Em had spoken through a thoroughly disapproving frown, she turned to head up the stairs to the main deck. That turn was the exact opposite of what Flint expected and it caught him off guard. With a slightly panicked lurch, he grabbed Az's arm and said, "No!"

If Flint had been simply watching Az's reaction to being grabbed, he would have thought it was insignificant. It would have appeared to be nothing more than a flinch, but in some ways, her demonstration of self-control made her reaction even more terrifying for him. He could feel the muscles in her arm tense. He could feel the way she rose slightly up onto her toes, ready to strike, and when her eyes locked on his, her cold glare all but screamed murder.

"Sorry." Flint yanked his hand away as if it had been burnt, making an apologetic gesture. "It's just that it's probably best if you stay down here."

"Flint, I'm still too floaty!" Em shouted.

Flint nodded at the intercom speaker. "I have never heard Em get this wound up before. Now, the women that are strapped in upstairs are kind of scared of Em, so I don't worry about them, but you aren't intimidated by her in the slightest, and adding you to her current disposition just doesn't strike me as a good idea."

Az considered that, then nodded and took a half step back into the center of the room. After a moment, she adopted the strange, passive-but-about-to-spring-into-action pose that seemed to be her idea of just standing around.

Flint nervously went back to work, taking navigation sightings and checking them against the course he'd plotted for Em's plan.

"So how exactly does your crazy little pilot intend to extract more vomit from her passengers?" Az asked. Her tone was terse, and her words were clipped, but Flint guessed that she was trying to be conversational.

"There's more to cutting the Drift than just dropping a plow into the slower air below to pull you up the Drift or lofting a kite into the faster air above to pull you down the Drift. You can also trade off altitude and momentum."

"Like turning that dive into this coast up the Drift."

"Exactly, but right now we're turning that dive around backwards. Em's using our buoyancy to push our glide forward. She basically needs to keep our forward momentum up just enough so we can clear the nose of the city." Flint leaned over the control panel, peering up and forward as far as he could. "Trading altitude and speed off against one another is usually not a big deal. We work with all kinds of variations on that all the time, but this is going to be an eye-of-the-needle kind of thing. We need to be barely moving when we just barely clear the nose of the city, but we can't stall out. We need to hold onto just enough momentum and float to carry us far enough up and past the leading edge of the city so the flow of the Drift carries us up and over the dome instead of pushing us into the nose of the city or pushing us back under."

"Why does she have to cut it close?"

"Because she needs to give me a reasonable chance to get a cable hooked on something we can use as an anchor." Flint finally spotted the leading edge of the city. He watched it for just a second to get a feel for how they were going to fly past it.

"An anchor ..." Az considered that before concluding "You're going to use that anchor to turn the ship into a kite. That's how you're going to bring us back over the city and onto the dock without being noticed."

"In terms of maneuvering, it's more like substituting an anchor for the plow rather than turning the ship into a kite, but yeah, the idea is to use that anchor and the eight thousand meters of cable I wound onto the big nose winch to control our drift back over the city. With a little friction on that winch as it unwinds, I should be able to keep more than enough airflow over our wings so Em can maneuver."

Flint pulled the lever to release the small tow kite he'd made and worked the auxiliary rigging winches that he'd set up to control it. He swung it from side to side and up and down, trying to get a better feel for controlling it. It was awkward and twitchy. He let line out of all four control winches so the kite would pull the grappling hook farther off the stern of the ship. That helped. It slowed how fast it darted about in response to the controls, but it was still awkward. He should have set it up with a control stick and a lever for distance. As it was, he wasn't going to want to move it along both the vertical and horizontal axes at the same time, but still, it was functional enough to get the job done.

"Clearing the forward edge of the city in a few seconds," Em said.

Flint flipped the intercom switch over, so the intercom stayed on. "Thanks, Em. Hook's out and flying. Looking for something to snag."

"There." Az pointed. "That light."

The inverted tower that held the light didn't look ideal. Flint had hoped to find a big, thick strut or brace, but from the looks of things, it was the only reasonable target that was going to come into range.

Dropping the tow kite down, he swung it past the tower to make sure he had enough cable out, let another twenty meters or so out, and let it fly way out to the side before bringing it back at the tower.

The cable hit the guy wires that stabilized the tower instead of the tower itself, so even with the extra cable he'd reeled out, he'd left it short. The kite and hook didn't make it all the way around as it wrapped around the tower. The hook still caught on something. He could feel it pull some cable off the winch drum as they flew up and past the nose of the city, but he had no idea how secure it might be.

Cautiously, Flint pulled a lever, giving the winch the tiniest bit of brake. The cable seemed to break free only to catch again, sending the tiniest twitch through the ship.

"Flint! What are you doing?" Em shouted.

"I'm trying to get the damn hook hooked." He worked the winch lever again, this time getting a steady bit of pull before he released the brake to let the cable freewheel off the drum of the winch.

"Damn it, Flint! Stop that! I don't want pull yet."

The Drunken Monkey hit the stall point, losing the airflow over the wings that it needed for controlled flight. They were still rising past the nose of the city, but they were adrift, and it was obvious that they hadn't gained anywhere near enough altitude. A swirl of turbulence buffeted the ship and then another. They slowly spun around until the tip of their starboard wing was pointing straight at the steep, leading edge of the dome. With that, the flow of the Drift over the city took over, first robbing them of the last of their forward momentum and then pushing them back toward the city.

"Uhm, Em, small issue. The wing."

"I see it, Flint. Totally under control." Em didn't sound at all like she believed that.

Perhaps the worst part of their predicament was that even though the crash was unfolding with the agonizingly slow inevitability inherent to the movement of very large things, there was nothing he could do to stop it. He had dumped all the ballast and he had pumped all remaining lifting gas into the lift cells. He couldn't drop the plow to get some pull up the Drift without getting its cables tangled with the anchor's cable. Even if he could get the plow down, with the way they had spun sideways, when it started to pull it would swing them around into the city before it pulled them away. The kite would pull them upward a bit when it popped open, but it would also pull them hard downdrift and into the city instead of away from it.

His mind raced, but there truly was nothing he could do to divert them from what was looking more and more like it was going to be a catastrophic collision. The nose of the city was damn solid. It took a lot of structure to hold the skin of the dome in the blunted curve that formed the leading edge of an airfoil and drifting straight into it with the tip of the wing was the worst possible way to hit. Everything about the wings of a junk runner—all of the bracing, all of the connections to the structural core, all of the cabling and other reinforcement—was designed to handle the stresses from the lift the wings generated and the impacts from heavy landings. The only resistance to hitting the city wingtip first would come from the plastic skin covering the wing. That would be nothing. Hitting the city was going to wipe out the entire starboard side of the Drunken Monkey and if that happened, killing all the women in the starboard cargo bay was only half the worry. It would destroy all the lift cells in that wing, wiping out more than enough lift to send the Drunken Monkey and everyone aboard plummeting into the Deep.

"Uhh, Em, I'd totally love to see some of that undercontrolness before we crash into the city and die," Flint said.

"Crash into the city! Yeah, that'll work!" Em sounded desperately relieved.

"What?"

"Hold on. Dumping lift."

"What?" Flint shouted. "Why in the hell would you dump lift?"

A scant few moments before the starboard wingtip hit the city dome, the gauges for all of the lift cells in the portside wing dropped so fast that the needles clicked when they hit zero. Em must have pulled one of the emergency vent levers a second time.

Dumping the nitrogen from just one wing was an insanely genius move. When the port side of the ship suddenly dropped, the ship rotated around its center of mass, the starboard wing swung up, and they hit the dome with the bottom of the Monkey instead of the wingtip. That shifted the angle of impact, channeling most of it into and through the reinforcements meant to deal with rough landings.

Genius or not, the Drunken Monkey didn't like it. It creaked, groaned, and made a few noises that Flint had never heard before, but it survived the slow, springy impact, and the recoil from flexing all the ship's reinforcing added a little extra bounce to the rebound off the plastic skin of the city. That pushed them up and clear of the city's nose.

"Now I need the pull from that anchor, Flint," Em said.

Flint gently applied the winch brake, gradually adding friction to the unwinding drum. Em used that pull to turn the nose updrift. By the time the momentum from their bounce off the city's leading edge faded to nothing, the pull from the anchor gave her enough air flow over the Monkey's wings to bring the ship's aerodynamics back into play. It was a close thing, but Em managed to use that to raise the heavier port wing and get the ship back to almost flying level. Even before finishing that maneuver, Flint gave Em some more friction on the unwinding cable, which added to the airflow and gave her enough lift from the wings to keep the negatively buoyant ship off the surface of dome.

"Rebalancing the lift," Flint said as he turned valves and worked the pump controls to shift some nitrogen from the starboard lifting cells over to the cells in the port wing.

"Get me back to neutral as soon as you can," Em said.

"Yep, will do," Flint responded, cringing in anticipation of doom as he reengaged the turbines and restarted the compressor system.

In addition to bringing the aerodynamics of the old junk runner back into play, the return of airflow over the ship spun up the turbines under the nose. Spinning up the turbines broughtthe generators back online to recharge the batteries, and it let Flint restart the air sifters that filtered useful gases from the toxic stew that was Venus's atmosphere. Even with a minimum of airflow, it shouldn't take too long to sift out enough nitrogen to get them back to neutral buoyancy. The problem was that putting the load from the sifter's compressor back on the turbines created a buttload of drag and that was on top of drag from the aero lift it took to compensate for their negative buoyancy. He was pretty sure that the thin cable on his improvised anchor system could take that kind of strain, but he had to add it gently and keep it steady.

Flying as close to the dome as they were, turbulence was going to be a hell of a problem. The friction from the thick, heavy air of the Venusian atmosphere flowing over a dome twisted the air into a roiling knotted mess. That turbulence complicated any takeoff or landing, particularly with a leeward dock, but it was a hell of a lot more than a complication for someone stupid or crazy enough to fly in low over the surface of a dome. The turbulence could build into a wave roll from the slightly faster, unhindered air tumbling over the top of the air slowed by friction against the surface. With a dome's surface measured in square kilometers, those rolling crashing waves of air could grow surprisingly large, and they were one of the big reasons why no one ever approached a leeward dock by flying in over the top of a habitat from updrift. In theory, those waves could grow big enough to roll over the top of a ship and crush it against the dome. That was farfetched. They never grew that big, but a small wave roll, or even just one of the bigger twisty kinks of air, could jerk them around hard enough to snap a cable that was already near its limits.

Fingertips on the lever that controlled the winch's brakes, Flint closed his eyes, listening to his ship, feeling his ship, and trying his damnedest to both keep enough pressure on that brake to provide the pull they needed while also keeping turbulence that was buffeting the ship from translating into a sharp tug that might snap the cable. One minute, two, three. The turbines drove the compressors. The compressors fed the air sifters. The air sifters extracted the lighter trace gases from the toxic soup outside. A lot of what they extracted was nitrogen and with the valves on the reserve tanks wide open it was flowing straight through and into the lift cells. Still working the brake on the cable, Flint listened to the distant, muffled, roaring hiss of the nitrogen passing through the system. It seemed like it took forever, but eventually he heard the distinctive shift in the tone of that hiss as the nitrogen finished filling the lift cells and a valve diverted the flow to filling the reserve tanks. With that, he could finally breathe. They were back to neutral, maybe just a touch into floaty.

He eased the brake on the drum winch, locked it in place with just enough drag to give Em the airflow she needed, and stepped over to the controls for the turbine and gas system. Closing the valves connecting the lifting cells to the reserve tanks, he checked the balance between the wings. It wasn't right; they were having problems getting gas into a couple of the cells on the port side, but that was normal for the Monkey, and everything looked good. They had done it.

They were still being jostled about by the turbulence, and that was going to get worse when they got closer to the high-rises that had been built up through the dome. Just to be safe, he decided to shut down the compressors and the sifters. That would reduce their drag further. Unfortunately, it was also something he should have taken a second to think about before he pulled the lever. The instant he disengaged the compressor's clutch, he realized the enormity of his mistake. As counterintuitive as it might seem, the way a cable stretched when it was under strain meant that suddenly cutting the pull was just as bad as suddenly increasing it. The cable never went slack, but the effect was the same. Cutting so much pull so suddenly allowed the cable to spring back toward its unstretched length and that was when the monster that was momentum struck. It was just like getting a running start to yank on something. When the flow over the dome translated that slight pull toward the anchor back into momentum in the opposite direction, it was far, far too much of a shock.

"Flint! What in the hell did you do to my pull?"

Flint worked the winch control, hoping that they had pulled the anchor free rather than snapping the cable, and that it might catch on something else, but he got nothing. He let out cable. Pulled it again. And again. And again. Nothing. "We lost the anchor."

"Flint, we can't do this without the anchor," Em said it as if she thought he needed to be convinced to do something about it.

"And I can't do anything about the fact that we lost it," Flint explained, still working at the winch even though he was sure it was hopeless. "I either broke the cable or the hook pulled free or something."

It was several seconds before Em replied with, "Damn."

For Em, aborting the landing would mean losing her claim to pulling off the craziest thing a pilot had done in ages. Flint understood just how devastating that would be for her. He knew that she would think his worries over the loss of the commission for bringing Az and her women into the city was trivial, but it wasn't. Between the expenses they'd incurred and the loads they hadn't taken while they were busy flying the women all the way in from the very edge of the Commonwealth, aborting the landing would set them back years if it didn't bankrupt them.

"Yeah, damn," Flint said. "We'll have to abort the landing."

"No, you will not abort the landing." Az drew her pistol and pointed it at Flint's head just to make sure he understood just how much she meant it.

"Uhm, Em," Flint stuttered, trying but largely failing to stay calm. "I don't think our passengers are all too keen on aborting the landing."

"Em, you make this work, or he dies." Az spoke loudly to make sure that Em could hear her over the intercom.

Em said nothing.

"I think she's kind of serious on that point, Em." In addition to the unnerving experience of having a gun pointed at his head, Flint's shock was doubled by having failed to imagine that Az might threaten his life. It was doubled yet again by having completely failed to notice that Az was wearing a holster and sidearm.

"Flint, I told you that sneaking these bitches into the city would be more trouble than it was worth."

"Yes, you did, but how about if we save that conversation for when there's a little less gun pointing going on?"

"Fine … but we will have that conversation."

"I look forward to it," Flint said, knowing full well that there wasn't any real hope that he'd make it to that conversation. Without that anchor, they couldn't generate airflow over the ship, and no airflow meant they had no control. Even if Em could somehow avoid all the towers that extended through the dome, even if she could get them in line to hit the clear area waiting for them in the repair yards, without that anchor they had nothing to help them arrest their momentum so they could land on that spot.

<hr>

Willamette thought that the park below the terrace was far more crowded than it should be. Logically, she knew how unlikely that was. It was not as if people could wander in to watch the automation track the race. What they called the park was simply the garden section of the yacht club grounds, and invitations to celebrate the regatta at the yacht club were strictly limited. The same number of invitations had been offered this year as the year before, and the year before that, so there could not be more people on the grounds than was typical. Perhaps it felt crowded because the opening stage of the race had been unusually engaging. That could have encouraged guests and their servants to wander into the park to watch the automation instead of just listening to the commentary on the loudspeakers. Or perhaps the crowding was because she had always before accompanied her parents during their obligatory tour of the park. Without the intimidating presence of her father and his entourage, there was less around her to encourage people to maintain a respectful distance. Or perhaps it was all an illusion created by her struggle to focus on the task at hand.

She blamed Niven.

On one hand, it was a joy to discover that even in his teasing and in his subtle acts of mischief, he seemed to be a genuinely kindhearted man. On the other hand, it was infuriating that he seemed to be bereft of even the most basic understanding of the most mundane tasks and responsibilities of the elite nobility. Worse, his antics made it all but impossible for her to attend to those tasks. Not only did he mix and mingle with the rabble, including servants, he was an absolute master at finding clever ways to amuse, irritate, and distract her. She did enjoy that. She enjoyed it far, far more than she ever would have imagined possible, but it was also extraordinarily frustrating. All the diversions and interruptions he instigated not only unsettled her, they also served to turn what should have been a quick, obligatory tour of the park into a meandering and confused muddle.

Niven gently grasped her elbow and she gasped, startled. His touch was electric, sending a tingle up her arm. She could not fathom that, and that was yet another distraction.

"Little Princess," he said.

"Please do not call me that."

"Hey. You set the rules for a pet name and Little Princess is both technically affectionate and perfect for tossing about a whole heap of contempt and loathing."

"Yes, but it irritates me even when you say it nicely."

"That just means it's even more perfect." He grinned and she could not help but huff and scowl back at his obvious amusement. That made him laugh.

"I insist that you stop laughing this instant."

That was the wrong thing to say. Her demand just made him laugh harder and louder. That drew curious glances from the people around them and brought a flush of warmth to Willamette's face.

"Oh, you are incorrigible," she growled.

"Yes, I am, Little Princess," he said, agreeably. "However, I am also worried that your serving girl might die of desperation if you don't notice her soon."

Willamette followed his glance and saw a terribly distraught Ida attempting to gain her notice. Ida had retrieved the satin travelling cloak, but without a gesture of invitation, she could not approach to present it to Willamette.

Willamette silently cursed herself as she offered the gesture to Ida. How could she have forgotten about the cloak? And how much longer than she had planned had she been displaying her person in nothing but a flagrantly provocative dress? She could scarcely even begin to imagine the complications that would create. At the very least, there was a point where a tease became a taunt and the taste of jealousy turned to bile in the mouths of men.

"Oh, thank you, Ida. You know my mind better than I do." Willamette pivoted to the left as she crouched and offered her arm for Ida to dress her. As she turned, she swept her vision to the edge of the terrace where her parents stood. That turn was meant to give her a look at them without letting anyone see her looking in that direction, but her mother wasn't fooled. Her mother had taught that move to her and as Willamette used it, her mother gave her a brief but icy glare. That would be yet another complication that Willamette would need to manage.

Despite fumbling with the purse she carried for Willamette, which appeared to be far larger than the handbag Willamette had selected that morning, Ida worked quickly and professionally. The change of purse, which also looked oddly overstuffed, was a concern, but as Willamette rose from the crouch she brushed her hand casually across the cloak's hidden pocket and confirmed that the key was there.

"I see you have prepared this cloak exactly as I asked." Willamette gave Ida the smile they shared when the girl helped her lady misbehave. "I do believe I will make very good use of this tonight."

Ida did not return the smile. The girl looked horrible.

"Ida. You have changed your dress. Have you taken ill, or suffered a fall?"

"No, my lady, I, uh, spilled on my dress." Ida was obviously lying. She was sweating, breathless, and pale. She had most certainly taken ill.

"I have been running you ragged. How inconsiderate of me." Willamette smiled and pretended to think a moment before suggesting, "Perhaps you might wish to return to the family suite and rest for a short while."

"No, I have to stay." Ida glanced desperately around and clutched at the purse she carried for Willamette. "I have to stay right with you."

"I do suppose it would be unwise for us to strain my mother's tolerance any further than I already have with this scandalous dress," Willamette said, agreeably. "Please do stay in attendance."

Willamette nodded Ida toward a nearby cluster of servants, but the girl just stood there. Willamette gave her a severe frown and another nod, but still nothing. She finally had to give Ida a shove before she was obeyed, and even then her serving girl was blatantly reluctant to step away. That was not at all like Ida. And the purse was a puzzle. Willamette could not imagine what Ida had decided she needed to add to the money for tips and the handful of other things Willamette had asked her to have ready.

Jillian Lolofi was less concerned with her daughter flaunting her body than she was disappointed in the way Willamette had revealed her reaction to her mother's disapproving scowl. In fact, Jillian approved of what Willamette was trying to accomplish with her wonderfully scandalous dress. The tactical use of her sexuality was a bold move, especially for a girl scarcely old enough to be thought of as a woman, but by hiding the dress until immediately after her betrothal was announced, Willamette had invited the lust of men while twisting the narrative away from the context of inviting the lust of men. There was no doubt her daughter was hoping for as much lust from other men as she could possibly arouse, but she could easily pretend her display was all about girlishly romantic notions of marriage. She was telling the story of a clumsy and childish but sincere effort to ask for the gift of desire from the man who would become her husband. This would give Willamette even more leverage with which to manipulate the lust that her stunt had "incidentally" provoked in others.

"Niven was truly surprised by the betrothal," Morden said.

"Indeed," Jillian agreed, surprised that her husband would use the boy's name. "That was not the reaction of a young man who had secretly won the heart of a woman above his station."

"We can then rule out what Willamette wished us to think, but that just begs the question of why she so transparently schemed to manipulate me into picking him." Despite the wording, Morden was asking his wife to explain.

"Does the why matter?" Jillian answered Morden's non-question with a question. "The only real worry was that she might have been chasing another of her childish notions."

"True," Morden said, agreeably. "I have worried that I let you coddle her too much."

"Ah, yes, dear husband. You just keep telling yourself that I was the one who coddled her." Their marriage was every bit the cold, distant, and formal union that was typical of a political match, but they had still managed to create a partnership out of it. Physical intimacy had vanished when age took the hope of more children from Jillian, and even though sex had never been anything more than a cordial necessity, she did miss it. Still, even without that side of marriage, they had sustained some room for a friendly prod and tease.

"Do we still wish to encourage the rumor that this is all about us indulging a foolish girl swept into the insanity of young love?" her husband asked. It was a sincere question. He had always deferred to his wife's deft touch with the more delicate side of diplomacy.

"Yes," Jillian said. "That story fits with their obvious rapport, and it will make her a far more sympathetic widow."

The idea that the passage of time could be stopped seemed less and less ridiculous the longer Flint stood there with Az's gun pointed at his head. Eons slid glacially by, giving him more than enough time to contemplate every tiny detail of the little weapon. Little was the operative word. Short little darts fired from a short barrel; it wouldn't be very accurate. There was also no room for a combustion chamber, so it had to be a cold gas gun, which wouldn't be very powerful, but those limitations offered small comfort to the man standing at the wrong end of the weapon. There would be more than enough oomph behind the darts to kill. And it was clearly a military weapon, optimized for use in close quarters. It had a big, autoloading clip full of darts and, judging by the numerous nicks, scratches, and other signs of hard use, it had seen more than a little action.

"Uhm, Em ..."

Flint looked at Az. There was no doubt she would pull the trigger, and, despite how slow the seconds seemed to be sliding by, there couldn't be all that many of them left before she did. The drag from the turbines down on the city's keel pulled Lightcastle into the

Drift at slightly under seven kilometers per hour. At that rate, it would only take an hour or so for the Drunken Monkey to drift all the way over the dome, and Flint was guessing that at least half of that was already gone.

"Em ..." Flint said again, pleading.

"Maybe we could drop the plow onto the dome." Em finally broke her silence.

"Yeah, the plow." Flint's reach for the plow controls was so abrupt he was lucky it didn't startle Az into pulling the trigger. Desperately relieved by the mere thought of having an option, he dropped the plow.

"You're going to have to land it on the dome as gently as you can," Em said. "Then you'll need to let out just enough rig to get an angle on the cables so the way the plow slides across the dome gives us steady drag and a consistent pull."

"Uh. Em," Flint said. "Maybe you should have led with the gentle part of that suggestion."

"Oh, son of a bitch, Flint! You dropped it through the dome! Didn't you?"

"No, I'm not that stupid," Flint lied.

"I can see the cable going down through the hole it punched in the dome!"

"Okay, maybe I did drop it through the dome, but on the upside, that'll probably give you all the pull you could possibly want." Flint worked the controls on the plow, surprised when adding some drag to the winches for the cables controlling the plow didn't give him any resistance.

"Give me some of that pull now."

"Uhm, yeah, working on that." Flint carefully worked the plow controls. If he was very gentle there was some pull, but as soon as he tried to get more, that small amount of pull seemed to vanish.

He took all the drag off the winch, gave it a couple of seconds and then tried again. Again, a bit of drag, but it was nothing close to what he would expect for basically having dropped a great big anchor through the dome and into the city.

"Flint, I need that drag!"

"I know!" Flint released the drag on the winch again and tried desperately to just stop and think. It wasn't easy. In addition to the whole gun-to-the-head thing and Em's snarling, they were drifting straight at one of the office towers that projected up through dome. On the good side, the aft control room would be the point of impact, so he wouldn't live long enough to have to listen to Em bitch about how it was all his fault that they crashed into that tower and died.

"Plow went through the dome," he muttered. "That makes sense because the pod would drop nose first and punch through, but it wouldn't come back out that way. The cables would pull it up flat, so the pod would hit the dome flat. The wings on the pod aren't all that big, but surely they're big enough to keep it from pulling back through the dome. As long as I didn't pull it back into the dome too fast …"

Flint looked out at the dome, wondering if he could have been so stupid. The dome was a good four hundred meters above the city streets at its highest point. It was far less than that where he'd dropped the plow through, but it was still a long way down to the streets below.

"If it fell straight through and all the way down to the ground, then I never pulled it far enough back up to get it up to the dome," he muttered as he slammed the winch into full rewind and watched the revolutions count down on the meter.

He didn't dare just let the plow hit the dome at full rewind speed; if it didn't rip through, the impact would probably snap it off the end of the main cable. But he also couldn't afford to spend too much time playing gentle. There was the small matter of the office tower waiting to kill them. They had, at most, another hundred meters to drift before impact.

He slowed the winch, slowed it again, and then it suddenly made a horrific squeal and the ship shuddered. Flint resisted the urge to crank up the power going to the winch motor and instead let go of it entirely and used the brake on the drum instead. The pull suddenly returned, and this time he held on to it. The ship decelerated abruptly, and Az crashed into him from behind, knocking the air from his lungs as she drove his stomach into the edge of the control panel. He managed to hold the drag somewhat steady. The brake squealed, but differently from the motor when it had hit the resistance of the plow hitting the dome. Cringing at the noise and the thought of what it might be doing to the winch, he gradually pulled harder and harder on the lever. The plow cable and winch were designed to transfer a lot of force into the ship and now that they had survived the initial shock they should hold, as long as he didn't push any more sudden or sharp forces through them. Yes, they should hold. He prayed they'd hold. They'd built a lot of momentum.

The brake lever was shuddering and the ship was making horrific noises. Groans and creaks, pops and bangs, things were crashing about and there was a weird subsonic rumble seemingly intent on shaking his teeth loose. The tower was looming, closer and closer, and then it all just stopped.

The noises vanished. The force from Az crushing him against the side of the control panel eased, and she fell back. The tower grew no closer. In fact, they pulled away slightly as the plow cables reclaimed some of the stretch they had surrendered to the strain of arresting their momentum.

"Flint," Em said. "That was unnecessarily dramatic."

"Yeah, but you know me, it's no fun without the drama." Flint gave the winch motor a little power, pulling them away from the tower. "Why don't you swing us starboard so I can get a sighting on the landing spot we arranged?"

CHAPTER 3

Having tidied the mess Ida had created, both by getting everything they had smuggled into the club out of the Lolofi suite, and in making sure no one would prematurely discover the bloody nightmare that had once been Mattie, Kofi was busy helping his team put the packages into the right hands. He had other things he should be doing. There were all kinds of things he should be checking and double-checking, but it all would be for naught if they didn't get every single package distributed, and soon.

Kofi carried one satchel under the tray of nibbles he'd brought from the basement kitchen and a second under his arm. The first was passed to a servant in club attire by handing him the satchel along with the tray of nibbles. The second wasn't quite as easy to hand off.

Kofi spotted the small blue ribbon on the butler's lapel, but he couldn't just hand him the package. The old man was in close attendance to one of the fat, inbred buffoons that had come to typify the devolution of the nobility under generations of Lolofi rule.

Kofi bumped into the butler and dropped the satchel.

"Pardon me," Kofi said, picking up the satchel and handing it to the butler as if the man had dropped it.

The old butler gave Kofi a curt nod of appreciation for the apology and then glanced briefly but nervously at the beefy bodyguard who stood just behind his fat and ugly master.

The yacht club's nearly perfect security measures had been a formidable obstacle for the plan, but security, no matter how robust, was a known factor and like almost any known factor it could be overcome with a plan. The number of personal bodyguards on the grounds, however, was a surprise and a significant worry. He had known that conflicts between the second- and even third-tier noble families had increased dramatically during the years he had been away; however, the yacht club was universally thought of as a safe little playground for the nobles. He had never imagined that their bickering and their occasional indulgence in a bit of violence might drive so many to pay extra servant admission fees just to bring a guard or two to the regatta. With all the extra muscle on the grounds, it wouldn't take too many shaky old butlers fumbling their opportunity away or flighty serving girls losing their nerve to turn everything into a chaotic mess.

Not for the first time that morning, he hoped Az would come through. Not only did he want his first and most experienced Blade at his side, he also wanted the tested and proven Blades she was smuggling into the city. He had full confidence in the skills of the women he had been able to bring in using traditional means of transport, but the reason most of them had clean identities was because they'd never done anything more than train.

Kofi gave the old butler a friendly, reassuring pat on the shoulder and a furtive glance at the ribbon. The nervous servant removed the blue ribbon as he tucked the satchel under his arm and took a deep breath.

Kofi walked off to retrieve more of the satchels. Even though there were already a lot of satchels under the arms of supposedly loyal servants, there were still dozens of the packages waiting downstairs and time was running out.

Phila wasn't at all upset about having to work through the regatta. She would have loved a daylong party, especially after the year she'd had, but the money was too good to turn down. Regatta Day paid triple wages, and just as she had hoped, all the no-shows had gotten her bumped up to a supervisor's desk. That not only gave her a higher wage to triple, it also made it just about certain she'd get a second shift. That one double shift added up to more than a week-and-a-half's wages and it put her into overtime for the rest of the week. With hangovers and a little luck sending a few more extra shifts her way, she could very well end up taking home an extra month's worth of pay. Even back in the days when the only thing she cared about was partying with friends, she would have had a tough time passing that up. Besides, as far as workdays went, Regatta Day was one of the few almost pleasant ones.

It was all juvenile and quite stupid to be honest, but that was also part of the fun and everyone working in the central telephone exchange played along, even the supervisors. The girls working the switchboards got to wear authentic regatta gowns. They were discards, stripped of glass or metal or anything else that that might be valuable, and some of them had been pulled from garbage cans, but they were still the real thing. Everyone acted all snooty and called each other lady this and lady that, and they had a contest for the most ridiculous hairdo, which Phila suspected she might win. Everyone said that they loved the way she'd threaded her hair through a whole bunch of severed doll heads. She'd even spread some red sauce on the necks of the doll heads for blood. Which was why she also smelled like pizza.

She might also win a small share of the contest for the most ridiculous call of the day. The girls in her switchbank had agreed to share that prize if any of them won it, and the call that had just been diverted to her as a floor supervisor had a pretty good chance.

She flipped the switch to alert the duty manager and let the caller babble on while waiting for the click of another party connecting. As soon as she heard her supervisor join the call, she interrupted the caller. "So, you're saying that someone tried to murder you by dropping a ship's plow on your head?"

"Yeah, nah, not murder, and it was just the pod part not the parachute. A parachute wouldn't bash or smash much, but it was some serious gonna kill someone doin' all that with it." The caller wasn't quite slurring, but he was obviously drunk.

"Sir, may I ask what you are doing down at the docks?" Phila asked even though she could tell from the routing switches that he wasn't at the docks. "The docks are supposed to be closed during the regatta."

"I'm not at the docks. I'm at my place. Nice place when the woman's not here."

"And why didn't you call this in while you were at the docks?"

"It didn't happen at the docks!" he shouted. "Like I said to that lady before, the plow fell on the roof of the building while we was up there listening to the race. It smashed down and almost onto us and then went up, and while we was looking at what parts of the roof it smashed, it came back down, and that double almost killed us."

"And then you say it flew away?"

"Yeah, nah, it smashed on the roof another time and then fwooop, up and away. And it almost hit us when it fwooped up, so that was like triple almost killing us."

"But you think that someone was trying to murder you?"

"Nah, maybe not trying, but we almost got accidentally killed, that was for sure."

"So, sir, I need to ask, to whom do you wish to be connected?"

"Like I said already and before, I need to talk to the police."

"But I'm not sure if I should connect you to the police if the person flying the magic ship around inside the city wasn't trying to murder you with their plow. It is Regatta Day, and that means that there's a pretty big fine if you lodge a call to the police when the situation isn't urgent or life threatening."

"Well, yeah, nah, yeah but ... I don't know, but I gotta tell someone."

"How about the Port Authority?" Phila suggested. "They inspect ships."

"Yeah, I suppose."

"Well, good. Their main office is closed today, but if you call back day after tomorrow, we can put you through."

In sharp contrast to most of their approach to Lightcastle, there wasn't even a hint of drama in the final part of sneaking the Drunken Monkey and its passengers into the city. Az didn't know all that much beyond the basics of cutting the Drift, but everything she saw Flint do and everything she heard Flint and Em say to one another seemed to fit with his earlier explanation of how they were going to bring the ship in over the dome. Once they got the plow to work as an anchor, they just flew the Drunken Monkey like a kite and they backed it into its landing space. Flint watched out of the rear and called out their position relative to the clear space on the dock as he slowly unwound the plow cables. The movement of the Drift over the dome pushed them backwards, and the only real challenge he faced seemed to be making sure that he unwound the winch slowly enough to give Em a steady flow of air over the aerodynamic control surfaces on the ship.

The landing was so gentle that Az barely noticed the bump as they touched down, and as Flint had promised, it didn't look like anyone out on the docks had noticed. There wasn't a soul to be seen or hint of movement anywhere in the section of the dockyards where they had landed. That was a big reason why, even though it had left them almost no room for error, they had waited until after the regatta was under way to fly in. Everyone who could was using the pretense of celebrating the regatta to stay as far away as they could from work.

The general state of distraction created by the regatta was also why Flint dropping the plow through the city dome was unlikely to disrupt the plan. The hole wasn't big enough to cause any noticeable amount of air loss, and the monumental extent of mass inebriation that was typical on Regatta Day would have the Lightcastle police stretched to the breaking point. The chances that they would rush to investigate any reports about the plow were near zero. Flint was obviously thinking the same thing.

"We've probably got at least a few hours, probably a full day before anyone sobers up enough to come looking for the owner of our plow, so the real problem is …" Flint's mouth kept working, but the sound stopped the moment he turned enough to see that Az was again pointing her gun at his head.

"No, Flint, the real problem is that I have to guarantee you stay quiet," she said.

"I can be quiet," Flint's voice trembled as he tried to sound flippant. "So quiet you can't imagine …"

"Flint, the drunken stories you tell about Em are how I found you."

"People can change. I can change. I want to change. I think quiet would be a great change. Might just stop talking altogether."

"Shut up, Flint." Az glanced pointedly at the cargo bay controls and Flint pushed a button, starting a red light flashing in the bays, warning the Blades they would soon lose their breathable air. "In the long run, the reputational benefit of letting you scuttle off to babble drunkenly about how well you were paid would have been quite valuable. Services like those you offer are far less expensive when people believe they'll walk away both alive and wealthy."

"Hey, we'd be very happy to help with that," Flint said, never taking his eyes off Az's gun as he worked the lever to open the cargo bay doors. "You wouldn't know it, but Em is also surprisingly good at drunken babble."

"And there's the problem. If either of you babble into the wrong ears too soon, we'll never get to the long run," Az said. "I'm sorry about this Flint, I truly am, but there is too much at stake and these first few hours are too critical to take any risk. Do you wish a moment to pray? Or perhaps you have a request. I will try to honor a last request."

"A last request, you mean like, please don't kill me?"

"Make your peace, Flint."

"Wait, those wrong ears would be on the sides of a cop's head, right?" Flint emphasized the word "sides" in his desperate rush to speak.

"Presumably the ears would be on the sides of the head, yes," Az said.

"Then that's your guarantee." Flint pointed out the window, then at the floor and in the other direction, obviously trying to indicate that he was talking about the cables that trailed back to the plow he'd dropped through the dome. "Even if you thought we were stupid enough to run and tell anyone in charge of anything that we just smuggled a shipload of very scary ballerinas into the city, dropping the plow through the dome is game over for us. It's a death sentence. I have no idea what Em and I are going to do, or how we're going to use whatever time we've got before someone comes looking for the owner of that plow, but I can guarantee that telling anyone anything, least of all the police, is not even going to be a consideration."

Az considered that. Flint and Em could very well decide that running to the authorities might be their only chance to rectify their situation. Then again, history offered them little reason to think it would do any good. At best, the Lolofis might let them skip being tortured before they were executed for damaging the dome.

"That's not a guarantee, but it does give me an excuse to let you live." Az holstered her weapon. "Thank you."

"Uhmm, you're welcome, I guess."

"I enjoyed your company," Az said.

"You did?"

"Yes, I did, and I truly prefer not being the person who kills you," Az said. "You will find the balance of our agreed fee in the bottom of our shipping containers."

Flint looked into the cargo bay, his jaw dropping as he saw the women removing assault rifles and pistols from the big plastic trunks that they had brought on board.

Az donned the hood and breather of her cheap, disposable deck suit and stepped into the air lock.

Willamette pulled slightly on Niven's arm in a vain attempt to steer him away from the hedgerow. He did not appear to notice.

"You truly have no understanding of formality or propriety, do you?" Willamette scolded him as their leisurely stroll carried them out of the view of the distant chaperones who were watching from the terrace.

"Understanding and caring are two completely different things, Little Princess."

"Then perhaps I should explain to you why you should care," she snarled.

"Or, perhaps, I should explain to you how me feigning such blatant ignorance of propriety now will create a first impression that will make it far easier for us to deflect or diminish the consequences of any real mistakes in protocol that I might make in the future."

"That makes sense." Willamette ran his words through her head again. "Wow, that makes a great deal of sense."

"You know, you don't have to sound so surprised." He guided her around a corner toward a mad scramble of servant children. "Even if my ability to think caught you off guard, I know full well that you've had a lifetime of tutors teaching you how to conceal your thoughts and feelings."

"Yes, but I would rather not hide my feelings from you," she said, surprised to realize she meant it.

"Well, that would probably be a first for a noble wife," Niven quipped. "When it comes to feelings, my mother has the habit of acting like my father is the most gifted psychic in the Drift."

They reached a small clearing full of children, and despite the bits of mess they had failed to fully clear away, it was a remarkable scene. A pair of mismatched chairs had been set next to a small table, which was crowded with enough cocktails and trays of food to serve at least a dozen people. The clearing was hidden on three sides by ancient hedges while the fourth side was bounded by a flower garden that sloped down from the clearing to offer a perfect view of the automation that tracked the race.

"This is nice," Willamette said. "It is inappropriately private, but nice."

"This used to be one of my favorite places to watch the automation track the regatta," Niven said. "The servant kids who snuck away from their jobs to watch it from here were always far more fun than the children I was supposed to socialize with."

"You preferred the company of low-class delinquents," she said. "Why am I not surprised?"

"And as a bonus, the eyes of a dozen gossips should be more than sufficient to safeguard your maidenly honor." Niven waved merrily at the women watching them from the far side of the expansive flower garden. Their reaction to his wave made Willamette desperately wish she could allow herself to laugh.

"Your serving boy is an impressive lad," she said, nodding toward the young boy who seemed to have organized the last-minute clearing and setting up of the space. "This could not have been easy to accomplish."

"He's not my serving boy," Niven said. "I don't have a serving boy."

"But … how could you have possibly arranged all of this without an experienced and trusted serving boy?" She frowned and glanced back at the boy. "For that matter, how could you have arranged this at all? You obviously had no idea we would be betrothed today, so you could not have arranged this in advance, and you have been at my side since then, giving you no opportunity whatsoever to arrange this. And even if this is all the boy's doing, which I find difficult to believe, you have had no opportunity whatsoever to secure his services."

"You don't even see the servants around you, do you?" Niven asked, chuckling.

She gave him a questioning, confused frown.

"You honestly didn't notice the way he followed us around the park with his tray of drinks, or the way he kept working his way around in front of us, or how he waited for the perfect moment to rush in to offer you a fresh cocktail, or the way you crushed his soul when you waved him away without taking one?"

"But …" She did not try to hide her bewilderment. "Why would he care if I took a cocktail from him?"

"All he wanted was the chance to serve you." Niven glanced at the boy, who was still working to get the last of the garbage cleared away from the edges of the clearing. "Serving a Lolofi is big-time bragging rights for the adults. For a kid who is probably working his first regatta ever, it would have been a tale he would have told over and over for the rest of his life."

Willamette shook her head, having trouble comprehending that.

"And you didn't notice when I stooped down to talk to him?" Niven asked.

"I do think I remember that he replaced the drink you dropped."

"I dropped that drink to give me time to talk to him as I took a new one from his tray." Niven thought a second. "Though I am going to have to be careful not to drop any more. I don't want to create the impression that I'm too clumsy to hold on to a glass."

"I agree. To have people think that you are a clumsy drunken fool would not be as useful as the belief that you are ignorant of the norms of propriety."

"Mitch." Niven called to the boy.

"You learned his name?" Willamette was stunned.

Another frown from Niven. It was unquestionably disapproving.

"Okay, Mitch, these are for all the kids who helped." Niven handed the boy a fistful of nearly worthless little coins. "You divvy them up fair."

Mitch nodded, gobsmacked by the treasure in his hands.

"And this one is for you." Niven held up a single coin with a crystal of glass embedded in its center. That one coin was worth at least a month's stipend for a high-ranking adult servant. "Now you can just keep this if you want. However, the Grand Lady Willamette thinks I need a serving boy and don't tell anyone, but the job is yours if you want it. All you have to do is take this coin to the offices of the Independent Estates Cooperative and use it to buy passage to the Lister Estate."

Mitch was overwhelmed. He probably did not dare believe what Niven was saying. To become the personal servant of a man about to marry a Lolofi was beyond the bounds of anything that he could have possibly dreamed his future might hold.

"Now I'm serious about not telling anyone," Niven said. "Don't tell your friends, or your parents, or anyone else. People can be horrible when they get jealous. So if you want the job, you just sneak away and once you're on my father's estate, I'll send your parents a letter. You understand?"

Mitch nodded.

"Good, now open your mouth," Niven commanded.

Mitch obeyed without hesitation.

Niven popped the coin into his mouth, and then pinched the boy's nose shut.

"Swallow it," Niven whispered before shouting and shaking Mitch like he was angry with him. "And do not ever sass me again you little toad!"

Mitch swallowed the coin. It looked to be a difficult and unpleasant thing.

"Now you go share those other coins with the other kids and ask a couple of the bigger boys to stay nearby and make sure no one disturbs us," Niven said. "Make them earn the extra share they're going to bully out of you."

Mitch ran off, but not too far. Even with that bit of theatre to protect him from losing his real reward to a shakedown, Mitch was still smart enough to stay in Niven's view as he handed out the coins, and he was smart enough to make sure that all the bigger boys saw that he had given all the coins away.

"And you, Ida." Niven gestured toward a corner of the clearing where Ida could stand in attendance but still be out of earshot. "Please step away."

Ida did not move.

"Ida!" Willamette scolded the girl. "You will obey Sir Niven as you would obey me."

Ida reluctantly walked over to the edge of the clearing, clutching the overstuffed purse and glancing around as if she was afraid to stand there. She was behaving so oddly that Willamette was certain the poor girl must be feeling quite ill.

"And now that we have some semblance of privacy ..." Niven handed Willamette one of the drinks from the table. "Forgive me for saying this bluntly, Little Princess, but this makes no sense."

"Is my fiancé truly befuddled by a champagne cocktail?" she teased. It was clumsy, but his chuckle suggested he appreciated the effort.

"Well, yes, these things are disgusting, but I was referring to our engagement," he said. "No matter how I consider it, I cannot imagine why you would choose me."

"Why I would choose you? You believe that the betrothal that our fathers negotiated is my doing?"

"I know it is."

"Truly?" Willamette smiled sweetly, hoping that her expression would make it obvious that she was teasing him. "Oh, do tell me the story, young Sir Niven. I do love fairy tales."

"Willamette, you know that I have two sisters," he said, gruffly.

"I may have gathered a great deal of information about you and your family," she said, abandoning the attempt to tease him.

"So, knowing I have two sisters, you should also have deduced I would have plenty of experience spotting the smug smirk of a little girl who has manipulated her daddy into giving her exactly what she wanted."

"I am not a little girl," she huffed.

"Yes, yes, that dress has left no room to doubt just how much of a woman you are and trust me no one is happier about that than I am," he said. "But the little girl smirk is immune to age and no matter how I turn this over in my head, I can't figure out why you would want me for your husband, or why your father would let you have me."

"My father's choice is easy to understand if you consider my betrothal in terms of politics."

"Politics?"

"Yes, politics." Willamette said it as if it should have been obvious. "Three of the Big 12 families currently have eligible sons and are several generations removed from direct marriage ties to the Lolofi family."

"And if your father sold you to one of them, he'd stir things up, or maybe even risk losing the support of the other two."

"I have not been sold," she snarled.

Niven continued his thought as if he had not heard her. "So your father went along with this because it allowed him to take you off the market, by selling you to my father."

"For the last time, I am not chattel! But ..." Willamette took a breath, using that as an excuse to soften her tone. "Yes, you appear to grasp the basic idea. The true mastery of politics lies not in the clichés of taking action or making hard choices, though that is something that has served my family well. The true mastery of politics lies in manipulating the choices you leave for others, and there is no one better at that than my father. So, I knew I could count on him to see that our marriage would, temporarily at least, remove my hand as something for those three families to fight over."

"Temporarily?"

"Yes," she said, failing to consider the matter-of-fact tone she was using. "My father will wait until two of the three families marry their sons and then ..."

"And then turn you into a widow."

"That would be the simplest and most efficient course of action, yes."

"You picked me to be murdered." Niven was aghast, horrified, and the way he was looking at her was heartbreaking.

"No ... well, yes, but ... no." She held up her hands, pleading with him to give her a moment. She could not believe how easily he could fluster her. It took several seconds before she could continue. "I chose you because I desperately hoped the young man who dreamt up the idea of building whale-sized shipping containers for his whaling ship was as clever as he seemed."

She took his hands in hers and stood facing him, trying to command his entire attention. "And, Niven, do not let this go to your head, but as soon as my agents began investigating you, I discovered that you are even more clever than I had first hoped. The cargo pods were clever but disguising them as ballast and making them neutrally buoyant so you could drop them to chase a whale without losing the cargo was brilliant."

"How do you know that? I've never told anyone that part of it."

"If you combine the records of your whale landings with the shipping manifests and the tonnages delivered with each trip—including the shadow company you set up to hide the extent of the cargo you were hauling with your whaler—it is not that difficult to figure out."

"Those are confidential business records!"

"The detail that is important is that you set up a system where you could drop the pods if you spotted a whale rising, chase the whale down, haul it to the nearest landing station, and then go back later to retrieve the cargo. That has allowed you to catch your share of whales while making enough money shipping extra cargo to be the only whaler in the Commonwealth who is not currently facing financial ruin."

"I don't just leave the pods," he said. "I have them set up so that after I secure the whale, I can hook a cable to them and tow them to my father's estate for safekeeping while I drop off the whale."

"Which is even more clever than I imagined," she said, disturbed how much that excited her, and unnerved by the way it excited her.

"So ... you wanted to give your father a clever boy to murder?" Niven asked, confused. "Why? To give him a challenge?"

"Niven! What I want is you!"

That bought her a moment to regroup. She tried a different approach entirely.

"My parents thought the study of history was an odd, but safe hobby for a young girl," she said.

"Okay, bizarre tangent, but I'll play along," he said. "I take it your parents were wrong."

"Indeed, they were. Sex and all manner of scandalous things abound in the tales of history, but the truly horrific thing I found is something the historians back on Earth called a tragedy of the commons."

"I doubt if it is more horrific than waiting to be murdered by your father-in-law," he grumped.

"One, my father would not murder you," she said. "He would have you murdered."

"Not an important distinction for the victim."

"And two, in our case, the tragedy of the commons will be a

catastrophe that is far worse than the gruesome death of any one person."

"Gruesome. Now my murder's going to be gruesome?"

"I will find a way to make it gruesome, and I will find a way to make it happen right this instant if you do not stop interrupting."

Niven pulled his hands from hers and held them up, surrendering as he stepped back. Willamette did not blame him for being scared, and it made her feel guilty, but she had already cast the die.

"To describe it succinctly," she said, "we, the big we, the hundreds of millions of people living in the Drift, have maneuvered ourselves into a situation where we cannot invest the resources needed to sustain a critical resource. Indeed, we are already seeing that resource fail ..."

"The whales," he whispered.

"Yes, the whales have become so rare that our economy, and I mean the economy of the whole world, is on the verge of collapse. The price of minerals has risen to the point where the iron and calcium in a peasant's body are worth more than the labor they can offer an estate owner. And it is only going to get worse," she said. "The whales are vanishing because we long ago quit constructing the automated mining machines that gather minerals on the surface, then build, load, and release the whales to float up to the Drift."

"No." He shook his head in disbelief. "That would be insane."

"No, it is not insane. It is horrifically rational, which is what makes it a tragedy in the classic, Greek tragedy sense of the word," she said. "Even though we can predict the catastrophe, we cannot avoid it."

"Why the hell not?"

"Think about how many thousands of empires, kingdoms, federations, and independent cities exist across the Drift." She stepped back to him and took his hands in hers again. "The Commonwealth is big. It is probably one of the biggest things in the Drift, but if we were to build a dozen of those mining machines, the odds that our whalers would catch a significant number of the whales the machines produce is vanishingly small."

"And no expectation of return makes any investment in the machines that create the whales irrational," he finished the thought.

"And I would bet building one of those mining machines is a monumental investment."

"Yes, The cost of just one is indeed monumental," she said. "There are ways to make it rational to produce them, but those methods are no longer viable. The taxation system we used to use to finance their construction collapsed generations ago."

"And you've got some kind of plan for restarting it or something?" He was doubtful, but hopeful.

"No," she said. "I doubt reconstructing the old system is possible. To make that taxation scheme work we need near-universal compliance, but the institutional mechanisms for accomplishing that are gone. We do not even have a good guess at how many habitats there are floating about the Drift. Getting all of them to agree to be taxed and then policing that taxation system to ensure compliance is not possible, but I do have some ideas."

"Ideas? That's it? All you have is a few ideas?"

"Niven, the only other historical solutions I have found involve different ways of riding out the collapse and building a solution into the recovery, but if we were to let the entire world's economic system collapse, I worry that humanity might not survive."

"But you think I can help you find a clever way to save the world?"

"I believe that the obligation to try is inherent to the privilege of my wealth and power. And I wanted ..." Quickly, before she lost her nerve, she rose onto her toes and kissed him. It was awkward, stiff, and rushed, but she hoped it got the point across. "And I wanted a partner. I need to have a partner, a real partner, to have any chance at all of succeeding."

She was embarrassed, and she wanted to pull away. She wanted to run away, but he had closed his hands on hers and she could not let go.

"I had solid, logical reasons to pick you, but I had hoped for something more than that. I had hoped ..." She had to take a breath. "Niven, I do know that this is foolish, and childish, and ... and I truly will murder you if you ever again smirk when I admit to something childish, but—"

He kissed her. It was soft, warm, slow, and exactly what she imagined a kiss could be. It left her breathless. That surprised her.

She had assumed that being left breathless by a kiss was just poetic hyperbole.

"Never underestimate the value of foolishness," he said. "But please tell me you have an actual plan to keep your father from murdering me."

"I have some ideas." Again she felt guilty, and it must have shown.

"Ideas? Oh my god. Are you kidding me? A few ideas? That's it?"

"They are quite good ideas."

There was nothing metaphorical about Kofi's distaste for getting blood on his hands. The warm slick feeling, the way it found its way into every crack and crevice in his skin, the way it clotted under his nails, the stains, the smell when it was fresh and the stink when it dried—he hated it. It didn't matter if the blood flowed from the heart of his enemy, or the belly of a parasitic noble, or the throat of a servant suffering the profound misfortune of working for the family that owned the suite with the balcony he needed; he disliked getting blood on his hands.

After he finished washing and drying his hands, Kofi quietly cursed himself for not doing his own recon of the yacht club. It would have been a tremendous risk. Most of the club's security personnel were retired military and sneaking in twice doubled the chances of stumbling into someone who might recognize him, but it probably would have been worth it. At the very least, he would have taken the time to determine that the sniper rifle the club was displaying as a war trophy was an HK44E rifle, not an HK44M. They looked so much alike that he hadn't noticed the error until he started to work on the old gun, but if he had been the one conducting the recon, he would have damn well double-checked that detail. The M and the E used the same darts, the same gas cylinders, and most of the same spare parts, but the difference between the mechanical trigger and the electric trigger was a huge problem.

He had every other part necessary to turn the old rifle into the deadly weapon he needed. He had a 900cc firing chamber to replace the 200cc quickfire chamber on the gun. That would up the power enough to allow him to use 30cm darts instead of the 15cm darts in the old quick loader. Thirties not only had more penetrating power than the standard fifteens, they were more accurate, and they could also be made to splinter. Splintering darts created an impressive mess out of whatever they hit, and the psychological impact of that was almost as valuable as their effectiveness at taking out the target.

All that, however, assumed that the final part that he needed to get the rifle in working order was the new mechanical spark trigger assembly he'd brought. Unfortunately, it was the wrong part and there was no way to make it fit. What he needed was the battery and capacitor electric trigger assembly that the E model used.

The battery was dead, and well beyond hope of revival, but for what he meant to do from the balcony, that was a manageable problem. The capacitor and spark mechanism in the rifle weren't all that fussy about voltages. Kofi broke open the small reading light over the desk and pulled the wires out as far as he could. They wouldn't stretch all of the way over to the railing, but there were four similar light fixtures around the suite. Without the right tools, stripping the plastic insulation off the graphene fiber conductors in the wires and splicing them together was a tricky job, but it was doable, and it would give him plenty of length to get the rifle to the railing. He wouldn't be able to use the rifle after he left the balcony, but hopefully, by that point he wouldn't need it.

Kofi checked the clock over the desk. He still had time.

Flint stared at the underside of the Drunken Monkey, unable to convince himself to do anything.

"Flint," Em spoke, from just behind him, her voice oddly compassionate.

"I don't know what I thought was in those crates they brought with them, but I never thought it might be guns," he said. "And I never imagined I might have a gun pointed at my head, twice, or that I would feel like being allowed to live was a favor. I always kind of just expected that not being murdered was implied in a passenger charter contract."

"With the money those bitches paid us to smuggle them into the city, how could you not realize they were up to something seriously ugly?"

"I know, but why couldn't it be a freaky outlawed ballet cult with a weird marriage thing or something?" He finally lit the small torch he'd brought out to cut the cables to their plow. "On the bright side, smuggling a heavily armed dance troupe into the capital makes dropping our plow through the dome seem a whole lot less catastrophic."

"No, it doesn't."

"Well, it's not like two death sentences are worse than one, and like you said, they did pay us pretty damn well," he said. "Assuming we can limp our way out of the Commonwealth without a plow, we should have enough money to buy a new one and get back up and running."

"Or maybe, if we were quick about it, we could just steal ourselves a plow. Or maybe even find an upgrade." Em said it as if it was perfectly reasonable. "This is a repair and refit berth. There's got to be a decent plow or two sitting around in one of the workshops around here."

"You want to steal a plow?"

"It shouldn't be all that hard. The whole reason we arranged for this yard to be clear was because this part of the docks is pretty much abandoned for the regatta, and it'll be late tomorrow or the next day before anyone even thinks about getting back to work."

"When someone finds a cop sober enough to come looking for the owner of the plow we just dropped through the dome, do you really think he's not going to notice that we stole a replacement?"

"Two death sentences, Flint. Getting caught stealing the plow we're going need to run away is not the relevant part."

There was a lot of truth in that.

"And, just this once, if you find any good tools in those workshops when you're looking for a plow, you can steal them too."

"I could use a new impact wrench."

She patted him on the shoulder. "And you deserve one."

CHAPTER 4

Phila survived just long enough to know that she was dying. The knife was so sharp that she felt no pain. There was a sudden sense of choking as it sliced through her windpipe and there was a flood of warmth pouring down over her chest, but there was no pain. It was only when her vision faded that she understood that she had been murdered. By then, the loss of blood supply to her brain had left her giddy and lightheaded, and her very last thought was how ironic it was that her joke of a fancy hairdo included a bunch of severed doll heads with bloody necks.

Phila died without noticing how many of her girls had added bright blue armbands to their outfits. She died without knowing that they called themselves Bluebands, or how easy it had been for so many of them to position themselves in the central telephone switchboard simply by volunteering to work the holiday. Mercifully, she also died unaware of which of those women had slit her throat. That tidbit of knowledge would have crushed her.

Willamette was surprised when Niven put his arm around her. It was a simple thing, but that quite nearly socially acceptable display of affection spoke volumes, and it was pleasant. It was astonishingly pleasant. The warmth, the gentleness, the comforting sense of being possessed but unconstrained. There was a simple but profound joy in it and it troubled Willamette to discover that she could not remember the last time someone had held her.

"Thank you," she whispered, not even daring to let Ida hear her utter those words to him. "I cannot imagine how difficult it must be for you to pretend that marrying me is something you desire, but I deeply appreciate the charade."

"It is pointless to curse your fate. Although, there is something cathartic about swearing at it while you roll up your sleeves," Niven said, quoting.

"I have never heard that one before," she said. "Who said it?"

"My grandfather, a lot," Niven said. "I don't know if he made it up or stole it, but I do know that he meant it when he said it."

"And are you swearing, Niven?" she asked.

It was a long time before he answered. "To be honest, Little Princess, I don't want this, not at all. So if I thought there was a way to run from it, I would, but we both know that from the moment you set your sights on me I was well and truly trapped in it. So, yes, I am silently offering the universe a tirade of profanity that is so filthy and so vile that it verges on the poetic, but I have also decided to roll up my sleeves."

He paused, but she could tell that he had more to say, so she leaned into him and let him take his time.

"It helps that you don't seem to be the same kind of soulless demon spawn that your mother birthed with your brothers, and I'm ashamed to admit that it also helps that you are a truly beautiful woman, but I also can't possibly describe how furious I am that you made me a pawn in your scheme weeks, if not months, before I even knew there was a game being played. The words simply do not exist. So, yes, I am angry, and resentful, and scared, and you are to blame for all of that. But I am trapped in it, so I'm not going to allow my anger to trick me into making matters worse. Instead, I am going to do everything I can to make this the best damn whatever this is going to be that I can."

The arm around her waist moved, and she was suddenly afraid that he might step away, but he was just taking a deep breath.

"And I also think that I shall drink, heavily," he said. "Yeah, I think I'll find a nice pub, with pretty barmaids who will hand me the next round before I even ask, and I'm going to just stay there until the wedding. Maybe I'll bring in a cot. No, I could run straight there after the regatta and have Mitch bring me a cot. That's the sort of thing a serving boy does, right?"

"I will have to consult the serving boy owner's manual," she said. "However, I do believe that anything enabling the excessive consumption of alcohol is allowed."

He gave her a bit of squeeze with the arm wrapped around her. It was just enough to acknowledge her attempt at returning his jest.

"Speaking of the wedding," he said, back to solemn. "I have decided that part of making the best of this is for me to make our marriage something like a real marriage."

Her heart leapt.

"I am acutely aware that we have no control over who we love or who we cherish," he said. "So, I cannot promise that those vows will be sincere. And do not for a moment allow this gesture I am about to make fool you into underestimating just how angry I am about all of this, but to forsake all others ... That is a simple, if sometimes challenging, choice. So, fidelity is a vow that I can honestly make, and it is one that I will choose to keep. Think of it as the only real wedding gift that I can give to the girl who can have anything she desires."

"I will treasure it as the best wedding gift that any man could have possibly offered." Again, he had caught her off guard, or, more accurately, he had put her off guard and then taken her by surprise. The tears were mortifying, but she was powerless against them. "Oh, this is so childish and foolish."

"Never underestimate the value and beauty of foolishness." He dutifully handed her his handkerchief, but it wasn't until she felt him cringe when she blew her nose into it that she realized that the delicately embroidered square of silk was probably a family heirloom. He had probably expected her to turn to Ida for one that was meant to be used, and she cursed herself for overlooking such an obvious social grace.

"It is too soon to be certain," she said, her voice trembling. "But I suspect that when I vow to cherish you, I will mean it."

"I don't suppose there's any chance you'd consider trading cherish for obey, is there?"

"Not a chance in the Deep," she said, chuckling through the tears.

On a whim, Willamette turned her teary gaze out over the flower garden to where the gossips had gathered. When she caught the eye of one of the drunk old birds, she gave her a smile and a wink. The woman smiled back and added an approving nod. Even though that same woman would concoct an ugly story about Willamette and Niven, in that moment even the most cynical of noblewomen could not help but appreciate that in Niven, Willamette had found the one thing that most of them did not dare even wish for.

The day had not unfolded exactly as Willamette had imagined it might. Far from it. Niven had kicked her intricate web of expectations, plans, and contingencies into a shambles, and some incidents would prove troublesome in the days, weeks, and possibly even years to come, but all of that was worth the joy of discovering that Niven was a better choice than she had hoped. She relaxed, for the first time that day; for the first time in weeks, if not years, she relaxed. Closing her eyes, she imagined that moment and that feeling lasting forever. And that was when the automation that tracked the progress of the race exploded.

Aside from a fair bit of drunken leering, no one had paid much attention to the women dressed in bright blue and carrying loosely wrapped bundles. That was expected. With all the costumes, drinking, and other foolishness of Regatta Day, and with all the people running around trying to make a coin or two off all of that drinking and foolishness, it would be difficult for anything or anyone to stand out enough to be noticed. Even so, it had been a challenge to find a way to linger near the yacht club's main gate without drawing too much attention. Only the best of the best were good enough for the yacht club's security team. They were alert and their security systems were well designed. Fortunately, the explosion that Az had been waiting for was also far more than just a go signal.

Even though Az was well away from the main entrance to the yacht club, the shockwave that burst through the open gates hit her with enough force to take her breath away. Fortunately, she had been waiting for the bomb to go off, so the surprising ferocity of the explosion didn't delay her reaction in the same way that it stunned the guards. That almost made up for the extra distance she had to cover. She was fifteen meters into the sprint before the first of the guards shook it off. She ignored him. He was outside the gate. She had covered twenty meters before the first of the men stationed inside the outer gate regained his wits.

Rifle shots flew past her from behind. They passed so close that the shrieking zip made her ears ring. The guards outside the gate were going down, but she scarcely noticed. She stayed focused on the guard that had sprung into action inside the outer gate.

Just like she would expect from a pro, he checked his zone of responsibility first. She covered five more meters in the half second it took for his still-confused mind to recognize the sprinting woman as a threat, and she covered another five in the half second it took him to decide on a course of action.

He went for his weapon instead of the gate controls and that turned her almost impossible shot into something simple. She let him draw his pistol, and in the time that took she both cut another five meters off the range and opened the angle through the arched gate opening. That brought his whole body into her view.

Az fired two quick darts, both hitting the guard dead center in the chest. Unlike the rifle shots taking out the guards outside the gate, Az's pistol wasn't powerful enough to punch through his body armor, but the darts still packed enough of a kick to send him sprawling.

With four shots left in her pistol, she covered another five meters before she put two darts into the guard that was moving to shut the gate. That was enough to get her through the outer gate. She unloaded the last two darts in her pistol into the nearest person who might be a threat to close the gate. Judging by the way the darts ripped through him, he had no body armor. That meant that he was probably just a noble who thought that a military-looking outfit made him look important.

She tossed her pistol and had one of the fallen guard's weapons in her hand before hers hit the ground. A dart went into the guard's head, and a second into the head of the other guard she had knocked down with the darts from her pistol.

The main entrance to the yacht club looked like it was just a lavishly landscaped portal of welcome for the patrons of the club. However, all the guards had to do was close the inner gate and the thirty meters from the outer gate to the inner gate became a kill zone. Scramble a few guards up to kill perches on top of the walls surrounding that space, and a few men could hold off an army.

To leave nothing to chance, everything about the landscaping between the gates was carefully set up to give the guards manning the inner gate ample opportunity to get that gate closed in the event of an attack. The pond across the middle was two meters deep and six across, and a shrubbery on either side made the leap across impossible. The bridge over that pond was set at an angle and it curved back and forth as it crossed the pond. That looked decorative but it was meant to make the attackers shift directions twice as they charged across.

When all of that was combined with the well-trained guards, who almost all recovered quite quickly from the surprise of the explosion, Az and the Blades with her had no chance to storm their way into the club. Az was able to get through the outer gate and keep it open so the Blades could follow her through, but the inner gate was closed well before the first of them could make it to the bridge. Guards were already rushing to man the kill perches and they would soon open fire. Once that happened, the women would have no option but to retreat.

Fortunately, they had no intention of fighting their way through the inner gate. Their goal was to establish a significant threat inside the outer gate.

Everything about the yacht club's security was designed to stop threats from outside, and that was its fatal flaw. All Az and the Blades under her command had to do was be that threat from outside. There were only a few men with military experience in the motley menagerie of servants that Kofi had been able to recruit, arm, and position inside the club, but the guards had almost nothing in place to protect them from an attack originating inside the yacht club. It was a slaughter, and they had the inner gate reopened in seconds.

In those few seconds, some of the club's guards made it up to the kill perches with rifles, but that was expected and because it was expected, it wasn't a problem. The Blades that followed Az in through the outer gate carried smoke grenades—dozens of them. In the confines of the walled garden courtyard that was the Lightcastle Yacht Club entrance, the smoke from those grenades created an impenetrable haze. If the inner gate had remained secure, that obscuring smoke wouldn't have mattered. If the Blades had been forced to fight their way in through the inner gate, they would not only have become stationary and trapped in the kill space, the fight itself would have given away their positions to the guards firing down into the murk. However, because that inner gate was so quickly reopened, the Blades never had to stop, or gather, or otherwise turn themselves into an identifiable target.

The guards still fired into smoke, concentrating their darts on where they knew the bridge would create a choke point for the attackers, but countless runs through a mock-up of the courtyard had trained that space so deeply into the memories of the Blades that they didn't even have to think about where they were or where they were going. Despite being unable to see anything, they were sprinting through the entrance courtyard at full tilt, three meters apart, and not one of them tripped or crashed into an obstacle. It was inevitable that a few of them would take a dart as they dashed across the bridge, but with the inner gate open, a few guards firing blindly into the smoke couldn't stop enough of the Blades to matter.

In the end, Az only lost two Blades in taking the entrance.

Kofi did nothing to stop the Lolofi family's scrambling retreat from the terrace. He knew that there was no way they could escape the club, and by leaving the terrace, they were also removing eight of the best-trained and most dedicated men from the immediate fight.

Scanning the scene with the scope on his rifle he spotted a body on the terrace. It was the old butler who had been serving that particularly offensive fat slob of a noble. His neck was bent unnaturally and the satchel Kofi had given him was open but empty. There was no sign of either the pistol or the ammunition it had contained. That was a problem. The fat slob had a first rate, military-trained bodyguard.

Kofi lowered the rifle and took another look at the scene without the scope. Two men with blue armbands were lying in puddles of blood and another two were hiding behind an overturned table. Kofi traced back along the line that defined the cover that the two cowering men were getting from the table, and he spotted the cherry tree that was the only place where someone could be hiding and shooting at them. That was probably where the old man's gun had gone.

He watched the tree for several seconds but saw no movement. He searched the area around the edges of the tree's foliage, looking for shadows or other hints of where that bodyguard might be, but saw nothing. That had been a faint hope. If it if had been night or a dark day, there almost certainly would have been shadows from the artificial lights, but when the sun was up, the high thin clouds that always covered the sky scattered the light making shadows rare. He watched for another few seconds, hoping for some movement or a flash of color or anything else that might give him some idea of where the guard with the butler's pistol was hiding under the expansive canopy of the cherry tree, but watching and waiting revealed nothing.

Kofi aimed at a tangle of small branches in the cherry tree and pulled the trigger. The loud, cracking report of the rifle was echoed by the popping snap of the dart shattering in the treetop. The noble took the bait and bolted from beneath the tree. Kofi quickly, expertly reloaded, but even after he was ready to fire, he just watched the fat man desperately trying to run. He didn't care about the noble. He was using him to force the bodyguard to move. The guard had no choice and when he emerged from under the cover of the tree, Kofi shot him. Reloading, he looked for other threats to the amateurs who had been so eager to play soldier for him.

"Security Alert One Eleven," Az's voice blared from the room's intercom speaker. "Security Alert One Eleven."

Hearing Az's voice brought a wave of relief washing up from Kofi's gut. Technically, she wasn't mission critical. He would have never launched this attack if he had to count on her being able find a way to smuggle herself and all of the other Blades on the Port Authority's watch list into the city, but her success increased their odds by orders of magnitude. Those two hundred or so women would easily double the effectiveness of the three thousand young and inexperienced Blades they were joining.

Kofi spotted another bodyguard trying to be a hero and shot him before answering the intercom. "Good work, Az. Is One Eleven the main security office?"

"Yes, we've secured all the gates and all the club's security offices," Az said. "But it looks like they have a direct line to the local police precinct, so they almost certainly got a call out that would have bypassed the city's main switchboard."

"That was expected, Az," Kofi said. "Call the main switchboard and tell ops to initiate phase two."

The force of the blast had so completely knocked the breath from Willamette that her lungs refused to work. Rising to a knee, she was gasping but received nothing but a sharp pain in her side for the effort. Desperate to draw a breath, she panicked, and that just made it worse. Growing dizzy, she tried to stand but could not. She tried to scream but could not. Her lungs would not work.

Niven slapped her on the back, hard, and that seemed to shock her lungs into action. She was still trying to scream as she sucked in that first lungful. The shrieking croaking noise she made tore at her throat, the air filling her lungs felt like it was full of needles, but it was such a relief to breathe that she hardly noticed the pain. Falling to the ground, she gasped and gasped until the fear of suffocating passed.

A loud popping noise cut through the ringing in her ears.

"Was that a gun?" Niven was looking back toward the clubhouse. "That sounds a hell of a lot like gunfire."

Willamette sat back up. A flurry of sharp, popping noises erupted all around them. The noises were different than the first, but familiar, and they certainly did not belong on the yacht club grounds.

"Those are pistols." She stood and tried to regather her wits.

There was a strange, silent pause before the scream erupted from the park. It started near the automation as survivors of the blast rose from amongst the bodies, and from there it spread. It set off a churning stir of the crowd. Some people tried to move away in one direction, some in another, and some stood confused. Then there was a second wave of popping noises from pistols, some from nearby, and that transformed the churn into panic.

"Those are cold gas single-shot pistols," Willamette said, her voice sounding odd over the ringing in her ears. "Short range, slow rate of fire, and not very accurate, but small enough to carry in a purse."

"You know something about guns?" Niven asked, looking around. He looked confused, but he was controlling his fear like a man accustomed to dealing with emergencies.

"My father made a point of making sure that all of his children were prepared to help their security team if the need ever arose," Willamette said, trying to copy Niven's example and stay calm. She did not wish to stay calm. She wanted to run, and scream, and cry.

"In the belly. In the belly. In the belly." Ida chanted the words.

With a small knife clutched in both of her hands, Ida held her arms straight out in front of her. Grimacing and crying, she closed her eyes and charged.

For Willamette, the attack provoked no thought, just movement. She turned her torso as she shifted to the left, narrowing the profile she presented to Ida and the knife. Planting her left foot, her right arm swept back in the other direction, down and across. She sensed, but did not feel, the impact against the middle of her forearm. The lack of significant resistance to the defensive swing of her arm translated directly into muscle memories that initiated the next move in the sequence. She crouched slightly as she filled the space cleared by the defensive swing of her right arm with a strike from her left. The springing thrust started deep in the ground and erupted up through her, her wrist cocked back, hand open.

The punch was meant to angle upward. An upward angle not only took advantage of the planted foot, it brought all of the energy loaded into the spring of all the tendons, muscles and ligaments into the movement. The angle would also drive a man's jaw up and across, maximizing the rotational force imparted into his skull. She knew that it was the rotational force that had the greatest impact on the brain, and the more she generated, the greater the chance of stunning an assailant. Ida, however, was a little girl, and the base of Willamette's palm hit her across the brow instead of the jaw.

Amazingly, the logic of why she was supposed to hit a man in that way passed through Willamette's head before the realization that it was her beloved little Ida who was trying to murder her.

The conscious recognition of that betrayal shattered the surreal, mystical, and distanced moment of action, and when it vanished, it took all of her finely honed instincts with it. In desperate moments, thought was a poor substitute for reaction. She remembered that she needed to bring her arms up and set her feet as she turned to follow Ida's headlong crash into the flower garden, but then a thousand unwanted thoughts stampeded in, and she noticed the blood. The defensive swipe of her right arm had caught the blade of the knife instead of Ida's wrist. Worries about tendons and arteries flashed through her head and it took a supreme effort to fight the rising alarm. The cut was bloody, but it was in the fleshy part of her forearm and probably not too bad.

Ida scrambled to her feet, tears streaming down her face as she held the knife out in front of her again, her arms stiff and straight. Lowering her head, she again chanted, "In the belly, in the belly," as she closed her eyes and charged at Willamette.

This time Willamette's reaction was to fall headlong into the crushing, paralyzing heartbreak of betrayal. Her mind refused to accept what was happening. If it had not been for Niven, Ida would have probably killed Willamette with that second attack.

Niven's tackle was straight from the sports field, but like Willamette's punch, it was a skill honed for confronting someone far bigger and taller than the young serving girl. He missed Ida with his shoulder, and his reach down at her brought a swinging forearm across her face, hitting her so hard that her feet flew up and over her head. Twisting as she flipped, her arms flailed, and her feet tried to run in the air. She landed on her face, and her body bent grotesquely, her heels slapping against the back of her head. It seemed impossible that her torso could bend that far without snapping her spine, but the unspringing of her body tossed her into a flopping, scrambling, frantic roll. She ended up on her belly and immediately tried to rise to her knees, but Niven's polished black boot slammed into her gut. That not only flipped Ida into a shrubbery, it quashed any inkling the girl might have had to try to stab Willamette again. She just curled up and whimpered.

"Ida tried to stab me," Willamette muttered, clutching at the cut on her arm. "She did stab me. My Ida stabbed me."

Niven grabbed Willamette. Wrapping his arms around her he pulled her backwards into the nearest shrubbery. The sharp ends from where the branches had last been trimmed dug into her flesh. That hurt even if it caused no real injury, and for some perverse reason, Willamette worried over the damage those sharp branch ends might do to her dress.

The leaves snapped back into place in front of them, and she noticed that the shrubbery was far bigger than it seemed. There was ample open space inside, and the individual bushes had trunks as thick as a man's thigh. The hedge must have been ancient.

"I loved Ida," Willamette said, more to herself than to Niven.

"Shhhh," he said.

A noble child ran through the flower garden and that unleashed a torrent as the crowd of others who were running away from the carnage near the automation followed him. Their feet churned the soft dirt as they fled through the garden and through the grotto, obliterating the flowers.

"I know that a servant is never a friend," Willamette said. "But I so enjoyed the way Ida helped me misbehave, and I thought she did too. I know she did. How could she even think of hurting me?"

Niven clamped his hand over Willamette's mouth, cutting off her mindless muttering. She screamed into his hand, and he clamped it harder over her mouth.

"Shhhh," he whispered, soothingly. "Shhhh."

There was a pop and a zip as something ripped through the shrubbery, and then another, and then a third, and then one of the zips ended in a thunking noise as a pistol dart hit the thick trunk of a nearby bush. That finally did it. That deadly, quivering little arrow embedded halfway into the hardwood brought Willamette back to her senses. Niven was pulling her down to a crouch. He was pulling her away from stray gunfire. She quit fighting him and crouched with him.

"You back in control?" he asked, whispering.

She nodded. She was still trembling, but she was back in control. He relaxed his grip and removed his hand from over her mouth, but he kept his arms around her.

"I truly cannot believe that my Ida tried to kill me," Willamette whispered.

"And now maybe you understand why I'm so upset about your father wanting me dead," he muttered, also whispering.

"Niven, I have lived with people wanting to kill me from the day I was born."

"Yeah, I guess you have, haven't you?" He removed the

decorative strip of silk that he wore around his neck, which was neither necktie nor scarf, and wrapped it around her lacerated arm. "Your reaction to that knife was beautiful, but the time to react has passed. Now we assess, analyze, and then act."

"Agreed," she said.

The people who had fled through the garden and clearing were gone, leaving their grotto empty again. The pistol fire was slowing and becoming more sporadic. The screaming was less panicked but there was wailing, and perhaps pleading, and that was punctuated by an occasional shrill shriek. Willamette had heard shrieks like that before and she knew that they were the cries of people realizing that they were being killed. Whatever was underway was grotesque, and it was well beyond the scope of someone planting a bomb in the automation.

Three men wearing bright blue armbands entered the clearing. Two carried brushcutters—the large sturdy knives that gardeners used to trim shrubberies—and the third carried a small pistol. The men were not searching, it was more of a quick check of the area.

A terrified little noble girl ran into the clearing from around the far hedge. She could not have been more than five years old, but her youth meant nothing to the men. The man with the pistol quite casually shot her as she turned to run away. It was an atrocity. The girl was so small that even though the pistol was not at all powerful, the dart still ripped right through her shoulder, leaving her to clutch helplessly at the exit wound as she fell to her knees and then the ground. Whimpering, she stared at the blood oozing out through her fingers.

"Was that one on Kofi's list?" one of the men carrying a brushcutter asked. He was wearing the colors of the club servants, and his uniform was stained with ground-in dirt. He was probably one of the groundskeepers.

"Kofi," Willamette whispered in horror, getting a warning squeeze from Niven.

"They're all on someone's list," the man with the pistol grumped as he reloaded the weapon. "The Colonel's list is just the priorities."

"Whatever," the groundskeeper said. "Still probably best not to leave her suffering like that."

"Oh boo hoo." The man with the pistol reloaded. "You want to put that thing out of its misery, then you can go right ahead."

Annoyed, the groundskeeper stepped over and cut off the girl's head with a quick swing of the brushcutter. The bastard at least had the good grace to look disturbed by the act. The other two were utterly indifferent.

"Let's go," the man with the pistol said. "We gotta check out our whole area quick-like."

The men walked off, chatting casually.

"You think we can get something to eat as soon as we're done checkin' our area?"

"Maybe we can wander over by the clubhouse and grab something if it's lying around."

"Yeah, but no booze. The Colonel was real clear that we can't touch the booze until he gives the okay."

"My gut says we need to run," Niven whispered as soon as the men were out of earshot.

"Your gut?" Willamette chided him. "Is that your idea of analysis?"

"You want analysis, fine," he whispered with a huff. "One, they sent your servant to stab you, so they clearly want to kill you. Two, this whole thing was carefully planned. Three, they've already taken enough control of the situation to move on to things like quick sweeps of the less obvious places around the club grounds, so I can't imagine that there's anyone or anything that will stop them from getting around to a real search of the grounds. Four, the club is built like a fortress. All of the security that is meant to protect us from something like this will now prevent the police and anyone else from getting in to help us. Taken as a whole, that means that no matter where we might hide inside the club grounds, they will find us and murder us, so our only choice is to get out."

"All true," she said. "However, if they are in complete control of the grounds as you presume, then they will have every gate and service entrance locked down."

"Who said we'd use an exit?" He gave her a nudge to urge her forward. Exiting the hedge was far easier than entering. She grabbed the purse that Ida had been carrying and nodded for Niven to lead the way.

CHAPTER 5

Chief Constable Huffer ignored the precinct's pitiful excuse for a captain and took charge. The word that had come in over the dedicated line to the central police dispatch was the stuff of nightmares and he knew that he only had moments to step in if he wanted to stop the precinct from descending into chaos.

"Throw them all in the drunk tank," he shouted as he climbed onto his secretary's desk. That was awkward. He was far too old and far too fat to be climbing around and standing on furniture. "Drunks, hookers, thieves, brawlers, people here to bail them out, lawyers, I don't care who they are, just lock them all in the drunk tank and we'll sort it later."

Two of the younger officers followed his command and their obedience was contagious. As the response to his orders spread, there was a noticeable reduction in the panic and pointless activity. That was a start.

"We don't know what's going on, but no matter what it is, milling around in here and yammering on about it isn't going to help. So everyone, and I mean everyone, gear up," he said, easing back from the earlier bellow. "If you aren't authorized to use a firearm, grab crowd control prods. Hell, I don't care what your job here is, gear up. If you don't know what you're doing you can take the place of the properly trained officers we pick up along the way to the yacht club. Just having people geared up and standing on street corners will look reassuring."

A sense of purpose pervaded the room, and the last of the chaos vanished. It only took minutes before everyone was ready to go.

"Are we ready?" Huffer shouted to the crowd as they gathered by the doors. There were noises of agreement that almost sounded like a cheer, and with that he led his small battalion of patrol officers, detectives, and office staff out the front door. Most of the qualified men were retirees who had come in to earn a little pocket coin and half of the rest were women. Still, Huffer thought the group looked impressive in riot gear, and he hoped that they would be a reassuring sight as they spilled out into the oddly empty street.

Word of the attack on the yacht club must have already started to spread and smart people were hunkering down. That was good. That should make things simpler, and it should make it easier to get his men over to the club.

"Anyone who has ever worked a security detail at the yacht club, walk with me," Huffer said as they turned toward the club. "We're going figure out a plan on the way."

Huffer heard rather than felt the arrow strike his chest, and for the briefest moment, he was bewildered by his stumbling step to the side. It wasn't until the second arrow embedded itself in his body that he understood what had knocked him off stride. He heard the distinctive noise of arrows finding a home in meaty targets. His posse was being ambushed by men with homemade crossbows.

Huffer took a third arrow and went down, never to rise again. He wasn't dead. Regardless of the weapon used or the nature of the attack, most wounds were slow to kill, and the Manganui Precinct's Chief Constable would live for several hours. Most of the thirty men and women he had pulled in under his command would live even longer than that, but they were all too severely injured to do anything other than think about dying.

Valarie screwed another two-meter length onto the rod and pushed the thermal charge farther down the pipe. She had to be close.

Adding one more length did it. When she pushed the rod, the charge hit what had to be the valve. The distance was about right, just under forty meters. She gently jabbed at the resistance a couple of times just to be sure it wasn't catching on a flaw in the pipe. The charge would go no farther so she set it off. It hissed and whistled, the sound resonating oddly in the pipe. Just as the first puff of acrid smoke burst out of the pipe, the sound vanished and most of the smoke was sucked back in. The charge must have burned through the valve at the other end.

She pushed the rod farther into the pipe to confirm it. Even adding another length to the push rod, she found no resistance. The pipe was now open to the modified elevator shaft that the Special Services Division called the garbage chute. Working methodically, despite her trembling hands, she disassembled the rod section by section as she pulled it out of the pipe.

The SSD Headquarters was probably the only building in the Commonwealth that treated Regatta Day as just another day. After all, if the enemies of the Lolofi regime didn't take holidays how could its most ardent defenders? Regatta Day or not, communications needed to be monitored, persons of interest needed to be interrogated, and prisoners need to be executed. Protecting the power of the Lolofi family was an ugly business, and Valarie was proud that she had dreamt up a way to turn the most wretched part of that building against the monsters that worked inside of it.

Neutralizing the SSD was a hell of a challenge. The Headquarters may have been built to look like an ordinary office building, but that appearance hid a fortress. The artistically cubic and overly robust design of the fountain served as a blockade to prevent the use of a truck for a ram raid. What looked like a lone security guard was the only man who was visible from the entrance. There was a large and well-manned security office situated behind a nondescript door just beyond the elevators. The decorative filigrees where the walls met the ceiling were camouflage for security cameras. Cameras and other electronics were rare and incredibly expensive bits of tech in a world that was starved for minerals, but there was no expense spared when it came to the SSD. The potted plants in the lobby were both barricades and shrapnel bombs that could be set off remotely by the team that monitored the security cameras from their bunker on the fourteenth floor. The security guard's desk was a blast- and dart-proof barrier that he could duck behind.

The coffee shop was just a coffee shop.

Structurally, the building was even more formidable. The windows were blast proof, several centimeters thick, and set in heavily reinforced frames. The structural support beams and connecting girders were encased in alternating layers of shock-absorbing foam and shrapnel-slowing, fire-resistant gel. The fourth floor didn't exist. It was a void that was designed to function as a buffer to isolate most of the building from fires, explosions, or any other threats that might originate from below. Similarly robust and layered defenses were built into the walls of the basements and subbasements, which were almost completely isolated from the network of utility tunnels that housed the air, water, power, and sewer infrastructure of the city.

Almost completely isolated.

Once the rod was out, Valarie put another thermal charge in the pipe, connected the detonator wires, and carefully began the process of pushing it through with the rod, adding length after length.

The garbage chute was a truly hideous nickname for a truly hideous thing. The garbage was people, and the chute was essentially nothing more than a convenient way to dump them into the Deep. No one knew for sure how long someone might fall before the pressure, heat, or toxic atmosphere of the Deep killed them, but for however long that was, the wind from the fall would drive the sulphuric acid that permeated the Venusian atmosphere through their clothing, burning them alive.

It took several breaths and a few tears before Valarie could settle back down enough to continue with the task at hand. She still had nightmares of Quinn falling down that shaft and to that hellish death, but that had been the point of making her watch them toss him into the chute. They wanted his death to hurt her beyond the grief of losing him, and that was why she had to do more than endure it. She had to make the SSD pay for that pain.

She carefully pushed the charge the last few meters, keeping tension on the wires to make sure that the transition from the pipe and into the shaft was as gentle as possible. The last thing she needed was for a small drop to yank the wires loose. Tying off her end of the wires to hold it in place, she pulled the rod back out. Once the rod was out, she secured the soft plastic adapter over the end of the pipe and checked the hoses as she followed them back to the service truck and started the gas.

There were security measures in place to prevent the unlikely possibility that someone might try to fly in under the city and use the chute to infiltrate the building, but it was the chute itself that was the weakness of the building. Like any other opening to the Drift, the chute was essentially an air lock, and the pipe that Valarie had discovered was the low-pressure, high-volume nitrogen supply used for the purging system. Normally, when the valve she had burned off was open, the pipe she was using would supply nitrogen to displace any of the caustic atmosphere that had drifted into the shaft when they opened the external hatch to drop someone out the bottom of the city. It was a simple system. Nitrogen was far lighter than carbon dioxide and it would push most of the heavier gas, and the acid that it carried, back down the shaft and out through a purge valve. Now the methane that she was pumping in through that pipe was doing the same to the nitrogen.

She watched the pressure drop on the methane tanks. The displacement of the nitrogen wouldn't be anywhere near perfect. Methane wasn't that much lighter than nitrogen, and nitrogen was prone to mixing with other gases, but it would still work.

The hiss from the tanks dropped in pitch as the methane ran low and she started the oxygen. Several minutes later, the hiss from those tanks dropped in pitch and that was the optimal moment. Smiling, she closed her eyes and set off the thermal charge.

Valarie had turned the garbage chute into a giant fuel air bomb. Three-quarters of a ton of methane and a ton of oxygen pumped into a space that was three meters by three meters, and twenty-one floors in height. An explosion across such a huge volume created a monumentally powerful shock wave.

The blowback through the one hundred–millimeter pipe that she was using was on the scale of a cannon being fired. In the confines of the alcove just off the utility tunnels, it was more than enough to render Valarie unconscious and rupture both of her eardrums. She would never hear again, but she would live, and a few days later, shortly before a stray dart killed her, she would have the satisfaction of learning just how much damage she had done.

It wasn't just the size of the explosion that made the blast so destructive, it was the way the building was designed to resist attacks from outside. Not a single window blew out, and confining such a massive explosion like that created a concussive force that was beyond what even she might have imagined. It crushed any compressible space within the building. The bones, cartilage, and flesh of the SSD officers' faces were driven back into their sinuses. Their ribs shattered and the shards were thrust into their lungs and hearts. Their tracheas collapsed, their internal organs were liquefied and injected into their intestines. Even the cartilage in their spinal column succumbed to the pressure. It was squeezed inwards with such force that it penetrated to the center of every vertebra.

If there was one thing that Colonel Kofi understood better than just about anyone, it was that everything about a military that relied on conscripted soldiers was focused on making sure that when you threw those reluctant soldiers into battle, their behavior was predictable and reliable. Reactions had to be so ruthlessly trained into them that they became undeniable responses to the stimuli. They had to be taught to fear their officers more than the enemy, and, most importantly, they could not be allowed to think of the lethality of the threats they faced.

That focus on throwing them into battle was necessary, but it was also a weakness. Little thought was ever given to all of the other situations and circumstances involved in military service. Most notably, no effort was made to win their hearts and minds. That was rational because it was usually pointless to try to create any sense of devotion, dedication, or patriotism to the government that had essentially enslaved those men. Further, to win their hearts and minds would involve developing loyalty to their fellow soldiers and camaraderie within their ranks. That was a danger because conscripts who cared about one another were halfway down the road to a revolt.

As a result, Larry was unremarkable. He was just one of the hundreds of young, conscripted soldiers stationed around Lightcastle who spent every moment of his enlistment boiling with resentment and counting down the days until discharge. It didn't bother him in the least to shove a knife into the back of his watch partner, and he was thrilled by the thought that the Bluebands attack on the capital's barracks would be a complete surprise. That same scene played out thousands of times around the Commonwealth that day. Those betrayals didn't destroy the Commonwealth's military, but they did cripple the bulk of the forces that the Lolofis might have called upon.

Kala seethed. She was a Blade, an elite soldier, but one awkward twist of her arm by an overzealous sparring partner and half a lifetime of training had been rendered pointless.

Even from her station deep in the service tunnels under Lightcastle, she had heard the explosion of the automation and she knew that her sisters would be launching attacks all over the city. Most would be small, quick, and simple assaults to secure critical locations or disrupt the responses of the various functionaries of the Lolofi regime, but those would still be real fights. No matter how insignificant they might be, joining one of those skirmishes would have finally given her the chance to test herself in combat. That first trip through the gauntlet of battle, that first ride on the cycle of anticipation, fear, death, and survival would have stripped away all the uncertainties, doubts, and rash presumptions that haunted an unblooded soldier.

She wasn't foolish enough to think that the Commonwealth would vanish in a day. Someone would try to hold it together, or claim it for themselves, or resist the Colonel's authority. There would be plenty of fighting to come and as soon as she managed to recover enough strength and mobility in her shoulder to be an asset, she would get the chance. Unfortunately, that knowledge didn't diminish her frustration in the slightest. She had been one of the best, and now she would forever be behind all of those she had worked so hard to surpass in training.

She fumed, but she didn't let it distract her. She attended to her assigned duty with fastidious care. No one told her why the utility junction was critical, or what the greasy-haired man with the ragged blue band on his arm had done in there. All she knew was that it was her responsibility to make sure that his handiwork remained untouched. She was determined to excel at her role, no matter how insignificant it was, and perhaps it was her conscious intent to remain completely focused on that task that drove her ill-considered reaction to the man carrying the toolbox. She was already leaping from the shadows with her knife drawn when she realized that he was walking past, not into, the utility junction.

Startled, he dropped the toolbox and staggered back, frantically digging at his pocket. She thought he was reaching for a weapon, but then she saw the wallet in his hand.

"Easy, easy, girl. We've all hit some desperate times along the way." His shaking hand offered her the wallet. He was on the far side of forty, world-weary and worn out. "There ain't much in there, but it'll get you a good meal or two."

She knew that she didn't need to kill him. It was obvious that if she just took the wallet, he'd run, relieved to escape unscathed, but she told herself that there was a chance that he might run for help. That was unlikely, and it was even more unlikely that he'd be able to find a police officer that would investigate a mugging in the utility tunnels during the regatta. Still, no matter how vanishingly low the odds might be, that possibility did exist, and that gave her an excuse.

He gasped as she drove the knife into his belly, but he didn't cry out. Instead, he wept, sobbing uncontrollably as he fell to his knees and then to the floor.

"Please." He held the wallet out to her, pleading as if she could undo what she had just done by taking it. "Please."

She felt dizzy, the world blurred, and she had trouble breathing. She fell to her knees, and it wasn't until she saw her tears falling onto her bloody knife that she realized that she was weeping along with the man.

Panicked, she tried to save him. She pressed her hands against the wound. She tried to think of a way to summon a doctor, or perhaps get him to a doctor, though she knew that it would do no good. The killing thrust had been perfect. The blood welling up through her fingers was black, straight from the liver. There was no way back from that. Except for the dying, he was already dead.

"Forgive me," she pleaded.

His last words were "Fuck you."

The rowdy gang of Bluebands thought they were soldiers. They were wrong.

The real soldiers were old, drunk, and unarmed, but they were also trained and determined to avenge the people they had just seen killed when the Bluebands had seized the dockside air lock just outside their favorite pub. Distracting those wannabe soldiers with a couple of rolling beer kegs, they enticed most of them to fire their ungainly homemade crossbows by flinging a barrage of beer mugs at them. The instant those weapons were neutralized, the old men charged. The Bluebands didn't know whether to reload or pull their knives, and the hesitation gave the soldiers more than enough time to plant the pub's kitchen knives in their bellies.

With that, the old soldiers went from outnumbered to the superior force. In the end, only three of the old men were killed and the survivors, armed with those makeshift crossbows, secured and held the air lock.

The Signal Corps was one of the reasons that the Lolofi family had held power for so many generations. The information the Corps sent and received was the thread that sewed the thousands of estates, towns, and cities into the single entity that was the Commonwealth. The family had gone to great lengths to make sure that they maintained absolute control of that signal. Only the most loyal of loyalists were allowed to serve as a Signal Corps officer. The job was only open to veterans who had voluntarily enlisted in the Lolofi Home Guard, and it was generally considered to be a reward for a distinguished military service record. That loyalty was further bolstered by making it the most coveted job in the Commonwealth. The pay scale started near the top of the standard civil service grades and increased in double increments, with no caps or limits. The children and grandchildren of Signal Corps officers were allowed to enroll in any school, free of fees, and spouses were allowed to join the Social Corps, giving them the same privileges as the wives of minor nobles.

The Signal Corps couldn't be infiltrated or corrupted, and it was all but impossible to disrupt their work. Countless practical measures had been put in place to keep it functioning no matter what. The signal rooms in all of the major habitats were fortified to the point that they couldn't be taken by force, and the headquarters was buried so deep in the foundation of Lightcastle that it was probably the most impenetrable bunker in the Drift. The signal lights and scopes on the outside of the Commonwealth's habitats were not only physically robust, they were also multiply redundant. There were over two hundred sending and receiving arrays situated around just the city of Lightcastle, and even the smallest of estates was required to have three or four. Further, that robustness extended beyond just making it impossible to disrupt the signals; it was also impossible to starve the Signal Corps of information. It had its own telephone switchboard with direct lines to dozens upon dozens of critical locations around the city.

Unwavering loyalty, however, was not the same as intelligence. In fact, blind loyalty often led to an obsession with routine and procedure, and that was what Kofi exploited. The officers responsible for the Signal Corps Headquarters were paragons of loyalty and exemplars of its flaws.

"Commander, I've got a call asking for urgent reinforcements," the watch officer reported.

"Log it and refer it to Special Services Division like the others," Commander Lisp ordered, annoyed.

"It's on the dedicated line from the Marine barracks."

"And the call claiming that giant ducks were attacking from the Deep came in on a dedicated line, and the call reporting a diseased pack of disrespectful sheep came in on a dedicated line, and the dozens upon dozens of other crank calls we have fielded today came in on dedicated lines. Obviously, someone has figured out a way to jack into those lines."

"But this has a verification code."

"Which you will pass on to Special Services Division, as per procedure," Lisp snapped. "And once they sort it, we will do as they advise."

"Special Services Division is not responding, sir," the watch officer reported.

Commander Lisp considered that for several seconds before he stepped through to the next option in the procedure manual. "Then send a runner."

The watch officer nodded and sent a man to convey the message.

He was sending that runner straight at a small team of Blades that was lying in wait along the route. He had no way to know that Colonel Kofi knew that a runner was the next step through the procedures.

Word of the coup would eventually spread beyond the confines of the capital, but there were dozens of steps through the Signal Corps' procedure manual that were still to come before that was likely to happen.

CHAPTER 6

Colonel Kofi didn't believe in perfection. He did not believe in black or white, good or evil, right or wrong. Reality was messy, uncooperative, and unpredictable, and that was before you involved people. The motley collection of disgruntled servants, petty criminals, and other castoffs that he had assembled as a force of irregulars didn't understand any of that. They were locked in an escalating spiral of grander and grander commentary that would soon lead to the claim that not a single dart had missed its target.

The handful of former military men who were rushing to claim rank in the mob had an inkling of how much he disliked that sort of thing. They had heard enough stories about the infamous Colonel Kofi to know that a messy but accurate report was far safer than offering him a shiny lie, but they didn't believe it. They lied less, but still polished off the roughest edges and exaggerated the things they thought the Colonel would praise.

Kofi's Blades were the only ones who truly understood. He had personally trained most of the senior officers, some of them from childhood, and they were the only ones who trusted him enough to give him the accurate and sometimes ugly facts and updates that a commander needed.

"We lost more Bluebands than we had hoped, but that hasn't caused any mission-threatening problems," Az reported as soon as she finished conferring with Dodi, her second in command.

"Bluebands?" Kofi was momentarily confused.

"My apologies, Colonel." Az nodded at the nearest man who was proudly sporting a blue armband. "That is what the irregulars have started calling themselves."

"I guess that makes you my Blueblades," Kofi said.

"I am your blade," Az said reflexively, though she looked almost embarrassed that the words had escaped her lips.

The selection of a bright cobalt blue had been as much an accident as anything else. It had been the base color of his family's uniforms, and when he had started to rebuild, the cloth had been lying around everywhere. There had been closets full of Kofi servant uniforms in all of the family's hidden homes and retreats that Morden Lolofi had never found, and there were countless bolts of the cloth sitting in the storerooms of tailors and seamstresses in the towns near the Kofi estates. However, even after that supply ran thin, the dyes needed to create that shade of blue were cheap and that meant that it was easy to obtain despite the destruction of the Kofi family.

He also liked it. As a noble family color, that bright shade of blue had always been distinctive, particularly in comparison to the more expensive darker blues that were common among the uniforms of the nobility. The color was also particularly striking when it was used for the bodysuits and short-skirted jumpers that the Blades wore, and it brought out the blue in the organic crystal blades of the women's knives. It also suggested that he was acting out of vengeance for his family, which might someday evolve into another useful myth.

"We're still in the process of accounting for all of the nobles who signed in at the gates today, but we have moved one of the families to the west dining room as you requested," Az said. "It is the Yassims, I believe."

"Good," Kofi said. "Move their uniformed servants in there as well."

Az nodded the order to an assisting Blade and walked to the west dining room with Kofi.

Yes, Blueblades. Kofi liked that.

"I only have the reports from the Bluebands, but even if you presume they are self-aggrandizing to the point of delusional, it still appears that phase two is going reasonably well," Az said. "I suspect that they have suffered far more casualties than they should have, and there are some objectives that are a concern due to their absence in the heroic tales, but we also have yet to see any significant number of police or other security units approach the club, so they are at least proving to be an effective distraction."

"Good," Kofi said. "Assign a small team of ... Blueblades to gather a more accurate assessment."

Az nodded at an accompanying Blade whose arm was in a sling. The woman nodded acknowledgement and ran off. It was then that Kofi noticed that except for Az and Dodi, all of the Blades he'd seen were injured.

"How many Blades have we lost?"

"There were only six killed and two dozen seriously wounded in the assault on the yacht club grounds." She gestured at the Blades around them as they walked through the main ballroom. "And about twice that many who are too wounded to continue fighting but capable of other tasks. I have no idea on the status of the other units around the city."

Kofi nodded, making sure Az understood that he approved of keeping those wounded women engaged. It wasn't just efficient; it was good for morale.

The west dining room was one of the more useless of the spaces in the yacht club. It was too big to be comfortable for intimate, single table dining and too small for what most of the nobles would consider a modest function. It was occasionally booked for business meetings, but for the most part it was just used as a staging area for big events. That had obviously been the case for the regatta. It was a mess, as were the Yassims. The ridiculously ornate costumes of the wife and two daughters had not been intended for rough handling, and the fat bastard looked like he was on the verge of a coronary. The servants were holding up better than the family, but they were terrified.

"Lord Yassim, I do not have time for pleasantries or subtleties so I will make this simple," Kofi said. "I have no use for you unless you can prove unflinching, immediate obedience to my orders. Do you understand me?"

Yassim nodded, his jowls flapping obscenely under his chin.

"Good." Kofi untied the man's hands and handed him the cord

that had bound him. "Kill that servant, the youngest boy over there, and I will let you live."

Yassim didn't hesitate. He didn't even have the good grace to feign reluctance or even shame. In one swift and agile move he leapt over to the boy and wrapped the cord around his neck. It was obvious that the fat bastard didn't know what he was doing. He hadn't looped the cord before throwing it over the boy's neck, so he was pushing his hands across each other rather than pulling. He also had too long a length of cord between his hands, so he was out near the extent of how far his arms could cross before the rope pulled tight against the boy's throat. However, if anything, that just emphasized how comfortable he was with murdering a servant.

The boy fought, frantically, desperately, sickeningly, but Yassim didn't relent. He didn't let any hint of empathy or concern bother him. Neither did the wife. The daughters appeared to be disturbed, but it looked like they were annoyed with the boy for failing to die quietly rather than disgusted with their father.

It went on, and on. The boy was gasping. His face turned red, and his eyes bulged, but the fat noble just wasn't cutting off enough air or blood to get the job done.

Finally, Yassim started yanking the boy around with the cord. He pulled the boy to the left and then the right. When the kid lost his footing, it finally ended. It still wasn't immediate or even quick, but once the boy's weight was added to the pull on the cord it tipped the scale toward death.

Kofi turned to Az. She looked stoic. She and her lieutenants were doing their damnedest not to let their disgust show, but Kofi knew them well enough to see what they truly felt, and he was pleased. It was important that his women believed that killing should be efficient and that suffering should only be inflicted when it served a purpose. When they started to enjoy it, they became dangerous.

"Have the irregulars …" Kofi hesitated. "What did you call them? Bluebands?"

Az nodded.

"Have the Bluebands take the Yassims out to the courtyard behind the kitchen and kill them," he instructed Az. "Set the rest of their servants free and tell them that they and their fellow servants may take anything they can carry from the properties of their former masters."

"You said we'd go free!" Yassim bellowed.

"Life isn't always about you, you fat, soulless bastard, and that is the real irony of this test," Kofi said. "It was your willingness to kill that boy that saved the rest of your servants. A noble who would refuse to kill a servant to save himself is the kind of person who is truly noble, and that just might inspire loyalty and devotion in his servants. We can't risk having devoted servants running loose, trying to help cousins and second sons hold on to this corrupt and inhumane system you've constructed. So, if you had refused to murder the boy, then we would have had to kill both your family and all your servants, just to be safe. But after witnessing what you did to that boy, there isn't a servant in the world who would be stupid enough to side with you or your kin."

Yassim wailed and begged as the Bluebands hauled him and his family away. The women managed to display a little more dignity, particularly the youngest. She spat, threw vile, defiant curses, and kicked with some effect. Kofi could appreciate someone who fought to live instead of begging. In another life, another circumstance, she might have grown into a real person instead of the caricature of nobility she had become.

"The Lolofis?" Kofi asked Az as he nodded an acknowledgement of the thanks offered by the exiting servants. He doubted if their looks at him were thankful. They were obviously upset about the boy, and one of the women was rocking him and wailing away like the world had just ended. Still, Kofi chose to act as if the ungrateful bastards were thankful.

"Morden, Jillian, and the two sons who were here, along with their families, are in the small ballroom," Az said. "We have confirmation that their youngest son was killed by the team you sent to his estate."

"And their spoiled little princess?" Kofi asked.

"There has been no sign of Willamette," Az said.

"Find her, Az. Find her now," he said. "I doubt if she's capable of much, but her existence is a threat. She could be used to great effect."

"We know she's still on the grounds and we have all the exits," Az said. "It is only a matter of time before we have her. She cannot escape."

"Be that as it may, she is a loose end that must be tied off. The

Lolofis are masters at installing true loyalists in key governmental and administrative roles, so we don't dare try to take control of the Commonwealth until we confirm, without any trace of doubt, that we have killed every single person who can claim the loyalty attached to that name."

"And it would also be foolish to make the same mistake that the Lolofis made with you," Az said, humorlessly.

"There is that as well," Kofi agreed, grinning.

"I'll get a team on it." Az nodded to Dodi who leapt into action.

"And check bodies. She might already be dead," Kofi shouted at the woman running to organize the search for Willamette. "She should be dead. I put a little knife right next to her."

Niven continued to impress Willamette. The servants who had gathered near the groundskeeper's workshop did not rush to murder them. That was a good thing, and it was probably to Niven's credit. A few of the boys who had helped set up the clearing recognized him, and they stopped the others from attacking.

"You need to get out," one of the club's older servants hissed. "They'll find you here."

"That's exactly what I was about to say," Niven said. "If you aren't with those men with the blue arm bands then it's not safe for you anywhere inside the club. They're after the nobles, but they've killed a hell of a lot of servants, too, so you need to get out."

"Easier said than done," a younger servant said. He looked like he had become the group's de facto leader. "They control all the exits."

"That doesn't mean that they control all of the ways to get out." Niven pointed at the groundskeeper's workshop. The workshop was built against the wall and the moment Niven pointed at it Willamette could see how a teenage boy might use it to sneak over the wall.

"Over the wall?" the servant asked.

"The wall and all the fancy spikes along its top were designed to keep people out, not in." Niven smiled. "And I know for a fact that a person can sneak out that way."

"What was her name?" a servant shouted from the crowd.

Niven grinned and made an exaggerated hushing gesture as he nodded comically at Willamette. The crowd laughed, but then fell into a hush when they realized who she was.

Niven, again, came to the rescue.

"My whaling ship is parked on the merchant docks," Niven said. "Help us get over that wall and we'll take anyone who wants to leave the city with us."

Agreeable murmurs were followed by a nod of agreement from their unofficial leader.

"Okay," Niven said. "We need a ladder or something to make it easy for everyone to get onto the roof, and we need a bunch of bags or tarps or whatever else we can find to lay over the spikes along the top of the wall, and we need ropes or something else for everyone to climb down the other side."

It should not have surprised Willamette that it went remarkably well. She had long ago learned that people were remarkably good at getting things done when they wanted to. That usually meant that an incentive system that rewarded accomplishments in a meaningful way paid for itself several times over, and at that moment there was no reward those servants wanted more than the chance to escape the club grounds. They worked at it like demons.

"Berth T-57," Niven told the woman who followed them over the wall. "If we're not already there when you get there, tell the captain of the Crystal Star that Niven says his wife's cooking is lethal and that I promised you a ride off the city."

The woman nodded.

"Say it," Niven demanded.

"T-57, Crystal Star. Niven says captain's wife's cooking is lethal," the woman said.

"Good," Niven said. "You make sure the next ten people off the wall know that before you head there, and you make someone stay to tell the next ten, okay?"

The woman nodded and Niven pulled Willamette into a run. They crossed the wide boulevard that encircled the yacht club and were quickly into what looked like a working-class residential neighborhood. It was a sharp contrast to Niven's noble family uniform and the simplistic but still extreme finery of Willamette's clothes, not to mention her hairdo.

"That was gallant, offering them a way out of the city,"

Willamette said, pulling her hand free of Niven's to make it easier for them to move quickly.

"It wasn't gallant. It was a diversion." Niven frowned as he looked up, using the structure of the dome to get his bearings amongst the tall buildings. "The captain of the Crystal Star will take them. He owes me a few favors, but it's not my ship. I sent them that way because I was sure that some of them will get caught or would sell the information."

"Regardless of that selfish motive," she said. "For the servants who do escape the city by that means, the effect is still the same."

Niven clearly did not agree with her, but he let the matter drop. They reached an intersection and he started to turn left, but then he stopped and frowned.

"My ship is in the J-docks, but I don't think we can run there either," he said.

"Agreed," she said. "If I was executing a coup, I would have sent someone to watch your ship the moment our engagement was announced."

"You think this is a coup?" He seemed surprised by the idea.

"I am certain of it." Willamette nodded pointedly at the bodies of two police officers. "If this was about attacking the club or attacking my family, they would not have bothered to kill any police officers outside of the club."

"Gruesome, but it makes sense." Niven nodded. "So, if we can't run to my ship, what other options do we have? I can't imagine that it would be a good idea to run to the palace."

"If you mean the Chairman's City Estate, I have to agree," she said. "If we could get inside the estate, or inside the Commonwealth Council Chambers, all of our problems would be solved."

"Which is exactly why they'd make sure we couldn't get to them or any other obvious place you might run," Niven said.

"We could pay someone to hide us. Perhaps you have a criminal friend in the city? I had Ida include some money in my purse, for tips and ..." Willamette gasped as she opened the purse that Ida had been carrying. It was stuffed full of jewelry. "And we have a small fortune."

"That's nice, but it doesn't help all that much at the moment," he said. "Putting aside your assumption that I have criminal friends, we don't dare trust anyone we'd have to bribe. We need to find someplace to hide on our own."

"How about a hotel room booked under an alias, and instructions on how to sneak in through the servants' entrance?" Willamette pulled the hotel room key and the note from her cloak pocket.

"That might just work," Niven said.

Willamette read Ida's tidy but still childish handwriting. "The room is in the Kelly Tower, in the Titahi district. Titahi ..."

"Shops full of ridiculously expensive shoes," he muttered, pointedly.

"Oh, yes, I know where the Titahi district is."

"Of course you do."

Flint was deeply disturbed by how much he was enjoying stealing a plow. The brazen wrongness of it all was exciting. Which shops should he break into looking for a plow? Why only the best shops, of course. How would he get the plow to the ship? Why not steal a truck? If he was going to steal a truck, he may as well make it a brand-new service truck that was loaded with a compressor and all the tools a man could ever need.

Between the excitement of stealing and the work of getting those ill-gotten gains moved to the Drunken Monkey, he even managed to briefly forget that the reason that his crime spree didn't matter was because he was already facing a death sentence or two. The reality of those death sentences, however, haunted him as he started the work of installing the new plow. Even if he was right in thinking that it would be several hours before anyone came searching for the owner of the plow they'd dropped through the dome, replacing a plow was a four- or five-hour job for a crew of experienced mechanics. Even with Em's help, he'd be lucky to finish in a day. Knowing that made the urge to rush all but overwhelming, and rushing led to mistakes, and mistakes cost time, and that increased the urge to rush. Every dropped bolt, every stuck nut, every setback felt like it would be the thing that cost him his life.

Every few minutes he decided to just pack it all on the ship and fly off without the plow, and every few minutes he reminded himself that they'd never make it out of the Commonwealth without a plow. With only a kite, they would be limited to downdrift runs and cuts, which meant that whoever came after them would know exactly the direction to search. They'd also be unable to land on any of the outposts or little estates that didn't have proper landing facilities, which would rule out all of the places that might be willing to hide them.

Then again, it was highly likely that it would be late tomorrow before anyone came looking for them. Fourteen or fifteen hours on a moderate downdrift cut would put a hell of a lot of distance between the Drunken Monkey and Lightcastle. That distance would feel good even if they would still be a very long way from escaping the Commonwealth.

"Hey Em, what would you think if I suggested we abandon the Monkey?"

Flint used a stolen forklift to lift the big spool of main plow cable up so Em could lock it into the spool stand. Given the forces the cable would transfer from the plow to the ship, the cable was surprisingly light, but a kilometer and a half of even the lightest cable still weighed a lot.

"I don't think that would be anywhere close to my list of good ideas," she said as she worked the length of pipe through the center of the spool. "This is the capital, Flint. No matter how much money those blue-frocked bitches paid us, it won't do us much good unless we can get away from the city, and this old beast is our best chance. I certainly wouldn't bet on buying a ride out of the city once the cops start looking for us."

"Yeah, but what if they weren't looking for us?" Flint lowered the forks, setting the spool on the stand, ready to unwind cable onto the Drunken Monkey's main plow winch.

"Flint, they're going to come after us." Em began cutting away the plastic that kept the cable from unwinding off the spool. "And when it comes to finding people facing death sentences, I wouldn't expect them to leave any corner of the city unsearched."

"They aren't going to be searching the city for us if they think we've already left." Flint rolled one of the spools of control cabling over to a spool stand.

"So ... what? You're thinking of taking up mass hypnotism?"

"No, I'm thinking that we launch the Monkey on a downdrift run without us."

That got Em's attention.

"We could secure the ship to the dock with the main plow cable, inflate the lift cells in the wings, launch the kite, scramble out, and cut the cable," Flint said. "It would look like we made a run for it."

"And a ship taking off like that, when the docks are closed, will set off a scramble to chase after it, even today. And it'll just be running down the Drift, so it'll be easy to catch. Figure it'll take them a couple of hours to get to it, and when they find out that it's empty, then they'll know were still here, and that means that they'd start searching the city for us even sooner," Em said.

"I hate it when you go and make sense," Flint muttered.

"The smart thing to do is stick to our plan," Em said. "We wait until after the regatta is done, use the alias for the Monkey that we set up to get a departure clearance, and hope it takes another day or two for them to track down the records that show who owned that plow."

All of that made sense and having a reason they couldn't launch immediately helped. Normally, Flint wouldn't think that reducing their options was a good thing but knowing that getting the plow installed before they took off was their best option helped him focus.

Az felt old. By any reasonable standard she was still a young woman, but there was nothing reasonable about the years that weighed upon her. It wasn't just the physical toll from the fighting, or the wear and tear from all the training it took to stay sharp. It was more as if a gritty weariness had seeped into every intangible corner of her being, grinding the edge off everything. Pleasure, pain, thrills, desires, and all the other things that turned living into something more than existing all felt soft and dull compared to her memories.

Just a few years ago she would have been infuriated by how little fighting she had done in the taking of the yacht club. She would have been gnawing at the leash that her own experience had put around her neck and begging to be released from the burden of command, but things had changed, profoundly. She wouldn't say she was happy to leave so much of the fighting to the younger Blades, but she no longer cared who pulled the blade across the throat, either figuratively or literally. All that mattered was that someone cut the head off the rotting corpse of the Commonwealth.

She followed Colonel Kofi into the ballroom where the Lolofis were being held. Unlike the Yassims, every single one of the Lolofis exuded the fiery, confident, and commanding presence that befit people who claimed to be noble. They were terrified. That much was obvious. But they still managed to cast an imposing presence upon the room.

Kofi considered the Lolofis, but his attention immediately locked on a girl hiding in amongst their huge herd of servants.

"You! Stupid little girl!" Kofi shouted. "Did you kill Willamette?"

"Not completely," the girl said, trembling.

Zo, one of the youngest of the Blades, rushed in and whispered in Az's ear.

"What in the hell does not completely mean?" Kofi bellowed, right in the little serving girl's face.

"It means that Willamette escaped," Az relayed the message from Zo. "She and her new fiancé went over the wall."

"Over the wall?" Kofi scowled. "How is that possible?"

"I don't know, but we caught a mob of servants following them, and several confirmed that she was one of the first who went over," Az said. "Dodi is organizing a small team to pursue."

It took a moment for Kofi to find a target for the fury that was provoked by that news and, unsurprisingly, it was the little serving girl.

"I warned you what would happen if you didn't do your job, didn't I?" Kofi growled menacingly at the girl before nodding to Az. "Take her into the kitchen and give her a good taste of the pain that she's going to suffer for the rest of her very long and unpleasant life. There should be plenty of things in there to burn her with."

"Burn her" and "the rest of her life" were Kofi's code for "get a good scream out of her and don't let anyone know you killed her." The illusion that the Colonel had a dungeon full of eternally suffering people was a powerful fiction that he worked diligently to maintain. He was also asking Az to handle it directly.

"But I did cut her," the girl shouted as Az grabbed her arm. "I tried to stab her, twice, and I cut her once. I tried, I really did, but she just got away."

"I told you before, Ida, it's too late for trying," Kofi said. "Failure has consequences. Now I have to waste time and effort searching all over the city for Lady Willamette."

"I know where she went!" the girl shrieked just before Az pulled her out of the room. "My cuzzie booked a room for her. A secret one, so Lady Willamette could sneak away with her new fiancé and, you know, fiancé him."

"Oh really?" Kofi asked. His tone made Az pause at the door.

"Yeah, I remember the name of the hotel from writing it on a note for her, but I'm not going to tell you that unless you promise to be nice to me." Ida was frantic, desperate, but also surprisingly brave. She was bargaining, not pleading, and Az could see that it impressed Kofi.

"You can write?" Kofi asked the girl.

"Lady Willamette made me learn so she could sneak me notes and get me to do some naughty stuff for her that her mum and the other serving girls wouldn't know about," Ida said.

Jillian Lolofi gasped, mortified.

"Okay," Kofi said. "Writing and brave enough to bargain with me are things that might even be worth more than showing everybody how much it hurts to fail, but you only get to live if you can start doing your jobs right."

"I can," Ida said. "I know I can."

It looked like Kofi was just going to use Ida as a serving girl. They could always use someone for that. However, when Kofi expectantly held out a hand to Az, she realized that he had far different plans for the little girl.

Az handed Kofi one of her knives. It wasn't the smallest she carried, but it was perfect for the girl. Its blade was about as long as Az's hand was wide, and it was narrow. The edges were more than sharp enough to cut a throat, or allow it to be used as a knife, but its needle-sharp tip was designed so that even someone as small as Ida could shove it between a person's ribs.

Kofi made a show of using the blue-bladed crystalline knife to cut Ida's bonds before he put the handle in her hands.

"Start with Lady Jillian," he said.

Ida didn't understand, and then when it dawned on her what Kofi wanted, she was horrified.

"Ida, we know all about the time that Lady Jillian beat you half to death, then locked you in a closet and forgot about you," Kofi said. "Mattie told us all about it. You were in there for days, in the dark, alone, starving, crying, dying. It was only an accident that Lady Willamette found you."

Ida trembled from head to toe. Tears streamed down her face and Az could see her falling back into the darkness in that closet.

"Now take all that dark and all that scared, put it in that blade," Kofi said softly but commandingly. "Put it all in that blade and shove it into that evil bitch's belly where it belongs."

Screaming, Ida held her arms out straight in front of her, lowered her head and charged at Lady Jillian. It was wretched technique, but against a helpless opponent, it did allow the girl to put all the weight and momentum she could muster into the thrust of the knife.

The impact not only pierced the Grand Lady Jillian's corset, it drove her back a step.

"How dare you?" Lady Jillian's voice was loaded with fury and disdain rather than pain or fear. "I own you."

"Again, Ida," Kofi said, again using that soft but compelling tone he used to demand action.

Ida yanked the knife out and wailed like an animal as she thrust it back at Jillian's belly. The corset deflected the blade, almost knocking it from Ida's grasp, but Ida reacted without hesitation. Jumping to the side she stabbed at the woman's flank and with that, Ida was consumed. When she chose to use her knowledge from dressing Willamette to kill Lady Jillian, she became the weapon that Kofi wanted. There was nothing left of the little serving girl. She was just a mindless, manic little human-shaped animal that shrieked unintelligibly as she frantically stabbed and stabbed and stabbed at the thinnest part of that corset.

"You are my Little Knife," Kofi said, his voice booming. "You are nothing but my Little Knife."

It took a dozen thrusts, but Lady Jillian finally fell to a knee, allowing Ida to stab her throat.

"Next!" Kofi shouted. "My Little Knife will cut the next one down. My Little Knife will cut them all!"

Ida attacked the oldest son. Again, she held her arms straight out, put her head down and charged. It didn't work the second time. Even though her target was hobbled and had his hands tied behind his back, he managed to knee her in the chest, knocking her back. She responded by scrambling to her feet and stabbing at his crotch. That made Az wonder if Ida might have suffered some other horrors at the hands of the Lolofis. It could have been that Ida's small stature put the belly of the tall and imposing man out of her reach, but sometimes, when girls had been sexually abused, just killing a man never seemed to be quite enough.

On the second thrust at his crotch, Ida cut his femoral artery, unleashing a spray of blood that shocked her and sent her staggering backwards.

"Next!" Kofi shouted.

Ida wiped at her eyes, confused.

"Kill the next one!" Kofi shouted, and Ida leapt at the youngest son's wife. That woman didn't have the heart of a Lolofi. Her fierce facade crumbled. She shrieked and pleaded, but Ida didn't notice.

When Ida ignored the pleas of the woman, she passed the second of the critical tests. The girl had been freed of the innate compassion that restrained people in even their most unhinged moments. Kofi asked Az the question with a raised eyebrow. Az shrugged and shook her head. She knew what Kofi was thinking. Regardless of how few Blades they had lost, they were staring at a war, and they would need to expand their ranks. Still, it was a bad time to start a new project, and Ida would be a project.

Ida was too young, for starters. No matter how much pain there might be in the girl, it hadn't settled into her bones like it would in another four or five years. There was nothing like the combination of the overblown teen angst of a hellish puberty and the abuse thrown at a servant or street kid to set the foundation needed to turn a woman into a weapon. There was also something about Ida that didn't fit the proper mold for a Blade. Maybe too much fear and not enough anger. Az wasn't sure, but the girl didn't feel like she was ready or right for it. Regardless, it wasn't her decision to make, so Az and the other Blades would either make it work or kill Ida trying.

Now that Ida had been broken, the most important thing was to make sure she didn't burn all the way through the fire that was driving her. They couldn't let exhaustion be the thing that pulled her back over the line between raw animal fury and the real world of human beings. Az would let the girl kill one more, the next son's wife, but that was it.

Az stepped up to Morden Lolofi and in one smooth motion she drew her knife and pulled it across his throat. It probably would have been more dramatic if they had exchanged a few pithy words, or if Az had done something to mark the moment, or if she had just made him suffer, but that wasn't the purpose of a Blade. A Blade's purpose was to cut, so that was what she did, leaving no chance that she might fail to kill him.

Az felt her knife nick one of the vertebrae in the evil bastard's neck, and with that realized that she had been wrong. She did care who cut the head off the rotting corpse of the Commonwealth. It felt good to be the one.

Willamette had more than a few doubts about just how stealthy she and Niven were managing to be as they worked their way across the city. It had been easy to find empty streets by simply avoiding shouting and screaming that suggested fighting, but the people that they did encounter noticed them. They were careful not to let any of those people get close enough to recognize her, but it still had to be obvious that they were nobles on the run.

Sneaking in through the servants' entrance to the hotel did not ease her worries in the slightest. On a normal day, the staff would have just chuckled to themselves and played along, pretending not to notice, but word must have spread that it was not a normal day. Every pair of eyes in the kitchen followed her as she and Niven walked through to the service elevator.

"Maybe we should find someplace else to hide," Niven suggested, quietly.

"I agree," Willamette said. "However, we should visit the room first. When Ida's cousin prepared it for us, she included some less conspicuous clothing."

"I'm not sure how much good it will do for you to change," Niven said, annoyed. "Except for that hair, you're already far less conspicuous than I am in this uniform. Maybe I can buy something from one of the staff."

"Ida's cousin prepared the room for us." Willamette scowled as she emphasized the word "us." "You were part of every element of that preparation, including arranging for clothing that would allow you to depart the building in a manner that would go unnoticed by gossips and rumormongers."

"Oh," was all that Niven could manage to say.

"I cannot believe that I thought you were clever," she grumbled, playfully.

Kofi wasn't upset by the need to pursue Willamette halfway across the city. He wasn't even annoyed. It was one of the more improbable complications that could have arisen, but chasing down a stray noble or two had always been expected. He hadn't expected to lead the chase himself, but he also hadn't expected the stray to be a Lolofi.

"What do you mean you can't tell me what room she's in?" Kofi threw all the menace he could into the words.

"I mean that I do not know what room this young couple might be in, and without a name to look up in the registry, I have no way to find it," the clerk snapped back. That was a mistake. The man was scared out of his wits, especially by Ida who was covered in blood, twitchy, and spastically pointing her knife at anything that moved. Still, insolence was unacceptable.

"Ida," Kofi said. She didn't respond so he shouted, "Ida!"

That startled the vacant look out of Ida's eyes, but she still had trouble focusing. She hadn't been drugged, but she may as well have been. Breaking a girl affected her mind and body in ways that were remarkably similar to the high and withdrawal of stimulants.

"What name did your cousin use to book the room?" Kofi demanded.

"I don't know the room number," Ida said. "It was on the key thingy."

"I know that you don't know the room number," Kofi said, sternly, forcefully. "I didn't ask for the room number. I asked for the name your cousin used to book the room."

"The room number is on the key thingy," Ida said.

Az strode in from the back. Kofi didn't even have to ask the question.

"The kitchen staff said that a young noble snuck a prostitute in through the servants' entrance about twenty minutes ago," Az reported. "If Willamette abandoned the more ridiculous parts of one of those regatta gowns they wear, she might look like a prostitute."

Kofi closed his eyes and thought back through his first meeting with Ida in Willamette's dressing room.

"Ida was fetching Willamette a travelling cloak, satin, delicate, creamy gold," he said, opening his eyes and looking at Az. "Get a better description of this prostitute from the kitchen staff and see if you can confirm that it was her."

Az nodded at a Blade and the woman dashed off to the kitchen.

Kofi thought about reminding that young and enthusiastic Blade to be gentle. For the moment at least, servants were their allies. The thought came too late, however. The Blade was gone before he could say anything.

"And get all the exits locked down," he reminded Az.

"Exits are already locked down." Az rolled her eyes at him, reminding him to whom he was speaking.

"Of course they are," Kofi said, then nodded at the insolent desk clerk. "Should we sharpen my Little Knife?"

Az thought a moment and then shook her head ever so slightly. Kofi replied with a frown. The disapproval in Az's expression vanished as she took the frown as an order, but she had made her point. Grabbing Ida by the hair, she viciously jerked the girl's head back and shouted, "What are you?"

"I am his Little Knife!" Ida shouted back.

"And what does a knife do?" Az shouted.

"A knife cuts." Ida's voice trembled like she was about to burst into tears.

Az savagely turned Ida's head toward the desk clerk and hissed, commandingly, "Then cut."

"I am his Little Knife," Ida said, the glazed vacant look of a drug addict returning to her eyes.

With just the slightest of shoves toward the desk, Az set the girl loose. It was like unleashing a manic and vicious little dog. Ida was over the desk with the kind of spring and scramble that only a child could manage, and she howled as she slashed and stabbed. The wild flailing was largely ineffective, but she was frenetic beyond measure and the clerk looked like he might end up dying from a thousand cuts.

"Very good, Little Knife," Kofi cheered her on. "It isn't so easy when they can fight back, is it?"

"She's too young," Az whispered, being careful not to let anyone else hear her as they watched Ida flail away. The desk clerk was still on his feet, but he was trapped behind the desk and already too wounded to have any real chance of escaping.

"You were younger," Kofi said.

"No, I wasn't, and that's why you should listen when I tell you that she's too young," Az said, sternly. "Besides, it isn't the years that make a girl old enough, it's the pain."

Kofi understood Az's reluctance. Ida needed a great deal of work. That reluctance to kill needed to be crushed into indifference before she could be built back up into a proper Blade, but the more he saw of her, the more he was convinced that his instincts had been right when he'd indulged the whim of pushing her to kill her seamstress friend.

He had imagined Ida as the perfect invisible and disposable little assassin. The youngest serving girls could wander into places that a woman or even a teenager couldn't. When children were playing or running about as they were prone to do, no one questioned the innocence of their incursions into forbidden rooms, passageways, or buildings. However, it was starting to look like Ida could be a hell of a lot more than just a disposable weapon.

She didn't have the seething anger that he usually looked for in recruits, but her other merits would certainly make it worth working around that imperfection. No one would think that such a young serving girl could read and write. She could be the perfect spy. He also suspected she would blossom into the kind of woman who could flirt her way into any man's bed. That wasn't something he would normally ask of a Blade, but Ida was not going to be a normal Blade.

Ida jumped back up on the hotel reception desk and it was like a dog shaking off a bath. She shook her hair wildly, flinging droplets of fresh blood. She was horror incarnate, but soon she would be more.

"They knew it was Willamette all along," the young Blade that Az had sent back into the kitchen reported. Kofi noted the blood on the woman's hand and on the handle of one of her knives.

Kofi acknowledged the young Blade—Mikka was her name—with a nod and pondered his next move. There was no way out of the hotel and the only real issue that remained was the mechanics of finding Willamette.

"Bottom up, Az," he said. "She has no chance to escape, so all you have to do is find her. Search every nook and cranny, no matter how small and no matter how long it takes."

"We should concentrate the search on the upper floors," Mikka blurted. "All of the suites are on the upper floors."

Mikka was obviously afraid to speak out, but she pushed forward anyway. Kofi approved, mentally noting her name for when he reviewed the day.

"Willamette is a Lolofi. She would almost certainly book a suite," Mikka added, mistaking his moment of thought for skepticism.

"Almost certainly," Kofi said, gently but also emphasizing the word "almost." "And even if she did buy a fancy room, what if something, or someone, has tipped her off and she isn't hiding in that room anymore?"

Mikka nodded, chastened but still standing proud and looking directly at Kofi.

He thought for a long moment, considered the situation, and considered Az. The search would be tedious, but it was also straightforward. In many ways it was an insult to Az's talents, but it was also so critical to the mission that if he didn't handle it personally, he dared not leave it to any other.

"This is your responsibility, Az," he said. "Willamette is the last Lolofi. You will not stop until you extinguish that name from the Drift. Nothing else matters until you complete that task. Am I understood?"

"Perfectly," Az said.

Kofi took Dodi and a couple of additional Blades with him as a personal escort, but he left knowing that Az could handle the final moments of eliminating Morden Lolofi's princess at least as well as he could, perhaps better.

CHAPTER 7

For Willamette, stepping into the suite was bittersweet in so many ways. The hotel tower was one of the tallest in the city. It stretched at least thirty stories beyond the dome, and even though their room was nowhere near the top, it was above the dome and the view out over the city was breathtaking. The room wasn't quite what she expected, but it was still wonderful, and her despair over Ida's betrayal became strangely mixed with an appreciation for the work the girl's cousin had put into preparing the room. In addition to the satin sheets, robes, and wines that Willamette had requested, there was a selection of massage oils beside the bed, and a basket of fruit and other foods, and there were flowers. The flowers were a very nice touch. Unfortunately, all that effort put into securing and preparing the room would go to waste and for some perverse reason, that bothered Willamette more than Ida's horrific betrayal.

"Whoa," Niven said. "I did not expect this."

"Innovative and successful men also tend to be stubborn and rebellious." Willamette tossed the overstuffed purse onto the bed, struggling to get her mind to settle into a more reasonable state. "There were several scenarios where a hesitant reaction to our betrothal might make it necessary for me to ... more assertively entice your interest in our marriage."

"Necessary," Niven muttered. "How romantic."

"There were also a few hopeful scenarios where seducing you might be desirable," Willamette said.

"Hopeful is good," Niven said. For some reason, the warmth in his voice helped.

"Indeed, hopeful is good." Willamette tried to reciprocate his tone.

Ida's cousin had paid similar attention to detail with the clothing she had placed in the closet. Not only had the appropriate undergarments been included, but footwear as well. Willamette had not thought of shoes, and she was pleased to see several pairs in the closet. Ida's cousin appeared to be a bright and industrious young woman. If not for the events of the day, that would have tempted Willamette to employ the young woman further and at a much higher rate of pay.

Willamette selected the shopgirl dress. It was sturdy but still tailored to flatter a woman's figure.

"You know, there's no reason all this has to go to waste," Niven said, impishly. "A couple extra minutes wouldn't matter one way or another."

"The man who frees me from the shackles of chastity had damn well better be committed to investing far, far more than a few minutes in the task." Willamette's words carried far more venom than she had intended.

"And the little princess shows just how scary she can be," Niven quipped, unnerved by her outburst.

"You have yet to see anything even remotely resembling how scary I can be," Willamette shot back, again with far more emotion than she intended. She knew he was joking, or at least trying to make light of her snarl, but for some reason, at that moment, his levity irritated her beyond measure.

"And she takes scary up to terrifying," he muttered, stepping past her to select an outfit. Stopping just short of the closet, he frowned, surprised and confused. "Wait. Did you just say chastity?"

His surprise angered her so much that she literally growled. The depth of the fury in that animal noise unsettled them both.

Willamette was not sorry that she felt as she did, so it did not feel like she should apologize, but she was also unable to find an alternative. She tried, but in the end, she decided that it could wait until time was less precious. She needed to change her outfit so they could be on their way. That, however, presented another difficulty, and as soon as she shed her silky travelling robe, she was again in a corner. The solution was obvious, but with all the tension in the room, she still dithered.

"Niven, would you please?" she finally asked, turning to present her back to him.

"Would I please what?" he asked. "I don't see a zipper."

"You will have to tear it," she said. "I had Mattie sew me into the dress to make certain that it fit perfectly."

He slipped his fingers in under the thin lace collar and very gently pulled at it, testing it until he found the weak spot that Mattie had left over the back of her neck. Forcefully, but still careful to avoid yanking the front of the dress into her throat, he ripped the delicate fabric, splitting the back of the dress all the way down to her tailbone.

"And that is how clichés are born," Niven said, breathy.

Mattie had been rather impish when she told Willamette that Niven would have to tear the dress off, and Willamette had thought it might be the kind of comically masculine thing that a man would find titillating, but she could not have possibly imagined that she would find it to be so arousing. The sound, the way tearing the dress pulled her toward him just enough to make her feel off-balance, the feathery touch of cool air against her back; the surge of desire it sparked surprised her, and when he tenderly slid his fingertips down her spine, she was all but overwhelmed. She wanted him to finish tearing the dress away. She wanted his hands on her, firm and forceful, but still gentle. She wanted nothing more than to indulge her most primal desire to let him take her. And when he kissed the back of her neck, she could feel her heart thundering away. Reluctantly, she resisted. She could not indulge herself, not then. Not until they were safe.

She stepped away from the exquisite sensation of his fingers caressing her back and took a breath before she went back to changing. They did not have the time.

The instant she slipped the dress off her shoulders, she stopped, catching the dress before it fell. He was watching her, intent, lusty, possessive. It helped her to know that she was not alone in the struggle to hold desire at bay.

"Niven, my love." She hesitated. She meant it when she said he was her love. She knew that was foolish and that she was probably just caught up in the moment, but it was still a stunning thought. Even in those times when she hoped that love was something more than girlish foolishness, she had never believed that anything close to a feeling of love could be possible for a woman born into her station. However, if love was anything like what she felt at that moment, it explained the turmoil in her head. It also explained why his quip about taking a few minutes had angered her so. The thought of love terrified her almost as much as it thrilled her. It also changed what she wanted to say to him. It changed what she needed to say to him.

Holding the front of the dress against her chest, she turned to face him. It took a long moment and a few deep breaths before she could trust her voice enough to speak. "Niven, please do not, for even a moment, think that this is anything other than romantic selfishness, and I will admit that I probably think about this, and obsess over it far more than I should, but for everything intimate that we are to share, even the little things, I desperately want leisurely, luxurious, and indulgent to come before casual and familiar."

He nodded and she retreated to the bathroom to change.

Az was nowhere near as meticulous as she allowed others to believe. While there were some aspects of her commitment to intense personal discipline that required extreme focus and precision, she was acutely aware that tasks like the search of the hotel required a distinctly different skill set. Most significantly, she found that tracking everything that had been done, everything that was being done, and everything that needed to be done was a challenge that bordered on the nightmarish.

"Tenth floor, cleared." The Blade's voice came from the speaker on the hotel intercom system.

"Roger," Az said, and then remembered that she had to push the intercom button for the tenth floor to talk back to the Blade. "Roger, tenth floor cleared."

A report from the tenth floor wasn't what she had been expecting and that threw her. She held the intercom button for several seconds and then let it up and stared at the array of intercom buttons, ten across and eleven tall. Each connected to the service closet on a guest floor. A second panel next to it offered a row of carefully labelled larger buttons for the various service centers around the hotel. None of that was relevant. She was at a loss for what to do.

"Az, write it down, but like a picture." Mikka whispered so only Az would hear. When she saw that Az still didn't understand, she cleared the blood-spattered mess of hotel paperwork off the desk with a sweep of her arm.

"We've cleared the tenth floor," the Blade said from the intercom. "Which one's next?"

Mikka pushed the tenth-floor button and spoke into the intercom. "Just a moment, dealing with an issue down here."

"Roger."

"Floors, one on top of another," Mikka grabbed a felt tipped marker and started writing numbers across the desk. Next to the ten she added an A. "We call the team on ten Alpha. So how many teams do you have?"

"Four," Az said.

"And where are the others searching?"

"Nine and eleven and … maybe eight, but maybe twelve."

"So Beta on eleven and Delta on nine." She added a B and then a D. "You'll have to cheat a little and wait for Gamma to report because you don't know where they're searching, but it's going to be either eight or twelve, right?"

Az nodded.

"Ten is cleared." She crossed out the ten, drew an arc from ten to thirteen, and wrote an A next to thirteen. "So Alpha goes to the next floor that you're sure is unsearched, which is thirteen. Now if a team reports from eight, you know that twelve hasn't been searched, so you send that team to twelve, but if a team reports from twelve, you send them up to the next unsearched floor above Alpha. Get it?"

Az nodded, but when she didn't do anything, Mikka pushed the intercom button for the tenth floor. "You are now team Alpha. Search thirteen."

"Team Alpha, confirming search thirteen."

"See how that picture tracks the cleared floors, who cleared them, where the teams are searching, and what needs to be searched next?" Mikka asked Az.

"Thank you, Mikka. That simplifies things a great deal."

"Yeah, it's one of those things where it seems complicated until someone shows you the trick," Mikka said.

"I'm going to make you my second on this," Az said. "I want you to double-check everything for me. We can't afford a mistake."

Mikka nodded, thought a long moment, and then said, "I'll check our coverage of all the possible exit routes. Make sure there's nothing we missed."

Az nodded and Mikka trotted off.

Willamette knew that she had taken far too long to change, and she was embarrassed to admit that at least part of the delay was because she had no servant to help her. While she took pride in not being the helpless cliché of nobility that her mother had become, the moment she tried to rush she discovered just how accustomed she had become to having Ida and her other girls there to help. That was particularly true for things that were small and intricate and better suited to a little girl's nimble fingers, like her hairdo.

"Willamette," Niven said, loud and pointedly from out in the room. "Even though we aren't in a tremendous rush, we do need to get moving."

"I know, but I have never tried to deconstruct one of these intricate hairstyles on my own before." She exited from the bathroom, still struggling with the buttons on her dress. "It was far more difficult than I would have expected, and this shopgirl dress is a nightmare. All these buttons down the front are difficult to fasten, and it seems like there are a thousand of them."

"A thousand?" Niven chuckled. "I bet your seamstress has never made an actual shopgirl's dress before, has she?"

"I cannot imagine how that would matter. Mattie is the best young seamstress in the Commonwealth. Truly gifted."

"I'm sure she is, but anyone who has ever had their hands on a real shopgirl's dress would know that most of the buttons are just there for decoration." He undid the top few buttons of her dress and refastened them. "Only seven or eight of them are real."

"Of course, that makes far more sense than this … Wait, how do you know that?"

"Shhh." He smiled as he playfully put his fingers to her lips to silence her. She flinched and shuddered when he touched her.

"Sorry," she said.

"It's okay." He said it like he meant it, but the expression on his face told a completely different story.

"No, it is not okay," she said. "I can think of no way to describe your touch other than to say it is electric. The slightest brush of your fingertips sends a shiver and chill through me, and I cannot help but flinch."

"Willamette, it really is okay." He tried to sound reassuring.

"Perhaps it would be okay if that was all it was, but it is far more than that. It has my head in a whirl, and I feel completely off-balance and …" She was frustrated by the rush of words and tried to reset, forcing the words to come slowly and deliberately. "I am repeatedly discovering that many of the things from the bawdy stories I have read, things that I had cavalierly dismissed as comically overwrought prose, are disturbingly literal. I would not say that I am consumed by desire, but I can certainly appreciate how lust might overwhelm a young woman's better judgement. And the fact that my heart can flutter in my chest unnerves me more than anything. Your kiss leaves me breathless, and I swear if my loins were to at any point quiver, I might just lose my mind altogether."

"Willamette!" he said, firmly but also softly. "Relax. It's okay."

"No, it is not," she insisted. "It is weak. A grown woman should be able to control herself."

He kissed her and wrapped his arms around her, holding her until she relaxed and kissed him back.

"It isn't weak," he said when they finally ended the kiss. "It's human. And after the emotional chaos that has engulfed you today, from the theatrical extravaganza you made of our betrothal, to having a trusted servant try to murder you, and now being on the run from a very real conspiracy to kill you, I would be worried about your very humanity if you weren't struggling with every bit of the entire spectrum of emotions."

"Please tell me that you have thought of a place where we can hide," she whispered, breathy. "Someplace with a big warm bed."

"I doubt if there will be any beds, big, warm, or otherwise, but I think we should be able to find someplace to hide in the below decks," he said.

"The below decks?" She released him from the hug. "I had not thought of that."

"Exactly." He grinned. "No one would think to look for Morden Lolofi's little princess down in the mechanical guts of the city, but down there somewhere, we just might be able to find the perfect place to hide. The gasworks, sewer works, and water works will all have crews on shift, but they'll be as thin as they can be on Regatta Day, and pretty much all the rest of the tunnels below the city should be all but abandoned. No one would dare schedule any maintenance, cleaning, or construction work for today, so we should be able to find a lonely, safe, and tolerably comfortable spot to hide for a day or two while we figure out our next move."

"Or we might even be able to escape the city," Willamette said. "There is a small ship, hidden in a secret hangar in one of the keel struts. It is meant as a last resort for escaping a siege of the City Estate, so I would expect that the passage down to it would be well disguised, if there is even a way to get to it from the utility tunnels, but if we could find a way to get to that hangar, and if you could fly that ship ..."

"I could fly it," Niven said.

"But how do we get into the below decks?" she asked. "If anything, with all the drinking on Regatta Day, security at the entrances will be even tighter today than it is on most days."

"And she answers her own question." He showed her the wine and the blanket he had packed in the leather tool bag that went with his mechanic's uniform. "It's Regatta Day. A bottle of wine, a giggly, drunk, and amorous shopgirl who wants to see the big machines ... If I tossed a fiver or two to a security guard who's annoyed about pulling the holiday shift, he wouldn't think twice of helping a young mechanic make his Regatta Day very, very memorable."

"I believe I can manage to appear giggly and intoxicated," she said.

"And amorous."

"Oh, yes, and amorous." She returned his smirk. "You packed the food, as well?"

"Yep," he said.

"We may be on the run for several days," she said. "Let me retrieve ..."

"Underwear," he finished the thought for her. "I already packed all the plain stuff." He shifted to a conspiratorial whisper. "And I added my favorite from the ridiculously fancy sets."

"How in the world could you possibly know that I would wish to take clean underwear?" She gave him a suspicious questioning frown.

"I have older sisters," he reminded her. "And one of their favorite ways of tormenting me is to casually discuss things that a little brother does not want to hear. I truly know far more about the unmentionable aspects of being women than any young man should."

"That still does not explain how you knew about the buttons on a shopgirl's dress," she shot back.

"No, it doesn't." He gestured for her to lead them out the door.

The lights on the buttons that summoned the elevator were flashing and pushing the buttons did nothing to change that. That worried Niven. He was scowling when he led her over to the stairs and the moment he opened that door, that scowl turned into a grimace.

She could hear people running up the stairs. The sound was distant but distinctive, and with a quick look down over the rail, Willamette caught a glimpse of her worst nightmare. The arms of the people climbing up the stairs were clad in Kofi blue.

She pulled Niven back to the hall. It took everything she had to retreat from the stairwell without making a sound. Once the door shut, she could not help but whimper as she ran back to the room.

"It's them isn't it?" Niven asked as he followed her into the room.

"Yes, they are wearing some kind of uniform. It is Kofi blue, just like the arm bands of those men who murdered that little girl at the club." Willamette darted over to the closet and pulled a thin leather belt off one of the outfits. She tested its strength before asking, "Do you think it would hurt to be strangled?"

"I think it would be horrific."

"You are probably right." She threw the belt down and looked around, searching, pacing. "A solid blow to the head perhaps. That fire extinguisher out in the hall looked heavy and hard."

"Willamette ..."

"No, the tub. You could hold my head under for me. People who have nearly drowned say that after the initial choking, it is quite peaceful."

"Are you out of your mind?" He grabbed her arm before she could dart into the bathroom. "I'm not going to drown you."

"Niven! That shade of blue is Kofi blue!"

"Yes," he shot back. "You already said that. So what?"

"So what?" she hissed, her eyes filling with tears. "Use that bloody clever head of yours and think. The Kofi family is the noble house that my father executed."

"Executed ... a noble house ..." Niven muttered. "Wait, are you talking about the nobles he threw into the Deep after the Skyhook Rebellion?"

"Yes, but there was one of the nephews that was never captured, a colonel in the Tactical Expeditionary Force, and Colonel Kofi is a monster. During the rebellion, some of the things he did to the people loyal to our family were so horrific that it made my father ill to hear of them."

"It made your father sick?" Niven was taken aback by that. "Your father?"

"Exactly," she said. "And if Kofi gets his hands on me ..." Willamette lost her battle against the tears with a hoarse sob. His arms were around her before she collapsed. "I desperately want to live, Niven. You cannot imagine how terrified I am by the thought of dying, but I cannot let him take me alive."

"Shhh," he whispered. "Settle down. Assess, analyze, and act."

"Go to jump into the Deep. And take that stupid saying with you."

He laughed and squeezed her. "How about we put that off for a while and think this through?"

"A quick and compassionate death is the smart choice," she said. "I know that it is my only choice, but I do not have the will. I need you to help me."

"No," he said, firmly.

"Please," she said. "To fall into his hands alive risks unspeakable horrors."

"The chance to live is worth the risk of any horror, any pain," he said.

"I do so desperately wish to live."

"Good."

"But reality does not care about wishes or dreams," she whispered. "Perhaps we should make use of the bed."

"No. If we did that, we would both be far too distracted to figure this out."

"I would like one last distraction," she said. "And then, I would like you to run, leave me and run."

"No. I will not leave you. And there will be none of this one last anything rubbish, not yet." He tried to hide the tremble in his arms by squeezing her tighter. "Besides, before I can get at the woman under the dress, I'd have to deal with all of those stupid buttons, and I don't think I'm up to such an arduous task."

Willamette laughed. She did not wish to laugh, but she could not help it.

"Better," Niven said. "Now what options does this Colonel Kofi think we have?"

"He would not leave us any options. He would methodically search every possible place to hide, and he would guard all the exits just in case we found a way to sneak down to the ground floor. And if he did not find me, he would probably burn the tower and everyone in it just to make sure he killed me. He might have already started the fire. He likes burning people."

"Fire," Niven said. "Oh, it can't be that simple, can it?"

"Niven, you should flee."

"The Kofis were one of the snooty-as-hell noble families, right?"

"They were not one of the Big 12, but they were more than powerful enough to make their execution a terrifying example to all the noble families with a seat at the council table."

"So, like you and your button-loving seamstress, this Colonel Kofi has probably never been the friend of anyone who had to work for a living. Right?" Niven dashed over to the window, pressing his forehead against the pane, and looking as straight down as he could.

"He would have had servants, obviously, and I believe that his commission as a colonel was earned, not gifted or inherited." Willamette shook her head, confused, not daring to hope that he had thought of something.

"That's not the same as working for a living or being friends with people who have to." Niven shoved a washcloth and her purse into her hand before he pulled her out of the room. They were at the stairwell door before she realized that the washcloth was meant for her to dry her tears and wipe her nose.

He signaled for her to be silent, she nodded her understanding, and they entered the stairwell. The activity in the stairwell was dozens of floors below, but walking down toward it was still unnerving.

Three floors down, Niven stuck his head into the hall and looked around before he led Willamette down another floor. He did the same on the next floor, but it was on the floor below that where he finally led her into the hall. There was a thick, heavy closet door across from the stairs. The small sign next to it read Emergency Access Only.

"Niven, I do not understand what working for a living has to do with any of this."

"My point exactly. There are all kinds of things that you and this Colonel Kofi would never know even existed unless you spent some time drinking and trading stories with people who do the tough jobs." Discovering that the door was locked, Niven pulled the fire extinguisher from its rack and hefted it. "You were right, these are plenty heavy enough to bash in a skull."

With a running start and a mighty underarm swing, he drove the bottom of the extinguisher into the door, just below the knob. The lock gave way so easily that the door bounced off the doorstop and swung back at him hard enough to knock him down.

A soft chime sounded, and a small red light flashed above the door.

"Damn, it just had to have an alarm," Niven grumbled.

The closet was large enough to be considered a room of its own. Dozens of heavy-duty deck suits hung on the wall, firefighting equipment and maintenance gear was stored in racks, and there were shelves loaded with hundreds upon hundreds of single-use emergency suits. It baffled Willamette until she saw the air lock on the far side of the room. That had to lead to the surface of the dome. They were at about the right height and that was the only possible reason to need an air lock short of the roof of the tower.

"Suit up. Quick," Niven said. "I don't see a way to lock this door."

Willamette started putting on the smallest of the heavy-duty work suits. "How could you possibly know about something like this?"

"Firemen are hard-working, normal people who drink heavily and tell all the best work stories," he said. "And if evacuating people from the upper floors of one of these towers is anything like what Darrel described, they are also truly heroic."

Mikka's trick had helped Az get on top of the floor-by-floor search for Willamette. That freed a few minutes between each call down from the floors. It wasn't long enough to allow her to do anything constructive, but it did give her ample time to worry about other things.

Were her teams missing someplace that Willamette might hide? Or worse, was there some kind of passageway that they didn't know about that Willamette might be able to use to move between floors? The hotel staff had already demonstrated some allegiance to the girl. Might they be helping her in some way? Was she even up in the tower? If Ida did manage to cut Willamette, then Willamette would know that she'd been betrayed. Could Willamette have been wily enough to anticipate that Ida would tell them of the hotel room? If she was, she seemed like she might be smart enough to show up just to convince the kitchen staff to say that she went upstairs, then run off to hide somewhere else. Or what if she never intended to come here at all? What if this hotel room was all a ruse to begin with? Willamette had been known to do things like that, using look-alikes to confuse the gossips and catch them out by proving their stories to be false.

More than anything, Az's promise to remove the last trace of the Lolofi name from the world weighed upon her. All missions mattered, but that command from the Colonel was no idle homily. Az knew just enough of Kofi's larger plan and strategy to understand how much of a nightmare it would be if Willamette managed to hold the loyalists together. At the very least, that would keep most of key security and police forces in play against them. At the worst, it might let her rally a few of the Big 12 families to the defense of the Commonwealth. That wouldn't be a catastrophe, but it would certainly turn their coup into a war, and if that happened, it would be the kind of war that would drag on for years.

"We'd probably be better off just holding the fifth floor as our line instead of covering all the exits," Mikka said when she returned. "It's a utility floor so all the air ducts converge there. Put a couple of teams on the ducts, a team on the fifth-floor landings of the stairwell, open the doors to the elevator shafts on the fifth floor so we can watch them, and then there's no way down."

Az thought it through and nodded. "That would free enough Blades for another search team, and we'd still have a few to rove below the fifth."

"Az, what's that alarm?" Mikka asked.

"What alarm?" Az asked.

"Don't you hear that alarm, or chime, or alert, or whatever it is that's beeping at you?" Mikka cocked her head and followed the sound. She ended up frowning at a panel behind the reception desk. "That wasn't going when I left."

Az read the label next to the flashing light. "Emergency and maintenance access door on floor seventy-six."

"Maybe someone's breaking in to one of the servants' closets?" Mikka said.

"That can't be it. There's a service closet on every floor, and there's only a light on this panel for the seventy-sixth," Az said.

"Wait, this tower is over a hundred floors, right?" Mikka asked. "It would have to go up and through the dome, right?"

"An emergency exit out onto the dome?" Az was skeptical, but the knot in the pit of her stomach wouldn't let her deny that it was the only logical explanation.

"If there was a door onto the dome, it would have to be about seventy-some floors up," Mikka said.

"Mikka, take over here," Az leapt over the reception desk and gestured at the other Blades in the lobby as she ran for the elevator. "And you three with me."

The elevators were all parked in the lobby, their doors open and waiting, but it still took forever to get up to the seventy-sixth floor and what Az saw when the elevator doors opened was a kick in the guts. There was a smashed-open door across the hall and even from the elevator she could see through the open air lock doors on the far side of the room.

She heard someone moving in the closet, and with a quick dash across the small foyer she discovered a petite young woman, struggling to finish putting on one of the deck suits.

"Hello Willamette," Az said, as she drew her pistol. There was no mistaking that face, but if Az was going to murder an unarmed teenager, she wanted to be certain.

The woman's reaction was unmistakable, absolute confirmation that she didn't just look like Willamette, she was Willamette.

A burst of water slammed into Az, knocking her back into the hall. When she instinctively rolled to a crouch, the spray from the fire hose hit her chest with such force that it lifted her off the floor and drove her backwards.

The stream of water stayed on her chest, pinning her to the wall, driving the air from her lungs, suffocating her. Az rolled along the wall and the water moved with her. It wasn't until the hose moved to knock back one of the Blades she'd brought up with her that Az managed to escape the pounding crush of the water. The three Blades that had come up in the elevator with Az tried to rush the door to the closet, but it was a hopeless effort. The blast of water from the fire hose was more than enough to keep them out of the emergency closet.

The spray suddenly quit, but Az could hear the water flowing, and something was thrashing around inside the closet. With a quick peek in through the door, she saw that the hose had been abandoned and left on. The nozzle was flying around in the room, spraying water everywhere and smashing whatever it hit.

Protecting her head with her arms, Az ran in and dove on the hose, crawling along it until she was close enough to the nozzle to get it under control. Directing the spray out through the open air lock, she waited for the Blades she'd brought with her to shut it off, but nothing happened. They were still standing at the doorway, unwilling to enter the closet.

"Get in here and help!" she ordered.

"But the outer door's open."

"Relax," Az said. "There's always a little extra pressure inside structures to keep the acid and noxious gases out if something springs a leak. You can even feel the breeze through here."

The hesitant Blades considered that, and then nodded, but they still didn't move.

"Well then get in here and shut this damn thing off!" Az shouted.

The Blades were still hesitant, but they obeyed.

Az leaned out the door. Biting back the dizzy, unbalanced feeling from the glance down through the dome, she assessed the situation. There were two people in deck suits headed down the leeward slope of the dome toward the docks. They were already well out of range of her pistol, and they were moving quickly.

Az found the intercom. "Mikka, it is an exit onto the dome. They're out there and running toward the docks. Recall the Blades from the search and get them over to the docks as quickly as possible. I'll follow the targets from here."

"Should I still set up our line on the fifth floor?" Mikka asked. "Just in case it's a ruse?"

"The idea is right, but it's not a ruse," Az said. "I got a good look at her and confirmed that it is definitely Willamette."

Willamette was scared, out of breath, dizzy from the height below her feet, and above all else, she was thankful that she had taken the time to tighten all the straps on the suit, particularly the boots. The surface of the dome was too springy and soft to run across, so she had to use the bounce and take big bounding leaps. That was fast, but it was also difficult. The surface of the dome was so clear that it was almost impossible to see, turning every landing into at least a bit of a guess. Add to that the way the soft-soled boot covers of the deck suit seemed to want to cling to the dome, and add the odd slowness of the way the dome absorbed her landings and then rebounded, and then add the downward slope toward the docks, and it was a wonder she could stay on her feet at all. It also did not help that she was struggling to restrain an irrational fear that her feet were going to plunge through the dome. That was ridiculous. The dome was incredibly strong, but that knowledge did not stop the flinch every time the clear plastic hesitated before springing back.

Niven did not seem to be bothered by the sensation of height, nor by the bounce of the dome, but he was also moving more slowly, and he was struggling. His bounds were smaller than hers and he was absorbing a great deal of the spring from the dome each time he landed. She tried not to worry about how quickly he was falling behind.

One of Willamette's shoes shifted inside the deck suit boot. It was not much, but that unexpected bit of slip, combined with the clingy grip of the outer boot was enough to pitch her forward when the dome launched her into the next bound.

She knew that she could not hope to retain her feet, so she did not try. Reactions from years of martial arts training kicked in and triggered the muscle memories for taking a throw. She tucked her shoulder under and brought her knees up to speed her rotation. She had no hope of flipping all of the way over. Instead, she was trying to land on her back rather than falling forward onto her face. It was a close thing. She hit the dome much sooner than she expected. She had not rotated anywhere near far enough and she just managed to land on the back of her neck instead of the top of her head.

The air tanks for the breather dug into her upper back and the mask was the only thing that kept her knees from slamming into her face as she folded in half instead of rolling.

She resisted the natural response to let her legs spring back. Instead, she clenched her gut and grabbed her legs to keep her body tucked through the slow-motion bounce. Once she was in the air again, she relaxed, extending her legs and arms, her knees bent, using her legs to absorb as much of the energy as she could with the next landing. Again, it was imperfect, but it worked well enough. After two more flips and bounces she managed to arrest most of her momentum, regaining her feet just in time to jump out of the way of Niven as he tumbled past.

Unlike Willamette, Niven was doing everything wrong. He kept trying to regain his feet, but he was bouncing down the slope of the dome far faster than he could run, so every time he tried to get his feet down, it pushed him forward and upward, throwing him further and further out of control.

Willamette chased him, but she was losing the race. The slope of the dome was just steep enough to impart more momentum than his flailing limbs absorbed. His bounces kept growing higher and his uncontrolled tumble toward the docks just kept spinning up faster and faster. The violence of the twisting, bending, and flopping of his body was beyond what she imagined a person could withstand. It was so horrific that even before she realized that he was destined to collide with a large shed at the bottom of the dome, she feared for his life.

The collision with the shed was as dramatic as it was violent. The wall exploded on impact, shattering into countless shards of brittle corrugated plastic that flew in all directions as the shed recoiled, shuddered, and slumped into a heap.

CHAPTER 8

The real beauty of seizing Lightcastle's central telephone switchboard was not that it severed most of the links between the different arms of the Lolofi beast that had terrorized the city. It also gave Kofi a flexible and robust means of sustaining operational communications without committing any significant resources to the task. With that tidy little bit of infrastructure in his pocket, he didn't need a base of operations. He could move around the city as needed or desired without giving any thought to being able to stay in touch, receive updates, or issue commands. No matter where he went, he could just pick up a phone, call the main switchboard, and with a code word or two he was connected to his ops teams. It was yet another gift from Morden Lolofi, as was the Buller House.

The Buller House was one of the many places around the city that the Lolofis had seized from its rightful owner on one pretext or another and then turned into a perk for their favored supporters. The former townhouse had been converted into a modest-sized but luxuriously appointed venue that offered visiting nobles and businessmen small offices, meeting rooms, and lounges that could be booked for a nominal fee. It had served the Lolofis well. Simply being allowed to book it was a powerful claim to status that all the minor families were desperate to secure. The key for Kofi was that it happened to be in a convenient location. It was not all that far from the Kelly Hotel, it wasn't something that would be booked for a

Regatta Day party, and it had everything he needed including dozens of phone lines and ample catering facilities.

"Get on the phone and let the ops team know that I decided to set up a temporary headquarters here," Kofi said, not bothering to direct the order at any one of his Blades specifically. "And tell them not to send anyone to join us unless they're nearby. I'm not quite ready to settle into a headquarters yet. I need to be able to react to events, so I don't want to be stuck here waiting for someone to arrive."

Dodi nodded and with a glance she sent a Blade leaping to a phone.

"And it's probably a good idea for someone to find the kitchen and stir up some food for us as well," Kofi said. "Always important to get the most out of the slow moments."

Again, Dodi assigned that task with a glance, and a Blade ran off as Kofi grabbed a phone and dialed the main switchboard. Dodi was an excellent lieutenant for Az. In the days ahead he would have to make that official. They would soon need a far more complex command structure than having countless ad hoc teams of Blades.

"Phoenix," Kofi said, the instant the operator answered the call.

"Yes Colonel." The operator was flustered. "It will be just a moment. I will patch you through to the coms team."

After a moment of muffled shuffling, there was a click, another click, and the phone was answered on the first ring.

"Yes Colonel, central exchange here." The woman's voice was familiar, oddly squeaky. She was probably a trainee, not yet ready to serve as a Blade.

"Updates," he said.

"Three updates flagged on the board as your highest priority. One: Ops team reports that sixteen groups of irregulars and two Blade teams have not reported achieving their phase two objectives and are now presumed to have failed and been lost. None appear to be operation critical. Two: The Signal Corps has not yet sent neighboring habitats any indication of distress in the capital and the commentary on the race continues uninterrupted. Three: We have a report from the Kelly Hotel. Reads 'Target on the run. In pursuit.'"

"Any more details on the last one?" he asked, unprofessionally abrupt.

"Details as follows: A subordinate reported on behalf of Az. She did not have Az's command code, but coms team considers the report to be reliable and valid. Full message from the Kelly reads: Target escaped through emergency fire exit onto dome's surface. Target is headed across the dome toward the docks. Az confirmed target's identity directly and is pursuing directly with a small team. Search teams have been redirected to docks to assist in pursuit."

"Son of a bitch!" Kofi shouted, kicking a chair.

The woman on the other end of the line didn't react to his outburst.

"Patch me directly through to ops," Kofi ordered the woman.

He managed to hold his rage in check long enough to direct the ops team to put the highest priority on responding to any and all requests from Az, and to make certain they knew to update him immediately upon any developments. As soon as he hung up, however, he let the monster loose. The furniture in the reception area was damaged beyond repair.

"Clean that up," he ordered a Blade. Turning, he found himself face-to-face with Ida. She was standing on a table, knife in hand, looking at him like an uncertain animal. He was certain that she would cut him, but she didn't move. She stared at him.

"You are my Little Knife," he said. "Do you understand that?"

She looked even more uncertain.

"That means you are a weapon. You are nothing more. However, and this is very important, it also means that you are nothing less," he said. "A weapon is a tool for changing the world, for fixing what is wrong and making it right. A knife cuts away what's rotten and that is how I will use you. When I say 'cut,' you cut. When I say 'kill,' you kill, and together, with my other Blades, you will help me save this city, the Commonwealth, and the world. You may be small, and the part you play may sometimes seem small, but you are not alone. You are part of something tremendous and that should make you proud."

Ida finally broke eye contact. She was still confused and uncertain, but he knew that he had gotten through to her.

"Now, a weapon must be properly cared for," he said. "You will wash that knife and have one of the Blades help you find a proper sheath for it, and then, once your knife is clean, you will take care of my Little Knife, just like you take care of your little knife. You get yourself cleaned up. You eat and then rest so that you will be ready to cut when I say 'cut.' Understand?"

Ida nodded and leapt off the table. Crouching like an animal, she peered around suspiciously before she scurried out of the room.

With that and the cathartic moment of violence behind him, Kofi was able to focus. Even if he had stayed to handle the search directly, this still would have happened. He could not have known that there was exit onto the surface of the dome. Even now that he knew of it, he found it hard to understand how the Lolofi bitch could have managed to find the damn thing. The only possible explanation was that she had somehow been helped by the staff, and if that was the case, the damage had been done before he left.

While none of that solved the problem, it did reassure Kofi that delegating the search of the hotel to Az was not the cause of failure and it clarified the situation going forward. He could not have done any better than she had done and even though he decided he needed to closely follow the impromptu operation being put together on the docks, he did not need to handle it personally. Az was his most trusted Blade and without question, she was the best subordinate he had to carry on the task of hunting down that infuriatingly resourceful Lolofi bitch.

Willamette managed to stay calm enough to keep her bounding run under control. It was a good thing she did. At anything close to full speed, she would have bounded off the top of the four-meter-tall wall at the base of the dome before she even realized that the dome did not extend down to the dock. If she had run or tumbled off that drop, she would have undoubtedly been injured. She might have even been killed. There were trucks and cargo trailers, giant spools of cable, and a plethora of other things that could have done some serious damage if she had fallen on them. As it was, the stacked spools of cable gave her a simple way to climb down. Two hops and she was on the dock, running to find Niven.

Expecting the worst, she let out a squeal of relieved surprise when she rounded the corner of the storage shed and found him struggling to escape from under a thick plastic tarp. Cursing yet another childish outburst, she assessed the situation. The thick plastic must have folded around him as it arrested his momentum. Grabbing the corner of the clear plastic sheet, she pulled it back over him. That made it reasonably easy for him to crawl out.

"You cannot imagine how relieved I am to see that you are well." She hugged him so hard he grunted.

"To say 'I'm well' is a bit of a stretch." He winced as he rolled his shoulders. His voice sounded odd, and it wasn't just the mask. It sounded like he was farther away than he was, but his voice was louder than it should have been, and the timbre was off. The higher pitches were more pronounced. "I feel pretty damn shattered, but after that little tumble, I'm more than happy to settle for reasonably intact."

"Little tumble?" She scowled at him. "Niven, that was extreme and violent to the point that I cannot fathom how in the world you could have possibly even survived."

"Well, there isn't much to these sheds. All they're really meant to do is to give you someplace that's protected from the acid to work or store things."

"You were incredibly fortunate," she said. While it was true that the shed was not all that substantial, the posts holding up the rafters were still more than solid enough to have killed him.

"Nah, it wasn't luck." He took her hand and pulled her into a run that almost immediately slowed to a strained and stiff trot. "It was astoundingly skillful."

"Of course it was," she said. "Now what?"

"The Lightcastle docks are a mess of fenced off yards, blind alleys, and shortcuts that can easily lead you around in a circle." He nodded at the four people who were working their way down the surface of the dome. "So, if none of our new friends are familiar with navigating their way through this place, we might just stand a decent chance of getting ourselves completely and thoroughly lost."

He led her into what looked like a dead end but somehow he managed to go straight to a gate that was disguised by the way two different fences met. Weaving through the piles of junk on the far side of the gate, he led her into a narrow alleyway and from there to a road lined by what looked like small warehouses. This time he looked at the surface of the dock before picking which direction to go. It seemed like the wrong way.

"Niven, are you sure we wish to go this way?" she asked.

He gestured at the road. "See the way the tire tracks all turn the same direction from the vehicles driving in and out of the doors to the garages and warehouses?"

"Yes, they all turn the other way."

"Which means the main thoroughfare is in that direction and I would bet that someone chasing us is going to expect us to head that way. So, we need to go in the other direction."

"But what if this is a dead end?"

"It probably is a dead end, for vehicles at least. If you could get a truck through this other end, you'd see at least a few tire marks turning to drive this direction."

At the end of the road, he found a narrow passage between two large workshops and, almost as if by magic, that passage led them to another open area, a turning circle at the end of a short road.

"You knew there'd be a way through," she said.

"Yeah, the one thing that you can count on out here is that no one wants to risk walking too far down a road or alley only to find that it's a dead end," he said. "If you're low on air, that sort of thing can kill. So, no matter who's fighting over ownership of what, or who's sneaking a bit of alleyway into their yard when they replace a fence, any road over about a hundred meters long will always have a way to walk out the other end."

"And is that another one of those things that only hard-working people and their drinking buddies know?"

"I learned about it when I was running around getting someone to build whale-sized shipping containers while having someone else modify my ship to carry them and, obviously, doing everything I could to stop either of them from figuring out what I was doing."

"Where are we going?" she asked.

"I don't know yet," he admitted. "But I've got a few ideas."

"Ideas?"

"Hey, they're good ideas." Even with the breather masks, she could see that he enjoyed throwing that one back at her.

When she reached the wall that separated the dome from the docks, Az took a long moment to survey the layout of the streets and buildings below. It wasn't a pretty sight. Roughly every thousand meters or so there were wide streets that connected the big air locks to the landing berths along the trailing edge of the city, but everything else was such a jumbled mess that it didn't look like there had ever been any kind of plan to it. If the chase devolved into a search, it was going to be a nightmare.

Hopping onto a stack of meter-wide spools of cable, then onto a shorter stack, and finally onto the dock, she caught up with the three Blades who had joined the chase just in time to hear the last of their comments on the destroyed shed.

"It's hard to believe that the person who did this managed to walk away," the Blade with the raspy voice muttered, getting nods of agreement from the tall one and the busty one.

Az knew it was unreasonable for her to think she should know the name of every Blade, but labelling women like that, even if it was just in her head, irritated her, and that irritation must have shown. The tall one suddenly stood at attention and looked worried and the other two rushed to copy her.

"Human beings are capable of amazing things when they're running for their lives." Az tried to sound conversational, but that didn't put them at ease. At a loss for what else she might do, she gestured for them to follow as she made a beeline to where they'd watched their quarry exit the yard.

Even knowing that there was a gate there, it took several seconds to find it, and a few more to get it open.

"How could she possibly have known that this gate was here?" the busty Blade asked as they fell into the loping run of people who ran and trained all the time.

"I can't imagine that Willamette was the one who knew," Az said.

"It's just as unbelievable that whatever noble asswipe she's picked up as a fiancé could have known about it, or about that exit from the hotel," the Blade with the raspy voice said.

"For that matter it's just as implausible that one of her family's bodyguards knew those things," the tall Blade added. "Our brief said that all the family's muscle is elite military, recruited from the minor nobility to reward distinguished service. Those are not the kinds of people who know about the quirky secrets of hotel architecture, or how to find hidden passages through Lightcastle's dockyards."

"So where is all that knowledge coming from?" Az asked.

"It must be her new fiancé," the raspy-voiced Blade said. "These could all be quirky things a noble might learn from real estate transactions or property development."

They reached the wide street that ran from the air lock to the landing berths, but there was no sign of Willamette or her fiancé.

"It looked to me like the one who crashed through the shed was hobbled, possibly seriously injured," Az said. "Right?"

"Limp on the left side," the tall Blade confirmed. "Best they seemed able to manage was a moderate walking pace."

"Which means they should be here somewhere." Az gestured angrily at the empty roadway.

The Blades nodded.

"We'll have to use the thoroughfares that run from the air locks out to landing berths to set a perimeter. That'll trap them between the streets, the back of the dome, and the fences separating the repair yards from the Port Authority's landing zone." Az paused just long enough to give the Blades a chance to nod their understanding.

"And the tunnels?" the raspy-voiced Blade asked.

"Shouldn't be too hard to cover the ones they can get to," Az said. "Most of the entrances are out in the landing zone beyond the Port Authority perimeter."

"Still, that's going to take a hell of a lot of personnel," the tall Blade said.

"My one and only mission is to erase the Lolofi name from the Drift, and I will see that happen, no matter what it takes," Az said directly to the tall Blade.

"Yes, but ..."

"But nothing," Az snapped. "You were with me in the lobby of the hotel when the Colonel said there is no higher priority, right?"

The woman nodded, taken aback.

"Until the Colonel says otherwise, we will use every resource it takes to carry out that mission. Is that understood?"

The Blade nodded.

"Good, now run to the nearest air lock. Call ops and tell them to send every damn Blade and Blueband they can muster to help. Then stay there and personally organize the perimeter and the search. You do it exactly as I have laid it out and you make damn sure that everyone knows that they are supposed to just kill Willamette the moment they spot her. It's not dead or alive. It's dead, is that understood?"

The tall Blade nodded.

"Good, now go."

She ran off.

"You two, stay with me." Az turned to run back down the side street.

"Objective?" the busty Blade asked.

"Recon," Az said. "Imagine you're smart, desperate, running for your lives, and you have some knowledge of the docks, and then shout out anything that comes to mind, no matter how insane or trivial it might seem."

Both Blades nodded.

"And what the hell are your names?" Az finally just asked.

The shopgirl dress and the deck suit did not work well together. The dress was made of heavy cloth, which made it far too warm to wear under the suit, but that might have been manageable if the skirt had been shorter. Willamette had pulled the skirt up and tucked it under the belt of the dress, but with all the bouncing, falling, and running, it had come loose and worked its way down to bunch at her crotch, where it kept trying to work its way down the suit's legs. The heavy purse wasn't helping either. Wrapping it in the skirt when she tucked the skirt into the belt had seemed like a clever way to carry it, but after the skirt worked its way loose, the purse had shifted around to wedge itself over her tailbone. That pulled the crotch of the suit tight against her inner thighs, making the chafing and binding from the bunched-up skirt that much worse. She knew that in the context of the day, that discomfort was trivial, but that did not stop it from slowing her down, and it did slow her quite substantially. After Niven's tumble through the shed, she should have been the one who occasionally had to wait for him, not the other way around.

Niven suddenly stopped, but he was not waiting for her. He was excited, looking around, taking half steps to nowhere and making half gestures at nothing.

"I take it that you have discovered a plan from within your idea," she said.

"Yep," he said. "We're going to steal a ship."

"We cannot steal a ship!"

"We most certainly can." He returned to walking and she fell in step with him. "I may not be a good pilot, but I can get the job done. And today is the one day of the year when there isn't anyone one out here to stop us."

"That is not what I meant," she said.

"I know that's not what you meant, and that's part of what makes it the perfect plan," he said. "The more the people chasing us know about you, the less likely they are to imagine that you might steal a ship, and what are the chances that they know anything about me at all? No matter how fast the news of our betrothal spread, I'm not even the heir to my father's estate. I can't imagine they've had much time at all to figure who I am, or what I might be able to do."

"I must admit, that does make a great deal of sense."

"We're going to need to find a ship that the two of us can get off the dock by ourselves," he said as he led her through yet another narrow alleyway. "Ideally, we want a ship that's on the smaller side and parked near the back edge of the docks, but we can make do with one that has a fair bit of space to leeward to give us room to float with the Drift as we lift off."

"Well, if we wish to find a ship by the leeward edge of the dock, then might I suggest we turn the other direction and walk toward the leeward edge of the docks?"

"You can't get there from here," he said.

"That makes no sense whatsoever."

"All of the landing and docking berths are on the other side of the Port Authority security perimeter." He turned and walked toward a main thoroughfare. "So we need to get to one of the places where we might be able get over or through the fence."

Niven slowed, then stopped.

"What is it?" Willamette asked.

Niven pointed at several cables draped over buildings on either side of the street. They were slack and sagging almost down to within reach. "That is profoundly odd."

"Az, there is no pattern to this, what exactly are we doing?" one of the Blades searching the docks with her asked.

"We're hoping we get lucky," Az said.

"Lucky does not sound like an objective." The Blade wasn't being critical. Her tone made it clear that she was asking for clarification or an explanation.

"Primary objective is recon," Az said. "All of our planning for operations on the docks focused on neutralizing the military dockyard, attacking the Marine barracks, and seizing the operations center from the Port Authority. We didn't prep for these civilian parts of the docks, so I need to learn this terrain, and fast. Once we're sure the perimeter will hold, we will need a plan that will allow us to be certain we find them."

"They're going to be air-limited," Monique said.

"And all of the buildings that might offer fresh air tanks or a refuge with breathable air appear to be locked down pretty tight," Gemma Lee added.

Az nodded and mulled over what that might imply for a search strategy.

CHAPTER 9

Flint was starting to feel hopeful. The regatta would be ending soon and with that their optimum window for launching was approaching. That made him acutely aware of every second that ticked past, but that pressure didn't seem to be slowing him down. If anything, it was helping him stay focused. He already had the new cables rolled onto all the plow winches and he had replaced the old plow's docking cradle with the one made for the new plow. All that was left was to thread all the cables through the control harnesses, hook them to the plow, and tune them up. That was the hardest part of the job, but he was feeling good about it.

"Hey, we need a ride," a man shouted as he ran toward Flint.

Flint managed not to panic. At least, he hoped that his panic wasn't obvious. He dropped the pneumatic wrench on his foot and leapt backwards a step, knocking his head against the wing of the new plow.

"We'll charter your ship." The man slowed and stopped. He was out of breath. "Real good money for private and fast."

"To where?" Flint asked. "Because we've got a … a job we gotta get to and it's a … it's nowhere near a lot of places."

"That's perfect," the man said, and he sounded like he meant it.

"It is?" Flint asked.

"Yeah, let's go." The man grabbed Flint's arm and pulled him toward the ramp to the open cargo bay.

"I'm kind of in the middle of something." Flint pulled his arm free and gestured at the truly monumental mess that he had made under the Drunken Monkey.

"I know, but we have to leave now."

"Trust me, buddy, I would love more than anything to leave now, but—"

"No, you trust me," the man said, almost shouting. "You want to leave Lightcastle, this instant."

"Buddy, this ship does not currently have a plow."

"And we both know that you can fly without a plow, don't we?"

"Well, I did, and I guess that you saying that just now means that we both know it, yeah, but we can't … uh, afford to stop anywhere to pick up a plow."

"Look, I meant it when I said it would be real good money," the man said. "You'll be able to afford any damn plow you want, but we've got to leave now."

"Money's not the issue," Flint said. "I mean. It is an issue but it's not the issue."

"Then what is the issue?"

And with that, Flint was boxed in. How could he explain why they couldn't stop somewhere else for a plow without explaining what had happened to their old plow?

"Look," Flint said. "You are just going to have to be patient. The port is closed and isn't going to open until after all the yachts from the regatta are back on deck."

Simon held no particular hatred for the Lolofis. He was not by any measure a supporter, but he also had trouble imagining that it mattered all that much which gaggle of rich pricks was in charge. Nor was Simon a supporter of the Colonel. Even if the stories about him were only half true, the man was a monster twice over. No, the only reason that Simon was wearing a blue armband was because he had been unlucky enough to pick the wrong shortcut after a double shift.

On the good side, despite having been exhausted from nearly twenty straight hours on the job, when he made that wrong turn he had been awake enough to realize that the men he'd found making weapons would be deadly serious about keeping their hobby a secret. Giving them a few helpful pointers on the designs and pretending like he thought that their revolution was a great idea had gotten Simon out of that alley alive, but it had also sucked him in, and ever since that fateful evening he had been struggling to keep enough distance from them and their insanity to give himself a fighting chance of talking his way out of the long drop into the Deep that the Lolofis would give all of these Blueband idiots. However, that was a dangerous game to play because he also had to make sure that his new friends didn't think that they needed to cut his throat.

Surprisingly, it was starting to look like Simon might just be able to thread that needle. His seniority at the Port Authority gave him access to all the secure yards along the leeward edge of the dock and that had made him too valuable to send into a fight. So other than some sore feet from all the walking around all day, he hadn't run into much of anything dangerous enough to worry about.

His seniority with the Port Authority would also serve him well when this idiotic revolt failed. He had been able to schedule his vacation for the two weeks surrounding Regatta Day, which made the timing of this whole adventure rather fortuitous. Add to that his well-known disdain for drunken debauchery, and it should make it easy for him to convince people that he'd been home quietly reading a novel and had missed out on the whole thing. And if these fools should somehow manage not to fail, with all his wandering around on the docks, he'd done just enough to earn some credit for wearing the blue armband. That should put him firmly on the good people list if they took over.

"That's them!" Jammal, or Jemmel, or Jomma, said, jumping around like a damn toddler. Simon wasn't sure what the kid's name was. He hadn't been all that interested in getting it right. "Look! Look! It's got to be them!"

Simon looked in the direction of the kid's wild gesticulating and saw that there were indeed three people standing around under an old junk runner in the repair yards.

"I don't know if that's them, Jimmy, but it sure as sunshine doesn't look like those two are helping that mechanic work on that junk runner, so I suppose I can't imagine who else'd be out here today."

"Simon, open the gate for me," the kid pleaded, gesturing at the people with his crossbow. "I've gotta kill 'em."

"I can't open that gate," Simon lied. He wanted as little to do with murdering people as he could manage. "That's a double-ex, code orange security gate. Only the port master can open and close one of those."

"Then help me climb over."

"Jimmy, them spikes on the top of that gate ain't just there to look pretty," Simon said. "They'll shred that suit so bad that the acid will be eatin' on your bones before you can run halfway to a decon station."

"But just think if I was the one who killed her!" the kid shouted.

"That's exactly what I'm thinking about, kid!" Simon shouted back at him. "Killing a person is the sort of thing that'll ruin you."

"She's not a person," he snarled. "She's a Lolofi."

"You can tell yourself that all you like, but none of the things you think make sense about that are gonna matter one damn bit," Simon snarled back at him. "Even if killin' was an accident and everyone tells you it was her own damn fault for doing something stupid it still rips your guts out."

"Accident?" the kid muttered, confused.

"You won't see it coming, but something will happen. You'll see someone who looks like her and suddenly you can't stop thinkin' about how she was just a twenty-year-old girl. You'll just be havin' a beer and figurin' on what you want to do on the weekend, and it will hit you that she had a whole life full of weekends that she didn't get to live. Thinking about what she felt in those seconds after she knew that she was dyin' will give you nightmares so bad they'll make you afraid to go to sleep. And just when you think it's all driven you as low as a man can get, it'll hit you with somethin' else and you're gonna find out just how much deeper the Deep can be. You go and do that to yourself by killing someone on purpose, and you'll never be a whole person again."

"Willamette's eighteen. Not twenty," Jimmy, or Jemima, or Jerrod said. All the eagerness and bravado that had filled him, gone.

"Yeah, so how about we just leave all the killin' to someone else." Simon pulled the emergency kit out of the thigh pocket of his deck suit, fished out the flare and offered it to the kid. "You can claim the glory of finding her and maybe not doin' the killin' yourself will let that be something you can live with."

"What's that?" the kid asked.

"An emergency flair," Simon said. "Standard piece of kit for anyone working out here. I'm sure the Colonel's ballerina murder girls are more than smart enough to figure out what it means."

The kid took the flare, twisted off the cap and pulled the string, sending a bright yellow spark about thirty meters into the air.

"Jerome," he said.

"What?" Simon asked.

"My name is Jerome."

Willamette understood why Niven was avoiding playing the obvious trump card. She probably could have just ordered the man, or his captain, to leave immediately and they would have obeyed, but with no idea who this man was, or to whom he might be loyal, or what he might know about the events in the city, revealing her identity before they were off the dock would be a huge risk. Regardless, it might be a gamble they would have to take. Niven and the man who had been working on the ship were finishing a second lap around their circular argument and they seemed determined to carry on for a third. Of course, the moment she thought she knew what to expect, Niven surprised her.

"Why don't we load the plow and the control harness in the cargo hold?" Niven suggested. "Then, if we took the ends of all the cables in with us, we could take off now and finish the install on the fly."

"That won't work." The man shot back, and then he cocked his head. "Wait. Why wouldn't that work, Flint?"

"It will work," Niven insisted. "So, Flint, that's your name, right?"

Flint nodded.

"Well Flint, let's get that plow back on the forklift and get it inside so we can get the hell off this dock."

"You know, that's just insane enough that it could work, and I am a certified expert at spotting insane things that just might work," Flint said. "It would be impossible to tune the control cables, but if we're careful, we should be able to get everything close enough to get the basics out of it. Dropping the pod out of the hold while we're flying without futzing everything up would be tricky, but damn, that could work."

There was a sharp popping noise and they all turned to look at the flare rising just a short distance away. Below the flare, just beyond the gate to the Port Authority yards, two figures wearing blue armbands on the outside of their deck suits were looking intently at them.

"Oh, that can't be good," Flint muttered.

"We need to get off this dock, now!" Niven said.

"Yeah, maybe that's a good idea." Flint nodded, hesitated a moment, and then ran for the forklift. "You two, get the ends of the cables into the cargo hold."

"No, let me do that. You need to work the winches," Niven said.

"Why can't you? I thought you said you knew ships!" Flint shouted.

"I do, but that doesn't mean that I know all the details of how you've got all the controls set up on yours!"

"Oh, yeah, then maybe you should run the forklift," Flint said. "And you, girl. You're a girl, right? Oh, never mind, it doesn't matter. I mean it does but ... grab the ends of all those cables and keep some tension on them all the time or they'll turn into a tangled mess."

Willamette grabbed hold of the cables. However, she had no idea what she was expected to do with them.

Flint tripped over a pneumatic impact wrench, getting the hose wrapped around his ankle. "Oh, damn, the tools ..."

"Flint!" A woman shouted so loud over the intercom that the speaker buzzed. "There are some people running this way from the city."

Flint turned to look toward the city and when he saw the three people running toward the ship, he dropped the tools that he was frantically gathering up.

"Run!" Flint ran toward the back of the ship and the cargo ramp. "Forget all that and just get in the ship! Em, fill the floats. Fill all the floats! Let's go! Let's go! Let's go!"

Niven and Willamette dropped everything and ran. Flint only had a couple steps on them, and even though he was neither quick nor graceful, he still beat them up the ramp and into the cargo hold by a significant margin. He was already entering the air lock leading into the ship by the time Willamette made it past the truck that was parked on the loading ramp.

"Shut the door, while I help get this thing off the dock. The controls are over there," Flint shouted just before he slammed the air lock door.

Niven knew what Flint was pointing at, and he also knew how to work the controls. Unfortunately, the truck was too heavy for the winches that lifted the cargo bay door, which was also the loading ramp.

"Willamette, move the truck!" Niven shouted. "Pull it into the cargo hold."

Willamette ran and climbed into the cab of the truck. It took up most of the width of the ramp, and with the skirt bunched around her crotch, and the purse jammed against her backside, it was awkward. However, none of that was nearly as awkward as what dawned on her as soon as she was in the driver's seat.

"Niven, I do not know how to operate a vehicle!" she shouted.

"Damn it!" Niven ran for the truck, stumbling as the ship shifted and started to lift off.

Monique upped the loping run into a sprint the moment she saw the ship that was parked in a repair yard. Two of the people that she'd seen standing under it were wearing deck suits from the hotel closet and it didn't take a genius to figure out that they had to be Willamette and her companion. It also didn't take a genius to know that she and Az and Gem were just a minute or two too late to do anything about it.

Not one to give up easily, Monique ignored the burning muscles in her legs and kept sprinting for the ship even though she knew it was pointless. When the ship's starboard side lifted she admitted defeat and slowed to a trot, and then immediately cursed the handful of steps she'd wasted. The ship rotated around the portside landing skids as it lifted and she saw that those skids were dragging because there was a service truck parked on the portside cargo ramp, weighing that side of the ship down. That ramp also served as the cargo bay door, and they'd never be able to close it with that truck parked on it like that. That still wouldn't have mattered, except that they were also trailing a line of some kind from that open cargo bay. If she could just catch hold of it, she could climb up into the ship.

Az shouted for her to wait, but Monique was determined. She could be the Blade that cut Willamette's throat. She could claim that glory, but she had to move fast. There was no telling how long that trailing line might be, and the ship was moving away as it rose and caught the flow of the Drift.

Twice she was sure she'd make it, and twice she was sure she'd failed, but she didn't waver in her resolve. In the end, with an extra push to get a last burst of speed and a leap, she managed to grab the air-tool that was hanging from the hose trailing from the rising ship. The hose stretched and the rebound almost pulled it from her grasp, but once she had a second hand on the hose, there was no amount of bouncing or swinging that would shake her loose.

The secret to climbing a thin rope, or pneumatic hose for that matter, was to understand that your grip was your weakness. No matter how fit you might be, the muscles in your hands and forearms weren't robust enough to repeatedly generate the kind of friction it took to lift your bodyweight. It just took far too much effort to squeeze your hand that hard on something that small. Your hands, however, were not the only way to create friction.

Reaching up with her right arm, she swung it around the hose twice before gripping the hose loosely with her hand. When she put some tension on it, the two wraps around her forearm cinched down and provided all the friction she needed to hold her weight. Pulling herself up, she did the same with her left arm. A few more iterations and she was up far enough to get her feet on the hose. Crossing her legs, she snagged the hose with the outside of her left foot and pulled it over the top of her right. The wrap under her left foot and over her right gave her feet something to grip. Locking and unlocking that grip allowed her to climb with the strength of her legs. That was far slower than climbing with just her arms, but she needed to conserve as much strength as she could for the fight. She did not expect Willamette Lolofi to die easily.

The first moments of flight were unsettled and unsettling. The ship was unbalanced and when one side lifted before the other, the flow of the Drift over the city caught them, spun them around and then dragged them along the deck. The shuddering, grinding noise set Willamette's teeth on edge. However, once they cleared the deck, the ship rose reasonably quickly, and the crew was able to compensate for the imbalanced load.

With that, Willamette could finally take a breath and with that breath came a rush of elation. Just over an hour earlier, escaping the hotel was something for which she had dared not even hope. Now, to be sailing away from the city was such a relief that she felt giddy. She knew that it was far from over. Just finding a safe haven in the web of loyalties and betrayals that must now define the Commonwealth was going to be a challenge, but it felt manageable, surmountable.

"Pretending you have no idea how to drive a truck?" Niven teased. He was obviously feeling relieved as well. "Don't you think that's taking the whole Little Princess thing just a bit too far?"

"I truly doubt if there are all that many of you lowly peasants who know how to drive," she huffed, exaggerating the snobby lift of her chin.

He laughed and bowed. "Might I shift thine truck for her Highness?"

"The grand lady does believe that she might find pleasure in allowing the peasant boy to attend to her needs."

"Oh really?"

"Though it remains to be seen if the peasant boy is sufficiently virile for the task." She took a step back to allow him to get past the door of the truck but just as she did, the ship lurched. There was a cable that served as a railing along the edge of the loading ramp, so there was no real danger that she might be thrown off, but it still put her face-to-face with the Deep and all its dreadful glory.

The Deep was an endless, sickly yellow blanket of clouds that looked as if it was close enough to touch but still so far away that you could fall toward it forever. Its roiling boil was frozen in time, but still seemed alive, lurking, evil.

"Let's not put so much trust in that cable." Niven grabbed her suit, but before he pulled her back he said, "Oh, son of a bitch!"

"What?" Before the word was even out of her mouth, she saw it.

The hose from the air compressor mounted on the back of the truck was hanging out of the cargo bay and a woman was climbing it.

Niven opened one of the big toolboxes that were built into the truck, rummaged for a few frantic seconds, and pulled out a small cutting torch. Sparking it to life with an expert flick of his fingers, he reached out to cut the hose, but hesitated. The hiss from the needle of blue flame seemed inordinately loud as he stood there, glancing back and forth between the woman and the hose she was climbing.

It was both a horror and a relief to see that Niven could not cut the hose. The woman would soon reach the ship, but that horror paled in comparison to seeing that the compassion in Niven's heart held sway. He could not take a life, even in such dire circumstances. Her fiancé was truly the antithesis of everything she despised about her family.

Willamette placed a reassuring hand on his arm and gave it a bit of a squeeze as she gently took the torch from him with the other hand. He shrugged apologetically but did not resist. He looked thankful.

Several very long seconds ticked past before Willamette realized that she could not do it either. The flame was less than a hand's-width from the hose, but that space felt impenetrable. She took a deep breath, reminding herself over and over that she was a Lolofi. She was born, bred, and raised to take exactly these kinds of ugly but necessary actions, but no matter how she tried to summon the courage of that heritage, she could not push the flame into the hose. All she could think about was the one and only time she had given Ida a beating. It had seemed like the grown-up thing to do. That was how misbehaving servants were meant to be punished, and Ida had truly misbehaved, but the justification made no difference. Hitting her had left Willamette feeling so guilty that she had been physically ill for several days. That could be nothing compared to sending a woman to her death in the Deep.

Willamette looked at the woman. She looked at the hatred and zeal in the woman's eyes as she climbed. She let herself feel the threat that the woman posed. She was certain that she could cut the hose if she just let the woman scare her enough.

A shrieking hiss startled Willamette. She had accidentally let the flame stray too close to the hose. It had melted partway through and now the hose was leaking a torrent of high-pressure air. Accident or not, it did the trick. The hose snapped a moment later, and just in time.

The woman was reaching for the bottom edge of the loading ramp as the hose in her hand went slack. In the space of that seemingly eternal heartbeat, the eager, murderous glee in the woman's eyes turned to surprise, and then horror. Her eyes stayed locked on Willamette as she fell, fearful, pleading, accusing.

For Willamette, there was no relief, just guilt.

Monique was surprised to discover that she feared death. Throughout all her training, and even during the fight to take the main gate of the yacht club, she had never given it much thought. It was just something that might happen. Before that, in the years before Kofi had found her, the nothing of death had often sounded better than the brutalities of life on the street, but when she felt that hose snap, she felt fear like she had never known before. It surged out of her guts with such ferocity that it took her breath and made her fingers tingle.

It was an instinct created by training that put her in the free fall position, knees bent, arms out with elbows bent. That arrested her tumble, and it was that same training that made her look for her drop target. That drove home the reality that even if she had a parachute, there was nowhere for her to land. There was nothing but the Deep below.

She felt the pressure build. Her ears hurt. Working her jaws, she popped her ears and then she set her jaws in the dive position, relaxed with the back of her mouth slightly flexed, keeping the tubes open.

The floating sensation in her gut made it feel as if she wasn't moving even though the low deep roar of the air rushing past and buffeting her told her she was falling. The Deep seemed to loom eternally far away. Seconds ticked past, perhaps minutes, perhaps hours. Her world was nothing but the roar of the thick air.

Her hands trembled. There was an ache deep inside the small of her back and she felt the tears on her cheek. They itched.

Suddenly the Deep rushed at her. She braced for impact but felt nothing as the clouds engulfed her. In the Deep, it was darker, and there was a new hiss in the throbbing roar of the rushing air, but nothing else changed. She just kept falling. It didn't seem to be getting any darker, but she could feel how much thicker the air had become. It resisted the small movements of her hands more than it seemed like it should. It felt almost as if she could swim in it. The roar of the air across her suit dropped in pitch. Her head and chest felt lighter and her legs heavier and she had to tuck her arms against her chest to hold the freefall position.

She felt the heat. It started as a warmth radiating in through the breather mask that quickly became uncomfortable. Then it began seeping in through the suit. First at the forearms and knees and then across her chest. Uncomfortable became painful and then it burned. The dull pain across her face grew more and more intense and then the atmosphere finally found a way in.

A component of the breather mask must have melted or broke. Monique's last moment was an explosion of agony as the searing-hot, acid-laden air shredded the flesh from her face.

Unlike in the city, where the utility tunnels were difficult to access, the tunnels that ran beneath the docks were the preferred way to move people out to the ships in the landing berths along the leeward edge of the docks, so they were set up to handle a great deal of foot traffic. Az was through the entrance and decon in seconds. She wished it could be hours, but she couldn't shirk her duty. She went straight to the security station and dialed the central exchange. Again, it only took seconds when she wished it could be hours.

"Willamette has fled the city." Az didn't even wait for Kofi to ask for the update. "The clever little bitch used the same damn junk runner that I used to bring the last of the Blades in."

To her surprise, Kofi didn't curse her failure. "And you are absolutely certain that she is on the ship that just lifted off without clearance?"

"Yes," Az said. "I had eyes directly on her, face-to-face at a few meters just before she escaped the hotel, and I had a clear enough look at the people boarding that ship to be certain that she was one of them."

"I can't wait to hear the story of how you managed to get that close without putting a dart through her," Kofi said, caustically.

"The story's not that interesting. Her fiancé used a fire hose to knock me back and hold us at bay while she exited the hotel," Az said. "By the time we got suited up to start the chase, they had a ten-minute head start, which they used to great effect. We still nearly caught them but fell just short."

"Well, if you want to stay in the chase, get to dock M23 before I do." Kofi ended the call before she had a chance to reply.

CHAPTER 10

Expecting a red light to flash a signal demanding that they return to the docks, Flint watched the F-dock control tower intently as he worked the rigging from the rear control room. He adjusted the inflation of the float tanks in the wings, trimming the ship to fly level despite the lopsided load. He also checked the work of their new passengers with occasional glances through the windows into the cargo bay. They seemed competent enough. They managed to move the truck inside and get the door closed, and they had run the decon for the cargo bay without his help. They hadn't been anywhere close to quick about any of it, but they had managed.

"Flint, where's my kite?" Em asked from the intercom.

"Patience, my lovely little flower," Flint crooned back. "It doesn't look like the Port Authority has noticed our illegal takeoff, so let's just play it safe and drift until we're sure we're clear of their control zone before we pop the kite."

"You call me a lovely little flower again and I'll pop your kite," Em snarled.

"Hey, you should be nice to me," Flint said. "I just snagged us a couple of paying passengers. They seem nice and they claim to be generously desperate."

"Passengers? How in the hell did you do that?"

"Magic, my lovely little flower, magic."

"And the plow?"

"That would be the bad news, and the reason I'm really, really hoping we can drift for another few minutes without getting tagged by the Port Authority."

"Roger that," Em said. "Give me as much float as you can so I can steal some speed from the glide up."

"That is an excellent idea, my ..."

"Say it again and you will not live to see tomorrow," Em said, calmly but sincerely.

"Roger that." Flint chuckled as he flicked off the intercom.

The air lock decon cycle started, and Flint listened to it run as he watched the control tower. Heavy rinse, spray of acid neutralizer, second rinse, a mist of acid neutralizer with the fans swirling that mist about and then a final rinse. He could hear their new passengers moving as the fans ran, shifting so that the acid that had found its way into the various crinkles and folds of the suits had a fighting chance of being exposed to the neutralizer. That was another indication that at least one of them had some experience.

When the air lock door opened behind him, he said, "You can hang those suits in the closet to your right. It's rigged for drying them."

They cleared the lights indicating the Port Authority control zone and he watched the F-dock tower for another few seconds before he decided it was safe to launch the kite. They had made it. It shouldn't have been possible to launch like that without being noticed, but somehow, they had, and that would give them a fighting chance of getting to somewhere safe, even without a plow.

"Welcome aboard the Drunken Monkey. I'm Flint and our pilot is ..." When he turned around to finally greet their passengers properly, he was so surprised that he couldn't even finish the sentence. Instead, he just muttered, "Whoa."

"I presume that 'whoa' is your way of indicating that you recognize me." Willamette Lolofi sounded disappointed if not resigned. She was wearing a rumpled shopgirl's dress, and she was a sweaty, bedraggled mess, but there was no mistaking who she was.

"Yeah, I've been licking the back of your head since you were a baby," Flint said.

"What?" her companion asked, bewildered.

"Stamps," Flint and Willamette said in unison.

"Oh, that's right," her companion said. "I forgot that your father put you on the intercity postage stamp. Hi Flint. I'm Niven."

Niven offered his hand, but Flint just stood there, staring at Willamette. He had no idea what to do, or what any of this meant, but he doubted if he was going to like anything that might come from having Willamette Lolofi on his ship, especially since she was desperate to flee the capital of her father's empire.

"Careful, she bites," Niven said.

"Yeah, she bites," Flint muttered.

"Flint, are you going to pop that kite or what?" Em snarled through the intercom.

"Yeah, pop the kite," Flint muttered. Then he was suddenly panicked by the thought of what Willamette might think of his reluctance to take off when they had first asked for a ride.

He stuttered apologetically at her.

"Flint." Willamette took his hand gently in hers, smiled sweetly at him and softly asked, "Will you be so kind as to do me a favor?"

"Uhm, yeah, of course, uh, Your Highness, ladyship, uh, ma'am," he stammered. "Just say the word."

"I would very much like it if you would …" Without warning Willamette went from soft and sweet to a commanding shout. "Turn around and help that woman fly this ship!"

Startled Flint took a step back and when he heard Niven laughing, he realized how foolish he'd been.

"Sorry about that, uhh, Grand Lady Willamette," he said, sheepishly. "Forgive me for being overwhelmed. Our clientele generally runs more along the lines of riffraff and scoundrels."

"That would be me." Niven offered his hand again and this time Flint decided to shake it properly. "Niven, certified riffraff and the Grand Lady Willamette's designated scoundrel."

"And my fiancé," Willamette added, emphasizing the possessive.

"Fiancé?" Flint was caught by surprise again. "Are you even old enough to have a fiancé?"

Willamette glared at him. It was almost as terrifying as Em's glare.

"Flint! My kite!" Em shouted at him through the intercom.

"Hey Flint," Niven said, chuckling and smacking him playfully on the shoulder. "Why don't you pop that kite and get it trimmed before one of the women on this ship decides that she needs to murder you?"

"Yeah, women threatening to murder me has been a bit of an issue lately." Flint nodded Niven toward the stairs and turned to the rigging controls. "Main cabin's up the stairs. I'll be up to get you sorted in a few minutes."

"Thanks," Niven said.

"Oh, and Niven ..." Flint said.

"Yeah ..."

"If you run into Em up there, be careful. She bites," Flint said. "And I mean that literally."

Kofi was finding it increasingly difficult to stay calm about the Willamette Lolofi situation. He had expected setbacks, but to have so much go so well only to have the straightforward task of killing a teenage girl go awry in such a spectacular way was nothing short of infuriating. Perhaps the most frustrating part of it all was that he wanted someone to blame. Unfortunately, no matter how he looked at the situation, there had been no failures. Except for Ida failing to drive the knife home when she had the chance, which had been far too much to expect of such a little girl, everyone associated with the elimination of the last of the Lolofis had executed their assigned tasks admirably. Every choice had been reasonable, every plan, every improvisation, every reaction had been appropriate. Still, somehow, Willamette kept slipping away and forcing him to commit resources that he wished to use for other purposes.

"Welcome aboard the Bluehawk, Colonel." The captain of the ship, Captain Roberts, saluted and then stepped forward to shake Kofi's hand. It was standard protocol, but Ida didn't know that. She leapt to intercept the captain with a slashing swing of her knife. She missed him, mostly, but if Az hadn't grabbed her, Kofi's Little Knife would have had a second go at giving the man more than a cut sleeve and a nick across the forearm. That protectiveness and possessiveness of the space around him was interesting. It was far different from the way any of the other Blades had acted when he first recruited them, and it further suggested that Ida might become something special once she was trained properly.

"The Bluehawk?" Kofi chuckled, as he strode toward the bridge.

"Blue seems to be a theme, sir," Roberts said, rushing to fall into step beside Kofi.

"As I have noticed," Kofi said. "Do you still have eyes on that junk runner?"

"Yes, sir. Navigation team is tracking them." Roberts directed Kofi to lead them up a stairway. "We can depart as soon as your people are aboard."

"Then let's get underway," Kofi said.

Roberts nodded at a junior officer who hustled back toward the air lock.

"And let me just say, Colonel, I know that we were only meant as a contingency force, and that as such you would rather not have found the need to use us, but we are thrilled to have this opportunity," Roberts said. "Training up with a bit of piracy is one thing, but the men on the boarding parties are going to be particularly excited by the chance to get into a real fight."

"I'm glad they're enthused, Captain Roberts, but you may wish to temper their expectations," Kofi said. "The only reason I asked you to wait for me was so that I could make damn certain that this complication was eliminated simply, completely, directly, and decisively. I don't need her alive. I don't even need a body. We know without doubt that she is on that ship so let's just knock that junk runner into the Deep as soon as it's in range."

"I would, sir, but I … uh, I'm sorry, sir, but we don't have any stand-off armaments, so we'll have to board," Roberts said, nervously.

"Why in the hell aren't you properly armed?" Kofi snapped.

"The only way we could get this ship onto the Lightcastle docks was to maintain the pretense that we were just a whaler that was making a little extra money by bringing people into the city for the regatta," the captain explained. "It was hard enough to disguise the special harpoons, ramps, ladders, cutters, and other gear we needed to be able to conduct boarding missions. Missiles or cannons would have been impossible to hide."

Kofi glowered at the captain but nodded his understanding.

None of that was the man's fault. Yet another person who could not be blamed.

"Az, get another couple of squads of Blades on board before we lift," Kofi ordered. "If there's going to be any hand-to-hand fighting, I want my best people involved."

Az nodded to a Blade who ran back to the air lock.

***

Willamette had no idea how long she had been sitting at the table. She didn't even remember sitting down at the table.

"Is the tea okay, uhh, Your Highness?" Flint asked, nervously.

"Flint, please call me Willamette," she said. "And yes. The tea is very nice, thank you."

"Says the woman who hasn't taken a sip," Niven teased. Standing behind her he gently placed a hand on her shoulder and gave it a reassuring squeeze.

"I cannot stop wondering what kinds of things might have made that woman laugh," Willamette said. "Did someone love her? Will someone miss her? What kinds of hopes, dreams, and desires did I dump into the Deep with her?"

"All of her hopes, dreams, and desires were focused on killing you," Niven said sternly. "She was climbing that hose because she wanted to cut your throat."

"A woman? Climbing up?" Flint asked.

"The air hose from the truck, it must have been trailing behind when we took off," Niven explained. "She was climbing up it, murder in her eyes; no choice but to cut the hose."

"Says the man who could not cut it himself." The words came out as bitter and petty, and she grasped the hand on her shoulder, giving it a squeeze of apology. "The look on her face when she felt the hose snap was terror as pure as terror can be."

"And the fact that it disturbs you so makes you more beautiful than you can imagine." Niven leaned down and kissed her on the cheek and then put his arms around her, hugging her tight.

"Not to ruin a tender moment," Flint said, apologetically. "But if you two need to get somewhere that's not straight down the Drift, then we kind of need to know now. We can't tack or pull ourselves up the Drift without a plow, at least not with any pace, so our direction of travel is pretty much limited to downdrift pulls and cuts."

"That rules out my dad's estate," Niven said. "It's well south and a bit updrift."

"Our betrothal has been announced so we could not run there anyway," Willamette said. "Nor can we run to any habitat or property associated with my family, and we probably should not look for help from anyone known to be a good friend or close ally of either of our families."

"What about running to someplace controlled by a noble family with some muscle?" Niven asked. "Like one of the Big 12. Someone that wasn't a close ally, but you still know would stay loyal."

"Even if we knew which nobles were still alive, we would not know which of them survived this because they were involved," she said. "Even if we could guess at which families were not involved, and who among them remained loyal, the stronger they are, the more likely they are to see an opportunity of their own in this. If I were to show up looking for help, they might see me as leverage for their own attempt to take the Commonwealth. Further, given Kofi's service in the military, I am even hesitant to run to a military base. There was a suspicious lack of response from the Lightcastle Marine barracks."

"So maybe we just cut the Drift for a while," Flint said. "Get a day or two away from Lightcastle before we try anything."

"That does not feel right either," she said. "The people chasing us saw us take off on this ship. I cannot imagine that we should remain passive and give them time to get things in order so that they can come looking for us."

"What in the hell are you two running from?" Flint asked. He looked deeply concerned.

"A coup," Willamette said. That disturbed Flint tremendously.

"And it appears to be a well-planned and well-executed one at that," Niven added.

"I believe we must do something bold," Willamette said. "Perhaps not necessarily bold, but something proactive and unpredictable. We need to avoid whatever additional contingencies and options that Colonel Kofi has in place. And we need to do something that will win us time and information that might help us develop some options."

"How about if we head for the nearest smelter?" Niven asked. "Smelters are dirty, hot, loud, industrial, and generally only fit for all the unsavory types of people that go along with that. It's the last kind of place they'd think you would run to. I would be surprised if they had figured out enough about me to imagine I would take you to one."

Willamette frowned and shrugged. The logic made sense, but it did not feel like the right option.

"Well, until one of us comes up with a better idea, why don't we set a course for the nearest downdrift smelter?" Niven suggested.

"I can also check the latest charts to see what options we'll fly past on the way," Flint added.

Willamette nodded. She was still not convinced that it was the right thing to do, but she had nothing better to offer.

"Flint, I need you at the nav station. I think we have a worry," Em said, climbing up from the helm. "Whoa, that chick looks exactly like the postage stamp princess."

"Yes," Willamette said, sighing. "We have had that conversation."

"Em, meet Niven and Willamette," Flint said.

"Hello," Em said, and then frowned. "Wait. Did you just say Willamette?"

"Yep, the one and only Willamette Lolofi," Niven said. "But she likes to be called Little Princess."

Willamette elbowed him in the thigh, digging the point of her elbow into the middle of the muscle.

"Ow." He jumped back, grinning.

"So, what's this worry you found, Em?" Flint asked. "Is the ballast compressor acting up again?"

"No, I think we're being followed," Em said, shaking her head in disbelief as she stared at Willamette. "Could just be someone else making a run straight downdrift, but it seems odd that the only other ship to leave the city while the port is still closed is on the exact same course that we picked."

Flint started toward the rear, but Niven grabbed his arm. "You're the rigger, right?"

Flint nodded.

"Then why don't you let me run rear spotter?" Niven asked. "You run the rigging."

"You know how to work a set of scopes?" Flint asked.

"Extremely mediocre," Niven said, as if it were the achievement of the century. "Extremely."

"Or we could just all walk over to the helm together, and Flint can strap his ass in the nav station and get a good look at them with the good nav scopes since they aren't in our blind spot."

"Yeah, I suppose that would work," Niven said.

"Well, I am so desperately relieved to hear that you approve," Em muttered caustically.

Willamette followed the others. The Lolofi family yacht may have been spacious and luxurious, but there was no place on it that offered a view out into the Drift that was anywhere near as spectacular as the view from the Drunken Monkey helm. It was essentially all windows. Starting at the floor of the helm's lowered deck, the windows curved up, over and just past the railing separating it from the main cabin, and they wrapped around in a curve that took them from wing to wing. It conveyed the vastness of the Drift in a way that simply could not be replicated by the view out of a normal, flat window.

Also, unlike the Lolofi family yacht, the Drunken Monkey heeled over a great deal when it turned. That caught Willamette by surprise and sent her sliding off the fold-down jump seat at the back of the helm, amusing everyone. Everyone else handled the shift without a thought and Niven just stood steady, not even bothering to hold on to anything.

"Damn, they matched our turn," Flint said, working the knobs that controlled the navigation station's sighting scopes. "Well, not quite matched it, but they shifted onto a cut that's going to bring them around in the same direction."

"Anybody got any bright ideas?" Em muttered.

"What kind of ship is it?" Niven asked.

"It's not a Port Authority Patrol Ship, if that's what you're thinking," Flint said.

"Why would he be thinking that?" Willamette asked.

"Because if it was a Port Authority Patrol Ship and it was chasing us because we made an unauthorized liftoff while the port was closed, we just happen to have a passenger who could tell them to kiss her ass and jump in the Deep," Flint said.

"Perhaps if this were a normal day," Willamette said.

"It's a moot point anyway," Flint said. "That ship isn't displaying Port Authority lights."

"I meant, what kind of ship is it?" Niven clarified. "A cruiser? A cutter?"

Flint took another look through the scopes, "It looks like a whaler."

"Really?" Niven was surprised. "Why would they be chasing us with a whaler?"

"The Battle of Cloud Nine," Willamette said.

It took Niven a minute to figure out what she meant.

"That's the one where your grandfather launched a surprise attack using modified whalers as boarding frigates," he said.

"That's what I would have brought in to Lightcastle if I wanted to sneak a fighting ship onto the docks," she said. "A whaler can sail just about anywhere, and no one will think twice about it."

Niven nodded.

"And whalers are fast," Flint said. "That bugger is gaining on us."

"Does it have any ballast in the whale rack?" Niven asked.

Flint flipped a lever, peered back into the viewer, and worked the knobs to control the scope. "Nothing at all in the rack. Why?"

"Because even though whalers are big and have a lot of room for crew, they have no cargo holds, or any other interior space big enough to hide big weapons. So, if that ship was equipped with missiles or cannons, they would be disguised as ballast and they would be hanging in the racks." Niven started to pace. "No one would think twice about something that looks like ballast in the whale racks."

"I am not sure what that tells us," Willamette said. "It fits with it being set up as a boarding vessel, which was already the most likely use for it."

"Yes, but the reason no one thinks twice about seeing ballast in the racks of a whaler is because there's a good reason that whalers often carry big blocks of garbage around with them," Niven said. "When a harpoon vents the lifting gas from the whale, a whaling ship needs to have plenty of extra lift available to compensate. At the same time, they don't want to waste weight on big compressors, or slow themselves down with the drag from pulling big turbines through the air to run those compressors. So their gas systems are barebones and their gas ballast tanks are slow to fill."

"So, without ballast in the racks, that ship will have trouble chasing a steep dive," Em said.

"Exactly," Niven said.

"But what happens after we dive?" Flint asked. "We don't have any way to use a dive to our advantage. No plow means we have nothing to drop down to get hold of the hard pull updrift from the Deep."

"That's irrelevant," Niven said. "A whaler can easily outrun and outmaneuver a junk runner on any course or cut, so our only chance is to lose them on the dive."

Flint nodded.

"Okay, strap in," Em said. "Everyone get ready for an emergency dive."

"Wait, hold off on that," Niven said, a bit too forcefully. He made a small apologetic gesture to Em before explaining. "That seems like the only choice, but this isn't the time to make a rash move. Let's take a few minutes to think through every detail of this and make very certain we give ourselves the best chance possible."

Both Em and Flint nodded.

Az focused on the virtues of patience. The pursuit of the Drunken Monkey was agonizingly slow. The Bluehawk may have been a fast ship, but junk runners were by no means slow, and Kofi's decision to personally oversee the pursuit, and then to delay long enough to bring a full contingent of Blades aboard, had gifted their prey a significant head start. Catching them had taken so long that Az had resorted to isometric exercises and concentration games to stay relaxed and alert. Ida, of course, had none of that training and whatever discipline she might have learned from serving Lady Willamette had been wiped away when Kofi broke her. She was just a scared little girl who had been cut loose from everything that she knew, stripped of any sense of right or wrong, and given a very sharp knife. She was dangerous and irritating.

Her fear was probably the real issue because that was what drove her to the Colonel. It was obvious that her fear was what he wanted. He was truly gifted at finding the perfect way to instill a desperate longing for the comfort of belonging in young women, and even though fear was not usually how he did it, Ida was living proof that it worked. She was also living proof that, just as Az had cautiously tried to warn the Colonel, today was not the day for adopting a stray. Kofi needed to be fully committed to dealing with other, far more urgent issues, but Ida was underfoot and unshakable. It was driving him insane.

Az grabbed Ida by the loose blue tunic that someone had improvised out of a wounded Blade's frock. Lifting the girl completely off the floor, Az held her aloft as she tried to run back to Kofi's side.

Az carried the squirming girl to the quiet and somewhat out-of-the-way area at the back of the helm, but just before they got there, Ida went for her knife. Az was expecting that. That knife had become the only source of power that the girl had over anything, and Az would have been surprised if she hadn't grabbed it. As the knife came out its sheath, Az tossed Ida into the air to unsettle her and she traded the grip on the frock for a grip on the forearm of the hand holding the knife. Az's fingers easily wrapped all the way around her forearm and even when she lowered the girl back to the floor, it was easy to lift her just enough to keep her on her tippy-toes so that she couldn't get any grip or leverage with her feet.

Staring Ida in the eyes, Az squeezed hard enough to make it hurt, and hard enough to cut off the blood flow to the hand holding the knife.

Sustaining the intense intimidating glare was a challenge. Regardless of what Kofi thought he saw in Ida, she was wrong for this. A Blade was wrought from a suffering and cynical soul. A Blade had to be a girl who had lost all hope for the future, and she had to feel nothing but disdain for the world she knew. How a girl arrived at that place was irrelevant. For many it was poverty and abuse, but for others it was a premature realization that the world that awaited them in adulthood was cruel, unfair, and uncaring. For some it was even a perverse reaction to a privileged life and the education that came with that. There was no hint of any of that in Ida's eyes. Even after the horrors Kofi had subjected her to, she still saw the world through a child's eyes. She wasn't angry; she was frightened. She wasn't jaded; she was adrift. She didn't cling to Kofi because she wanted the new tribe he offered; she saw him as the only thing that might reconnect her to the world she had lost. It was heartbreaking to look into those eyes.

Az gave the girl a slight shake. The hand holding the knife had gone weak from losing the blood flow, and the shake was enough to jostle the knife free. The girl whimpered in panic as it rattled on the deck. She stared at it, desperate to pick it back up.

"A knife cannot give comfort," Az said. "It cannot bring hope, it cannot offer strength. A knife can only cut."

"I am his Little Knife," Ida whispered, worried, trying to say the right thing.

"It is how the knife cuts that allows it to bring comfort, hope, or strength," Az said. "And knowing how to cut, when to cut, and what to cut is a matter of the mind. It is a matter of focus and discipline."

"Please don't hurt me." The girl winced, again reminding Az that she was still just a child. "I'll be good."

"Discipline is not about pain or being punished, Little Knife," Az said. "It is about learning to control your mind, your body, and your self. You must learn to control yourself, and your self. Do you understand?"

Ida nodded, but it was desperate and hopeful. She didn't understand. She just wanted to avoid punishment.

"We'll start with two rules," Az said. "First, your knife stays in its sheath unless you are told to use it. Do you understand?"

Ida nodded, again a desperate effort to give the right answer, not an indication of understanding. For now, Az was going to have to work with that.

"If I see you waving that knife around without being told to use it, I will cut your hand off with it. Do you understand that?"

Az heard Kofi chuckle, but more importantly, Ida's horrified glance at her numb hand told Az that she understood that one.

"Good," Az said. "Rule number two is called chain of command. The chain of command is the arm that Colonel Kofi uses to wield his Blades and you, Little Knife, are the smallest and littlest finger at the very end of that arm. You are at the very end of that chain. This means you will obey me as you would obey the Colonel. When I tell you to do something, that is the Colonel telling you to do something through me. And if another Blade tells you to do something, that is me telling you do to it through her, which is also the Colonel telling you to do it through me. Do you understand how that makes a chain?"

Ida nodded. She did understand that. The chain of command would make sense for a girl who had always been a servant.

"Good, now you will stand next to me, you will stay quiet, and you will stay out from underfoot."

Az let Ida go. She scrambled to pick up her knife, but she also immediately put it in its sheath and ran to the very back of the helm. She stood as far out of the way as she could, watching Az and waiting for instructions. Az recognized that as taking the station of a servant in attendance. That wasn't ideal because thinking in terms of servitude would interfere with developing the kind of goal-driven thought that was expected of a Blade, but it would do for the moment.

Kofi caught Az's eye and gave her an approving nod. Az resisted the urge to remind him that Ida was not suited to his needs. Instead, she gave him a curt nod to acknowledge his silent compliment.

"The junk runner is still rising, but the extra drag from inflating its external floats has slowed it considerably," the navigator said. "Estimate five minutes to harpoon range."

"Harpoon crews to the work deck." Captain Roberts was so calm he sounded bored. "Hull cutters and boarding parties on standby. This is what we trained for, boys. Let's go kick some ass!"

"Why did they inflate their external floats?" Kofi asked. "Surely, they knew that the drag would slow them down. And why is that ship still running a cut across the Drift? Anyone who's read a war story knows that running straight downdrift eliminates most of the speed differentials between ships."

"Using the externals and staying on a starboard cut are poor choices, but that's not all that surprising." Captain Roberts added a bit of a sneer to his bored monotone. "The pilots and captains of junk runners are never more than minimally competent."

That set off a thousand alarm bells in Az's head. "No, you are wrong, Captain. The pilot of that ship is insanely brilliant."

Roberts frowned at Az, questioning.

"Target maneuver," the navigator shouted. "They're ... packing their kite?"

"Captain, she is completely insane and utterly brilliant," Az said.

"That is the ship that I used to smuggle the last contingent of Blades into the city. That pilot flew us in over the top of the Lightcastle dome and managed to land that thing on the docks without anyone noticing."

"That's not possible," Roberts said.

"Nonetheless, she did it," Az said.

Everyone looked out the front of the helm, watching the Drunken Monkey as its kite pod was reeled into the rack on the top of the ship. The moment the rack's clamps closed on the pod, its external floats deflated, and it turned hard as it dove.

"Target maneuver. Hard dive updrift," the navigator called out.

"Recall the deck crews and prepare to pursue," Roberts ordered, no longer sounding bored.

"Sir, they're on a collision course with an estate," the navigator said.

"And they're on that course for a damn good reason," Az said.

Roberts looked at Az, thought another moment, and then gave her an acknowledging nod before turning to the navigator.

"I want a full tactical assessment of that course," he said before turning back to Az and speaking directly to her. "And I want you to tell me everything you know about that junk runner and everyone on it."

Az nodded. Captain Roberts was smart, flexible, and willing to put his ego aside when needed. He was exactly what she would have expected from a man that Kofi recruited.

Willamette had never appreciated a piece of advice in the way that she was grateful for Niven's insistence that she should secure all the straps and belts when she secured herself in a jump seat at the back of the aft control room. She knew something was afoot when he had stepped into the odd harness, tightened the belts around his waist and legs, and used it to lash his hips tightly against the edge of the control panel, but if he had not insisted, she still would have probably just used the lap belt.

The ship groaned mightily as Em pulled them out of the dive and the sensation of falling was suddenly replaced with crushing weight. Momentum pulled Willamette's arms down so hard that it ripped her hands free from where they were holding the shoulder straps and her arms fell toward the floor with such force that it hurt her elbows when they snapped straight. Her fingers and toes tingled and throbbed as the blood rushed down her arms and legs. The shoulder straps dug into her shoulders, and if not for the way they were buckled together between her breasts, she would have been pulled out of them. For a count of three, it felt as if the hand of a god was trying to pull her insides down through the floor, and then, without warning, up became down.

An invisible force tried to throw her into the ceiling. It was nowhere near as powerful as the earlier pull toward the floor, but it was still irresistible. Her head snapped back and up. Her arms flew upward, again hurting her elbows as they snapped straight. Her knees hit her chest hard enough to make her grunt and she struggled to breathe as her guts tried to crawl up into her lungs.

Through all that, Niven managed to hold his face to the viewer and keep his hands on the knobs that controlled the navigation scopes.

"Damn," he muttered, and then shouted, "North, Em! As far and as fast to the north as you can."

Willamette was thrown to the left and then pulled hard toward the floor again. The maneuver suddenly brought the underside of the estate into view out of the back of the ship and that visual reference steadied everything for Willamette. She could suddenly feel how she was orientated. She knew what was up and what was down and that made a world of difference, especially for her stomach. A few moments later, the pull toward the floor eased, and they settled into a steady dive downward.

"Just before we dove over the nose, they veered to the south," Niven said into the intercom before burying his face back in the viewer for the scopes.

"Did they follow us over the estate?" Flint asked from the helm.

"All I saw was the start of their turn, but I don't think they moved to cover the updrift run, no," Niven said, working the knobs. "And they made the turn south earlier than they needed to. I think they wanted to make sure we saw it."

"Damn, they must know that we don't have a plow," Flint said.

"Yeah, that would be my guess," Niven said. "Sorry, guys."

"Don't be sorry," Flint said. "You were right. Losing them with the dive was our only real shot."

"At the rate they were moving, I would guess we want to run about ten degrees downdrift of north to keep the estate between us and them for as long as we can," Niven said.

"Roger that," both Em and Flint said. Em added, "But I don't think keeping the estate in their line of sight will help. We all know that it's over except for the singing."

"One minute to the Deep," Flint said.

"Niven?" Willamette was not sure what to ask. Fortunately, Niven knew what to explain.

"Being heavier and able to dive faster would normally give us big advantage on an updrift run," he said. "In addition to the extra momentum we would get from the steepness of our dive. If we had a plow, when we levelled out down however far we dared go, we could drop our plow down even farther."

"And the farther down you can get the plow, the faster it will pull you up the Drift," Willamette finished the thought. "Yes, I understand that."

"Their counter to that move is to use a steep but much flatter dive to get as much updrift momentum as possible from their descent. They would want to use that to stay over the top of us so we can't outrun them updrift."

"That was why we waited on the dive as long as we did," Em said over the intercom. "We wanted their optimal updrift dive to force them to fly directly over the estate. That would give us the chance to turn downdrift while we were hidden from their view by the estate."

"But if they know that we don't have a plow, they also know that we can't make an updrift run," Flint said over the intercom. "So, they didn't try to get their own run updrift. Instead, they moved toward one side of the estate to limit where we could go while we were out of their sight."

"Which pins us into a fairly narrow wedge of courses toward the north," Niven added.

The light suddenly dimmed as their dive took them into the haze of the Deep. It was not dark, but it did become gloomy.

"I didn't get a visual on them before we hit the haze, so I don't think they got one on us," Niven said, finally looking up from the viewer.

The dive flattened out as Niven turned on the lights in the control room. Not all of them came on.

"Does that mean we made it out of sight before they saw where we are headed?" Willamette asked.

"Yes," Niven said. "But that won't do us much good."

"Surely we could make a turn now and they would not be able to see which direction we were headed," Willamette said.

"Yes, but—" Niven was cut off by a deep rumbling thump.

"Is that sonar?" Willamette asked.

"Yeah, whalers have active sonar," Niven said. "Most ships just use a passive array to listen for the direction of the pings from habitat beacons, but whalers use active sonar to help spot the whales that are rising out of the Deep."

"They turned like they did, because by narrowing where we could go into the Deep, they could make sure that they could get over us and track us with the sonar," Willamette said.

"Exactly," Niven said as the rumble hit them again, louder. "And that's them using the echo off our hull to aim the thumper directly at us."

"Now would be a good time for a clever idea," Em muttered over the intercom.

Several silent seconds passed before Willamette unbuckled the belts, walked over to the intercom, leaned forward, and spoke directly into the microphone. "We need to dive deeper."

"Princess, we can't dive deeper." Em growled. "Deeper isn't safe."

"You will not, ever again, call me princess." Willamette matched Em's growl with one of her own. "And yes, we can dive deeper. We must dive deeper."

"Princess, we are not diving any deeper," Em returned the growl and added a bit of a snarl.

"But we must." Willamette went gentle. Speaking sweetly and softly. "Dive deeper and head north. And you will stop calling me princess."

"Hey, Em ..." Niven said. "I'd bet that Willamette knows something we don't. She knows some monumentally weird stuff. So how about we set a descending glide to the north and then hear her out."

Em didn't answer, but Willamette felt the ship make a small turn and return to a descent.

"Thank you." Willamette spoke into the intercom microphone, but she was smiling at Niven.

"You're welcome," Niven said to Willamette, before speaking to Em. "And Em, Willamette likes to be called Little Princess. Not just Princess."

"Roger that," Em said.

"I will flay you alive for that." Willamette smacked him on the arm.

Niven grinned and winked, but the playful bravado faltered almost immediately. He sighed and his smile shifted to grim.

"Do not despair, my love," she whispered in his ear as she hugged him. "We are far from defeated."

CHAPTER 11

Flint's mind was darting like mad, and he didn't care for any of the things it was flinging about as it did. An obsessive desire to remember exactly how long he'd been meaning to fix the lights on the bridge kept resurfacing, and that was irritating as hell. The other odd things he was noticing were distracting, and the handful of rational thoughts he managed to churn up were, to say the least, distasteful.

The helm of the Drunken Monkey was gloomy in all senses of the word. The weary, overwhelmed mood felt dark and oppressive. The ship was making odd groaning and moaning noises, as if it was wailing in despair as it adjusted to pressure that it had never known before, and the dim light felt like a physical force weighing on Flint's shoulders. The layer of clouds that defined the Deep blocked just enough of the sunlight to leave the bridge at the threshold separating day and night vision. There was enough light to hint at some of the colors, but not quite enough to see them naturally and that was exacerbated by the yellowish-brown tint the clouds added to the light. His eyes were confused further by the small pools of clear white light cast by the handful of working lights that illuminated seemingly random parts of the helm. Or perhaps it was just the first touch of the madness of the Deep. He had never descended into the Deep before, so he had no way to know, but he had suspicions.

The most obvious and probably the most rational thing that he and Em could do would be to detain their passengers in some way and surrender them to their pursuers. That whaler wasn't a ship that would have been sent by either the Lightcastle Port Authority or the Commonwealth Navy, so dropping the plow through the dome couldn't have any bearing on why it was after them. That meant that it must be part of the coup, and that meant that they were chasing after Willamette and not the Drunken Monkey. That in turn meant that they just might be willing to let him and Em sail away in return for making it easier to get their hands on her. Of course, if he and Em were going to go down that dark route, they may as well go full on burnt midnight black. They could dump Niven and Willamette into the Deep, surrender to the whaler, and plead to the theft of the service truck as an excuse for running. No, that wouldn't work. Those people on the dock had seen her board the ship. They'd have to give them a body, or her head. Or had they seen her board? Yes, they must have. Willamette had said it was a woman trying to climb into the ship. That must have been one of Az's killer ballerinas.. Maybe it was Az who was after them. Maybe he should try to talk to her. No, Az'd kill him if she saw him again. He was sure of that.

Damn, they were down way too far already. The Deep was starting to muddle his head. Maybe he should quit looking out the windows. They said that looking out the windows made it worse, but the helm was pretty much all windows.

"First, the Deep does not drive you mad." Willamette sounded like a schoolteacher lecturing foolish children.

"Willamette, I've felt it myself," Niven said. "Most people say it's caused by the light, but I suspect that there's maybe something in the clouds down here that isn't in the air up in the Drift. I think it slips in through the air sifters. When I upgraded air sifters on my ship, it didn't seem to hit as fast or as bad."

"Let me guess, the madness feels like drinking alcohol," she said. "It gets worse the deeper you dive and the longer you are down, and if you let it go too long, it leads to hallucinations and reckless behavior. Right?"

"Yep, that's pretty much it," Niven said.

"Niven, that is the description of nitrogen narcosis," Willamette said.

"Nitrogen what?" Flint must have said that out loud because Willamette looked at him when she explained.

"Nitrogen narcosis," she said. "Some people used to call it the martini effect. It was a known danger encountered by people working below the surface of the oceans on Earth. When you breathe normal air at high atmospheric pressures, nitrogen becomes intoxicating. And it was said to get worse if the carbon dioxide in the air you were breathing was too high."

"Which would explain why the madness is worse on old or poorly maintained ships," Niven muttered.

"Great," Em huffed. "I'll try to remember that for the test but calling it nitrogen whatever doesn't make it any less real, and it certainly doesn't make it any less deadly. Like you said, it's going to get worse the longer we're in the Deep. And every meter deeper we glide is going to make it get worse faster."

"All true," Willamette said. "But knowing that the madness is nitrogen narcosis does tell us how to remedy it. If we remove the nitrogen from the air we are breathing, we should be able stay down here and remain sane for as long as we wish."

"We can't just remove the nitrogen from the air," Flint said, wondering if he should try to calm Em. She was a mean drunk, and if this nitrogen thing was like drinking, she could get nasty. Or nastier. Or … whatever. He took a breath and focused on explaining the point he wanted to make. "What I mean is, I could rig something with the air system to take all the nitrogen out of the air in here, but if we got anywhere close to pure oxygen, every greased joint and fitting on the ship would burst into flames."

"We do not just remove the nitrogen, we replace it," Willamette said. "I believe that on Earth they replaced the nitrogen with helium. They called it heliox diving."

"Hah. Helium." Flint laughed. Then Em started and that got him laughing so hard that his eyes watered and his side ached. Fortunately, Niven was better at handling the Deep. That made sense. Whalers would have had to dive down into the Deep any time they thought they might have competition for a rising whale.

"Air sifters on ships are generally set up to collect whatever valuable trace gases they can while gathering what a ship needs," Niven said. "Selling that provides a nice bit of extra income, but helium is so hard to sift out that it isn't even worth trying to catch."

"Argon then," Willamette suggested. "It is plentiful, and easy to catch, and it is also a noble gas."

"Argon won't work," Niven said. "You can use an eighty-twenty argon-oxygen mix as an emergency anesthetic."

"Yeah, that gets used quite a bit on ships out in the Drift," Flint said. Niven's story about knowing ships and being a whaler had some truth behind it. The argon thing wasn't the sort of thing that just anyone would know.

"Neon maybe?" Em gave Flint a knowing and questioning look.

"Yeah, we haven't dropped any neon off at Benny's in ages," he said. "So we've got heaps and gobs of it in the tank, and if we tuned the system to optimize for neon, we could probably sift enough out to keep up with leakage."

"So, if we can survive down here without going mad, why would sane people want to head north?" Em asked, snippy and bitchy. She was a horrible drunk. Flint decided that he should warn the others about that.

"We head north because there are three reefs that will soon pass Lightcastle, the closest of which should be about a hundred kilometers downdrift of the city and short distance to the north," Willamette said.

"A reef?" Niven muttered, gobsmacked.

"Yes." Willamette was back to her prime schoolteacher voice. "When an estate, or town, or sometimes even a city suffers a catastrophic breach, such as occasionally occurs in a war, it sinks until the density of the atmosphere matches the lift from the foundation foam and whatever air is trapped in intact buildings. Those sunken wrecks are called reefs."

"Yes, we all know what a reef is," Em grumped, emphasizing the word "we." "But how in the hell does a fancy little princess like you even know what a reef is, not to mention where we can find one?"

"Because as soon as this fancy little princess discovered that people could work under high pressures for extended periods without going mad, she explored the implications," Willamette said, infuriatingly sweetly. "Harvesting mobies was the most obvious of the practical implications of that discovery. As you undoubtedly know, 'moby' is the colloquial term for whales that were overloaded or leaked some gas and failed to float all the way up to the Drift. It is a name derived from an old Earth novel about whales …"

"Willamette!" Niven said, just forcefully enough to startle her. "Focus!"

"Yes, indeed." She pursed her lips and gave Niven a forced smile that looked like a prelude to cold-blooded murder. "As you know, mobies are plentiful and valuable, but they are out of reach, unless you are able to work in the Deep for extended periods of time. That seemed like a perfect way for the fancy little princess to exploit what she had discovered. However, when she explored how she might find mobies, she learned about reefs, and lo and behold, not only were reefs already being tracked by the minions of her villainous father, they held treasures far, far in excess of anything that could ever be plundered from all the mobies of the world."

"You could salvage a fortune off just one reef," Niven said.

"Or the fancy little princess could find a partner to help her refloat one and use it as part of a crazy idea that might just save the world." Willamette said that far too enthusiastically, and she was smiling far too happily. The Deep must be getting to her. She had an unnaturally eager gleam in her eyes, and she looked excited. She was probably a happy giggly drunk. If she'd ever been drunk. She was very young. Teenage girl kind of young.

Damn it, Flint.

"How about if we save the world later and work on staying sane enough to salvage a functional plow from that reef," Flint suggested. "Then we can make a long fast run up the Drift to get out from under these bastards."

Nods all around.

"The captain of a whaler would know how to use a passive sonar rig, right, Niven?" Flint nodded at the headphones at the nav station, getting a confident nod from Niven. "Good, you vampire the sonar pings off that whaler that's chasing us and see if there's a reef nearby. I'll get some breathers filled with a neon-oxygen mix."

"No, just do the whole ship," Niven said.

"Don't you think that maybe it would be smarter to have someone test some neon-oxygen mix through a breather before we replace all the nitrogen in the cabin with it?" Flint asked.

"No, that'll take time, and I think we need to hurry," Niven said. "Willamette just called herself a fancy little princess at least a half dozen times. So, obviously, the madness has already set in, and bad."

The descent of the Bluehawk had been smooth, steady, and uneventful. In other words, it had been perfect. Captain Roberts was perturbed by how close they had come to losing touch with the Drunken Monkey. It had extracted far more velocity from the dive than should have been possible, and that had carried it much farther north than they had anticipated. It had nearly moved out of range of their first pings after clearing the estate. Fortunately, nearly and almost didn't matter one bit.

"Target is turning but still on a northerly bearing," the sonarman reported. "Still carrying a lot of speed. A lot of speed."

"Match their course," Roberts ordered. "Level out at minus three thousand meters. Stay above the haze, four hundred meters updrift of them, and set all stations for depth siege."

"No. No siege, Captain," Colonel Kofi said. "We need to destroy them."

Roberts considered his response carefully. The old sergeant who had trained their boarding parties insisted that Kofi prized forthright officers above all other considerations, and the sergeant should know. He had served under Kofi back when he was actually and legitimately Colonel Kofi. Still, forthright was seldom what commanders wanted and Roberts was acutely aware of how much he risked if he should be relieved of command.

"Just spit it out, Captain," Kofi ordered. "Don't waste my time trying to find the right way to say whatever it is you're afraid to say."

"Colonel, the madness of the Deep is not some fairy tale," Roberts said. "It is more dangerous than you can possibly imagine."

Kofi frowned, skeptically.

"You hardly notice it at first, and that's what makes it so dangerous," Roberts explained. "It creeps up on you and you don't realize how clumsy and foolish you've become until people start dying."

"Captain, we will have to take the risk," Kofi said.

"Colonel, it is a foolish risk," Roberts shot back, calmly but assertively. "If you are trained to deal with it—which you and your girls are not—you can handle diving into the Deep for an hour or two, but no longer. If you spend any longer than that below the clouds, you're as good as dead. They've already been down there for twenty minutes, we've got them on sonar, they can't possibly escape, and the clock is ticking. The smart thing to do is to stay up here until they either come up, or the madness takes them."

"You think that it is impossible for them to escape," Kofi said.

"Yes, sir, I know that it is impossible," Roberts said. "Even if they had a plow and could outrun us updrift while they were down there, they'd have to rise out of the Deep long before they could lose us."

"Captain Roberts," Kofi said. "It was impossible for Willamette to escape from the yacht club grounds, yet she did. Then we trapped her in a hotel tower. Escape was again impossible, yet again, she did just that. Then we had her trapped on the docks, with no way out, yet for a third time in a matter of hours she managed to do something that was impossible. So, I am sure you will forgive me for being unwilling to offer her the opportunity to find a fourth way to pull off an impossible escape. You will take us down there, and we will finish them off directly."

"Yes, sir." Roberts saluted. He understood the final word when he heard it. "All hands, review protocols and procedures for the Deep. This is not a drill."

"Thank you, Captain," Kofi said, and those simple words said a great deal about the man. Firm, confident, polite, they indicated respect for the captain, and an acknowledgement that Roberts had conveyed his reservations about the chosen course of action, but they conveyed no indication that Kofi had ever thought he would be defied.

"Colonel, I will brief you and your girls on the basics of conducting an operation in the Deep and you will listen. I will not order the dive until I am convinced that you are as ready as I can make you," the Captain said, firmly. He needed to make sure the Colonel understood that just because he had accepted the given order, it did not mean he would follow it blindly.

"Of course, Captain," Kofi said, again with respect.

Willamette thought that the Drunken Monkey's sonar system was fascinating, and it was astoundingly simple for such an effective instrument. Niven had been able to describe its operation in minutes and she had encountered no difficulty in working it. That freed him to help Flint adjust the air sifter to extract more neon from the atmosphere outside.

Thankfully, replacing the nitrogen with neon appeared to be working. It had taken some time before it cleared Willamette's head, but once it did, it was frightening to look back at just how quickly the narcosis had affected everyone. They were all embarrassed. Most disturbing for Willamette was that she had not noticed how severely her behavior had deteriorated until after she recovered.

The thumps of the sonar from the whaler continued to rattle the ship but she ignored them. She had the headphones on and she was listening for distant echoes of those thumps. The latest was slightly louder in her right ear than in her left. She turned the knob to the left and the next echo was centered, so she read the numbers from the dial.

"Starboard six point five degrees," she called out, flipping a switch to change to the vertical microphone array, and moving her hand to a different control knob. The next ping was louder in the right ear, so she turned the knob to the left. She overshot and it took another echo to bring it back to the right enough to center the ping. "Minus two point one degrees."

"You do realize that you're only eighteen, right?" Em suddenly and abruptly asked.

"Yes," Willamette said.

"And that you're engaged to be married," Em said.

"Yes, I am aware of that as well," Willamette said. "You do know that a woman's age and marital status are two things that everyone would generally expect her to know."

"Yeah, but a teenage girl shouldn't have a marital status to know," Em said. "It's obscene."

"Oh, Miss Em, you should just say what you really think."

"What I think is that if a poor man sold his daughter to a brothel, your father would throw him into the Deep, but call the same damn thing a noble marriage and everyone thinks it's just fine and dandy. Including you. Don't get me wrong. Niven seems nice enough, but the whole idea that the privilege of raping you was sold to him because it suits your father's political interests should offend you, and the fact that your father rushed to whore you out moments after your precious peach was legally ripe enough to pick should infuriate every damn sensibility in your head."

"Contrary to what you seem to believe, Em, I spent several years manipulating my father into the rush to betroth me to Niven," Willamette said.

"Several years?" Em was stunned, slack-jawed.

"Yes. I was about fourteen or so when I realized that I would end up as nothing more than a trophy on the arm of a philandering old man if I didn't do something to influence the situation. So, I took action."

"You took action?" Em snarled. She always seemed to snarl. "At fourteen?"

"Yes, I began with tantrums where I threatened to publicly engage in the lewdest behavior that I could imagine," Willamette said. "Then, after I had established the impression that puberty had transformed me into a frustrated little animal that was perpetually in heat, I began redirecting my parents' worries toward a man I might find acceptable as a husband. I did a great deal of research, and once I decided upon Niven, I arranged several brief escapades to create the impression that we had initiated an illicit romance. Whenever he would dock at Lightcastle while I was in residence at the City Estate, I would slip away from my security when I was out shopping, or I would sneak away from the grounds, or otherwise vanish for several hours. I was always careful to make sure that I was noticed sneaking back into the estate with a satisfied smirk on my face, and sometimes, if I was returning late in the evening, I would even go so far as to look somewhat disheveled. I also forged some rather graphic love letters from him and hid them where my mother's servants would find them, and when I believed that the seed had been properly sown, crass pun intended, I forced the issue by asking my sister-in-law's midwife how I would know if I were pregnant."

"Whoa," Em said. "For a little girl, that was some seriously intricate and manipulative bitchery."

"Oh, those are just the highlights," Willamette said, dismissively.

"And Niven was happy to go along with all of this?"

"Niven had no idea whatsoever," Willamette said, dismissively. "Before this morning, I would have bet that he never even imagined he might meet me."

"Wait, you just met each other, for the very first time, this morning?"

"Yes, that is usually how these things work," Willamette said.

"That is so insane, in so many ways," Em growled. "And you're telling me that your father, the infamously devious Morden Lolofi, never even noticed that his little princess had him caught in this intricate web of manipulations?"

"Oh no, he knew that I was trying to manipulate him," Willamette said. "I left the letters in a place that would make it obvious to my mother that I was trying to manipulate my father into picking Niven. My mother is the scheming and manipulating master on their team, by the way."

"Oh god, I think I have to know why in the world you would do that, but I'm honestly worried that my head might explode if I even try to understand any of this," Em said.

"Em, even though I have only just met you, I am quite certain that your head could easily resist even the most powerful of explosions," Willamette said, smiling with mock sweetness before she explained. "As you intimated, it would have been impossible to hide such an intricate, and occasionally naive scheme from my parents, so instead of trying to hide it all, I picked which parts I wished for them to discover. I let them figure out that I wanted Niven because that would encourage them to think of my scheming in terms of a headstrong girl chasing the fantasy of love. If they failed to believe that—which was possible if not probable—I wanted them to believe that I just wanted to be in control. If they believed that, they would also believe that a tantrum could be avoided if they just went along and pretended they had let their spoiled little girl manipulate them into letting her pick her own husband. Either conclusion would allow me to hide the fact that my goal was to force them to betroth me as soon as I was of age."

"You wanted to rush to the alter?"

"Wanted … no," Willamette said, admitting more with her tone than she would have preferred. "What I wanted was to date a few boys who were all wrong for me. What I wanted was to risk having my heart broken, and maybe just once I would have liked to have gone to a party, picked a boy, and tried to seduce him."

"You wouldn't have to try. You'd just have to decide which one you didn't want to fight off." Em shrugged and gave her a look. "It's both flattering and a little scary. And it's also why you should always take a nice big stick with you when you go to parties."

"I would have loved to have been able to discover that and all the rest of it for myself, but those are things that the girl who can have anything cannot have," Willamette said. "The reality of who I am meant that I did not own that part of my life. I was to be married off by my father in a way that suited the politics of the Commonwealth, and the only thing I could do was manipulate that reality."

"But what could rushing possibly accomplish?"

"I made my father rush because I knew that no one would dare start politicking for my marriage before he made it clear that my hand was available. Forcing him to rush straight into a betrothal mere weeks after my birthday would catch everyone completely by surprise and would give the big families no opportunity to maneuver. That essentially eliminated all the men that I knew I did not want. It also made it easier to push my father to choose Niven, who was exactly the fiancé my father would have chosen for me if my sudden marriage was a political move he chose to make."

"Wait? You manipulated your father into picking Niven because he's exactly who your father would have picked for you if you hadn't manipulated him into picking Niven?" Em huffed. "Girl, you may not be anywhere near as smart as you think."

"The political appropriateness of Niven for my father's needs was one factor, but there are hundreds of young men who would have served that purpose," Willamette said. "I chose Niven because his cleverness seemed to be the reason he had so quickly become a successful businessman, and I needed a clever partner. It was simply good fortune that he also turned out to be kind and, in his own infuriating way, pleasant."

"So, you two aren't in love or anything," Em said.

"I am not the sort of woman with whom a man could fall in love." Willamette's words were far more heartfelt than she wished.

"He's not the one I was asking," Em said. "I'm asking the girl who is on a ship that could carry her right out from under the patriarchal systems of oppression that are forcing her to marry a man she just met."

"Despite a few recent doubts, I cannot honestly say that I believe love is anything more than poetic hyperbole. However, I can also say that the one thing that I currently fear more than anything is that the political marriage I worked so hard to avoid is the price I may have to pay to prevent this coup from devolving into a war over the Commonwealth," Willamette said. "A war over the Commonwealth would be horrific and bloody. If there was even a chance that I could prevent that through a diplomatic marriage, I would have no choice."

"Princess, from what I can see, you're just being a dumbass," Em said. "I don't care how wonderful you think that royal whisker biscuit of yours is, the chances that you could stop a war by letting the right noble plow your furry little estate are slim to none. There are twelve big families in the Commonwealth and at least three times that many smaller but powerful ones. I sincerely doubt that any of the sons, nephews, and cousins that didn't get the chance to butter your magic muffin would be all that keen on helping you avoid or even shorten a war."

"I believe that that was the crassest and crudest political analysis I have ever heard," Willamette said.

"Tell me I'm wrong," Em said.

Willamette fumed, but Em did have a point, no matter how crudely put.

"You know, you are not that much older than I am," Willamette finally said, choosing to let her annoyance show.

"It's not the years that matter, Little Princess," Em said. "It truly is not the years."

Niven turned out to be far more than an extra set of hands. He wasn't an engineering genius or anything like that, but the kid did have a reasonably functional head on his shoulders. He listened, dug down to the heart of the idea, and was pretty good at making the jump from the problem to what needed to be done. On his own, Flint would have never thought of isolating the mechanical core from the main cabin. The idea came together with Niven's suggestion for cutting neon loss by flushing the air locks with nitrogen from the float system, instead of leaving them hooked to the interior air system. That was brilliant, easy to do, and it would save a lot of neon. As a bonus, that idea led to them realizing that filling the cargo holds and the mechanical core with CO_2 would help with their growing buoyancy problem. The deeper they dove, the floatier they became, so less space they filled with lifting gas was a good thing.

"I think we're good," Flint announced as he and Niven returned to the helm, bearing coffee.

"You found a way to catch more neon?" Willamette sipped the coffee and quite nearly managed to hide her cringe at the taste.

"A little bit," Flint said. "But the real solution was to reduce the volume we need and cut the rate of loss."

"Helm, main cabin, and the aft control room are the only areas with the nexi mix," Niven said.

"Nexi?" Willamette thought for the briefest moment before answering her own question. "Neon and oxygen."

"Yeah," Flint said. "Everything we could shut off from those areas is now full of CO_2, so if you need to go into either of the cargo holds or the mechanical core, or the upper air lock prep area, you'll have to wear a breather loaded with nexi mix."

"That sounds workable," Em said. "And the timing's good, because I think those lights up ahead must be our reef."

"It's got lights on?" Flint asked, surprised.

"It makes sense that it would have at least a few lights still on," Niven said. "The same wind speed differentials that spin the power turbines on the keels up in the Drift would also work down here."

"So, unless someone took the time to shut everything down as this place sank, the lights would stay on until the last one burnt out or the last turbine broke down," Flint finished the thought, again impressed by how quickly Niven jumped straight to the details.

"How long would that take?" Willamette asked.

"Light fixtures can last decades, so it would probably depend on how long a turbine can keep running without maintenance," Niven said, shrugging. "They're amazingly robust so … who knows."

"Air's clearer than I expected down here," Em said.

"Is that normal?" Flint asked Niven.

"Beats me," Niven said. "This is far deeper than I would ever even think of diving after a whale."

"This reef looks like it's pretty damn big," Em said. "It's hard to get a sense of scale from a distance but take a look at the docks. If those are repair cranes, then that's a good-sized repair yard."

"A factory town would be a prime strategic target in a war," Willamette said.

"Yeah, that would be my first guess," Niven said.

"If it is a factory town, then we're about as lucky as we could have ever hoped to be," Flint said. "Unless someone managed a massive salvage operation before it sank too deep, you've got to figure that there's going to be a plow sitting around down there somewhere."

"So now, in order to get to that plow, we have to work out how to make an unassisted landing without a plow, which is impossible because you absolutely have to have a plow in order to make an unassisted landing," Niven said.

Em cackled, gleefully.

"Uhm, Flint, are you sure the nexi is working?" Niven asked.

"Yeah, that's just normal Em kind of crazy," Flint said.

"Crank up the ballast system, Flint," Em said, a gleam in her eyes. "I want to go in as heavy as possible."

CHAPTER 12

Em was not a natural pilot. She was a coordinated and athletic woman who constantly worked on her skills. She treated every takeoff, landing, cut, and turn as a chance to practice basic skills, or explore the boundaries of how their lumbering little beast of a ship could be controlled. That was what she was doing as she flew a winding and weaving glide down toward the reef, and it was a good thing that she had developed that habit. The Deep was affecting the ship in ways that she hadn't expected.

She had thought that she had known what to expect from the thicker air. On updrift cuts she often dropped down a couple thousand meters from the middle of the Drift so she could grab hold of a deeper, faster pull. That had given her a feel for how the thicker air would create extra drag, and how smaller control surface inputs would create bigger pushes. That was an even bigger thing in the Deep, but it was also different. The density of the air was so extreme that it was fundamentally altering the balance of the ship.

The Drunken Monkey was generally a bit nose heavy when it was empty and butt heavy when it was loaded. That was largely because the turbines were up front and the cargo bays toward the rear. In the soupy, thick air of the Deep, however, the balance of the ship had shifted toward the aft. That made the tail feel heavier, and it made the downward glide feel unstable. Maxing out the ballast tanks helped some, but it still felt oddly like they were being pushed along rather than gliding, and the nose of the ship felt like it wanted to pop up. All of which made the maneuver she had to pull off just that much trickier.

Unassisted landings were a bog-standard normal thing for the pilot of a junk runner. Most of the outposts, estates, bases, and small industrial installations that a junk runner was built to serve only sent or received a few shipments a month, so it didn't make sense for them to invest the money it took to set up winches, kite tugs, control towers, and all the other things it took to provide any kind of decent landing assistance. Instead, they built a landing space that would make it reasonably easy to land unassisted. There were countless variations but the most basic was a dock projecting from the front or the side of the habitat. With the plow down, a ship could fly around in front of the dock, ease off the pull updrift, and back its way in. It was always rough. Turbulence was an absolute bitch in close to habitats, especially the smaller ones, but it was still the sort of thing that any decent pilot could manage.

Towns, cities, and most of the larger estates had leeward docks, and landing on a leeward dock was an altogether different ballgame. Those bigger habitats were usually served by bigger ships; it was just a hell of a lot safer to keep those behemoths downdrift. Let a little too much momentum build up and big freighter or transport coming in from updrift could take the dome right off a town. The problem with leeward docks was that you needed landing assistance. The dock itself was in the way of the cable connecting the ship to the plow it needed to pull it updrift. So, at the very least, you needed some way to get a tow cable on the incoming ships so you could pull them in. Theoretically, with a small ship, it was possible to land unassisted on the very port or starboard edge of a leeward dock. You had to fly the plow out as far as you could to the side of the dock while you flew your kite in over the dock to counter that offset pull while you crept in sideways. It was as insane as it sounded, and as far as Em knew no one had ever tested that theory, but it was possible if you had a plow.

As they approached the town, Em pushed the Monkey's nose down, then pulled it up to the edge of a stall, then pushed it back down into the glide while making small smooth turns. The maneuver she had in mind would be tricky, and she needed to train the feel of the thick air moving over the control surfaces into her muscles. She'd only get one shot at it.

The reef had clearly been an industrial town. In addition to looking industrial, with big squat buildings that must have been factories, its docks were oversized, it had several big exhaust stacks jutting through what was left of the dome, and it had what looked like some huge dump chutes for dropping waste into the Deep. It was also clear that it had indeed been sunk in a war. Several burnt and bent buildings were visible through the ripped open dome and the docks were littered with ships.

"Jackpot, look at all those ships," Flint said. "There must be at least a dozen of them."

"And imagine how many people died if this thing went down so fast that not even the crews of those ships had the time to escape." Willamette voiced the exact thought that sprang to Em's mind.

"There we go," Em said. "There's a nice, big, clear space just off to port there, see it?"

"Em, that space is neither all that clear, nor is it big," Flint said.

"Hush, and double-check your belts," Em said. "Everyone double-check your belts."

"I hate it when you say that," Flint muttered.

"Quit being a baby and let me concentrate," Em said.

"I would, but you're going to miss that open space entirely," Flint said.

"Yes, I am," Em said. "Now drop some cable off the nose winch and hang on."

"What?" Flint asked.

"Nose winch, drop cable, now!"

Flint pulled the lever and let cable unwind off the winch while Em glided down over the open space, flying straight at what looked like a small hangar. It might have been a storage shed. Whatever it was, she just hoped it was as flimsy as it looked.

"Em," Flint said, and then more urgently, "Em. Em!"

At the last moment, Em lifted the nose, bringing them up just enough to clear the front edge of the building. As soon as they were directly over it, she pulled the controls back hard, stalling their glide completely. Yanking the big red levers for an emergency dump of the lifting gas, she dropped the Monkey onto the hangar roof. The grinding crunch of the ship crushing the hangar, or whatever the building was, was oddly satisfying.

"Lady, gentleman, and Flint," Em said, using her captain-talking-to-passengers-over-the-intercom voice. "Welcome to Dante's sixth level of hell. If you happen to be a heretic, do watch out for the rain of fire on your way to the burning tombs. For all of you regular old sinners, do note that it really is as hot as hell out there, and thank you for choosing the Drunken Monkey."

There was a long, stunned silence before Willamette said, "You have read Dante?"

"She just crashed this ship into a building, and her snarky reference to *Dante's Inferno* is where your head goes?" Niven rolled his eyes and shook his head. "Really?"

"Wait, you knew that I was talking about *Inferno*?"

"Again, the ship you were flying in just crashed into a building and your issue is that you're not the only survivor who has read some ancient literature?" Niven was incredulous.

"I didn't crash. I landed," Em snipped.

"Tell that to the hangar," Niven shot back.

"Look," Em said. "Physics say that you can either control your speed forward over the dock by balancing the downward glide against the flow over the dome, or you can control your rate of descent by lifting or dropping your nose. Doing both at the same time to get a zero-velocity, zero-altitude stall is pretty much impossible. Best you can hope for is to get a zero-speed stall low enough over something squishy so you don't die when you drop the ship with a lift dump."

"That hangar wasn't squishy," Niven said.

"Are you still alive?" Em shot back.

"Mostly," Niven said. "I'm a little dead inside, but that's from a nasty philosophy accident I had back when I was a teenager."

"You never recover from those," Flint said, amicably.

"Niven, can you walk away?" Em asked.

"Yes," Niven admitted.

"Then the hangar was squishy enough, and it was a landing," Em said.

"I think she's got you on the technicalities," Flint said as he stepped up to the very nose of the ship and peered around, particularly interested in how the front of the ship was situated in the wreckage of the crushed building. "And I also think that you and I had better get out there and get that cable from the nose winch hooked to something. Em can't refloat the Monkey and get it set down into that open space to leeward until we do, and I think we want that to happen ASAP. With our nose buried in the guts of this shed, there's no way we're getting much if any air flowing through the turbines, and I'd hate to find out how fast this old bucket of bolts heats up down here without the turbines spinning the cooling system compressors."

"I did wonder if the cable thing was just to distract you and shut you up," Niven said, climbing the ladder to the main cabin.

"As did I." Flint stopped at the top of the ladder. "How about if you come back and help us as well, Little Princess."

"Certainly." Willamette climbed primly, but swiftly, up the ladder and walked quickly after the boys. "And quit calling me Little Princess."

Alone on the bridge Em could finally let go of the bravado. She took a deep shuddering breath, and then another. The relief washing through her was so powerful that it brought tears to her eyes and her hands were shaking.

"You did good, you creaky old bitch," she said to the ship. "You did good."

The ship responded with a groan and shudder as what was left of the hangar collapsed under its weight.

The difference between discipline and experience was exposed in stark terms as they dove into the Deep. The Blades under Az's command endured the creeping touch of the madness with stoic resolve. They stood that little bit straighter, moved with that little bit of extra purpose, and they thought for that extra moment before acting in even the smallest way. They were calm, quiet, focused, and introspective, using every mental trick they knew to buttress the core of sanity in their minds. The veteran soldiers of the Bluehawk did the opposite. They talked, laughed, and joked while they threw themselves into mindless but intricate tasks with gusto.

Az thought it was an odd if not foolish thing to do until she saw the way a squad of the soldiers reacted to an error made by one of its members. They called it out in no uncertain terms, acted as a group to demand its correction, and carefully inspected, then argued over the results of the individual's effort to correct the mistake. They were using the group to steady their minds, counting on the others to notice elements of madness that the men would not be able to see in themselves. The physical tasks also provided a means to further focus and anchor the mind.

Az doubted if any of the soldiers understood any of the logic that underpinned their procedures for engaging the Deep, but trial and error and copying what seemed to enhance the chances of survival had refined the military's approach to operating at depth.

"Dodi, Blades in squads of four," Az said. "Perform the yin taolu of balance, in unison. I want it perfect."

"Yes Az." Dodi set to the task personally. That surprised Az. Dodi was a delegator by nature.

A small creature tried to tackle Az and when it failed to topple her, it clung fiercely to her leg, squeezing her thigh with all its might.

Az had completely forgotten about Ida even though the girl had never strayed more than a few steps away. Perhaps that oversight was a sign of how the madness would take her. Regardless, she could not begin to imagine how the madness might affect a child's mind, or how it might compound the damage that Kofi had already wrought upon her.

"Little Knife," Az said, firmly but calmly, and with what she hoped was a compassionate tone. "You must perform a task that is difficult and requires your full attention but is something so familiar that you expect nothing less than perfection from yourself."

Ida looked up at Az.

"What do you think that task would be?" Az asked.

"Lady Willamette always liked the way I braided her hair," Ida said. "She said that my little fingers made me the best at it of all her servants."

"Then you will braid your hair," Az commanded. "Make it intricate and allow it to be nothing less than perfect."

"I can't braid my own hair," Ida said. "No one can braid their own hair. Not proper, that's for sure."

Az restrained the desire to scold the girl. If Ida was to become a Blade, the habit of communicating truths back to authority was essential and must be cultivated. It needed to be better controlled, but that control was yet another thing that would have to be put off.

"Then you will braid mine." Az sat on the floor to allow Ida to easily reach her hair. "The braid must be appropriate for fighting. Can you do that?"

"Yes, Lady Az." Ida immediately set to work on Az's hair. "I think that would be like braiding for dancing. Ballet dancing, not fancy dancing, I mean."

"That would be appropriate," Az said. "And Little Knife, there are no ladies here. You will call a Blade by her name or address her as ma'am if she is a superior."

"Yes, Az, ma'am," Ida said.

"And someday, when you become someone's superior, you can call your equals and subordinates sister if you do not recall their name."

"Yes, Az, ma'am. I will."

Az began the yin taolu of hands and space. It required extreme focus to move the hands, fingers, wrists, and arms through the space within her reach. A warrior must strive to accomplish many things, but the most fundamental of all was to control the space within one's reach.

Willamette liked the way Flint explained things. He added just enough of the logic behind why the control was located where it was on the control panel to give her that critical second hook to anchor its name, location, and purpose in her memory.

"Nose winch." Willamette placed her hand upon the well-worn grip of one of many levers on the aft control room's control panel.

"Correct."

Flint gestured at a set of four levers.

"Cargo bay cargo winches." Willamette placed her hands upon and rattled off the purpose of the rest of the controls he had shown her. "Controls for the port and aft cargo bay ramps, which are also the doors. Plow winch array, with main winch, port pull, starboard pull, forward pull, and aft pull control winches."

"No, the control winches are backwards of that. Remember, you're facing the rear," Flint said.

"And the 'the left port' mnemonic refers to port being on the ship's left side facing forward, not my left side facing the rear," Willamette said.

"Yeah, and it's important that you keep that straight for when you're helping us hook up the control harness for the new plow," Flint said. "If we ask you to snug up one control cable and you snug up its opposite that could cause all kinds of problems."

"Got it," Willamette said.

"Intercom controls are already set to broadcast in here, to the helm, the cargo bay, and the cargo loading area outside," Flint said.

Willamette pointed at a switch. "And that is the one for the speaker and microphone directly under the ship, which we do not wish to be active now, because who knows what kind of a racket the microphone will pick up when we lift off the building, but I will need to turn it on once we begin installing the plow."

"Right again." He gave her a pat on the shoulder, flinched as he worried that he might have done something wrong by touching her. "If anything else happens to come up, I'll describe the control's location on the panel in relation to one of the controls that I know that you know."

Willamette nodded.

"Now for the lift and relocation, you are mostly going to serve as Em's eyes because she can't see if the area under and behind the ship is clear," he said. "But if the turbulence gives her any trouble, she might have you control the nose winch and get the ship over a clear landing space so she can focus on the rest of flying the ship. If that happens, just do what she asks and pretend that you don't mind being yelled at."

"Got it."

"Damn I wish I had my deck suit," Niven said as he tightened the last of the adjusting straps on the deck suit they'd taken from the hotel. "Even when you take the time to get these utility suits adjusted properly, they're still awkward and uncomfortable."

"Try cramming three-kilos worth of a shopgirl's dress into the crotch of one, then we can talk about awkward and uncomfortable," Willamette grumped.

There was a long moment of stunned silence, then both Flint and Niven grinned at her.

"What?" Willamette demanded.

"The whole princess thing is still a bit of an issue," Flint said to Niven as he nodded toward the air lock. "But she might be a keeper."

"Yeah, there's a droll primness to it that catches you off guard," Niven said.

"Delivery still needs work though," Flint said.

"True, but she shouldn't overrefine it," Niven said. "I think that one of the reasons it works so well is because the realization that it is a sarcastic snipe comes a second or two after she's said it."

The rest of their conversation was cut off by the closing of the air lock door. Willamette resisted the urge to turn on the air lock intercom. As it was, she was embarrassed by how pleased she was that not only had she found a way to tease Niven, but also that he honestly seemed to enjoy it.

"Port cargo bay, intercom check," Flint said as they exited the air lock.

"I can hear you," Willamette said, resisting the urge to lean over and speak into the microphone. Flint had assured her that there was no need to do that unless there were other noises in the room that she needed to mask with her person.

"Roger that," Flint said. "Will you open the portside cargo bay door for us?"

Willamette pushed a lever and was pleased to see that the appropriate door opened. It would not open all the way, but it did open enough so that Flint and Niven should be able to walk out onto what was left of the roof of the shed.

A pounding, ripping noise reverberated through the ship.

"What the hell?" Flint shouted.

A flicker of motion caught Willamette's eye and she looked upward to see the whaler that had been pursuing them flying in from the rear. Another hammer blow struck the ship.

"I think those were harpoons!" Willamette shouted.

The whaler fired more harpoons, one of which tore all the way through the top of the ship and penetrated into the cargo bay, narrowly missing Flint. The cable yanked it back and Monkey shuddered as the expanding barbs on its head caught the ceiling of the cargo bay.

Willamette was thrown about as the momentum from the whaler's swooping dive yanked the Drunken Monkey forward and dragged it through the remains of the shed. The noise was horrendous. Grinding, screeching, snapping, shattering, groaning—it was deafening.

The nose of the ship must have caught on something because that forward movement suddenly stopped, and the ship tipped forward. The groaning increased and the ship kept rolling forward onto the nose until Willamette felt like she was lying flat on her back, and then the momentum of the whaler was exhausted. The energy stored in the stretching of the harpoon cables pulled the attacking ship backwards and as soon as that happened, the Drunken Monkey started rolling back toward horizontal, which added more energy to the pull on the whaler.

The momentum of the whaler dragged the Drunken Monkey backwards through the wreckage of the shed and all the way into the clear area where they had intended to park the ship to work on the plow.

Willamette scrambled back to the control panel, but she was lost for any thought of what she might do. The whaler loomed just above and behind the Drunken Monkey, looking like a predator poised to strike the fatal blow.

CHAPTER 13

Flint had become so accustomed to Em's affection for less than gentle maneuvers that he never lost his sense of place as the Drunken Monkey was yanked around by the whaler. When the ship was back on its landing skids, he was completely unsurprised to see the open area of the docks through the partially opened cargo bay door. He was also completely unsurprised when the whaler took up the slack in the harpoon cables and started lifting the Drunken Monkey off the dock.

"Going heavy," Em shouted through the intercom. "If we let them haul us up to the Drift, we're dead."

He heard the whoosh of lifting gas being vented. That surprised Flint. He thought that Em had already dumped it all. A moment later there was a soft impact as the Drunken Monkey settled back on the dock.

"Turbines are clear and spinning." Em sounded more in control with that shout. "Going max on the ballast pump and filling the tanks fast as I can."

The rising thrum of the turbines spinning up slowed as she engaged the compressor starting the two-stage process of converting the atmosphere outside into liquid ballast. The thick air flowing over the city was providing plenty of power, so even under the maximum compressor load, the turbines quickly spun back up.

"It's not going to be enough," Niven said. "Whalers have a hell of a lot of lift capacity."

Niven and Flint looked at each other and then looked around as the lift from the whaler reduced the friction with the deck enough to allow the flow of the atmosphere across the dock to start pushing both ships toward the leeward edge of the reef's dock.

The Drunken Monkey collided with a small truck that had been abandoned on the dock, and that seemed to give Niven an idea.

"The cables from the cargo winches." Niven pushed Flint toward one of the winches. "Willamette. Unlock the drums on the cargo winches. There's probably a switch by the base of the control levers. Flip that and open both the cargo bay doors."

By the time Flint grabbed the hook on the end of one of the cargo winch cables, Willamette had the drum unlocked, and she was already lowering the cargo bay door the rest of the way.

"What exactly are we doing?" Flint asked as he followed Niven, running down the ramp, pulling a cable with him.

"We're hooking these to something heavy," Niven said as he jumped out.

"Oh, you are nuts," Flint said as the whaler lifted the ship off the dock. It was already over a meter to the dock and jumping that far was more than enough to hurt his knees. "Why is everyone but me crazy?"

"They can't stay down here. We can," Niven shouted. "All we have to do is hang on until they lose their minds or give up."

"I know, but this is still insane," Flint said, running as best he could. "And I am way, way too old for this."

Flint hooked the cable onto the roll cage of a forklift. It wasn't that far from the cargo bay, but even that short run, combined with the atrocious heat, had left him sweating so bad that it felt like he was melting.

"There!" he shouted. "Hit the winch, Little Princess!"

Willamette was ready and waiting. She slammed the winch into action and that nearly killed him. He ducked as the cable snapped taught, but he had grossly overestimated the weight of the forklift. The winch was more than powerful enough to yank the machine over, and he had to dive out of the way as it came hurtling at him.

The dive was another thing that was tough on an old man's body, and it surprised him that when he scrambled back to his feet, he seemed to be unbroken. Everything hurt, but all the important parts of his person were still in working order.

Niven picked a better anchor for his cable. It was highly unlikely that the cargo winch would be anywhere near strong enough to pull the small cargo crane off its foundation and drag it about like the forklift. Still, Niven also hadn't been kidding about just how much lift a whaler could produce. The pull from the ship hovering overhead was already straining that cable, and the whaler was rapidly inflating even more external floats.

Flint ran back to the Drunken Monkey. It was more of a swift walk that was nearly a jog, but it was the best he could manage, and it wasn't going to be anywhere near fast enough. The bottom edge of the loading ramp was already out of reach.

Fortunately, Niven was a young man. He not only sprinted fast enough to leap and catch the starboard cargo ramp before it was pulled out of reach, he also pulled himself up and into the bay like it was nothing. Flint thought that he maybe could have dreamt of doing that when he was Niven's age. He could never have done it, but at least when he had been young the possibility would have been vaguely imaginable.

Niven dropped one of the starboard bay's cargo winch cables down to Flint, but when Flint clipped the hook to the tool belt on his deck suit, no one winched him up. The cable just stayed slack, and that confused him. It wasn't until Niven jumped back down from the cargo hold with the second winch cable from the starboard bay that Flint realized that he was meant to find an anchor for the cable he'd clipped to his belt.

The Drunken Monkey was swinging around the anchor provided by the cable attached to the crane, rotating around so its nose pointed toward the lee of the dock. It was also slowly lifting farther off the dock and that one cable would be nowhere near enough to stop the whaler from carrying it away. Willamette was already letting the cable pull itself slowly off the one cargo winch to make sure it didn't snap.

"Oh, you are a clever one, aren't you girl?" Flint muttered.

"Yes, she sure as hell is," Niven said as he scrambled to his feet and gave Flint a small push to get him moving. "Now get that cable hooked to something heavier than a lard-assed old navigator."

"I'm also a decent rigger," Flint shouted, hobbling as fast as his aching knees and now aching hips would allow.

Flint pulled the cable in the general direction of the crane that Niven had used for an anchor. The second and third cables needed to pull in that same direction as much as possible if they were going to take the strain off the first. He considered just hooking his cable to the same crane that Niven had used, but he had no idea how much upward pull the crane's base might be able to take, so he picked a light tower instead. The nearby light tower looked to be bolted solidly to the dock and it was also closer, which was more of a consideration than Flint wanted to admit.

Niven found a bollard a short distance away. That would sure as hell work. It was meant to serve as an anchor for pulling ships about.

Unfortunately, it wasn't clear if the strength of what they anchored the cables to would be what mattered. The cargo winches were meant to pull pallets of cargo up the loading ramp and that didn't require all that much power. Flint had never bothered to consider what they were rated to pull, but four-millimeter carbon-fiber cables, even when they were new, couldn't be expected to hold more than a couple of tons, and the Monkey's cables were nowhere near new.

"Willamette, give me slack on the winch hooked to the forklift," Niven shouted as he ran toward the toppled machine.

Niven clearly intended to hook that cable to something that would provide a better anchor. That was a good idea, but Flint doubted if it would be enough. The whaler could probably generate more lift than the four cables combined could counter, and the captain of the whaler would have far more than just lift to work with. All he had to do was lift the nose and when its wings caught the flow of the atmosphere rolling over the dock, the force generated by all that heavy air would easily snap a dozen of those cables. In fact, Flint was surprised he hadn't done that already. Whatever. What they needed was a cable and winch that could handle tons and tons of force.

The instant that thought crossed his mind the answer was obvious.

"Willamette, unwind the main plow cable," Flint shouted as he ran as best he could back toward the ship. "We need it now!"

Niven must have understood exactly what Flint was thinking. He abandoned the fourth cargo cable, sprinted in under the ship, grabbed the plow cable and ran for the bollard with it.

Flint left that to the young man and took over the task of getting the fourth cargo winch cable off the forklift and anchored to something solid. It may not have been much, but every little bit extra they could do to handle the strain couldn't hurt.

Kofi was both impressed and enraged as he watched the Drunken Monkey winch both itself and the Bluehawk back down toward the dock.

"I can only guess that they have the main cable from their plow anchored to something on the dock and are using that," Captain Roberts said. He was glassy-eyed and blinking like mad, but he still managed to look steady, focused. "If we pull too much harder, we'll rip the harpoons loose."

"All this damned cleverness is uncalled for," Kofi snarled. "It is impressive as hell, but still uncalled for."

"It is impressive," the captain agreed.

"And you need to impress me with how you deal with it," Kofi shouted. Even though he knew that it was the madness of the Deep that was making him feel so angry and aggressive, it was still almost impossible to restrain.

"Colonel, we have already been down here too long," the captain said, whining. "We need to cut the harpoon lines, retreat, and set siege. It shouldn't take long for a siege to work. The madness will surely take them soon. We're barely hanging on and they have been down here longer than we have."

"How does any of that cleverness you're seeing in any way make you think that they are about to succumb to the madness?" Kofi shouted.

"The madness doesn't make you stupid," the captain shot back. "It makes you foolish, rash, and reckless. That is what kills and that is what staying down here is, foolish, rash, and reckless."

"Captain, we will go nowhere until Willamette Lolofi is dead," Kofi said. "So, I suggest that you find a way to kill her. Now."

"And that is foolish, rash, and reckless," the captain said, firmly.

"You have your orders, Captain." Kofi drew his sidearm and pointed it at the captain's face. He wanted desperately to pull the trigger.

"Boarding parties to the work deck. Prepare for action," the captain said.

Willamette was fighting to stay calm and think through the problem. There was no way she could pull the ship all the way back down to the dock using the variety of winches and cables that anchored them to the sunken industrial town. The lower they were the more sideways the different winches pulled toward the different locations where the cables were anchored and that reduced how much pull was directed downward toward the dock.

She would have to suit up, and go out into one of the cargo bays, and lower something that Flint and Niven could climb up. That should work, but what could she use? She did not see a ladder, or a cargo net, or a rope, or even another cable that she could use. Maybe there was something on the service truck. Maybe it had a winch of its own.

"Willamette. It's getting a little hot out here," Niven said.

"I know but the closer I pull the ship to the dock the more the winches pull laterally rather than vertically. This is about as close as I can manage," she said. "Flint, is there a ladder or something that I could lower down to you? Maybe something on the service truck? Or maybe we could use one of the cargo winches?"

"Flint," Niven said. "Flint, are you okay?"

"Yeah, yeah," Flint said. "Just a little dizzy and tired. Really tired."

Willamette leaned forward so she could look under the edge of the cargo ramp. Flint had fallen, and he was lying awkwardly on the dock.

"Niven! Should I slack one of cargo winches so we can pull him up?"

"No, winching him up won't work." Niven said. "He would just get caught on the lip of the ramp."

"I can get up," Flint said, standing and falling again. "Although, it seems that I can't stay up."

"Niven, what shall I do?"

"Ease the tension on all the winches except the plow winch," Niven said.

"Okay," the ship shifted upwards as Willamette eased the tension off the cargo winches.

"More plow winch," Niven said.

That brought them down and pulled them to the side a few meters.

"Less on the starboard cargo winches."

The ship moved farther to the side and the rear tilted down some as they moved backward. That was when Willamette saw what Niven was doing. The portside cargo ramp was only a few meters from a light tower.

"I see what you want, Niven," Willamette said. "You are going to use the light tower to climb in."

"Yep, I just need to get Flint up above the level of the ramp," Niven said, his voice strained. "Climb, Flint."

"I'm heavy."

"Yes, you bloody well are. Now shut up and just help me help you climb this thing," Niven said. "Foot up."

Willamette worked the winches. More slack on the starboard winches moved the ship sideways. More pull on the plow cable pulled it backward. She could easily pull the ship backward into the tower if she wanted, but the pull she could get toward the side wasn't going to be enough to get the ramp aligned with the light tower.

"Em, is there anything you can do to shift the back of the ship three meters to port?" Willamette asked.

"Yeah, maybe. Hold on," Em said, as the rear of the ship skewed toward the port, putting the tower dead center behind the middle of cargo ramp.

"Sorry, too far," Em said.

"No, that is perfect. Please hold it there," Willamette said. "Where are you, Niven? I cannot see you."

"He can't climb," Niven said.

"Niven ..."

"Give me slack on one of the port cargo bay winches," Niven said. "Lots of slack."

"I thought you said that would not work?"

"Just give me slack!"

Willamette hit the switch that let the drums on one of the portside winches spin free and a few seconds later Niven climbed into view on the tower. He was by himself. His back was toward her so she couldn't see exactly what he was doing, but it was easy to put the pieces together. He was running the cable over one of the struts near the top of the tower. He was going to use that like a pulley to pull Flint up.

"There, put some tension on that winch," he said as he climbed quickly back down. "And then pull gently."

"Pulling gently," Willamette confirmed. "Is that good?"

"Yes," Niven said. "Now climb, Flint. There you go. Light as a feather."

It took another minute or so to winch Flint up so that Niven had him above the level of the cargo ramp. Flint was still functioning, but he struggled mightily.

"I will pull the ship backwards into the tower and you two jump as we hit," Willamette said. "You give me the go signal."

Niven unhooked the winch cable from Flint, freed it from where he had draped it over a strut in the light tower and rehooked it to Flint's belt.

"If you can, snug that up as soon as we jump," Niven said.

"Will do." Willamette took a moment to think through the control to be certain she worked the correct winch before she asked, "Are you two ready?"

"Yeah, go," Niven said.

Willamette pulled with the plow winch, backing the Drunken Monkey's port cargo ramp into the light tower.

The timing for Niven's push on Flint was about right, but his own jump was a bit late. The ship hit the tower just before he leapt. That sent the tower swinging backward as he tried to jump off it and it turned his dive into an awkward flop. His gut landed on the edge of the ramp next to Flint's knees. When the ship sprang back from its collision with the light tower it was only the hand gripping Flint's tool belt that kept him from falling back to the dock.

Willamette quickly worked the winches to move the ship to the side. That almost shook Niven off the back of the ramp, but it kept him from being crushed against the swaying light tower. Once she was sure he was ready, she very gently used the cargo winch hooked to Flint to pull both of them into the cargo bay.

Niven scrambled to his feet, took a moment as if he was dizzy, and then shook it off. He helped pull Flint up the ramp and by the time both men were in the cargo hold proper, Flint was able to roll over onto his hands and knees and crawl to help Niven get him into the air lock.

Marines were always the first ones thrown at the most dangerous missions. Dropping onto a dome, onto a dock, or onto a ship out in the Drift, they were the tip of the spear, and they inevitably faced the fiercest fight. Because of that, their training was entirely focused on finding the safest way to fight past those lethal risks. Nine times out of ten, all of that training boiled down to making sure you were equipped with the perfect tools for throwing some extreme aggression at someone. If not for the madness of the Deep, he would have remembered that.

"Repeat that order?" Chiles shouted into the intercom.

"Boarding parties one through four, drop to the dock, we'll take the ship from below," the captain said.

"Understood," Chiles said into the intercom before shouting to his men. "You heard the crazy bastard. Relocate your winch connections to the drop straps on your harnesses and set your winches for friction drop. We go on my order."

Switching the point of attack like that was a nightmare. They were set up to board through a hull breach, so they were carrying all the wrong weapons for fighting on an open area like the dock. All the weapons they carried were meant for hand-to-hand, interior fighting. They didn't have a single rifle amongst them, and they had nothing heavy enough to blow through light cover or blast a hatch open.

The work deck of a whaler was also the worst place that Chiles could imagine for launching a long winch drop onto a dock. It was set up for safety, which in turn made jumping off of it a pain in the ass. Harpooning a ship and bringing it in for a breaching attack was basically the same as hauling in a whale, so it wouldn't have been a problem for that. For a drop to the dock, however, the little winches that were meant to provide a bit of extra safety for jumping onto a ship had to lower them a good thirty meters. They weren't designed for that. They were mounted in awkward places, they had the wrong type of brakes, and there was no real way to adjust them if you didn't get the setting right before you jumped. None of that was good at the best of times. With men who were also fighting the madness of the Deep, it was insane.

"Go!" Chiles started his leap before he shouted the order, just to make sure that he was the first one off. Leading your men into a fight was mostly symbolic, but every little thing helped when it came to the razor-thin line that separated tomorrow's veterans from today's casualties.

He fell a couple of meters before the brake kicked in to slow his descent. Unlike the connection they used for a safety cable, the drop strap connection on the harness was designed to pull from a spot between the shoulder blades. That kept the soldier facing the enemy and dropping feet first.

A soldier to his right plummeted past. He had jumped over the railing without hooking to a winch. Jesus, how far gone did you have to be to forget to hook yourself to the winch? Especially having just been told to hook up. A few others were still connected to the safety ring instead of the drop strap connection and were being lowered ass first toward the enemy.

Fortunately, there didn't appear to be any enemy resistance. It was a long way to the dock, but no one took a potshot at any of them while they were dangling and at their most vulnerable.

On the dock, Chiles crouched and assessed the situation as he unhooked from the winch. No resistance, no sign of enemies anywhere except a lone person, possibly a woman, manning the helm of the junk runner. So far so good. It was better than good, actually. Now that they were on the dock and below the level of the junk runner, he could see that its cargo bay doors were down.

"Go! Go! Go!" he shouted. "Get in behind the bugger."

The bottom edge of the starboard cargo bay door and loading ramp was no more than four or five meters from the dock, but that was more than enough to put it out of reach. Chiles cursed. He needed a man with a grappling hook and climbing winch, or a man with a harpoon that could be fired with a rifle. He should have thought of that. If he had just sent a couple of men back in through the air lock to grab some of the right gear before they dropped, this assault would already be over.

"Stop that!" a woman shouted over the ship's intercom. "If you cut those cables, they'll just pull us up to the Drift and leave you behind to die down here."

Chiles spun around and nearly fell. He was dizzy and his ears were ringing. Just a few meters away, three men were hacking at a thick cable with their combat knives.

"Stop that you fools!" Chiles shouted.

"The captain wanted to haul them up to the Drift so we could fight them up there!" one of the men shouted back.

"That's not why we were ordered down here!"

"We've got to get back up to the Drift!" the man shouted, drawing a pistol.

Chiles shot the man drawing his weapon, and then he shot the one who was sawing at the cable tying the junk runner to the dock.

"Anyone else want to cut at those cables?" Chiles shouted.

The other men near the cable ran away.

"We were ordered to board and take that ship from the dock, so we are going to find a way to board and take that ship from the dock," Chiles said. "With those cables coming out of the cargo bay, they'll never be able to close those doors, so find a truck, or a portable crane, or ladders, or something else that we can push, pull, or carry over here. We'll use that to get up to one of those cargo ramps."

Chiles knew that it was a pointless effort. The junk runner was slacking its winches, letting the Bluehawk pull them out of reach. They'd have to climb the cables, somehow. Again, he hadn't brought the right gear.

There was a moment of extreme despair, but then Chiles saw what the famous Dread Captain Roberts must have had planned all along and he couldn't help but laugh.

"Forget that last order and form up over here with me!" he shouted. "Prepare for boarding action!"

The cool water felt like it was burning as it washed over Flint's face, and when Niven forced the shower under his chin to fill his deck suit, the initial rush of water across his chest hurt. It went warm almost instantly, but that first touch was a shocker.

The water sprayed on his face again. It felt better the second time, and then someone was pushing and shoving him into a closet. No, Niven was taking off his deck suit, unsealing it and pulling it down enough to spray more water on his chest. That felt better the second time as well.

Flint's head cleared as the water washed over him and cooled him. Niven was using the wash in the air lock to cool him off. The boy was alternating between spraying Flint and spraying himself down. The boy may have dealt with it better, but he was just as overheated as Flint.

"Roll more cable off the plow winch, Little Princess," Flint heard Em say over the intercom. "Another meter or two higher should be enough. I can't see anything that they might be able to use to get up that far."

"Would you please stop calling me Little Princess," Willamette pleaded.

"No," Em said.

"Maybe we should do something about the cargo bay winch cables so we can get the cargo bay doors closed," Willamette said. "Just to be a little safer."

"I doubt if a closed door would make much difference to soldiers trained to board ships," Em said.

"Yes. I understand," Willamette said. "So now what should we do?"

"Now we just wait for the Deep to do its thing," Em said. "We might want to be ready for them to do something stupid. That's the sort of thing that I'd guess would happen with the madness, but I'll bet that they'll cut and run once they realize that we're not going to let them haul us up or get to us from below."

"What will we do if they leave those men behind?"

"We worry about that when it happens," Em said. "How's Flint?"

"I'm fine," Flint said, as upbeat as he could manage. He was, however, far from fine. His head was pounding. His guts were in knots. His heart felt like it was struggling to keep time. His limbs both ached and felt like they had melted into nothing, and he was trembling. The shock of overheating and suddenly being cooled was just starting to hit him.

Willamette took a worried step toward him, but he stopped her with a smile and a wink. "I feel like going for a walk."

Willamette gave him a wry smile and then frowned at Niven. "I expect that the two of you are going to cause me no end of despair?"

"Hey," Em said, annoyed. "I'm good at causing despair, too."

"She is." Flint pulled himself to his feet. It was a struggle, and once he was up, he didn't dare let go of the railing.

Something hit the Drunken Monkey and it suddenly slewed to the side, throwing Flint back to the floor.

"What was that?" Niven asked.

"Oh. That's trouble," Em said. "Big, big trouble. They're cutting lift and winching themselves down on top of us."

"Look at the soldiers," Willamette said, pointing at the dock. "They are getting ready for something."

"They're getting ready to board us," Niven said. "The whaler is going to push us back down to the dock so they can board us."

"Lift." Flint stumbled and fell as he tried to get back on his feet. He gestured Niven toward the control panel. "Lift. We can't let them push us down."

Niven rushed over to the panel and started working the lift control valves, frowning as he read the gauges.

"No pressure readings from one, two, three, four, five, six of the lift cells in the wings," Niven said.

"One of the gauges is broken," Flint said.

"That still leaves five cells that those harpoons must have destroyed," Niven said.

"Oh yeah, we were harpooned." Flint shook his head. "We have twenty cells and no cargo to speak of, so we should be able to lift out of here pretty easy, and we've still got the external floats."

"Yeah, I would believe that, but it is certainly not going to be enough float to keep both us and a whaler off the dock," Niven said.

"Em!" Flint shouted. "Em!"

There was no answer from the intercom.

"Do you have any guns?" Niven asked Flint.

"Yeah, we've got a couple of pistols and one nasty as hell rifle that Em thinks I don't know she's hiding in her cabin. Why?" The moment Flint asked why, he knew what the answer had to be. "Upstairs. The pistols are upstairs in the kitchen."

Niven ran up the stairs.

"One's in that stupid drawer under the oven," Flint shouted at the young man's back. He finished by speaking quietly to Willamette. "The other's behind the cleaning stuff under the sink."

"Come on." Willamette forced her shoulder under Flint's arm and took some of his weight.

Flint accepted Willamette's help even though he was starting to feel steadier on his legs. He could have made it without her, but he was still thankful for her help.

When they made it to the kitchen, Niven handed him one of the pistols, frowned at him, and then took it back and gave it to Willamette.

"Good call," Flint said, watching Willamette give the gun a quick once-over. She knew what she was doing.

The fight, if it could be called a fight, was bitterly anticlimactic. The soldiers fired so many darts as they advanced that all the defenders could do was cower. Willamette managed to reach out and blindly fire a couple of darts in the general direction of their attackers, but that was it.

The only remotely good thing was that it was only the three of them who were captured. There had been no sign of Em and the soldiers didn't find her when they searched the ship.

CHAPTER 14

The little angel of rationality in the back of Kofi's mind was having a rough afternoon. Usually, she was nothing short of a domineering bitch that always got her way, but Willamette Lolofi's miraculous ability to pull off one impossible escape after another had left his little angel a bit battered, and the madness of the Deep was threatening to finish her off. Rationality was still prominent in the workings of Kofi's mind, but instead of defining how he thought and constraining the impulses, it had been perverted into a servant of his desires. His little angel was giving him excuses to do what he wanted rather than defining what he needed to. Strangely, even though he knew that, it made no difference.

"You said that all you wanted was to see Willamette killed," the captain shrieked, sending foamy spittle flying as he stepped between Kofi and the exit out onto the work deck of the whaler.

"Yes, Captain, but the point of ordering her to be killed was to make sure that no one risked letting her escape by trying to take her alive," Kofi snapped back at him. "Now that we have her, alive she has value far beyond what she would have had as a corpse, and I will take full advantage of that."

"Colonel, we have already pushed our luck far too far." The captain pushed his own luck, refusing to step aside as Kofi took a half step toward him and made it clear that he wanted to pass. "The Deep is not to be toyed with like this."

"Captain, prepare to depart," Kofi said, physically shoving the captain aside. "This will take no more than a few minutes. Hell, I may even be back before you are ready to leave."

"Prepare to lift," the captain ordered, finally stepping out of Kofi's way. "Make haste. Prepare to cut free and lift."

"Bess." Az spoke from somewhere behind Kofi. "Stay close to the captain and make sure he doesn't get too hasty in his rush to leave."

Bess, the young squad leader, didn't answer. She stared at Az, confused. For that matter Kofi was confused.

"Don't let the captain leave without us," Az said.

Bess nodded and now that he understood, Kofi took a moment to nod his appreciation to Az before gesturing for her to lead the way. She in turn gestured for three Blades, including Dodi, to lead them onto the work deck.

Az looked good with her hair braided. The tight-plaited weave looked far more mature than the simple ponytail she usually adopted when training or fighting. It conveyed a formality and regalness ... regality, that fit her fierce stature as a powerful woman. Come to think of it, Kofi pretty much always thought that Az looked good. No one would call her beautiful, but Kofi had always found her attractive and in that moment, he resolved that he would act upon that as soon as circumstances allowed.

"You stay with Bess," Az said to the girl that everyone had started calling his Little Knife.

"No," Kofi said as his angel of rationality finally found an excuse for his desire to confront Willamette. "My Little Knife needs to come with us."

Az clearly disapproved but she was smart enough to know that now was not the time to say anything or act upon that instinct.

The work deck under the Bluehawk had been transformed into a staging area for boarding. There hadn't been any need for any kind of boarding action from above, but the crews had still dropped the plastic tent to seal the gap between the two ships, and they had pumped that tent full of breathable air. That was probably done to make it easier to bring the marines back onto the Bluehawk. Or it might have been routine, or it might have been something that someone had just done because they could. It was hard for Kofi to tell anymore. Regardless of the reasoning, a ramp had been lowered to the top deck of the junk runner and it was a simple, but steep, walk down to the captured ship.

"Don't touch anything until we're inside the other ship," Az said to Ida. "There will be acid on everything out here."

"Yes, Az, ma'am," Ida said.

The topside deck of the junk runner was little more than a narrow walkway that ran most of the length of the ship. It was a precarious and inherently dangerous place. There were no railings or anything else that might add weight and drag in the name of something as unprofitable as safety.

The upper air lock was built into the extension of the ship's structural core that projected up to support the topside rigging structures. The air lock was tiny, scarcely large enough to accommodate one person per cycle. The prep room beyond it was similarly cramped, a couple of meters in each direction, with lockers, benches, and nothing but a ladder down to the main deck inside the ship. That might have been the reason for lowering and sealing the boarding tent, assuming that there had been a reason. Simply being able to open both the upper air lock doors would have alleviated that bottleneck.

"Well done men," Kofi said to the soldiers in the small common area around the kitchen. "You may return to the Bluehawk."

Kofi's words surprised the men. They were reluctant to let Kofi's Blades take their place and they tried to linger. Fortunately, Az was not one to put up with that kind of behavior and she managed to send them scurrying off with a pointed glare.

There was something that felt wrong about the three prisoners. The small woman in the shopgirl dress was unquestionably Willamette Lolofi. Even if her face had not been one of the most recognizable in the Commonwealth, her fierce, confident, and proud bearing would have given her away. The young man to her right must be the fiancé. Even dripping wet and bedraggled, he managed to look like her protector, but he was too young and scrawny to be a Lolofi bodyguard. The old man was with the ship, and he was a mess. Not only was he soaking wet, he looked like he was about to pass out. They all fit the place and circumstance, but something about the trio of prisoners felt wrong. There was something that Kofi was sure that he knew that clashed with what was before him, but no matter how hard he tried, he couldn't put his finger on it. That bothered him.

"Ida?" Willamette exclaimed. Horrified, she glared at Kofi. "What have you done to her?"

"You should probably be more concerned about what my Little Knife is about to do to you," Kofi said.

Something was missing, Kofi's little angel of rationality whispered. Something that Az had mentioned in briefing the captain of the Bluehawk. That didn't help. Kofi's deepness-addled mind could not even begin to guess at what was not there.

Em hurt.

Irrespective of Flint's cavalier attitude, piracy was a reality out in the Drift, and she had long ago prepared for the possibility that they might be boarded. In addition to buying and learning how to use the rifle, she had sussed out the hiding spot she would use if worse came to worse. Her spot was at the point where the hall between the passenger cabins joined the lounge. Above the end of that short hallway, there was a place where the weave of supporting cables that ran through the structural ribs of the ship converged. There was more than enough room between the cables and the outer hull to allow a small woman to crawl around up there and hide. More importantly, once she was up there, she was basically invisible. The light fixtures in the hall were mounted below the cables, which meant that even if someone happened to look up, which no one ever did, they still wouldn't be able to see her in the shadows behind the lights.

Unfortunately, just because she could lie on those cables, that didn't make it comfortable. They dug into her flesh, and it didn't take long before shifting around was just moving the discomfort from one set of bruises to another. To make things worse, to get the rifle aimed at anyone that she might want to kill, she had to scoot partway off that web of cables so that she could lean her head and shoulders and most of her torso out and down from her hiding spot. It only took a few seconds for that to start hurting.

Em used the rifle sight to check her firing lines. The rifle was a repeater, but the autoloader only held three darts. That gave her four shots and eight targets, not including the little girl. The bastard who was obviously in charge of everything was going to get the first dart, that was for sure, but who was second? She wanted to protect Flint, but it was probably smarter to take out the woman standing behind Niven first. Niven was not only in far better shape for fighting than Flint, he would also probably try to protect Willamette. So, if she shot the blue ballerina bitch standing behind him, that should give him a chance to mix things up.

Az was the obvious choice for shot number three, but she was standing next to the bastard in charge and that back-and-forth swing from shot one, to two, to three, seemed stupid and awkward. Maybe she should take Az out with the second shot.

"Kill her, Little Knife," the bastard in charge said.

"I can't," the little girl said.

"Did you forget about the consequences of failing me?" the bastard in charge growled menacingly as he drew a big, cheap, black-bladed knife.

The little girl trembled and drew a small knife from its sheath. Crying, she held the knife out in front of her with both hands and tried to build her courage.

If the little girl attacked, that would be Em's moment. She practiced the movement of the aim of the rifle, imagining the sequence of shots as she did. Bastard, then blue bitch behind Niven, then back to Az was too much swinging around. Bastard, Az, then the blue bitch ... but maybe not the one behind Niven. The woman behind Willamette might be a better third shot. Willamette might be a fancy little princess, but there was also a heap of badass in the girl. She'd probably put up a decent fight if Em gave her the chance.

Em leaned down farther to make it easier to swing the aim and rehearsed the sequence with the woman behind Willamette as the third shot.

Willamette was glancing around, desperately, as if she thought one of the bastard's women might step in and help her. She caught sight of Em and held eye contact for just an instant. In that instant, Em could see that the Little Princess was up to something.

"I told you to kill her!" the bastard shouted at the little girl.

"Wait!" Willamette shouted, making eye contact with Em again.

Em pulled back up into the shadows and waited for Willamette to give her something to follow.

"Please do not make Ida do it," Willamette pleaded with the bastard. "She is a child. You are destroying the soul of a lovely little girl."

"She is my Little Knife," the bastard said, cackling. He was manic. "And killing you will finish cutting her free from her past."

"Please just let her go, Colonel," Willamette said, with a calm but forceful and confident tone. "If you leave her with these people and let them all go, I will—"

"The only thing you have that I want is your life," the Colonel said.

"Have you thought that through?" Willamette said. "Can you imagine how helpful I could be if I chose to help you consolidate your power?"

"You want me to believe that you would help me just to save these three?" The bastard Colonel laughed. "Why would I possibly think you would be sincere about saving a serving girl, a man your father forced between your legs, and the half-dead captain of a derelict ship?"

"If I helped you, it would also save the thousands, if not tens of thousands, who would die in a war for control of the Commonwealth," Willamette said.

"As if I believe that a Lolofi could care about that," the Colonel said.

"Yes, it would be hard to imagine that." Willamette smiled as if she had been caught in a lie. "However, if I were to help you, I would obviously wish to retain my wealth along with my life. You would have to seize some of the Lolofi assets, for appearances, but—"

"Stop it!" the Colonel shouted. "I know that you're just stalling, and I will not let you play this game long enough to let the madness of the Deep give you a chance to make another impossible escape."

"Colonel …"

"Little Knife, kill her now or I swear that you will spend every last moment of a very long life suffering pain beyond your worst fears!" the Colonel shouted at the little girl.

"I can't." Ida held out the knife, arms straight, but she shook her head, crying.

Willamette glanced back up at Em and raised a questioning eyebrow. It wasn't much, but it was enough to get a suspicious glance in Em's direction from Az. Em froze. Az didn't seem to notice her.

"Ida," Willamette said, forcefully but soothingly. "Ida, I am going to die here no matter what, and Colonel Kofi is an evil man. I have no doubt that he will punish you in horrible ways if someone else has to kill me. Do you understand that?"

Ida nodded.

"I cannot bear the thought that you might suffer so horribly when I will die anyway," Willamette said. "I need you to do what he says."

Ida shook her head, flinging tears and snot.

"Please Ida. It will be a mercy if you can make it quick." Willamette spread her arms, exposing her chest to Ida. "Stab me in the heart with all your strength. Please. Straight in the heart, and hard as you can, so I will die quickly. Then neither of us has to suffer."

Em wasn't sure what the hell Willamette was thinking, but whatever it was, she was ready.

Willamette was thinking about the way Ida was holding that knife. Ida had been holding the knife the same way when she first tried to stab Willamette back in the park.

"Do it Ida! Now!" Willamette shouted commandingly. "As hard as you can!"

That set Ida into motion and just as Willamette had hoped, she attacked in the same way that she had back at the yacht club. Eyes closed, head down, arms straight out in front of her, she held the knife like a spear and charged blindly.

Willamette waited until the very last moment to react.

Spreading her arms and exposing her chest to Ida had been about more than inviting the lethal thrust. Willamette had also used that bit of theatrics to shift from both knees to one. She had one foot planted solidly on the floor and that made it possible for her to turn, lean, grab both of Ida's upper arms, and direct the knife up into the gut of the blue-clad woman standing behind her. She then used the foot she had planted on the floor to lunge to the side and drive her shoulder into the woman standing behind Niven.

The thundering crack of Em's rifle rang out so loud that it reverberated in Willamette's guts, but her entire being was focused on driving her shoulder into and through the woman standing guard behind Niven. It didn't work perfectly, but the impact was enough to send the dart from that woman's pistol wide of Niven's head.

From there, Willamette wasn't sure what happened.

Kofi never knew what hit him. He saw the Lolofi bitch redirect Ida's knife up and over her shoulder. Then he was knocked sideways by an overwhelming force, and that was it. There was no reaction. There was no pain. There was no moment of clarity as death closed in. There was just a flicker of overwhelming surprise and then nothing.

Despite being so confused that she felt like she had to focus her entire being on the task of staying on her feet, Az saw enough to know that Colonel Kofi had been shot with a high-power military rifle. The hole the dart cut through his body expanded as the dart splintered, blasting shredded flesh, organs, and bone out of an enormous exit wound. It looked like a bomb had gone off in his chest.

Az dove at Willamette but as she did there was another report from the rifle and she was flung around into a twisting spin that slammed her into the kitchen cupboards.

A surge of adrenaline added a surreal sharpness to the murky mess that engulfed her. It didn't bring any clarity, but it did help her force her mind to think. She had been shot in the thigh. The rifle dart had failed to splinter. It had stayed mostly intact as it passed through her leg, but the wound was still so bad that it didn't hurt. The blood loss would kill her, but not immediately. It had missed the femoral artery. She had time to act.

She evaluated the tactical situation, locating everyone and assessing their status. It took a second look to locate Ida. Why did she do that? Ida didn't matter.

Another shot rang out, but she had no idea who, if anyone, that dart hit. Everything around her was chaos.

Az lunged and managed to grab a fistful of Willamette's hair. She swung the girl around to use her as a shield. It shouldn't have done any good. Willamette's petite body wouldn't even slow a dart from that rifle, but maybe the person with the rifle wouldn't want to kill Willamette. Yes, that made sense. Kofi had been shot first.

"Stop!" Az drew her pistol and pointed it at Willamette's head. "Stop or I swear I will kill her!"

It took a few seconds, but the fighting stopped.

"Em, that's you up there with the rifle, isn't it?" Az yelled. "Get down."

Em swung down, hung by one hand from a cable, and then dropped to the floor with surprising grace. She didn't quite manage to hold her weapon always at the ready, but she had it pointed back in Az's direction the instant her feet were on the floor.

"Az, if you kill Willamette, you're dead," Flint said. He was pointing a pistol at her, and so was the fiancé. Where had they gotten pistols?

"I know," Az said.

"And I swear to god if you kill her, I'll die just to make sure that none of you blue bitches get out of here alive," the fiancé said.

"Really?" Az pulled Willamette backwards so she could get her back closer to the wall and reduce their firing angles to make sure that none of them could get a shot past Willamette. She also needed something to lean against. She felt weak, and the very idea that the fiancé would feel so strongly about Willamette was distracting her from the struggle to just stay upright.

She took a breath, held it a moment and then exhaled slowly.

Kofi was dead, two Blades were disarmed and had pistol wounds, one of which might be life threatening. The Blade who had been guarding Willamette was down with a belly wound that looked survivable but would become fatal if she wasn't helped soon. That left three Blades, including Dodi, who could still fight, but they all looked sick, unsteady, barely hanging on. That was a remarkable contrast to the fiancé and Em who both looked steady and alert. All things considered, she guessed that it would be a toss-up as to who might prevail if the situation devolved back into a fight.

"Dodi, get these Blades back aboard the Bluehawk and tell the captain to depart immediately," Az said.

"Az …"

"Dodi, Flint doesn't want to kill anyone, so he's going to let all of you just walk out of here," Az said. "Isn't that right, Flint?"

Flint thought a second, then nodded.

"I'm ordering you to get our wounded Blades out of here," Az said. "Once I know that you and the Bluehawk are away, I'll complete the mission."

"Yes ma'am." Dodi hesitantly holstered her weapon, and when no one shot her, she hurried over to the Blade that Ida had stabbed.

"And, Dodi," Az said. "Back someone who cares about people."

"Ma'am?"

"Dodi, once I finish extinguishing the Lolofi family …"

"Extinguish?" The fiancé started at Az, and almost got himself killed.

"Niven, no!" Willamette barked and her fiancé obeyed. Obviously, Morden had chosen the perfect husband for his princess to boss around. "Look at those pistols pointed at you. One more step and you are dead."

There were indeed three pistols pointed at Niven, and the Blade with the belly wound had raised hers, even if she wasn't managing to point it at anyone.

"Let them leave," Willamette said. "She's giving all of you a chance to live. All you have to do is let them leave."

Willamette may have managed to sound calm, but the girl was trembling like a leaf. Az held her tighter to make sure Niven didn't see that. He was a young man, and he would react like a young man if he saw how scared she was.

"Dodi," Az said. "Once the last remnant of the Lolofi name has been erased from the Drift, there will be nothing holding the Commonwealth together, and with Colonel Kofi dead, there will be no one in position to seize it. There will be a war, a long war, and I think that the Blades backing someone who cares about people … I think that would be a wise choice."

"Yes ma'am," Dodi said.

"Oh, and you are to take my place as First of the Blades," Az said. "Did I say that part?"

"No, you did not," Dodi said.

"Well now I have, so get the hell out of here," Az snarled.

"Yes ma'am," Dodi said.

The retreat of the Blades from the Drunken Monkey was swift and efficient, and the Bluehawk's departure was remarkably immediate. There couldn't have been more than a count of ten between the slamming of the outer door of the topside air lock and the lurching shift of the Drunken Monkey as the Bluehawk cut the cables and lifted.

"If your mission is to finish murdering everyone in the Lolofi family, that means you can let all the others live, right?" Willamette asked.

"As long as they don't try to stop me, I have no reason to kill them," Az said, wondering why she hadn't already pulled the trigger.

"Thank you," Willamette whispered, and with that, she broke. The trembling became weeping, the weeping became sobs, and she would have collapsed if not for Az holding her up by the hair. That breakdown didn't surprise Az. What surprised Az were the tears of the fiancé.

"You actually wanted to marry her?" Az asked him, incredulous.

Niven nodded, and then shrugged, staring at Willamette with longing and despair.

"That's foolish," Az said. "You don't even know her."

"You should never underestimate the value and beauty of foolishness," the fiancé said, getting a sad chuckle from Willamette as she cried.

Az hesitated and then the hesitation became a delay, and then they just became stuck in that moment. She wasn't sure why she let it drag on. The end was predetermined. She would pull the trigger and then Em would kill her. That was inevitable. Despite all of Az's doubts, she couldn't bear the thought of failing to carry out her mission. She had been ordered to extinguish the last remnant of the Lolofi name from the world and nothing would stop her from finishing that mission. She needed to just do it. Leaving Willamette staring at death was cruel and there was no need to be cruel. The girl didn't deserve that.

Still, Az couldn't pull the trigger. Something was stopping her, and it wasn't just knowing that she would die as soon as she did, nor was it the reluctance to accept that her last act in life would be the cold-blooded murder of a sobbing young woman. Something was gnawing at Az, worrying away in the murk that had her mind had become. It felt like she was searching for a word that she could not recall.

Seconds and then minutes ticked past. Willamette managed to stifle the sobs, but the tears kept flowing. Niven was a teary mess. Em had every ounce of her being focused on getting a clear shot at Az's head and Az's head was a wandering, bewildered, frustrated mess. She looked to Flint. For some reason she hoped that he might offer her respite or escape or even just the willpower to end the cruel torture of holding Willamette on the precipice of death. Az focused on recalling the moment that Kofi had given her the orders, hoping that the memory would give her the impetus to act.

Flint was thinking insane thoughts. The least crazy of those thoughts was the idea that he might be able to creep close enough to Az to surprise her and save Willamette. The exact physical move he might use to accomplish that wasn't clear, nor was it clear how he might creep closer, or how he might surprise Az, but it was still his least insane of those thoughts. The second-least-crazy idea involved hypnotism.

"There must be some other way. There's always another way." They were meant to be thoughts, not words. They were meant to be kept inside, just for him, but Flint heard his voice ring out through the tense silence.

Az looked at him, her eyes shining and not seeming to focus correctly as they stared into him.

"Politics and all that rubbish be damned, when it comes down to it, they're just a couple of stupid kids, and ... and ..." Flint swallowed hard. He was desperate but couldn't even begin to imagine what to say. Finally, he just let desperation win. "Look, Az, I'll be honest with you. I have no idea where I'm going with this but now that I've started talking, I'm terrified by the thought that as soon as I stop, you're going to pull that trigger. I doubt if this means anything to a soldier like you, but all I can think about is how wonderfully young and stupid these two kids are. I mean, seriously, look at them. They both still look like kids, and they're both so incredibly stupid about all this romance crap. Hell, I would bet you anything that if we flew off into the sunset, got them both away from the Commonwealth and all the rest of that nobility garbage that was forcing them to get married ... I would bet you everything I own that they'd still get married. You can't get any more stupidly romantic than that. And naive. What does he think he's going to get by turning her into his wife? Does he honestly think that she's going to stay all sweet and flirty all the time? Hell no. When she becomes Mrs. ... whatever, she'll still be ..."

Az interrupted Flint's imbecilic monologue with a loud, barking, snorting, cackling laugh that abruptly ended when a smile pulled at the corners of her mouth. That smile was horrifying. It turned her into the comic book caricature of a villain, but scarier and real. She suddenly pointed the gun at him. It was more of a gesture than a threat, but at that moment, that distinction wasn't all that significant to Flint.

"Which one of you two lunatics is actually the captain of this ship?" Az demanded.

"Flint," Em said, rushed. "Flint's always been the captain."

"Thanks, Em, but right now is not when I wanted to win that argument," Flint muttered.

"Marry them," Az said.

"What?" Flint said.

"You said it. For some reason, this stupid boy wants to marry this stupid girl. And she seems to not want him to die, which is probably about as close as a Lolofi has ever been to wanting to marry someone." Az put the gun back to Willamette's head. "So, you, Flint, as the captain of this ship, are going to marry them."

Flint looked around, but everyone else looked just as confused as he felt.

"Now, Flint!" Az shouted. "Before I pull this trigger."

"Uh, Niven, to have and to hold and ..." Flint had no idea what the vows were. "Uh, and all the rest of the husband part, whatever that may be."

"I do." Niven's voice was a hoarse whisper.

"Classy, Flint," Em muttered. "That was pure class."

"And, uh Willamette, to have and hold, and the wife stuff."

"I do," she said, smiling sadly at Niven.

"I guess I now pronounce you Lady—"

"No!" Az barked. It was so sudden and loud and assertive that it made everyone flinch. "Mr. and Mrs. It has to be Mr. and Mrs."

"Okay, okay," Flint said. "I now pronounce you Mr. and Mrs. ... uh ..."

"Lister," Willamette said, holding her chin up bravely and proudly. "Mrs. Willamette Persephone Lister."

"I now pronounce you Mr. and Mrs. Lister," Flint said.

Az laughed heartily. It was hideous.

Willamette and Niven shared a brief, longing look before Willamette took a deep, shuddering breath, closed her eyes and cringed, trembling as she waited for Az to finally pull the trigger.

Az released her hold on Willamette's hair and gave the girl a gentle shove. "I believe that it is traditional for you to kiss your damn husband, Mrs. Lister."

Willamette stumbled to a stop in the middle of the kitchen. Confused, she looked at Az.

"My orders were to extinguish the Lolofi name from this world." Az pointed her pistol to her own head. "And, Mrs. Lister, while I may have used a technicality to let you live, I do expect you to honor the intent of the mission I was given."

"I will. I swear." Willamette nodded to Az, but it took her several seconds before she believed the turn in events. When she did, she shuddered in relief, cried in amazement, and shook her head, bewildered. It was too much for her, but Niven rushed in and caught her before she collapsed. He whispered in her ear as he rocked her gently, perhaps even lovingly.

Az slumped but caught the kitchen counter before she fell. There was a puddle of blood under her feet.

Az looked at Flint and with a wry smile, she said, "I trust that you will make sure she keeps her word. The Lolofi name must never again pollute this world."

"That's your mission," Flint said. "Your responsibility."

"Flint, I understand what you are doing and why you might feel obligated," Az said. "But it is ..."

"It is a good excuse," Flint said. "And I think we both know that, just like you once looked for an excuse to let me live, and now an excuse to let her live, you are also looking for an excuse to live."

Az frowned at Flint and shook her head.

"Az, if you wanted to pull that trigger, I would already be

cleaning up the mess," Flint said. "Making sure Willamette lives up to her part of the bargain is a good excuse for you to choose to live. You should take it."

He had to give Az an encouraging nod before she holstered her pistol.

"I will pledge no fealty," Az said. "I will obey no master, but I will repay the gift of my life if I am allowed to live."

Flint nodded and Az had to nod him at Em before he realized that she was still aiming her rifle at Az.

"Em," Flint said. "At the risk of sounding like an echo, we both know that if you wanted to pull that trigger, I'd already be cleaning up the mess."

Em slowly, reluctantly lowered the rifle and gave Az a nod, which Az returned with a slow, thankful dip of her head.

"Now, if we mean to keep you alive, maybe we should bandage that leg," Flint said.

"In a moment." Az hobbled over to where Colonel Kofi had fallen, but it became a stumble and she ended up falling to her knees by the time she reached him. At first it looked to Flint like she was grieving the Colonel, but then she spoke.

"Forgive me, child," Az said. "I should have found a way to protect you."

The girl, the one that Willamette had called Ida, peered from where she was crouched behind Kofi's slumped and contorted body. Covered in blood from head to toe, she was a sight straight out of a nightmare as she tried to scoop the blood off the floor and put it back in the gaping hole that used to be the left side of Kofi's chest.

"I am his Little Knife," Ida said.

"No, Ida, you are not his Little Knife," Az said.

"I am your Little Knife?" the girl asked, plaintively, grabbing her little knife off the floor and looking to Az as if she was begging for the order to use it.

"Ida, you are not a weapon," Az said. "And if I have any say in the matter, you are no longer a servant. You are a child, and for the next few years at least, I swear that you will get to play, and learn, and laugh, and get to do all the things that a child should be allowed to do."

"Promise?"

"Yes, I promise," Az said, her voice far softer and more

comforting than Flint would have believed the woman could manage.

"And I shall promise as well," Willamette said, sniffling.

"I hurt you and stole things and I'm bad," Ida said to Willamette.

"You are not bad, Ida," Willamette said. "You behaved badly, that is different."

"I did horribleness," Ida said, guilty, looking at her knife.

"Yes, you did," Az said. "And I won't lie to you, all that horribleness will feel bad forever. You cannot escape that any more than you can escape a wound that leaves you with a limp, but you can live with it, just like you can live with a limp. At least I hope you can, because I have done horrible things as well, but I am going to try to find a way to live with that. I am going to try to leave it behind and find a way to live my own life. And I was hoping that perhaps, we could do that together."

Ida leapt at Az and hugged her. Az, tears in her eyes, hugged her back.

"Ow, too squeezy," Ida squeaked.

Az chuckled and let Ida go. The chuckle was odd, as if it was something the woman was trying for the very first time.

Ida took a step back and then leapt back into Az's arms, hugging her with all her might.

"Perhaps we should bandage that leg now," Flint suggested.

"Perhaps we should also lock up all the knives." Em carefully pried the bloody knife out of Ida's bloody hand. "Hugs and hope are great and all, but I think we would all feel more comfortable if there weren't any stabby things lying around."

"Now, Willamette," Flint said. "Do you think we can stay down here long enough to salvage a plow? Or should we maybe just bugger off now?"

CHAPTER 15

Standing at the back of the helm, Az let her mind wander. Even though the throbbing ache in her thigh had grown more intense rather than abating, and even though the first hour of the morning gave every sign that the day ahead would be mundane to the point of boring, she was looking forward to it.

The ship shuddered and bucked slightly as they rose out of the layer of clouds that defined the Deep and Em levelled the ship.

"Flint, set neutral lift, with a full pull on a six-hundred-meter plow, straight up the Drift," Em said.

"We're a couple hundred meters above where the Little Princess's decompression schedule says we should be," Flint said.

"I know, but she said that she was just making a conservative guess on that, and I really wanted to get out of the Deep." Em glanced at the big official ship's clock that dominated the constellation of timekeeping instruments above Flint's navigation station. "The sun should be rising in a few minutes, and I didn't want to waste another eight hours in the gloom."

Az listened to the back-and-forth between Em and Flint, trying to absorb every detail of the conversation.

"You know, Em, it's been dark up here for the last forty-eight hours. So even though we've been down there for three and a half days we didn't miss out on all that much sunlight," Flint said.

"Just give me this one, would you, Flint?" Em said.

"Okay, but if we die in agony from that bends thing, it's your fault," Flint said.

The ticking clocks, the hum of the atmosphere slithering over the ship's hull, the creaks and groans of the ship's structure as it responded to stresses, it all added depth, context, and color to the voices. The stations of the helm, the worn levers, dials, and controls, the broken things that had never been repaired, the window frames and all the rest of the structure that held the expansive array of windows of the helm in place; it was the details that brought the moment to life. The small shifts and shudders of the ship, the slight flexing of the deck beneath Az's feet, it felt as if the Drunken Monkey was a beast striving to carry them out of the Deep and across the Drift.

"You think that bends thing is real?" Em asked.

"The Little Princess was right when she said that the madness of the Deep was caused by nitrogen," Flint said. "And she said she learned about the bends from reading the same historical stories, so I think we have to take it seriously, but it will be nice to see the sun again."

"So, we're going to fly at this altitude for the next eight hours, right?" Em asked.

"Yes, and like I said, if I die it's your fault," Flint said, working some of the valves at his station. "There, that should have us neutral."

The sky around them slowly brightened. Az couldn't see the sun, but it was clear that it was rising directly behind them. Or, to be more precise, it was appearing to rise directly behind them as the winds they called the Drift carried them around the world. With the growing light, Az expanded her world out from the helm of the ship to include everything within the clear layer of the Venusian atmosphere that they called the Drift. Wrapping around the world, it was an infinity bounded by the thin, wispy white clouds above and the soupy yellow-brown haze of the Deep below.

"Can I go see her now?" Ida asked as she ran in from the closet they had turned into a little cabin for her and leapt onto the railing separating the helm from the main cabin.

"No," Em said. "You just leave them be."

Em and Willamette had thrown out Ida's makeshift tunic and they had dyed her Lolofi servant dress with some juice to hide the bloodstains. The dye job hadn't worked all that well. If anything, it made Ida look more like a bedraggled mess than before. Securing new clothes for the child needed to be a priority.

"But I want to see Lady Willamette," Ida said, climbing upon and leaning precariously over the top of the railing.

"You can't call her Lady Willamette anymore," Em said. "She's Lady Lister now."

Az resisted the urge to correct Em. She was half correct. The lesser nobles appended their family name to their formal titles rather than their given names. However, unlike sir, which went to all sons of estate holders, only the wives of estate holders and the wives of the heirs to estates were allowed to call themselves ladies. Since it was Niven's older brother who would inherit the Lister Estate, Willamette was Mrs. Lister, not Lady Lister.

"But I want to see her and talk to her," Ida whined. "Please. It's been forever."

"Quit your damn whining, Ida!" Em snapped. "Only Flint is allowed to whine and whinge on this ship. Besides, it hasn't been forever."

"It has been two days," Flint said. "And I could use the boy's help with a few things."

"Niven is not leaving that cabin until the Little Princess decides that he has totally and completely satisfied her every desire," Em said.

"Or he dies of exhaustion," Flint quipped.

"I doubt if he'd complain," Em muttered.

"Of course he wouldn't complain," Flint said. "He'd be dead. Dead people hardly ever complain about anything. Which seems kind of odd because if something killed you, you've probably got plenty to complain about."

Em sighed, but Az could see that she was also smiling as she shook her head and rolled her eyes at Flint.

"Hey little one, how about we cook something yummy and see if the smell tempts Willamette and Niven to join us for breakfast?" Flint asked.

Ida answered with a childish celebration dance.

Az gave Flint a smile as he stepped past her to climb up into the main cabin, surprising him. She listened to him take Ida to the kitchen in the common area and then she returned to inviting the sensations of the world to fill her.

The world was not just in that moment. From the twenty-four-hour days they imposed upon the Drift's cycle of forty-eight hours of sunlight and forty-eight hours of darkness, to the three-hundred-and-sixty-five days they shoved into their years, it was the stories, the history and the habits of long-ago Earth that carried them forward through the present and into the future. History shaped everything, in big ways and small. It gave meaning to Az's desire to rush headlong at the challenge of a life free of the missions, orders, and responsibilities. Even the horrors that had driven her into that life as Kofi's Blade carried forward into and through the moment.

With that thought, Az understood that there was no such thing as a moment. It was only with her feet planted firmly in that past and her mind reaching to the future that she could find meaning in the sights, sounds, and feelings of every instant that flowed through her. She wanted to fill herself with every detail.

She wanted to live.

Em added a few degrees of starboard cut to their course. They were still a good three or four hours from getting anywhere near the cluster of habitats that they could hear pinging away updrift, but it was best to be safe and avoid them. Even though they would pass at least a couple of kilometers below the keels of those habitats, you never knew when someone might decide that it was time to dump a few tons of garbage into the Deep.

She made a few more very minor corrections, and when she was satisfied that it was safe to just let the Monkey fly for a while, she linked the helm controls to the altimeter and the windvane. Those simple mechanisms kept the Drunken Monkey's altitude steady and held the angle of its pull up the Drift. It was an effective and robust mechanical system, and with just two in their crew, she used it a lot.

The thought of a long and leisurely breakfast evaporated the moment she stood and turned to follow Flint up to the kitchen.

"You don't think that this is over, do you?" Em snapped, startling the serene smile off Az's face.

Instantly alert, Az crouched slightly and scanned the sky outside, wincing as she flexed her injured leg.

"Oh, for god's sake, Az. That's not what I meant, and you know it."

Glancing back and forth between her search for threats from the Drift and Em, Az gave Em brief glimpses of a questioning and bewildered frown.

"The symbolism of starting new lives by sailing off into a fresh morning sky would have been a poetically dramatic way to end this, but there's no way in hell that Willamette could possibly settle for that," Em said.

"Settle?" Az shook her head. "How can what she's been given be construed as anything less than far more than she could have possibly had a right to expect? Even if that girl is spoilt to the point that she is incapable of appreciating the simple fact that she still has a life to start anew, she also has secured the husband she so foolishly wanted, and all the evidence from the last two days would suggest that she is happy with that choice."

"Yes, she's spent nearly every moment since you let her live wallowing in the carnal delights of her new love monkey, but that's also why she could never settle for just sailing off into a new life," Em said.

"That makes no sense," Az said.

"It makes perfect sense once you understand that the compassionate Little Princess we all read about in those gossip magazines wasn't just some public relations story ginned up by her father. That's who she is. And there is no way that she could endure such a pleasantly mundane life when she knew people were dying in a war that she didn't try to stop. The guilt would destroy her, and the happier Niven makes her, the guiltier she's going to feel."

"How can you possibly believe that she could be so driven by concern for the fate of others?" Az gestured, dismissively. "She is a Lolofi. Or … She was a Lolofi."

"Az, you saw it yourself. When you had a gun to her head, she was worried about whether you would let the rest of us live after you killed her."

Az shook her head, refusing to believe.

"Yeah, if it was just that, I might be skeptical, too, but I see it in nearly everything she has said or done since I met her," Em said.

"There's been lots of little stuff, but the big thing that comes to mind was just after we fled Lightcastle. The very first thing we talked about was her worrying that she might have to marry into a noble family that could use her name to hold the Commonwealth together. She was horrified by the thought. It was painfully obvious that she truly thinks she's in love with Niven, but she was still willing to leave him, and abandon any hope of a happy life behind if it offered even the slightest chance that she could stop the rush to war."

"Truly?" Az asked.

"Yeah, truly," Em said, sarcastically imitating Az's stunned utterance. "A diplomatic marriage probably isn't an option …"

"It obviously is not," Az said, gruffly. "She no longer has the Lolofi name to trade upon. She swore."

"Uhm, yeah, if you believe that a promise that she made with a gun literally pointed at her head would stop her from saving people's lives, sure." Em rolled her eyes at Az. "But I was thinking that now that she's been right and properly harpooned by her handsome young whaler, the thought of letting some lecherous old pirate plunder her little treasure bunny is probably just too much to bear. Isn't that right, Little Princess?"

Em glanced pointedly toward Willamette, who had stepped up to the railing above. Judging by the shift in Az's ever-present scowl, she was both surprised and dismayed to realize that Willamette had managed to approach them without her noticing.

"Must you always speak so crudely?" Willamette huffed. Even though her face was scrunched up in a disapproving frown and her hair was still damp and hanging limp from taking a shower, she somehow still managed to add an air of nobility to her wrinkled shopgirl dress.

"Tell me I'm wrong," Em challenged her.

"I would honor my pledge regardless of the context in which it was made, but …" After a long moment of fidgeting, and a quick glance back over her shoulder toward where Az belatedly realized that the men's voices could be heard in the common area, Willamette softly said, "I will admit that the thought of enduring the physical aspects a diplomatic marriage seems far more unpleasant now that I have been given a tangible point of reference for what I would be abandoning."

"A tangible point of reference." Em chuckled. "Is that what the noble girls are calling it these days?"

Willamette frowned, confused.

"And just how tangible was the point of reference that Niven gave you?" Em asked, feigning sincere interest.

Amazingly, Willamette still didn't understand.

"Some women swear that it's all about how a man gives you a tangible point of reference, but I think it's foolish to pretend that the size of his tangible point of reference doesn't matter." Em gave Az a questioning look. "Bigger is just more … tangible. Don't you think?"

Stony-faced, Az refused to join in the teasing.

It took several more seconds, but when Willamette finally understood what Em was talking about, she gasped and was overwhelmed by a scandalized blush. That drew an eyeroll and shake of the head from Az, but Az's expression of disapproval was directed at Em, not at Willamette.

"Why are you like that?" Willamette demanded, angrily.

"I blame the structural violence inherent to the patriarchy," Em said, offhand.

"Cute," Willamette grumped.

"Instilling an innate belief in the inadequacy of the female is essential to normalizing the acceptance of male social dominance," Em quoted, confidently, swiftly, and angrily. "When that belief clashes with a young girl's self-recognition of ability, particularly if that ability is in a realm of endeavor commonly associated with male excellence, the cognitive dissonance manifests through challenges to authority and defiance of social norms of propriety. Over time, those behaviors are ingrained into the social-interactive habits of the woman and become fundamental to what is often called a dysfunctional female persona."

Willamette's jaw dropped.

"Surprise, Little Princess, naughty girls can be taught to read, too." Em loaded the comment with all the sarcasm she could muster.

"No … I am well aware that you are far better educated than you wish people to believe," Willamette said. "If you look past all your crass provocations, anyone can see that you think and argue like an educated woman. I am, however, surprised, and a touch embarrassed, that I had never considered any of those esoteric theoretical arguments together, or in such concrete terms. The behavioral and psychological ramifications women suffer from an authoritarian patriarchy seem painfully obvious once given voice. And the gendered label of a dysfunctional female persona … I have seen it so often in political and social analyses. How could I not realize that its common usage in educational and punitive contexts all but proves the point?"

"Don't get yourself too caught up in it, Little Princess. I might just be a snarky bitch," Em said, surprised by how uncomfortable she was with the twist in the conversation.

"The two are not mutually exclusive," Willamette said, primly. "Nor does the situation excuse your unkind behavior, but it is still …"

"How about if you just tell us how you intend to get us all killed?" Em demanded.

"What?" Willamette was thrown off by the demand.

"You've had the better part of two days to stew over your princessly duty to save the innocent people who would be killed in a war over the Commonwealth," Em said. "You must have come up with some kind of harebrained and hopeless scheme by now."

"I will never discuss what happens in my bedroom but let me assure you that I was far too engaged to spare a single thought for any distraction from beyond the door of that cabin."

"Except of course for the little girl who kept sneaking away to knock on that door," Az said, drolly, as she turned and started awkwardly climbing the ladder up to the main cabin. Her injured leg was almost unusable.

"Ida did have impeccably poor timing," Willamette mused.

"Oh, come on, Little Princess. You can admit it," Em shot back. "The instant Niven rolled off you, your mind went straight to worrying over saving all the people who would be chewed up and spit out by a war over the Commonwealth."

"I will admit no such thing," Willamette said. "That is simply untrue."

Az reached the top of the ladder and, bizarrely, put a reassuring hand on Willamette's shoulder.

"I believe you, Willamette," Az said, sincerely and warmly. "I cannot imagine that you are the kind of woman who would rush to contemplate issues of grand politics the instant your new husband finished making love to you."

"Thank you, Az," Willamette said, prim, vindicated, and grateful.

"You are obviously the kind of woman who would scoot off the wet spot before worrying about how to stop the war for control of the Commonwealth," Az said, walking away as she delivered the punch line with the same pretense of sincerity and warmth as the setup.

It wasn't until Em chuckled that Willamette realized what Az had just said, and when she did, the melodramatic, scandalized gasp that accompanied that realization was too much for Em. She burst out laughing. That laugh escalated with every new flush of red that found its way onto annoyingly beautiful shades of olive and tan on Willamette's face. And when Willamette's mortification from that perfectly delivered scandalous comment grew to the point that it threatened to buckle the Little Princess's knees, Em's laughter spiraled to the point where she cried. There were tears in Willamette's eyes as well, which ruined some of the fun, but still, a sidesplitting belly laugh was exactly what Em needed after the tense and wild ride she had endured over the last week or so.

"I'm starting to like Az," Em said, fighting to tame the laughter. "I'll feel a hell of a lot safer once we dump her and her stabby little friend off somewhere, but I have to say, the woman does have her moments,"

Surprisingly, Em's comment about Az and Ida upset Willamette nearly as much as Az's perfectly executed tease. The Little Princess was an odd young woman, and it was starting to look like she was deeply hurt by the rough little turn of their conversation. That probably shouldn't be all that surprising. Not only was Willamette a princess all the way to the core, she was also the youngest in her family, and she had no sisters. Em couldn't imagine that she had ever really been teased before.

"Willamette …" Em said, softly. "Willamette, it's okay."

Willamette glanced over her shoulder at the common area and after wiping her eyes looked back at Em. "What is okay?"

"It's okay if you could ignore everything beyond the door, but it's also okay if the troubles of the world found a way to creep in. It's okay if you scooted off the wet spot. It's okay if you didn't care about the wet spot. It's okay to admit that there was a wet spot. It's okay if it embarrasses you to talk about sex and you want to keep it all private, but it's also okay if you want to whisper and giggle over every naughty detail. It's okay if it wasn't perfect. It's okay if it was wonderful beyond what you imagined it could be. It's okay that you want him inside you. It's okay that there is something bizarrely magnificent about feeling crushed by the weight of a man on top of you. It's all okay because a woman is allowed to own her sexuality in any way she chooses, and you accepting and believing that is more important to me than you can imagine. No matter how much I enjoy teasing you, which is ... a lot. I mean, like, I enjoy teasing you more than you can possibly imagine, but still ... I will always be the first one to defend your right to own every single aspect of your sexuality. Do you understand that?"

Willamette gave Em the slightest nod, and with that, Em was at a loss for what, if anything, came next. They stared at each other for what seemed like an eternity before Em nodded curtly and flopped back into her chair. She unlocked the flight controls and swung them through some slow and gentle maneuvers. There was no real point to that. They hadn't decided where they were headed yet, so their course was irrelevant and the moves weren't big enough to help her refine her feel for the new plow, but she persisted in pretending like it was purposeful. As far as stubborn went, however, she had to admit that she had met her match in Willamette. The woman was not going to move from that spot at the rail.

"What?" Em demanded.

"Dumping us somewhere and flying off without us, is that what happens next?" Willamette asked.

"Flint says I'm supposed to call it disembarking, but, yeah, dumping people somewhere is the way the whole passenger thing works," Em said.

"So, we are nothing more than passengers?" Willamette sounded like a devastated little girl.

"Niven offered Flint an undefined but large sum of money for a charter flight out of Lightcastle, does that ring any bells?" Em said, pointedly and caustically.

Willamette was silent for what seemed like an eternity before she said, "I meant it when I said that I had not spared a thought for anything beyond the cabin door."

"Uhmm, okay, I'll play along," Em said. "And I meant it when I said that whatever you did or didn't do in that cabin was okay."

"No, it was not okay," Willamette said. "I could not spare a thought for all the people who are going to be chewed up and spat out by the fight over the Commonwealth because I was too busy worrying about what was going to happen to me. I know how selfish that is, but lying in Niven's arms, in that bed, in that cabin, on this ship … for the first time in my life I truly felt safe, and I could not bring myself to care about anything else or anyone else."

Willamette stopped and was obviously expecting a response. What she expected that response to be was an absolute mystery to Em.

"I think we need to get something straight, Little Princess," Em said. "I am not one of your fancy tutors. I don't give a damn about your command of the subtlety of language, and I am certainly not some diplomatic whore who is going to parse things clause by clause, so all of your fancy and flowery I'm implying this and that and this other thing is just wasted breath. If you want to say something to me, you need to just say it. If you want to ask me for something, you need to just ask for it."

"I wish to remain here, on the Drunken Monkey," Willamette said.

"See. Now I understand. Was that so hard?" Em asked.

Willamette shook her head.

"Good,'" Em said. "And no, you can't stay."

Willamette was stunned.

"Pick 'em up. Dump 'em off. Passengers are just a pain in the ass kind of cargo, they don't stay any more than a load of turnips stays," Em said. "Crew stay, but even if we needed crew, which we do not, you have absolutely nothing to offer. I could maybe see Niven being worth something. He's got some skills and knows plenty of things about ships and cutting the Drift, but, honestly, we don't have a lot of call for princessing. What are you going to do to earn your keep? Cook and clean? Hell, for that I'd pick stabby girl over you any day. The cookies she made were good. I mean, really good. She ate pretty much all of them and then puked them all over everything, but then she cleaned up the puke. When's the last time you cleaned up puke? We have to clean up a hell of a lot more puke on this ship than you might think. I don't know why, but we do. You up for that?"

"I gave you the way to survive the Deep," Willamette said.

"Yes, you gave it to us and now we've got it. Thanks," Em said. "Flint's a fair kind of guy, I'm sure he'll give you a discount on whatever it is he's going to charge you for the charter in return for that, but that's all it's worth. Actually, to be honest, he'll probably give you way more than it's worth. I can't imagine that we are ever going to put ourselves in a situation like that ever, ever again, so what's the value of knowing that, right? But Flint's kind of stupid with those things, and that's beside the point anyway. Passengers don't stay and you've got nothing to offer as crew."

Willamette's tears were back, flowing freely. She was devastated.

"Look, I'm not trying to be a bitch," Em said.

"You clearly do not have to try," Willamette snapped, huffy.

"There's more truth to that than you can possibly know, Little Princess, but my dysfunctional female personality doesn't change the reality of the situation." Em locked the flight controls back down, stood, turned, and took a breath before explaining. "We aren't a desperate crew on the run from creditors. We aren't holding the ship together with spit and stealing food to feed our passengers. That kind of desperate poverty is all comic book nonsense, but we aren't that many steps ahead of the cliché. Honestly, if we didn't have Kegley on the books so we could pretend to be legal with just two on the crew, I don't know how we'd do it. There just isn't that much money to be made in moving people and things around the Drift, and I can't imagine how we could find a way to pay a third crew member, or a fourth, since I'm guessing that it would probably take a crowbar to pry Niven out from between your legs."

Willamette glumly nodded her understanding.

"We aren't just going to fly in low over a dock and toss you out the back," Em said. "But whatever your future is going to be, you are going to have to make it happen yourself."

Niven hadn't realized how hungry he was. To be fair, he had been far too thoroughly distracted by Willamette to even think of something as mundane as food, but once he wandered into the kitchen area, he had been all but overwhelmed by how famished he was. He had snuck out of the cabin a couple of times to grab them snacks, but they hadn't really eaten in ages. That made the untouched plate that he'd dished up and set aside for Willamette all the more curious. She had to be starving as well, but eating was obviously less important than stomping about the ship, huffing, grumbling, and slamming doors. She might not have ever been an actual princess in title, but she sure as hell was one genuine drama queen. When she marched up to the table and slammed her heavily laden purse down, she was completely committed to that grand theatrical gesture.

"What the hell is that?" Em grumped.

"That is me, making the future happen." Willamette paused for effect before she upended the handbag and dumped its contents.

"Whoa, that is some nice something to have happening." Flint's jaw dropped as he picked up a thick gold chain. "Oh my god that's heavy."

"Yes, the density of solid metal is stunning, and the weight of gold borders on the unbelievable," Willamette said.

"That's gold?" Em grabbed the necklace from Flint, shaking her head as she tested its heft. "Like fairy tales, elves and goblins and magic and gold?"

"I assure you that there is nothing mythical about gold," Willamette said. "It is extraordinarily difficult to obtain, but it is a simple mineral, like iron, silicon or any of the others brought up by the whales."

"Willamette," Niven said, speaking softly but not bothering to hide his annoyance. "I know that you are new to this not being the richest girl in the world thing, but you should have kept your pile of treasure private until after we negotiated a charter price with Flint."

"Dear husband," Willamette replied with mock sweetness. "I understand full well the critical role of information and the use of its strategic revelation in the process of negotiations, but this is not a negotiation. This is a proposition, and I wished to make sure that I had everyone's full attention."

"Well, then, except for Ida, I do believe that you have succeeded in that." Niven took Willamette's arm and firmly directed her to sit in the seat that had been saved for her. "Right, Flint?"

"Uhm, yeah, pardon the drool."

"Ida is hiding because she saw me with the purse, and she is afraid that I might make her clean the jewelry." Willamette used a glance to direct Niven to pull out the chair for her.

"Or yell at her for stealing it in the first place," Niven muttered. After a moment of hesitation, he decided to attend the chair for Willamette. Their discussion of when acts of formality like that were and were not something she should expect from him could wait until they were alone.

"Yes, she might well fear that." Willamette ate a single forkful of eggs from the plate before taking a deep, performative breath to make it clear that she was launching into her pitch. "I thought it important to discuss this with everyone at once, so now that I have your attention ..."

"Let me guess, you have a plan for getting us all killed trying to end the war that is maybe probably happening," Em said, sarcastically.

"I have a few ideas." Willamette winked at Niven, getting a chuckle. "And yes, the most urgent of those ideas are focused on ending or limiting the extent of the war, if there is one, over control of the Commonwealth, but ..."

"Thought so," Em said. "Well then let's not waste anyone's time, because I am profoundly not interested ..."

"Em," Flint said, sternly, getting an annoyed, pouting gesture of surrender from her.

"It is okay, Flint," Willamette said. "If Em wants to take her share and go her own way, I understand completely."

"Take my share?" Em held up a necklace and nodded at the pile of jewelry on the table. "Of this?"

"Yes. Regardless of what any of us decide to do going forward, I intend to share this." Willamette took a dainty second bite of the cold eggs, taking her time before swallowing and continuing. "There is not as much here as it might appear. A great deal of this is the sort of thing that looks pretty to a little girl but is not all that valuable. Still, if you and Flint were to combine your shares, I am certain that you would have more than enough to set up your business in some distant kingdom where the Commonwealth is little more than a whisper on the wind. However, I am also just as certain that no matter where that place might be, you will face the same struggle you face now. As you so succinctly explained to me, Em, there is not all that much money to be made moving people and things around the Drift."

"And you think that we'd be better off throwing in with you on some harebrained scheme to save the world?" Em was skeptical.

"It is oddly apropos that you should mention saving the world, because in the long term the stakes may indeed be that high, but in a more immediate sense I believe we would all be far better off if we acted in concert rather than going our separate ways, yes," Willamette said. "The bigger picture and longer term are profoundly important to me, and yes, I want to do something about the nightmare that has been unleashed upon the people of the Commonwealth. However, I am committed to a joint effort, even if it is a stopgap arrangement to gather additional wealth before we go our separate ways."

"Gather additional wealth?" Em sneered. "Right, now you want to be the Little Pirate Princess. I believe that."

Willamette looked directly into Em's eyes, and said, softly but intensely, "If you are more than talk, and if you wanted to strike a real blow against the patriarchy of the Commonwealth, do not underestimate what we might be able to do together."

"Now you're just pandering," Em huffed.

"No, that was a challenge to your pride," Willamette said. "When I intimate just how much I desperately need to exploit your aptitude for piloting, that will be when I am pandering."

Em thought a few seconds and then shrugged. "Okay, I'm listening. Not interested but listening. And there better be some damn good pandering coming my way."

Willamette gave Em a slight, but thankful nod and seemed to contemplate all the troubles of the world as she took an eternity to eat another dainty bite of eggs.

"Az, you told that woman ... the officer under your command who you sent away ..." Willamette closed her eyes and cocked her head. "Darcy?"

"Dodi," Az said. She seemed impressed. She probably shouldn't be. Niven knew that his sisters had been taught to recall any name they heard. It was a common point of training for daughters of the nobility and Willamette was undoubtedly nothing less than a master at it. She almost certainly knew that the woman was called Dodi and not Darcy, but by feigning the need to be corrected, she had coaxed Az into investing in the conversation.

"Yes, Dodi," Willamette said. "Am I remembering correctly that when you passed your command to her, you told her that she should convince the other women in your … movement to back someone who cared about people?"

"Yes," Az said.

"Would she back me?" Willamette asked.

"I cannot speak for her, or the Blades," Az said. "But if you were to convince me that you indeed care about the many people who truly need and deserve your help, and that you can offer a real chance of bettering their circumstance, I would be willing to offer your argument to her on your behalf."

"I would be most grateful if you would," Willamette said.

"Don't get too excited, Princess," Em sneered. "Those women are scary as hell, but there's only a couple hundred of them."

"A couple of thousand," Az corrected her.

"Whoa, seriously?" Em asked.

"Yes," Az said. "I have no idea how many may have been killed over the last few days, or how many are loyal to their sisters after you killed Colonel Kofi, but we were over three thousand strong when we launched the coup attempt. It would be safe to guess that Dodi still commands a significant portion of that number."

"Well, thousands of murder ballerinas running around loose is truly the stuff of nightmares. And I could see that working pretty damn well for someone like Kofi trying pull off a coup, but we've got to assume that this has devolved into a war. And you, Willamette, of all people, would have to understand what a war over the Commonwealth entails," Em said. "Do you have any idea how many soldiers there are floating around the Commonwealth? Even if you could convince Az's women to support you, they'd be little more than a fart in the Drift."

"Yes, I know how many soldiers there are in the Commonwealth," Willamette said, with both slightly exaggerated annoyance and matronly patience. "Last year's military census counted roughly a million men in active and reserve roles, and that was almost certainly a gross underestimation."

"Three thousand against a million," Em said. "They do teach princesses math, right?"

"Em, if it was simply math, you would be correct with what that sarcasm implies, but the reality is nowhere near that straightforward. Those soldiers are spread across over eighteen hundred different commands, many of which have officers from one family commanding enlisted men from another." Willamette took another bite, and then, unexpectedly, she took another and seemed to have to force herself to stop before she returned to her performance. "My father carefully manipulated the military power, commands, and the security responsibilities that were given to every family. By doing this he made it all but impossible for anyone to make any big military moves on their own, or even talk about making big moves without exposing themselves to a strike from one of the others."

"Which was also probably a big part of why this Colonel Kofi thought he could take over with just a few thousand murder ballerinas." Em looked pointedly at Az, questioning.

"We knew that the most dangerous of the Lolofi loyalists were scattered across different commands and were being used primarily to keep the forces loyal to others in line," Az said. "I do not know the details, but I do know that Colonel Kofi was confident it would only take a few assassinations and mutinies to cut the head, or heads, off that snake and prevent an effective military response."

"And that's probably the real point," Em said. "You can't control most of the soldiers out there. So, adding a few killer ballerinas to whatever surviving loyalists you might be able to rustle up just isn't going to be enough to win a war."

"Yes, I know. However, I also know everyone out there will assume that if I take action, then I must be trying to take the Commonwealth for myself." Willamette gave Em a wicked grin. "After all, this is your assumption, is it not?"

"You're thinking something seriously crazy, aren't you girl?" Em said, smirking.

"There is nothing crazy about letting everyone think I am trying to win a war when all I wish to do is stop it," Willamette said, smirking back at Em.

"By your reference to what people will think when you show up, am I to assume that you no longer intend to honor your promise to me, Mrs. Lister?" Az said, pointedly.

"On the contrary, Az," Willamette said. "If you can allow me some flexibility in how I honor that promise, I intend to make certain no one could ever possibly doubt that the Lolofi name has been extinguished from the Drift."

"If that is true, I may be willing to negotiate on that point," Az said. "But it also depends on the details of your harebrained scheme."

"The details will depend on what we can do and what we decide we wish to do, but, if I were to summarize, I would say my basic idea is to princess the living shit out of it," Willamette said, with exaggerated primness.

It took a moment, but once it started, the laughter overwhelmed the table, and with that, Willamette finally dug into her breakfast. To Niven's relief, the moment she was done performing, she ate with a surprisingly casual gusto.

Dodi had thought that she was prepared to take command, but she had been wrong.

The situation aboard the Bluehawk was nothing short of catastrophic. Once they were back up in the Drift, the madness of the Deep had slowly faded, but as it did, they discovered that the mythical curse of the Deep was just as real as the madness. There was no rhyme nor reason to whom it struck, and there was no explanation for all the wildly different ways it struck, but that just made it all the more horrific. For some it was nothing more than irritatingly odd aches, pains, or cramps. For others it was debilitating, leaving them curled up in a puddle of their own sweat, convulsing in agony. And for three unlucky souls, it had been lethal, and oddly so. One had just died, as if a switch had been flipped. Another suffered what seemed to be a heart attack, and the third died gasping, as if she was suffocating in perfectly good air. For some the curse hit, passed, and was over. For others it lingered in ways that might well be permanent and the damage it left was bizarrely random. A mild headache might lead to blindness in one eye while a day of tortured writhing in bed could just end without leaving a trace. The numbers of afflicted weren't that high. Nine severe cases and maybe twenty minor cases out of the one hundred forty-six people on the ship, but the randomness of it all was haunting. There was no way to tell if it might happen to you, and that transformed every normal ache, pain, or twitch into a terror.

It seemed like they were past the worst of it. There hadn't been a new complaint in over a day, but just holding the crew together and maintaining order on the ship had been a monumental effort, and that was before Captain Roberts refused to sail them back to Lightcastle. The discipline of the Blades had won out in the end, but his men were experienced, and the fight had cost her a dozen healthy sisters and several days.

Dodi was exhausted to the point of collapse, but she could no longer put off dealing with the bigger picture. The reports that were being flashed to them as they approached Lightcastle were desperate.

It wasn't surprising that the situation had degenerated after nearly a week without Colonel Kofi there to manage things. His absence from Lightcastle, and now his death, left them without someone to step into the leadership vacuum he had created by decapitating the nobility of the Commonwealth. It also eliminated the one and only person who knew the whole plan. Dodi could scarcely even imagine how he meant to turn their opening move into revolution. Several of the next steps seemed obvious, and the Blades left behind in the city had done a commendable job of taking them, but the rest was a mystery to everyone.

Az would have known a lot more of Kofi's plan than Dodi. She might even have been able to carry it through and take the Colonel's place at the helm of whatever it was he meant to build out of the ashes, but Dodi couldn't. She could keep most of the remaining Blades together as a coherent fighting force, of that she was certain, but the rest was beyond her. At best she and the Blades could retain their hold on a few key strategic assets and try to use those assets to leverage themselves out of the mess that Kofi's death had created. At worst …

"Dodi?" Kirah prompted her.

Dodi looked out the window of the helm. That was pointless. They were still too far from Lightcastle to see any details that might be helpful, but looking at the city assured Kirah that she was thinking, weighing options.

"We consolidate," Dodi said. "Instead of trying to hold everything we have, we pick a few key things that will give us leverage, or give us something to work with, things we know we can easily hold."

"And then?" Yassim, one of the more assertive of the younger Blades, asked.

"And then we find a good person to back," Dodi said.

"The best person," someone said from behind her.

"No," Dodi said, placing her hand gently over her heart and turning to face the others. "A good person. A person who is good."

Nods from the four women who had fallen into the roles of her lieutenants.

"But that begs the question of what those few key things might be," Dodi said. "We need to answer that question before we do anything."

Flint double-checked that he had all the controls locked down like he wanted them and then his double-checking was immediately double-checked by Ida. She had no idea how any of it worked or what any of the settings meant, but she still inspected everything with great care.

"Okay Ida, are you ready for your first watch?"

"Oh, yes, yes, yes." Ida skipped over to Em's pilot station and leapt into the chair.

"Good, now what's the first and most important rule?" Flint asked as he buckled the lap belt for her.

"Don't spill your hot chocolate," Ida said, tapping the mug in the cup holder.

"Correct, and rule number two?"

"Don't touch any of the controls," Ida said.

"And what are you supposed to do if you see something we might crash into?"

"Yell for you, Niven, or Em," Ida said.

"Excellent. Your training for level one shipgirl is complete. The helm is yours," Flint said, heading to main cabin.

"Aye-aye, Captain Flint."

Em and Az were sitting at the table in the lounge examining a document.

"Where'd Niven go?" Flint asked.

"Where do you think Niven and the Little Princess are?" Em muttered.

Flint chuckled and poured a cup of coffee.

"So, what do you think of the Little Princess's plan?" Em asked Flint.

"I think that someone would have to tell me what her plan is before I could tell you what I think of it," Flint said. "Landing on a small industrial town to gather information, load a few supplies, send a few messages, and start a few rumors is all fine and dandy, and I believe her when she says she can't be sure of what we might be able to do until after she's had a chance to thoroughly assess the situation."

"But …?" Em said, using the tone that meant get to the damn point.

"But when she says, 'I cannot be certain' that's a hell of a lot different than her saying, 'I do not know,'" Flint said, imitating Willamette.

"Agreed," Az said. "There is something she intends to do, something significant and central to her thinking, that she's hiding from us."

"Or maybe she's just hiding it from Niven," Flint said, softly.

"Why would it be about Niven?" Az asked.

"Didn't you wonder how she intended to make certain no one could possibly doubt that the Lolofi name had been extinguished from the Drift?" Flint asked.

"Is it relevant?" Az asked.

"If she doesn't want Niven to know, yeah, maybe," Flint said.

"Blaze of glory," Em muttered, looking horrified.

"I can't imagine how she could twist making a spectacle of her death into something that ends or shortens the war, but it fits with what she said about her promise to Az, and it fits with the way she's doing everything she can to keep her actual plan a secret," Flint said.

"Niven would stop her," Az said, nodding.

"Yes, and she's probably afraid that she'd let him stop her," Flint said.

"What do we do about it?" Em asked. "What can we do about it?"

"Are we sure we should do something about it?" Flint asked. "I think that's the question we need to answer before we get to Donovan."

"Yeah, we're already pretty much committed to the small industrial town recon part of her plan, aren't we?" Em said.

"If we want to eat, we will need to stop somewhere," Flint said, shrugging.

CHAPTER 16

In the blink of an eye, Willamette was transformed from an embarrassed young woman unleashing the righteous hellfire of the Deep, into a foolish girl who was mortified by her childish fury. Screaming at a deliveryman bursting into the seamstress's fitting room while she was being fitted for her new dress suddenly seemed trivial, and with that, she finally understood just how unprepared she was to play the grand game of nobles. The countless hours spent studying the dynamics, complexities, and nuances of politics meant nothing. All of that knowledge, no matter how detailed and complete it might be, was little more than the faintest shadow of the vivid, visceral, and violent reality it represented.

"What did you expect, Princess?" Az's stern, uninflected question somehow sounded compassionate. "You knew that provoking something like this would be all but inevitable. That's why I had so much leverage in negotiating our contract."

"Yes, and do remind me to teach you a thing or two about negotiating," Willamette said. Despite recognizing her prattling, patronizing comment for exactly the self-distraction it was, she kept going. "You used that leverage quite poorly, but this is ..."

The man moved, startling Willamette so completely that she yelped and jumped away. Despite his wheezing and groaning, which had left no doubt that he was still alive, it had never occurred to her that he could still move.

Willamette turned away from the dying, would-be assassin but almost immediately looked back at him. She did not wish to, but she could not tear her eyes from whatever it was that was so irresistibly horrific about the lingering moment of his death. The way he tried to crawl back to the stairway; the slow wheeze of each desperate effort to draw a breath; the way the blood leaked through the fingers of the hand he pressed against the wound; it was all palpably, overwhelmingly, and sickeningly gruesome. There was so much blood. The pool had already spread so far across the floor of the seamstress's loft that it would be impossible to avoid it on the way to the stairs, and it kept growing. It seemed inconceivable that a human body could possibly contain so much blood.

"Willamette," Az said, softly but sternly, picking up the package the man had used as an excuse to barge into the shop and up the stairs. She inspected it to determine if it contained anything in addition to the pistol and, finding nothing, tossed it aside. "You cannot allow this to bother you."

"How can it fail to bother me?" Willamette asked. "As you said, this is my fault. The moment we … The moment I chose this course of action, this was all but inevitable."

The man lifted his head and then collapsed, his face hitting the puddle of blood with a sickening, thick, wet smack.

"Yes, your decision to instigate the rumor that you lived was all but certain to provoke a reaction. At the extreme that included the distinct possibility of assassination attempts, but that was a simple prediction of what others might choose to do. It does not in any way imply you are responsible for the choices and actions of others." Az took a quick, careful look down the stairs to make sure no one else had come with him. "He chose the path that led to his death. He is the only guilty party here."

"But …"

"But nothing!" Az snapped. "The very first clause in our contract states that I will not kill an innocent person for you. I killed him; therefore, he is not an innocent person."

With one last tremble, the would-be assassin died. His delayed but inevitable end was surprisingly abrupt, like a switch had been flipped.

"Guilt or innocence be damned!" Willamette hissed, inexplicitly angry at the woman who had just saved her life. "How can you be so unperturbed about killing someone?"

"And I might ask why you find this so much more disturbing than when Em killed Colonel Kofi," Az replied, raising a questioning eyebrow.

Willamette had no answer.

"But to answer your question …" Az began that statement with her usual terse and confident tone, but she faltered when it came to offering the promised answer. After a long moment, she pulled a second knife from a sheath hidden under the light travelling cloak that Em had lent her. She flipped the knife casually to hold it by the blade and offered the handle to Willamette. "I do not know why it doesn't bother me. However, as per the first clause in our contract, I believe that those two are innocent, so you will have to kill them yourself."

Three women gasped in horror: Gabrielle, the old seamstress; Polly, her young apprentice; and Willamette.

"I will not kill them!" Willamette all but shrieked at Az. After several half-completed, confused gestures, she turned to the seamstress and her assistant. "And I will not allow you to be killed. Do you hear me? I will not allow either of you to be killed."

The young apprentice, perhaps fourteen, nodded frantically and gratefully, her breath quivering as she tried to keep her silent tears from growing into sobs. Gabrielle, however, just pursed her lips, a look of resigned despair in her world-weary eyes.

"The sentiment is kind, Willamette, but you know that it is foolish," Az said, sheathing the knife she had offered Willamette. Casually, she then used an expensive dress on display to wipe the blood from the other blade before sheathing it. "It is the uncertainty inherent in a rumor that was the whole point of this escapade. If the noble houses and other political players of the Commonwealth cannot be certain if you are dead or alive, it will force them to cover both the possibilities."

"I know that!" Willamette snapped. "I was the one who explained it to you."

"Which is why I should not have to explain to you that this entire effort becomes pointless if you leave behind two women who can conclusively confirm that I killed this man to protect you," Az said.

"I do not see how this changes anything," Willamette. "Few would ever believe I would deign to even land on a run-down industrial town such as Donovan, and since we took such pains to avoid being noticed on the journey to this shop, there will be no credible witnesses to confirm any claim regarding my presence in this shop or even in this town."

"Witnesses, Little Princess," Az said, pointedly. "Even though there would have been a few people who knew that Gabrielle and Polly unexpectedly worked through the night, and there would have been a few who knew they had been paid handsomely for that effort, it would have still been easy for most to dismiss any claim they might make that it was you who bought the gown. However, that man's body turns them into witnesses, and the effort that will be put into investigating the truthfulness of their story will erase the uncertainty you wished to create."

"It is a formal day dress, not a gown." Willamette frowned at Az, then looked pointedly at Gabrielle and Polly. "And I am certain these ladies will agree to tell whatever tale I ask them to tell."

Polly gave Willamette another teary and frantic nod, but Gabrielle just held her despairing frown.

"And I am certain that no matter how sincere their pledge, it will wither to nothing when they are tortured," Az said.

"Tortured?" Willamette was aghast. "Why would anyone torture them?"

"Do you truly not understand how your father used terror to rule the Commonwealth? Or how deeply ingrained those things are in every aspect of life?" Az asked, shaking her head in disbelief. "Little Princess, if Gabrielle and Polly refuse to speak, or worse, if either is caught in a lie, no effort would be spared to extract the truth. And when their hands are in the fire ... when an inquisitor takes a torch to their hands and forces them to watch their flesh burn away, there is no detail they will not share."

"Then we will take them with us," Willamette proclaimed, making certain her tone left no doubt the matter was resolved. "You two will both depart the city with us, and you will remain with us until it is safe for me to allow you to return."

Both of the women nodded. The girl looked impossibly grateful, but Willamette's statement did little to change the look on the seamstress's face.

"That is a tactically poor, but … humane choice," Az said.

Willamette acknowledged Az's near compliment with a nod and then spoke to the old seamstress, "Gabrielle, please pack a travelling work kit with whatever you will need to finish my dress and my cloak."

"And we need a dress for a child." Az stepped over to the table by the window and mimed picking through the accessories displayed upon it to cover her glances at the street below. "Something durable, easy to clean, and suitable for robust play. The girl is eight or nine, petite, roughly one hundred and thirty centimeters tall."

"Ida is barely over one hundred centimeters, and she is a robust six-year-old. She is not petite," Willamette corrected Az as she looked around the shop, considering what options might be available. It took her a moment to realize Gabrielle and Polly were just standing there.

"Move!" Willamette said, her tone leaving no doubt that she was issuing a command to the seamstress and her apprentice.

"Polly, go fetch my big workbag," Gabrielle said. "And make sure you put everything in it that I'll need for hand-stitching delicate fabrics."

"And hurry. We leave in two minutes," Willamette added.

Polly ran for the workroom and Gabrielle turned back to the dummy upon which she had just finished hanging Willamette's marked and pinned dress.

"What do you think we should do?" Willamette asked Az.

"Perhaps you might wish to put on some clothes before we depart," Az said, drolly.

Willamette was surprised to realize she was still wearing nothing but her underwear, and her head was in such a muddle that it took a pointed nod from Az before she remembered where her shopgirl dress had been hung.

"Gabrielle, is there another exit?" Az picked a random scarf from the table by the window and made a show of turning to offer it to some imaginary person in some indistinct place in the middle of the loft.

"No," the seamstress said as she folded the tacked-together dress and gathered all of the unfinished bits that went with it. "The only way out of here is down the stairs and through the shop."

"Any other windows?" Az asked. "Maybe something that looks out over a courtyard or alleyway in back?"

"No."

"You led us into a dead end?" Az snarled at Willamette. It was an unnerving contrast to the big fake smile she had plastered on her face as she made a show of selecting another scarf to show to the nonexistent person in the middle of the room. "Really, Princess? You damn well know better than to do something like that."

"No one is supposed to know I am here yet." Willamette pulled the shopgirl dress on over her head. "Honestly, I can't imagine how anyone could have possibly discovered I am even in the city, not to mention in this loft."

"Well, someone found out, and the two men watching these windows for a signal from our leaky delivery man don't seem to be all that interested in sticking to your plan," Az said. "Damn it, Princess, you should always assume a plan will fail."

"Just two men?" Abandoning her fumbling effort to button the dress, Willamette stepped gingerly over to the edge of the pool of blood, stretched as far as she dared, and just managed to get the tips of her fingers on the assassin's pistol.

"Yes, there are two men watching these windows," Az said.

Willamette's balance was so precarious that the attempt to lift the pistol pulled her over, forcing her to plant her other hand on the floor. The thick, warm, and slippery feel of the blood under her palm was too much. Her stomach rebelled, her guts heaved and what was left of her dinner was added to the still spreading pool of blood. A second heave and prickles of cold sweat followed. It took a few breaths before she dared stand, and when she did, she took extreme care to regain feet. She did not wish to imagine what it would be like if her hand slipped and she fell into that puddle.

"The two of us could fight our way past two men," Willamette said. "They would not be expecting that."

"The two of us?" Az muttered, caustically.

"Yes, the two of us." Willamette held the pistol between two fingers, shuddering in disgust at the look and feel of the blood despite her determination to remain stoic. "Unless you would prefer that I wilt like a lily."

"I'm not a real fan of flowers, wilted or otherwise, so I do appreciate your misplaced confidence," Az said. "But ..."

"Misplaced?" Willamette was offended. "I will have you know I am well trained in the use of weapons and am fully prepared to act in my own self-defense."

"What makes you think you could kill anyone?" Az made a grand, exasperated gesture at the vomit in the dead assassin's blood and then at the way Willamette was holding the bloody pistol.

Willamette conceded the point with a scowl.

"Besides, if I can see two men watching the windows, that means there are more out there. I would have at least two out of sight watching the door," Az said.

"Regardless, the two of us could overcome four men, if we surprised them." Willamette grabbed a sample of woolen fabric from a table and used it to clean the blood off the pistol and off her hands.

"At least two more men." Az emphasized "at least."

"And they'll know how to fight," Gabrielle whispered.

Willamette and Az turned to Gabrielle. Willamette was stunned. Az looked annoyed.

"The Merchant Militia. Mostly retired soldiers and there will be at least seven or eight of them patrolling the merchant quarter tonight, with that many again walking the docks," Gabrielle said.

"Well, that explains how they found us." Az pulled her knife back out of its sheath and scowled at Gabrielle, disappointed in the old woman.

Polly returned from the workroom with the workbag and slowed to a stop in the middle of the fitting room. Wide-eyed, she looked back and forth between Az and Gabrielle.

"I thought they were loyalists." Gabrielle was looking at Willamette. She wasn't pleading. She looked apologetic. "I was sure they would want to help protect you, and that they would be furious if they were denied the chance to join you."

Willamette nodded her understanding and Gabrielle nodded back thankfully before closing her eyes and lifting her chin to expose her throat to Az.

"Mercifully," Gabrielle whispered. "Please."

"Az," Willamette said, softly. "Wait."

Az stopped. To someone else, she probably would have appeared to be simply standing there, casually holding the knife by her hip, but Willamette could see the stance for what it was. Az was perfectly balanced with her feet set to drive an explosive slash across the seamstress's throat. She probably expected Willamette to demand more information from Gabrielle in return for a swift death.

"Gabrielle, I accept your confession," Willamette said. "And given the circumstances I expect that these men will murder you as well, so I doubt this will make much of a practical difference. However, in consideration of your intent, I choose to spare your life."

Gabrielle gasped and choked back a sob. After a concerted effort to reclaim her dignity, she bent a knee and bowed deeply to Willamette. "You cannot imagine what it means to die at your side instead of by your hand, Grand Lady Willamette."

"Thank you, but I would sincerely prefer that we both lived long enough for you to finish my dress," Willamette said drolly.

Gabrielle chuckled, surprised. "Indeed, my lady."

Willamette gave the scowling, incredulous Az a dismissive gesture and said, "Do not bother to tell me how much you disapprove. I know and I do not care. Now find a miraculous means to escape from this dead end. That is an order."

"I do not take your orders," Az said. "But I will see if I can manage a miracle."

"Give me that, Polly." Gabrielle took the bag from her apprentice, looked in it, and scowled ferociously at the girl. "Now help the Grand Lady Willamette with all of those ridiculous buttons on that silly dress of hers while I fill this with the things that I asked you to fetch."

"And hurry," Az said, frowning as she paced and looked around the shop, searching for inspiration. "As long as they think their man still might be alive, they'll wait, but I can't imagine that it will be too much longer before they send plan B our way."

The seamstress stepped over to a curtained closet, pushed the curtain aside, and without an instant of hesitation snatched a dress from the wide variety on the racks the curtain concealed. Showing the short-skirted dress to Willamette, a dress that reminded Willamette of girls' sporting uniforms, Gabrielle said, "What do you think? It should be the right size for Az's little girl, and it should hold up. Messenger girls tend to be a bit rough on the uniform."

"That will do nicely," Willamette said. "Thank you."

The close attendance of servants, particularly in bathing or dressing, had always been something Willamette had endured rather than enjoyed, but in that moment, it was oddly calming to leave the fiddly buttons on the shopgirl dress to Polly.

The old seamstress tossed the dress for Ida and a few pairs of the stretchy trunks that went under the skirt into her work bag and set to gathering the rest of what she would need. By the time she was done, Polly had finished with the buttons and was helping Willamette into her boots.

"How tall is this building?" Az abruptly asked the seamstress.

"Eight floors," Gabrielle said.

"Eight …" Az muttered. "Where's the toilet?"

"The toilet?" The seamstress was confused.

"Yes, the thing that you pee in," Az said, irritated and sarcastic. "You do know what a toilet is, don't you?"

"Through the work room and into the storage room," Gabrielle said. "The bathroom is on the right, past the break room and kind of around the corner."

"And the break room has a sink?" Az asked.

"Yes, it has a small kitchen, including a stove," Gabrielle said. "Most of the lofts along this street used to be apartments for the merchants who owned the ground floor shops."

"There's our miracle." Az strode for the workroom. "Let's go."

"A toilet miracle," Willamette muttered. "This I must see."

Gabrielle picked up her bag and gave her loft a long, despairing look. It was the look of a woman who knew she was walking away from a lifetime of work, investment, and toil.

"It will be here, waiting for you." Willamette pulled a heavy bronze bracelet off her wrist and put it on Gabrielle's. "And when you return, you can sell this and add anything you desire."

Gabrielle's jaw dropped as she tested the heft of the bracelet with a shake of her arm.

"But now we must go." Willamette pulled the seamstress with her as she ran into the workroom.

The workroom was larger than Willamette had expected. It had two huge cutting tables in the middle surrounded by a half dozen sewing stations. Beyond the tables and sewing stations there was an array of comfortable chairs that were probably meant for embroidery or other kinds of fine stitching, and amongst the machinery, Willamette recognized a lacemaking machine. Gabrielle was more than just a simple seamstress.

"There isn't a way out back here," Gabrielle protested.

"In here!" Az shouted from well beyond the open door to what must have been the storage room. "And hurry, damn it."

Willamette, Polly, and Gabrielle trotted into the storeroom and rounded the corner past the break room just in time to see Az, who was standing on the sink in the bathroom, jump as high as she dared with the ceiling just above her head. When she came down, she stomped on the front edge of the sink with all her might. There was no way the sink could withstand that. Hung directly on the wall, with no cabinet to support it, it tore free, leaving a gaping hole.

"Az?" Willamette muttered.

Az landed catlike on her feet, grimacing. Tossing a towel over the thin mist of water spraying from the stressed and bent pipefittings, she favored her injured leg as she crouched and peered into the hole. "It's tighter in there than I expected, but workable."

"What's workable?" Willamette asked.

"Taller buildings are usually designed with utility runs for their plumbing," Az explained, stepping aside so that the others could see that there was a significant gap behind the hole in the wall. "They're just open shafts that run up through the inside of the building, so you can install new pipes between the basement and the upper floors without having to tear out walls or otherwise disrupt the lives of the tenants in between."

"But how could you possibly know that?" Willamette asked.

Az stuck her head and then her shoulders through the hole in the wall and started feeling around for something. "They're often overlooked when people set up security systems, which makes them pretty damn handy for getting into and out of buildings that seem secure."

"Ah yes, of course," Willamette sighed. "Between you and Niven I have begun to doubt if I truly know anything worthwhile about the world."

"No need to wonder, Little Princess. You don't." With some careful maneuvering, Az worked her way farther into the cavity behind the wall, twisting and turning until she was sitting on the bottom edge of the broken wallboard.

"That was an invitation to assure me that there is value in my knowledge as well," Willamette muttered.

"Yes, Little Princess, what you know has value," Az said, utterly insincere. After some more shifting and searching about in the cavity behind the wall, she pulled one leg at a time in through the hole. A few seconds later she stuck her head back out. She was standing on something below the level of the floor. "There's a ladder to the right as you face the wall from out there. If you enter backwards and reach through to grab that with your left hand, it should be easy for you to climb through, get your feet on the ladder and climb down to the basement. From there we should be able to escape through the utility tunnels."

"Easy?" Gabrielle grumbled. "Maybe for you young girls."

"You first, old woman." Az took the work bag from the seamstress. "I'll take that down for you."

"Wait," Willamette said, her mind racing. "Gabrielle, you called those men a militia, correct?"

"They're the Merchant Militia," Gabrielle said. "They watch the warehouses, small factories, and such during the night, and they provide some extra security for the business down by the docks."

"Yes, yes, and I know that their real purpose is to keep the local police from asking for too much protection money."

Gabrielle nodded, surprised.

"My father supported many of those kinds of groups for exactly that reason. It helped ensure the loyalty of both the veterans and the merchants," Willamette explained. "That is probably why you believed they were loyalists."

Gabrielle nodded again.

"And you are sure that they are experienced soldiers?"

Another nod from Gabrielle.

"Can we save this for later?" Az asked, annoyed.

"No, we cannot." Willamette took the workbag from Az. "Az, we need to climb up, not down."

"That makes no sense at all. We'll be trapped up there," Az said. "I don't have the tools to cut through the wallboard, and there isn't enough room in here for me to kick or bash a way out."

"Az, my father did not throw money at just anyone who wanted to form a local militia," Willamette said. "He only supported militias that were under the command of well-trained, experienced, and loyal officers."

"They don't seem all that loyal to me, Little Princess."

"True, but that does not negate the rest, and what do you think well-trained officers with combat experience will do when they see the mess you have made here and find that passage down to the basement?" Willamette asked.

"They'll scramble to cover all the exits from the utility tunnels, and once they're sure we're boxed in, they'll close in to finish us off," Az said.

"So, if we go up instead of down, once they move in to finish us off, we will be behind them."

"Clever, and terribly risky, but if it works, it might very well give us a chance to walk out the front door." Az finished the thought.

"I believe it is our best chance," Willamette said.

"And I would be a fool if I did not trust the instincts of a woman who has proven to be incredibly adept at escaping from impossible situations," Az said. Then she rolled her eyes at Willamette and huffily added, "Yes, I formally acknowledge that your knowledge might, occasionally, have some value."

Willamette had no idea how she might have prompted that sarcastic snipe.

"What?" Az snapped. "Do you want it in writing?"

"No." Willamette started huffy, but immediately retook control, pausing just the slightest of moments to make the intentionality of the shift clear before she said, "I wish to apologize for that horrible look I just gave you."

Az nodded her acceptance of the apology as she said, "The three of you climb up and find a place to wait it out. I'll climb down and make it look like we ran out through the tunnels."

Rather than wait for Gabrielle and Polly to climb into the wall and up the ladder, Willamette ran back into the workroom. She closed the door to the fitting room, jammed a pair of scissors under it, and kicked them to wedge the door shut. She did the same to the door between the workroom and the storage room. She even locked the door to the toilet before she climbed into the utility run to join the others. She knew that jamming and locking the doors would not stop the militiamen, but it would enhance the impression that they were escaping through the tunnels, and it turned out that they needed the brief delay it created. Someone was pounding on the door between the workroom and the shop well before Az returned from the basement.

The climb into the utility run was nerve-wracking. She kept thinking about the dangerous drop down to the basement. Should she slip, the fall would be fatal, and the ladder Az had found was not a ladder. It was a succession of rungs that had been bolted to the framework on the inside of the wall, and even in that it was a poor example. There was a disconcerting flex in the rungs as she committed her weight to them and many were poorly secured, wiggling when she grabbed them. Worse, some of the rungs had obviously failed over the building's many long years, because there were several that did not feel the same under her hands as the others, and some of them were bolted to the wall slightly out of position.

Willamette's heart leapt when a light came on below, but a quick glance told her that the light was well below the bathroom. Az had turned on some of the basement lights before climbing to join them.

There were no ledges or anything else inside the utility shaft, so there was nothing that might offer an even remotely comfortable place to wait it out. That left them no real option other than to climb to about the sixth floor, settle in and find a comfortable way to stand on the ladder. Willamette climbed until she was a few rungs below where Gabrielle and Polly had decided to stop, and then she did her best to get comfortable.

A minute or so later, Az whispered from just below her, "One more step up, Little Princess."

Willamette moved up to the next rung and was surprised when Az gently placed a hand on her buttocks.

"Now take your right foot off the ladder and stick your ass out," Az whispered.

Willamette did not care for the idea of taking either foot off the ladder or shifting her pose like that, but she did what Az asked anyway. The hand on her buttocks gently pushed her to the left, guiding her backside past one of the big drainpipes and onto one of the crossways members in the wall framing.

"Now reach out to the opposite wall with your right foot," Az whispered as she reached out and guided Willamette's foot to a crossways member on the opposite wall. "Now you can shift back and forth between sitting as best you can, and then mostly standing on one foot, then the other. It won't be comfortable, but shifting like that will help you save your strength."

As soon as Willamette was settled into position, Az gave her backside a little shake to make sure she was secure.

"Unless you enjoy fondling me, that was unnecessary," Willamette said.

Az ignored her quip and used the framing of the walls to climb past to help Gabrielle help Polly settle in.

"Voices travel farther than you can possibly imagine, so not a word, whisper, or whimper from any of you," Az said. "And all of you need to make sure you shift your weight around so you can avoid cramps. The only way this ends quickly is if they find us, so, hopefully, we are going to be stuck in here for a very long time."

There was a banging and crashing noise below. The militiamen had made it to the bathroom door.

***

Despite having never before set foot on Donovan, Flint could have described almost every detail of the dockside mercantile exchange before stepping through the door: A small, dingy reception area with flooring that was so dirty he could feel the filth in the gritty little bit of extra slip under the soles of his boots; an out-of-date calendar featuring a scantily clad woman in a suggestive pose who was advertising a product that couldn't possibly be further removed from any rational association with a scantily clad woman in a suggestive pose; a chest-high counter with crappy candy for sale in an honor box; a loudly ticking clock; a break room off to one side behind the counter; and a sign that said Fire Safety Door, Keep Closed over a door to the warehouse that was wedged open. Even the man who shuffled out of the break room to handle the after-hours customer was predictable: scraggly beard, wild hair, grubby hands, and a potbelly that threatened the structural integrity of his stained coveralls.

"So, buddy, what are you selling me tonight?" the exchange clerk asked Niven. That irritated Flint.

"Buying, not selling," Flint said, adding a bit of snip to it to make sure it was clear who was handling things. "Assuming your prices are reasonable."

"Captain, we could delay our departure until the afternoon if we have to go into town to buy what we need," Niven said, acting as if interrupting and suggesting it to Flint made him nervous.

"Most people think our markup is worth the convenience," the clerk said, hurriedly. "Five points on yesterday's buy and sell prices from the town exchanges and warehouses."

Five percent was a lie. Whatever price sheet or invoices he would show them would exaggerate the prices that people paid for goods in the town, and the dockside exchange would be getting an insider discount on top of that. To the man's credit, acknowledging a markup was generally a sign that the clerk wasn't going to try to get away with too many liberties.

"So, what am I putting on your ship?" The clerk nodded Flint toward the calendar with the nearly naked woman. "They make some of the Hoskins fittings in town. It's always a real good price on those and they're easy to sell no matter where you're off to next."

"We're looking to buy some food," Flint said.

"Perfect. How many in your crew?" The clerk gestured at some plastic-wrapped pallets out in the warehouse. "We've got prepacked crew kits. Everybody loves 'em. Two weeks of meals and all the other essentials, plus some beer, wine, and a few surprise extras. The pallets are already packed for crews of three, four, five, or whatever you need up to twenty. It's far cheaper than buying everything separately, and the meal packages were put together by a real chef. The spices, sauces and absolutely everything else you need —right down to the ketchup—is in there."

"Yeah, we'll take two of those for a crew of six," Flint said, trying, but failing, to imagine what kind of meal a real chef might think needs ketchup. "And four tons of beans, half-kg bags, packed in boxes, on pallets."

"Four tons?" the clerk was stunned.

"Yeah, and six tons of rice, same size bags in boxes if you've got'm, but we can work with one-kg bags if that's easier. And two tons of wheat flour, also bagged, boxed, and on pallets."

"Buddy, this is an industrial town. We buy food. We don't sell it." That statement sounded ominously final.

"You'll sell anything if there's enough profit in it," Flint said.

"That's usually true, but people around here are pretty damn nervous about a war breaking out," the clerk said. "There are all kinds of rumors about military call-ups, and fighting on the streets of Lightcastle, and the whole shebang. Everyone'll notice if I sell you twelve tons of staples and that kind of attention is bad for business."

"You're just ripping us off, aren't you?" Niven said. The interjection was almost as surprising as his biting, bitter tone. "Captain, he's ripping us off."

"No, buddy, I'm trying to tell you that it would cost me a hell of a lot more than money to sell you that food," the clerk said.

"You filthy, profiteering bastard!" Niven shouted, red-faced. "People might be nervous here in Donovan, but they're already starving over on the Jax Foundry! The Leonards didn't just cut them off, they stole damn near all the food out of the warehouses when they buggered off. And everyone's so afraid of losing landing privileges at Leonard ports, or getting their cargo stolen by the bastards, that no one will even carry any food into Jax. But a few thousand men and their families dying is just a way for you to make a few more coins, isn't it?"

"Calm down!" Flint stepped between Niven and the clerk, buying a few seconds to figure out what the hell Niven thought he was doing. It was easy enough to believe that the Leonards might jump on the chance to muscle a famously independent and defiant foundry like Jax, and Niven's melodramatic outburst was pretty damn believable. Hell, despite knowing that they weren't headed to Jax, Flint almost believed him.

"Calm down?" Niven kicked it up another notch, almost shrieking. "Those men and their families are counting on us! My brother's family is counting on us, and all this bastard can think of is getting his hands on more of their money!"

"Enough, boy!" Flint shouted, playing along. For whatever reason, Niven wanted the clerk to believe that they were headed to Jax on a very personal mercy mission. "I'm the captain, so why don't you just let me handle this while you go send those messages for me?"

Niven nodded, making a show of his supposed effort to regain his composure.

"Who handles the after-hours Signal Corps business around here?" Flint asked the clerk.

"Ask for Mazzy at the White Rose Hotel," the clerk said, unsettled.

"Go on, kid," Flint said to Niven. "Find this Mazzy."

Niven gave the clerk a withering glare, turned, and stomped out.

"Sorry about that," Flint said, reassessing the situation.

Flint knew that Niven wasn't foolish enough to think that the clerk might be moved by compassion for starving souls. The man had to answer to a boss, who probably had to answer to shareholders, so why the furious melodrama? The business calculation remained the same. An industrial town depended on food shipped in from elsewhere. The potential for the budding war to disrupt that flow of food would make everyone in town nervous, and the clerk was smart enough to know that no matter what kind of profit he might be able to extract, it could never cover the potential backlash from shipping off tons of that incoming food. When people were scared, making money was not a good enough excuse.

And that was it.

Flint's estimation of Niven went up yet another notch. The whole point of his outburst was to give the clerk an excuse to sell them the food. A mission of mercy was the kind of thing that even scared people would understand, and if enough people that mattered accepted it as the reason for the sale, it would limit the backlash.

"Look, buddy, I totally understand that you've got nervous people around town, and you don't want to get offside with them," Flint said. "But Donovan also has a reputation for being decent, and I think the people around here will understand that you're just helping us deal with what's turning into a pretty desperate situation on Jax, right?"

The clerk nodded.

"Good. So, as long as you're reasonably up front about how much you're ripping us off for that food, we can probably work something out," Flint said. "Just make sure that paying you your cut is worth saving us the day or two it would take to stop at an estate or farm instead."

The clerk nodded and Flint started trying to figure out how

much it might be worth to avoid the danger and lost time from a second stop to load up on food. That calculation would have been a hell of a lot easier if he knew why the Little Princess insisted that they secure as much food as the Drunken Monkey could carry, but for some reason, that was not something she thought he needed to know.

"Oh, and I have a service truck I need to sell," Flint said. "Kills me to do it. It's a beauty. Basically new, with a compressor, and it's loaded with every tool you could imagine, but I do need to get every kilo of food that I can on my ship."

The messages that Niven was sending all looked perfectly natural. Many of them looked like the standard business correspondence a small freighter would send whenever they stopped between cuts across the Drift, and others appeared to be personal letters asking how loved ones were coping with the turmoil, or assurances that this or that fictitious crewmember was safe and would endeavor to stay safe. That appearance of normalcy, however, was deceiving. They were all coded messages of one form or another, and because Niven knew that, he could figure out the gist of most of them. A lot of what he thought he saw disturbed him.

Az's first letter was addressed to her "Dearest Sister" and spoke about finding the perfect gift for their father. It was saying she had found something she thought the woman now in charge of the murder ballerinas would want to hear about. The details included a request for her sister to telegraph a commercial credit voucher to their supposed next port of call so Az could buy the gift, so on and so forth. Az's second letter, however, was an apology to a lover, admitting betrayal and telling him the baby she was carrying was the child of his business rival. Niven was surprised that the stoic woman could write something so melodramatic, but what worried him were all the different ways he could imagine the second message might be modifying what was in the first. The easiest interpretation was it was meant to turn a meeting into an ambush or otherwise set them up for betrayal.

The messages he was sending for Willamette were even more suspicious. She had written a whole stack of messages that looked like business correspondence. There were several buy and sell orders going to what Niven guessed were fictitious commodity brokers. Those were probably coded messages to core loyalists in the security forces, or perhaps messages to reliable family allies. He'd expected that, but the number of messages was disturbing, particularly since Niven was certain there were several orders of magnitude between what she thought of as a handful of key resources, and what a normal human being might think that meant. Regardless, whatever she was up to, which she adamantly refused to explain, the stack of messages made it abundantly clear that she was not making a small move. Even more disturbing was that several of the charter purchase orders he was sending for her were going to what Niven knew were real shipping and passenger transport companies. They all used the same preferred customer code, which probably identified the orders as official Lolofi or government orders, and each of those seemingly legitimate charter purchases was paired with what looked like real and very large money transfer orders.

The only thing Niven could imagine was that she was arranging the movement of a huge number of troops, which then made him worry that she might be making a pretty obvious and clumsy play to retake control of the Commonwealth. In convincing him and the others to join her, that was exactly what she had sworn she wasn't doing. Yet if she had far more military resources available than she claimed, which easily could be true, it made a scary kind of sense. It would be a typical Lolofi kind of move to both act so blatantly that it was difficult to take seriously until it was too late, while also deceiving their closest allies until it was too late for them to back out. That made her refusal to explain why they needed to load the Drunken Monkey with tons of food even more worrisome.

Niven would like to say he didn't believe she'd lie to him and manipulate him like that, but he wasn't sure if that was true. After all, she had gone to some incredible lengths to force her parents into arranging the marriage she wanted without bothering to even let him know, and in the end just because Willamette was now legally his wife, it didn't mean he knew all that much about her.

"My wife," he chuckled, shaking his head.

"Excuse me?" the matronly telegraph agent said.

"Nothing," Niven assured her. "I just got married the other day.

Spur-of-the-moment, girl I just met, seriously crazy stupid kind of thing. Every time I think about it, I'm just kind of flabbergasted that I have a wife."

"Married, you say." The woman smiled and sighed melodramatically. "Looks like I wasted the good makeup, again."

Niven laughed.

"Will this be everything?" the woman asked.

"Newspapers," Niven said. "The captain wants to get caught up on what's happening, so I'll take whatever you've got lying around from the last week or so."

"Yeah, been a crazy week, hasn't it?" the woman said.

"And then some," Niven agreed.

CHAPTER 17

E m waited until half the cargo was loaded before she went out and unhooked the Drunken Monkey from the berth's mooring anchors. In terms of dock rules, and safety regulations, and all the rest, unhooking the ship like that was about as naughty as you could get. Only Port Officials were allowed to release the moorings, and they were only allowed to do so after a ship was cleared to take off. The Drift might only flow over a habitat at about six or seven kilometers per hour, but the air in the crew and cargo holds of a ship generated more lift than most people realized, and when those holds were empty, that seemingly gentle breeze across the docks could be more than enough to slide a ship around. That was why she had waited until the ship was half-loaded to release its moorings. Even then, it was such a stupid thing to do that it was not the sort of regulation anyone would ever imagine a pilot might break. That was why, if Flint saw her, he would assume that she was just out conducting an inspection of the ship. He would wonder what had driven her to engage in such an uncharacteristic act of routine procedure, but he would never imagine she was out releasing the moorings. Of course, Flint also would have never realized that they needed the moorings released. Despite all the qualities that made him a good captain and business partner, he wasn't much when it came to imagining worst-case scenarios and thinking ahead.

Hanging the wet deck suit in the drying closet next to the air lock, she sensed the person hiding in the shadows on the stairs up to the main deck.

"Running away?" Em asked, trying not to sound hopeful. Az's stabby little sidekick seemed like she might have once been a nice enough kid, but even if Em liked kids, which she didn't, the girl was a deranged and scary beast. The leaps from happy, to morose, to glassy-eyed demon-possessed psychopath were just too quick, too unpredictable, and too frequent.

"No," Ida said. "There are monsters attacking the ship."

"I'll give you the monsters part," Em said. "Cargomen working a nightshift are a monstrous bunch, but they're just loading cargo, not attacking the ship."

"Are you sure?" Ida took a step down the stairs, moving into the light.

"Is that a knife?" Em shouted. "Where in the hell did you get a knife?"

"From the cupboard where you locked them up," Ida said, shrugging.

"They were locked in there so you couldn't get your stabby little hands on them," Em said.

"Oh," Ida said.

"Rule, no knives," Em said. "You understand that? You are not allowed to touch a knife."

"Why?" Ida asked.

"Because we're scared of you," Em said, immediately realizing how horribly hurtful that must be for a little girl to hear. "And we're scared of you because you had a horrible, horrible real-life nightmare, and that can make you scared of things that you shouldn't be scared of."

"Like cargomen?" Ida asked.

"Yeah, and when little girls who have had a real-life nightmare get scared, it's easy for them to panic. And if you have a knife when you panic, you might accidentally hurt someone really bad. Imagine how awful it would be if you were having a bad dream and Willamette tried to comfort you, but you had a knife and you stabbed her because you thought she was a monster from your bad dream."

"Oh, okay, here." Ida leaned through the railing to hand Em the knife.

"Thank you," Em said.

Ida showed Em the pistol. "So maybe I should give you your little gun back, too?"

"First off, the little guns are Flint's. I have a rifle," Em said. "And second, how in the hell did you get your hands on that! Give me that damn pistol!"

Az had been wrong. It turned out that Willamette was capable of killing someone in a fight. The Little Princess hesitated, and she was bawling like a baby even before she pulled the trigger, but she did manage to pull the trigger. Surprisingly, she also knew how to use the weapon. Her stance was perfect, and the dart had hit her target dead center, just below his ribs, taking him down before he could fire the shot at Az. Az had to handle all the rest of the fight, and finish off the man Willamette shot, but that one shot was the only reason she had stayed alive long enough to handle all the rest of it.

Despite her efforts to ignore the pain from her injured leg, Az grunted and cringed when she crouched to scavenge the pistols from the militiamen. It had been just over a week since Em had put the dart through her thigh and that was probably the worst point in the healing process to put any strain on a wound. The muscles felt like they were regaining their strength, but that was more illusion than reality. They were still fragile, and the wound was still vulnerable to tearing.

She shoved the pistols in the pockets of the cloak she had borrowed from Em and added the extra ammunition the men carried before she grabbed Willamette's arm and pulled her into a run. "Not the time for tears, Little Princess. If they left this many people watching the shop for this long, then they're probably also ready to react to us getting past this team."

Running was unnecessary, and it would draw unnecessary attention to them, but it would help Willamette. Az needed Willamette to be thinking, engaged and in control, and vigorous activity was the best way to shake a young woman out of an emotional state. When the physical effort passed the threshold that initiated a cardiovascular surge response, the body instinctively diverted resources to meet the physical demands. That tended to shut down energy-sapping things like emotional outbursts.

Willamette yanked her arm free of Az's grasp and wiped the tears away without breaking her stride. That was good, one less thing to worry about. Polly, who was carrying the bag, also looked like she wasn't going to be a problem. She was young and seemed tolerably athletic, but Gabrielle was neither of those things. A hundred meters into what was a modest-paced run she was already several strides back and gasping for breath.

Az considered dropping back to help Gabrielle, but she charged forward instead. Gabrielle was not her concern. Willamette was her concern. Az would take every reasonable step to give the old seamstress a chance, but if she didn't make it, she didn't make it.

"Run until you're past the bend in the street. When you are fifty meters from the intersection with the café, slow to a fast walk," Az said to Willamette, waiting for the acknowledging nod before adding, "You must get to the ship. Wait for nothing."

With another nod from Willamette, Az turned, and as she did her injured leg buckled. She had mistakenly used it to plant for the pivot, and the twisting strain sent a shock of pain through her that brought tears to her eyes. Itching prickles of sweat erupted all over her body and no matter how determined she might be, the muscles in her thigh wouldn't respond. Tumbling, she rolled to a crouch, popped back to her feet, and still managed to run at a reasonable pace, but the fall was embarrassing.

Az cut through an alleyway, heading away from the docks instead of toward them. With no chance for a full recon of the town, and with little more than a vague expectation of how Willamette's escapade might unfold, Az had worked as much opportunity for observation of the operational environment as she could into their indirect route to the town's only shopping avenue. Going one street farther forward gave Az the opportunity to approach the café at the intersection of Cargo Avenue and Market Street at ninety degrees to the direction where anyone stationed there would expect to see someone making a run from the seamstress's shop to the docks. She didn't expect to reach the café unnoticed. One of the reasons to put a team at that intersection was because it offered a clear view of the all the thoroughfares to and from the docks. The unexpected angle, however, should give her some options she wouldn't have had if she approached with the others.

The route Az took to the intersection was longer, but even with the limp, she was faster than Willamette. Slowing to a trot, which she hoped would make her look like a health-conscious person out for an early morning jog, she crossed over to the far side of Cargo Avenue. There was no one watching for someone running from the dress shop. The café was open, and a handful of people were inside, eating, drinking coffee, and being served, but there was no one sitting at the tables on the sidewalk.

"Why wouldn't you set up here?" Az muttered, and then silently cursed Willamette's refusal to allow an extra day. That would have given her the time she needed for a proper recon.

There must have been something she had overlooked. Clear lines of sight down both Market Street and Cargo Avenue; open around the clock; just busy enough so no one would think anything of a few men sitting at those tables for a few hours; it was also the perfect option for rotating teams between responsibilities, keeping everyone fed and rested.

There was a moment of panic when Az wondered if she had sent Willamette running straight into the hands of a team that had finished its break at the café and was on its way to relieve the team that had been watching the shop. That fear faded almost the moment it arose. Just a few strides after the thought crossed her mind, she spotted Willamette approaching from the other direction. Willamette and Polly had slowed to a walk and they were glancing back at the still running Gabrielle, who had fallen far behind. The Little Princess had not slowed to match the old seamstress's slow, shuffling running pace. That was a small surprise.

Az continued her jog past the café and down Cargo Avenue, looking for what she was sure she must have missed, but everything she saw just confirmed her original assessment. The café was the best place to post the second team. There was nowhere else between the shop and the only entrance to the docks.

It didn't make sense and she desperately needed to figure it out, but she didn't have much time to puzzle over it. It was only a hundred meters or so from the café to the entrance to the docks. Az slowed to a walk before she'd covered half of that distance. She needed time to think. Also, walking would be less likely to catch the eye of any of the men stationed at the security office at the dock entrance.

And with that thought, she laughed. The answer was so obvious. There was nowhere between the shop and the only entrance to the docks for men to gather and loiter without drawing undo attention other than the café … and the security office at the entrance to the docks. She had been stuck in the mindset of acting clandestinely when she had considered the options available to the men hunting them, but if the Merchant Militia patrolled the docks, they'd be the ones manning that security station, and the entrance to the docks was obviously the best spot for them put the backup team.

The architecture of the docks was simple and standard for a small industrial town. Beyond the entrance was a wide street that was cleverly called Dock Street that ran from port to starboard along the leeward edge of the town dome. On the leeward, dock side of that street, there were some necessities for moving cargo and a few dozen enclosed tunnels that went out to the landing berths. Those tunnels provided access to the movable tubes, tents and passenger bridges linking the ships to the town. All the taverns, hotels, brothels, eateries, and other shops you had to have along a dock were on the town side of Dock Street, built against the wall separating the docks and the town. There was always a wall between the docks and the town, and there were always buildings built against it on both sides, and there was always a building or two like the little green hotel Az had spotted on their trip out to Gabrielle's loft.

At the intersection just before the entrance to the docks, Az turned down the cleverly named First Street. Ten paces down the road, as soon as she was out of sight of the six men she had just noted in the security office, she broke into what was as close to a sprint as she could manage.

The little green hotel had a stucco wall and, most importantly, a big, tall sign that stretched from just above the main door all of the way up to the edge of the roof. Approaching the wall at a flat angle, she didn't leap, she ran up the side of the wall, using her momentum to gain purchase with two quick steps before she turned the third into a leap at the shop's sign. That provoked another spike of pain from her leg, and she cut her hand grabbing one of the brackets supporting the sign, but she managed to hang on long enough to get a firm grip with the other. That was enough for her to pull up just enough get a toehold on the lowest of the brackets connecting the sign to the wall. From there it was a simple and quick climb to the roof. The gap between the sign and the wall was just about perfect for jamming the toe of her boot between the two, and even with her injured leg, it was almost as simple as climbing a ladder.

The hotel rooftop was a typical little garden, slightly unkempt and half wild. At the back, the wall separating Dock Street from the city was only waist-high and the rearmost part of the garden was set up so that people could sit at a table and watch the activity on the docks. That part of the garden looked well used and comfortable.

The building on the dock side of the wall was shorter. The drop from the wall was a good three meters. The door to that roof was locked, and there was no obvious way to climb down. That left Az with a two-story drop to the walkway. That would have been painful at the best of times, but with her injured leg, it was a hell of a problem. She tried to tuck and roll out of the drop, but that still put far too much force into her injured leg. There was an instant where that leg was helping absorb the momentum from the drop and then nothing. She went over far harder and far faster than she expected and instead of rolling out and through, her hip, side, and shoulder slammed into the pavement. The arm she instinctively put between her head and walkway was probably the only thing that kept her from splitting her skull open.

She was unable to get her injured leg to do much of anything after that. She tried to stand but couldn't get it to support any weight, and when she tried to run, all she managed was lurching hops. Fortunately, she probably wouldn't need to run too much farther.

Like most small towns, everything about the design of the docks was oriented on quickly and efficiently moving cargo on and off the small and medium-sized ships that would normally service a town like Donovan. That was why all the hatches, tubes, tunnels, and tents that connected to the ships were big enough to accommodate the small tractors and cargo trailers parked along the street.

Az would have preferred to use just a tractor, or at least use one with an empty trailer, but in her condition, she had no choice but to take the closest one. It was hooked to a pair of trailers, which were piled high with goods that someone had unloaded from their ship during the night. Again, something typical for a small-town dock. Given the extremely limited options for buying and selling things in town, and with a militia loyal to the local merchants patrolling the docks, it was generally safe to leave cargo sitting around like that.

The weight of the trailers was almost too much for the tractor. It crept forward, and it took at least a minute before the big wheel of the electric traction motor spun up fast enough to pull the trailers at a walking pace. It was another couple of minutes before it was moving at the rate of a moderate jog, and even though it gradually accelerated from there, it never made it to anything close to full speed. Az would have liked to have had speed at her disposal, but the momentum of such a heavy load would have to do.

She took the turn onto Cargo Avenue as wide as she could, holding on to as much of that hard-earned momentum as possible. The trailers leaned ominously but didn't tip, and once she was clear of the corner, she steered the tractor straight at the small office where the militiamen stood watch. It wasn't easy to get the tractor and trailers to settle into a nice straight run. The trailers were unbalanced, and they wanted to snake back and forth. And leaping from the tractor with only one good leg was a challenge, but Az managed. Rolling clear of the trailers, she was up on the knee of her good leg just in time to see the tractor hop the curb and smash into the office marking the entrance to the docks.

The men in that office didn't stand a chance. They had spotted Willamette, Polly, and Gabrielle, and they were all busy trying to both watch the women and look natural as they pulled weapons out of hiding places. They never noticed the tractor and its cargo-laden trailers coming from the opposite direction, and the building was so flimsy that it provided no real protection. Az doubted if any of them survived what turned out to be a surprisingly catastrophic collision.

Willamette looked horrified by the carnage, but the girl had enough good sense to break into a run when she saw what Az had done. That was fortunate, because it looked like the men at the dockside watch office had managed to call for reinforcements.

Az turned and hobbled as fast as she could, heading straight for the tractor parked at the entrance to the nearest tunnel out onto the docks. The attached trailer was empty, which was fortunate, and she had it moving just in time for Willamette to jump on.

Az considered just leaving Polly and Gabrielle behind; the men chasing them were moving fast and would soon close to effective pistol range, but she waited instead. She didn't want to, but she knew that more time would be wasted if Willamette jumped off the trailer to force Az to wait for the other two, and Willamette was exactly the type to do something stupid like that. Still, Az didn't stop completely. She kept the tractor crawling forward. When the electric traction motors used in the tractors were already spinning, even if it was very slowly, they spun up to full speed far faster than when they started from a complete standstill.

Polly, still carrying the bag, leapt aboard the trailer a few seconds later, but the gasping, wheezing old woman didn't make it.

Gabrielle threw everything she had into covering the last twenty meters that separated her from the safety of the trailer, but she was still ten meters back when the militiamen opened fire. Even with high-powered military issue pistols, the militiamen were too far away to have any decent chance of hitting a moving target, and they were firing on the run, but one of them got ridiculously lucky. The long, heavy dart hit Gabrielle just below the base of the skull, and she was thrown forward as her face exploded.

In an unsettling way, the incredible luck of that shot was fortunate for everyone. For Gabrielle it was quick and painless. For the rest of them, the lethality of the gunshot was so obvious that it left no chance for anyone to think they should try to save her. Willamette howled with rage, but Az could speed away knowing that the Little Princess would keep her dainty ass on the trailer.

"Lay down, flat!" Az shouted.

Speeding away was a relative term. At best, the tractor's top speed was still somewhere short of a decent sprint, and even with a couple hundred meters of running already under their belts, the team chasing them weren't losing much if any ground. Darts zipped past, forcing Az to crouch to use the back of the seat for cover.

She was all but certain she would have to stop and make a stand to give Willamette a chance to make it to the ship, but then shots rang out from just behind her. For an instant she assumed the worst and glanced around for the ambushers she had failed to spot as they drove past. Instead, she saw Willamette lying on the trailer, facing to the rear, and returning fire. Again, the young woman surprised Az. She was being methodical about it, picking her shots, focusing her fire on whomever was closest or seemed to be gaining on them. She was buying as much time as she could with every single one of the darts left in the pistol she'd taken from her would-be assassin.

Az tried to carry too much speed through the turn into the tunnel that led out to the Drunken Monkey's berth. The tractor managed to take the corner reasonably well, but the trailer clipped the edge of the tunnel entrance. As the trailer lurched sideways it pulled the back end of the tractor around enough to flip the tractor.

Az was thrown clear, but she had to scramble, lunge, and roll out of the way of the trailer. That sent yet another surge of pain through her injured leg. Everything from her toes to the middle of her guts felt like a throbbing, useless mess and it took her several precious seconds to fight past it.

"Run." Az pulled a pair of pistols out of her pockets as she hopped around to take cover behind the tractor. "I'll be sixty seconds behind you."

Willamette didn't argue and Polly followed her. Seconds later, the first of the militiamen rounded the corner. He went down with a single shot, as did the second. The third was running too fast to stop before he reached the tunnel, but he did manage to react to the gunfire by diving, rolling, and crawling past the entrance. The reloading mechanism on Az's scavenged pistol worked fast enough to allow her to put a dart into his leg before he rolled all of the way out of sight, but the next man stopped short of the tunnel. When he reached around the corner and fired blind, that was Az's cue to run.

Despite her useless leg, she managed to hobble reasonably quickly, but it wasn't going to be anywhere near fast enough. The tube out to the tent enclosing the back of the Drunken Monkey was the last one, and even though it was only about thirty or forty meters farther down the tunnel, it may as well have been kilometers away. She was never going to make it, so she ducked into one of the other tubes that ran out to a cargo loading tent. She would make her stand there.

She was far enough down the tunnel to force her pursuers to abandon the cover of the wrecked tractor if they wanted to get a good shot at her. She could use that. Giving them enough time to cover about half that distance, she reached back out into the tunnel and fired a couple of shots blind before she rolled out. Rolling out left her exposed, but it also allowed her to aim and fire carefully. She took out one, but there were more coming.

Three of the men were down at the entrance to the tunnel, and now another, but that was four out of how many? If it was a total of six, she had a chance, but if it was any more than that, it was hopeless. Az was furious with herself for failing to note how many of them there were. That was an unforgivable mistake and it left her with only one choice. She had to assume there were too many. She had to assume that she had no chance, and her only viable option was to do everything she could to buy the others time. That was strangely comforting. Her obligation to fight for Willamette was contracted rather than a matter of fealty or loyalty, but Az still took some solace in knowing she would be able to save the young woman.

She rolled back into the cover offered by the tube entrance out to the cargo tent. The militia men wouldn't fall for another round of her firing blind. They'd be waiting for her to roll out before taking aim to fire. She could use that. That expectation would mean they were set to react to the second movement they saw, not the first. Shifting to set her good leg so she could push off with it, she listened, waiting for the momentary pause between the shuffling steps of overlapping approaches toward her position.

She timed it about as close to perfect as she could have hoped. The lead man still had a hand off his weapon from giving the move signal and the man behind him was just rising from his covering crouch as she fired. Her first shot took out the lead man, but her second missed. It was disappointing, but it wouldn't have mattered. There were three more men around the wrecked tractor.

She hit the dock hard, jarring her shoulder. It hurt but in that moment the pain seemed distant. The world slowed as the men turned their weapons toward her. She should be able to get off a couple more shots before they took her out, and if she was lucky, she just might take another one of the bastards with her.

The distinctive crack of a rifle was strangely distant, and the significance of one of the three remaining militiamen flying backwards didn't register until she heard the second rifle shot. It was behind her. She rolled toward the shot and up to her hands and knees. Staying low, out of the rifle's line of fire, she crawled as fast as she could toward the end of the tunnel. Willamette fired a third shot, then waited as long as she dared before firing the fourth and last dart in the reloader on Em's rifle.

"Go! Go!" Willamette shouted, dropping the rifle. With the rifle hanging from its shoulder strap, she looked like something out of a comic book as she drew Flint's pistols from the belt of her shopgirl dress.

Niven ran past Willamette, pulled Az to her feet, and forced her into a run, pulling her arm over his shoulders to help hold her up. Willamette fired one pistol and then the other. She knew how to cover someone even if she wasn't quite doing it right. An experienced soldier would have stepped farther out into the tunnel to get a better angle past Niven and Az. Az pushed that thought from her mind and focused on nothing but staying in sync with Niven's stride, making sure they could move as fast as possible. Down the flexible tube, out into the cargo loading tent, they hobbled up the ramp into the Drunken Monkey. Pulling her arm off Niven's shoulder, she let herself fall and rolled until she could point her pistol back out the cargo bay door. She wasn't sure if she had any darts left, another unforgivable mistake, but she would rather look foolish pulling the trigger on an empty weapon than leave a dart unused.

"Are you in?" Em's voice shouted through the intercom. "Are you in?"

"I'm in," Willamette shouted, two steps before she reached the loading ramp.

"Everyone hold on!" Em shouted. "Flint, pop the kite!"

There was a lurch as the kite yanked the ship backwards, and there was a god-awful shuddering, grinding, scraping noise as it dragged them backwards across the dock.

"Flint, pull hard to starboard with the kite," Em said, loud, demanding but focused, commanding. "Shift the pull to hard forward as we turn around."

The cargo tent crumpled, stretched, and strained against the clamps that secured it to the back of the Drunken Monkey, but it stayed in place as the kite pulled the ship around to put the nose downdrift. When they passed the halfway point in the turn, Az could see that the landing skids were leaving deep gouges in the dock.

The cargo bay door started rising. Finally, someone had thought to close it.

The door was about half closed when the cargo loading tent finally tore free from the back of the ship, and with that, Az decided it was safe to lower her weapon and hobble over to the air lock. Even if someone thought they could leap up far enough to catch the lip of the rising door, no one would dare dash across an open dock unsuited.

"Az, even though you didn't listen the last time, you damn well better this time." Em sounded gleeful, almost wicked, over the intercom. "Strap in or die."

Em's takeoff maneuver was as audacious as it was brilliant. She didn't even try to lift off. Instead, she used the kite to drag the ship off the back edge of the dock. It was far, far faster than increasing the lift until they floated off the dock, but it was also dangerous to the point of insane.

"Pack the kite," Em shouted.

The pull vanished but their momentum carried the ship off the back of the dock. The nose of the ship dropped, slamming Az into the forward wall of the air lock, and then they plummeted.

Fortunately, that initial drop was the only violent part of the maneuver. Em pulled partway out of the dive almost as soon as it started but the shift was gentle. She was preserving as much momentum as she could.

"No, Flint, no float yet," Em said.

"Em, we're way too heavy for this," Flint said. Even over the intercom, Az could tell that he was genuinely concerned.

"I know that, and I want them to see it," Em said. "I want them to think we screwed up, overloaded the ship, and just plummeted into the Deep."

"Which is exactly what is happening," Flint shouted back. "We're at least a ton over our rated maximum and we are plummeting into the Deep."

"Quit whining," Em huffed back. "I know what I'm doing."

Az grew heavier and heavier. The ship groaned, creaked, and shuddered in protest as the floor became ever more solidly down. Em's gradual pull out of the dive continued, and by the time the air and decon cycle in the air lock had finished, it felt more like a steep downward glide than a dive.

Willamette was just on the other side of the air lock. Her arms were wrapped in the belts of the jump seat, clinging to them with a desperation that went far beyond the fear of another violent maneuver. Whatever it was that had given Willamette her edge in the fight had abandoned her.

"Little Princess," Az said, softly. "You may cry now."

Willamette nodded thankfully. For a few seconds, it looked like she was going to hold it together, but then she burst into tears. Az wasn't sure what she should do, so she guessed, and pulled Willamette into a hug. It was awkward and stiff, but Willamette seemed to appreciate it nonetheless.

CHAPTER 18

E ven in the best of circumstances, the human mind was an unfathomably complex, fragile, and bizarrely unpredictable miracle of nature. As such, it should never surprise anyone that when a mind broke, it was impossible to even guess at what might emerge from the wreckage. The murder of an innocent man who was just heading home after a shift in the utility tunnels shattered Kala's belief in who and what she was, and from there she spun out of control. The abuse that had driven her to join Kofi's Blades and the way Kofi's training had included an intense indoctrination into his twisted code of honor mixed and then exploded into an incomprehensible mess. There were strict rules that defined her quest for atonement, and even though she knew that those rules did not fit together in anything close to a logical or coherent construct, she still followed them slavishly.

"Whoa, whoa, whoa, buddy." Kala pushed the soldier's hands away from the hem of her short little sequined dress. "Soldiers pay up front."

"I might toss you a coin or two after," the soldier said, laughing menacingly. "If I think you were worth it."

He was a uniformed soldier. She didn't recognize the family colors, but the condition of that uniform suggested that he had been on Lightcastle long enough to have seen at least a few skirmishes. That probably meant he was a member of a quick-response expeditionary force, an elite soldier with plenty of experience. On one hand, that suggested he was a dangerous man, but on the other, all that experience could lead him to be careless. He would let his guard down. He had obviously been in what he thought was exactly this situation before. He would believe he could do anything he wished, and he had no reason to even imagine he should fear any consequences for his actions.

"You really want to pay me up front," Kala said.

"Listen, bitch, unless you want to get yourself hurt or killed, you'd better just give me what this dress says I can have," he snarled, menacingly.

"I am obligated to remind you that you were warned, and give you the opportunity to reconsider your choice," she said.

He sneered and slammed the palm of his hand into her crotch so hard it lifted her onto her toes and sent a throbbing ache shooting into her gut. The sudden clenching of that hand added a sharp exclamation to that pain as his fingers dug cruelly into her tender flesh, but she forgave him for that. The spasming of his hand wasn't his fault. It was his body's reaction to the knife she had thrust into his gut and her rules said that she could not blame him for the pain she suffered from the clenching hand.

She twisted the knife rather than giving it the sideways flick that would have cut his aorta. Cruelty to those who failed her test was part of the same rule that said she would do everything she could to please the men who paid a fair price up front. She spent exactly as much time torturing him as she would have spent pleasuring him. To Kala that seemed fair and righteous, as did making sure that he survived for quite some time after she cut off his manhood and added it to the others that she carried in her bag.

Commodore Umptilla watched Vice Admiral Windemere interrupt his pacing just long enough to pour yet another drink. Windemere was a drunk, that was a simple and unquestionable fact, but Umptilla was one of the few who knew. Windemere had always been the very definition of a high-functioning alcoholic. Windemere was also the type where the drunk was a far better man than his sober counterpart. Drinking took just enough of the edge off

Windemere's aggressive, competitive, and uncompromising instincts to turn the monster into a surprisingly thoughtful man.

"Well Tilly, I think that it's fair to say we've been reading these orders through the eyes of loyalists," Windemere posited.

"Me probably more so than you, Vice Admiral, but yes, I would put both of us firmly in the loyalist category," Umptilla said.

"So as loyalists, we've both been reading Willamette's orders to harass the deGruens and the Malliks as a retaliatory action against the families she thinks were part of Colonel Kofi's coup, and we've taken 'to the greatest possible effect' to mean maximizing the damage we inflict," Windemere said.

"True, but I presume you intend to add a 'but' to that assessment."

"And so I do." Windemere saluted him with the glass before continuing. "But what if we stop and reread her message purely as military commanders rather than as loyalists? What if we consider these orders in terms of nothing other than military strategy and the current tactical situation?"

"Then we might conclude that she's ordering us to implement a guerrilla campaign," Umptilla said. "And 'to the greatest possible effect' would then mean she wants us to tie up as many of their forces as we possibly can, for as long as we can."

"Which would demand a completely different approach than any of those we have considered so far," Windemere said.

"However, to interpret her orders in that way, we would have to assume that a teenage girl who's been coddled like a delicate little princess for her entire life understands how dire the current military situation is. And that she understands she can only count on a handful of ships that are inconveniently scattered across the Commonwealth. And that she understands that a guerrilla campaign is the best way to affect the current situation with that handful of scattered ships. And it assumes that she has some kind of plan she is implementing. And it assumes she has some political or diplomatic resources available that will allow her to take advantage of a guerrilla campaign."

"She was obsessed with history," Windemere said. "Absolutely and utterly obsessed. Do you remember that tantrum she threw when her father reassigned the Admiral who was serving as one of her history tutors?"

"Not the kind of thing that any of us who saw her storm into that briefing is likely to ever forget," Umptilla said. "And that makes it quite easy for me to believe that she's once again throwing a tantrum, and that these orders are just her lashing out."

"The Admiral was Sundstrum," Windemere said, pointedly.

"Sundstrum?" Umptilla muttered, disbelieving. "Suffer no fools, beat some smarts into the dumb bastards, Sundstrum?"

"I doubt if he would have beaten her, but he would have taken a dive into the Deep before he would have put up with any spoiled brat bullshit from her," Windemere said.

"And if she wanted to keep him as her tutor, it suggests they got along, which would only be possible if he could see that she was learning what he was teaching," Umptilla said, thoughtfully.

"Which gives us reason to interpret her message as orders being issued by a competent military commander; it also gives us a damn good excuse for doing what we know to be the only reasonable thing to do in this situation."

"And it gives us an excuse for fighting in a way that gives us a chance to survive," Umptilla muttered, with caustic sarcasm.

"And that sarcasm is the loyalist talking instead of the soldier," Windemere said.

Umptilla had to nod. There was no arguing with that.

"Turn it around, Tilly. What if we're reading these wrong?" Windemere asked. "If we read it wrong when we presume that Sundstrum got her up to at least marginally competent, then she doesn't get as much punishment as she wanted. Boo hoo, the angry little girl wanted us to be meaner to the bad families."

Umptilla seized upon that thought and carried it forward, "However, if we treat this as a brat throwing a tantrum, and give her what that girl would want, but the reality is that she's competent, that could have dire consequences. Especially if she was using our distraction to do something like create a window to move the troops of an ally into Lightcastle."

"Or have an ally hit them from behind, or if she was trying to stir a revolt from the second- or third-tier families against a disloyal major family, or whatever," Windemere said.

"Now that is a logic that I … that we have to respect," Umptilla said.

Niven had sat through hundreds of night watches. Taking that despised shift was one of the easiest things a captain could do to keep his crew happy. Also, one of the first things he had learned, as a teenage shipowner and captain, was that just keeping his men happy paid handsomely. It was hard to nail down exactly how it paid off, but when the books were settled at the end of every month, his operating costs were always well below the standard budgets. Night watch on the Drunken Monkey, however, was nothing at all like the ones he knew. There was no need to check externally secured cargo or ballast, no need to monitor the sonar just in case they stumbled across a whale, and no need to make sure everything was ready for the scramble to chase one of those stumbled-upon whales.

That was why a night watch wasn't something you normally bothered with on a little freight hauler like the Drunken Monkey. Usually, Em or Flint would just take the ship well above or well below the middle of the Drift, set a course chasing some clear sky, and turn in for the night. At most, they might adjust their schedules slightly so that one of them stayed up late and the other got up early to limit how long the helm was left unmanned. However, with the rush toward war, and since it would be light outside during their flight from Donovan to Lightcastle, they had decided that they needed a night watch.

As a captain in his own right, Niven was the logical person to take that watch, but the question of why Willamette had decided to stay up well beyond the witching hour was more of a mystery. It wasn't as if they lacked for private time together. Everyone except for Ida had been incredibly indulgent in that regard. And it wasn't as if she was staying up to keep him company, or even that she wanted to share some time outside of bed with her new husband. In fact, she seemed to be going out of her way to find reasons to avoid him. She gave him a smile when she saw him climbing up from the helm, but it was tired rather than warm, and it seemed disturbingly obligatory.

When it came to Willamette, Niven was certain of two, and only two, things. The first was that no matter the circumstance, she had an incredible ability to project an aura of nobility. The gown that she had woken Polly up to work on was inside out, pinned, and marked; yet on her, it was somehow elevated into elegance. The second thing that Niven was certain of was that Willamette was at least a decade away from leaving behind the look of a little girl. Big eyes, little nose, pointy little chin, and cursed by an impish hint of a smile that forever tugged at the corners of her mouth, everything about her face was so inherently youthful that no matter what she wore or what she did, there would always be a hint of a child in her expression. Even when she scowled, she looked like a little girl.

"Polly, dear," Willamette said, sweetly. "Could I trouble you to stick the pins in the dress, rather than the princess?"

"Yes ma'am. Sorry ma'am," the exhausted girl said.

"Ah ha, are we admitting to being a princess?" Niven teased as he poured a cup of coffee and leaned against the counter. The coffee was surprisingly good for being part of a prepacked crew supply kit, and it held up pretty well to sitting for hours in a warm pot.

"If I am to succeed, I will have to embrace it, temporarily at least," she said.

"Are you sure about this plan of yours?" Niven asked.

"No, I am not sure of anything other than being sick to death of running away from people who wish to murder me," Willamette said.

"You should probably be careful what you wish for," Niven said. "What little I know of your plan involves a great deal of running toward people who wish to murder you, which doesn't sound better to me."

Willamette chuckled softly, careful not to move too much while Polly worked with the pins.

Niven changed his tone and tersely added, "Of course, since you won't tell any of us the whole plan, I have no way of knowing for sure what we're in for."

"Polly, I think we should probably call it a night," Willamette said.

"Yes ma'am." Polly kept working.

"Polly," Willamette said. "We are done working on the dress for the night."

"Oh, that's what you meant." Polly stood, hesitated, and gave an uncertain bow to Willamette. "Sorry ma'am."

Polly started to help Willamette remove the dress, but once again hesitated. She glanced at Niven and then froze, uncertain.

"Polly, just go back to bed." Willamette gave Niven a flirty grin. "I am sure my husband would be more than happy to help me remove my dress."

"Yes ma'am," Polly said, but still didn't move.

Willamette waited a few more seconds and then said, "Polly! To bed! Shoo!"

Polly finally scurried out of the lounge and down the hall to the little cabin she shared with Ida.

"You do wish to remove my dress, do you not?" she asked Niven, trying to tease him.

"Yes, of course, but neither that, nor the arduous task of extracting you from that ridiculous underwear is going to distract me from the fact that you are keeping me in the dark." Niven unpinned the seam of the dress, opening the back as if there had been a zipper there. "Everyone is worried by how much you're hiding from us, but if they knew some of the extra bits that I know, I suspect they would abandon you and this insane plan altogether."

"And what extra bits do you believe you know?" Willamette asked.

"I don't think any of the others would be surprised that you had me send some secret, coded messages to military units and a few other security forces. However, I suspect that the number of those messages you had me send would shock everyone on this ship, and they would be horrified if I told them that you also spent a fortune hiring a fleet of civilian transport ships." Niven held the gown by the shoulders, pulling the top open as he lowered the dress off her shoulders. He tried to avoid disturbing any of Polly's pins, but a few still came undone. "The only way those two things make sense is if you are bringing in an army to seize control of the city, and the Commonwealth."

"And such is the danger of choosing a clever husband," Willamette said, sighing as she stepped out of the dress and nodded him toward the makeshift seamstress's dummy Flint had cobbled together for Polly.

"Willamette, if the others knew what I knew, they'd turn on you in an instant, and even if that doesn't happen, their commitment to this plan of yours is far more precarious than you probably realize. Everyone is setting up options for bailing out."

"Wise," she said. "Never enter a war or a dinner party without an exit strategy."

"And I'm … insulted is the wrong word," he said, surprised he had no idea what the right word might be. "I honestly don't know how to explain how it feels to know you are deceiving me."

"You must feel betrayed," she whispered, hugging him from behind as he secured her dress to the dummy. "You have given up everything, risked your life to save mine, and not once have you asked for anything in return. You have been a paragon of nobility and now you fear that you have been taken for a fool."

"Willamette, it would be different if you just trusted me."

"I do trust you," she said. "I trust the people on this ship more than I ever thought I could trust anyone, and I trust you immeasurably more than any of the others. However, that is the reason I cannot explain any more than I have."

He tried to step away, but she held him tight.

"Niven, there is no plan, at least not in the sense any of you would call it a plan. There is so much uncertainty, so many unknowns, so many possibilities, and so many permutations that I will not even be able to guess what is possible until I learn how things are situated in the city. My so-called plan is just me building as many options as I can into a foundation for improvisation, and that is where my trust in you, and my trust in the others, is critical. Since I cannot possibly know what might happen, I have to trust that all of you will react honestly."

He tried to step away again, but again, she refused to let him.

"And yes, I am deceiving you and the others," she whispered, haunted. "I must because no matter how this evolves, my position is indescribably weak. Maximizing deception and misdirection will be the only way I will have any chance whatsoever, so I cannot allow any of you to know more than you do."

"Why not?"

"If any of you had any idea what my two highest priorities were or how I might pursue them, your actions, or reactions, or lack of reaction, might accidentally put others on guard and I simply cannot let it happen. I must catch everyone, absolutely everyone including you, by surprise or I may not be able to pull any of it off."

She relaxed her grip and it felt like she was stepping away from him, but before she could, he turned around and wrapped his arms around her, pulling her back in.

"That is a rubbish answer, and I don't buy it at all, but I still think you need to say at least that much to everyone," he whispered. "Even Ida and Polly."

"If you truly believe that, then I will," she whispered back, squeezing him with all her might.

She held him like she might never release him from her embrace, but he knew exactly how to fix that. It took a while, but, eventually, he felt her cock her head and she relaxed her grip slightly. "Niven, are you unlacing my corset?"

"I ain't stopping with the corset, Little Princess," he growled, playfully.

***

The Knightly family always made it too easy to believe they took the knight in their name too seriously. It wasn't just the black knight on their family crest, or that they bred and rode horses, or that they occasionally even fought from horseback. They also had an unfortunate tendency to live up to the claim that they could be counted on to charge first and plan retroactively.

As a result, it surprised no one, least of all their field commanders, that they were the first to commit a significant number of front-line troops to Lightcastle. It was also no surprise that the commanders of those troops had no idea why they were there or what the family hoped to accomplish beyond putting the first boots on the streets. They had nowhere near enough troops to take and hold the city for the Knightlys, but that wasn't an issue because they also didn't know if the Knightlys would want the city if they stumbled across an opportunity to take it. They didn't even know if they were there to keep the Commonwealth intact or help tear it apart. Their commanders knew only two things for certain. The first was doing nothing was not an option, and the second was no matter what they did, the family patriarchs would end up wanting them to have done something else.

"What's your guess this time?" Actus asked. Technically Actus Knightly was in charge, but unlike the family members sitting around the table at the Knightly capital city of Hearthstone, Actus knew when and how to defer and delegate.

Hamish shrugged.

"It'd be smart to take something that seems important and racks up a big body count," Actus said, before adding, "Their bodies, not ours."

That got a chuckle out of Hamish.

"Of course, there's no telling who the right body donors might be," Actus mused.

"And this ain't just a raid on some estate or town," Hamish said. "This is Lightcastle. One way or another, someone's going to decide to throw everything at taking it. When they do, I wouldn't want to be holding on to something they think they gotta have."

"So, we don't want to try to hold the docks," Actus said.

"Docks'd be the worst," Hamish said. "Twenty-four kilometers long, outside, and open to attack from ships, with none of our ships here to give us cover ... we may as well just march the boys off the edge and get it over with."

"But we want to hold something which is worth something at the negotiating table once it's obvious who's going to win," Actus said.

"How 'bout we go below decks and take some important part of the central utilities?" Hamish suggested. "Below decks is easy to defend, so we could hold whatever we took pretty easy."

"Easy to defend means hard to take," Actus said.

"Only if someone's defending what we try to take." Hamish shrugged. "Can't imagine anyone is, but if I'm wrong, we can jump to something else down there, or just say 'screw it' and try something different."

"Below decks would also just be a good place to be," Actus added, nodding his approval of Hamish's thinking.

"Oh, hell yeah," Hamish said. "From below decks we use the utility tunnels to pop to the streets pretty much wherever we wanted and kill whoever looks like they need killing, and when the fight'n's over, we could have control of something like the gasworks."

"Which no one would need to take in order to take the city, but would desperately want once they were in control," Actus said.

"And since it's so easy to defend, they'd probably be happy to give us some decent loot to get us to walk away," Hamish said.

"More likely the idiots around the table back home will trade it for some magic beans, but still … it's a plan that doesn't get us all slaughtered, and the men are fond of not getting killed too much," Actus said.

"That they are," Hamish agreed.

CHAPTER 19

Belatedly, Dodi realized they probably should have worn civilian clothes out to the dock. The cargomen were unnerved by the bright blue uniforms the women were wearing under their long cloaks.

"Relax gentlemen," Dodi said. "It's flattering that you're so terrified, but right now we're just another customer, and all we want from you is a standard service for a small cargo hauler: landing assist, tenting, decon and, if needed, unload."

The foreman nodded nervously, and he and his men just stood there, fidgeting.

"So maybe you should get over there, and you know, prep or something?" Dodi said, pointedly.

The men hurried over to the air lock and once outside, started preparing the tent and tunnel.

"Perhaps she has been delayed," Lisa said.

"Perhaps," Dodi said. "But I think it more likely she waited until darkness fell to approach the city. That's what I would have done."

"Assuming she knows we arranged for her to land here," Lisa said.

"The status light for the berth is flashing the code 'Az land here,'" Dodi said. "I think she's smart enough to figure that out."

"If she knows to look for something like that coming from a commercial berth," Lisa said.

"The small commercial berths are the first places she'd look," Dodi said.

One of the first lessons of war that Az had offered Dodi was that there was an astounding amount of normality to be found in a warzone. The specific locations that the soldiers decided to fight over needed to be avoided, as did the soldiers themselves, but for the most part, life went on. Supply chain disruptions were a nightmare. Any ship that could avoid flying into a warzone, would, and that led to all kinds of shortages in the city, particularly when it came to food, but life went on. Air, water, sewer, and other essential city services continued. Telegraphs and letters were delivered, newspapers were written and sold, garbage was cleared, banks banked, police policed, gardeners gardened, cleaners cleaned, and the whores whored. It wasn't exactly life as usual, but it was far closer to normality than most would expect. Since Az had been the one who first explained that to Dodi, Dodi knew that doing something normal, like renting a commercial cargo berth and flashing a blatant signal for Az to see, was exactly what Az would expect. Conveniently, it had also been the best way to conceal what they were doing from the other military forces in the city. While the flow of ships had dropped to almost nothing, the cargo that was arriving was coming in on small independent carriers who were looking to make good money off the risk of flying in past the patrolling warships. They landed at berths exactly like the one she'd secured, and she'd done what she could to make sure that everything about renting this berth had looked like it was just another ship tiptoeing in to make a quick coin.

Ten minutes later, Dodi's faith was rewarded. An old junk runner showing no lights, not even instrument lights on the bridge, flew up from just below the level of the dock, rising like a ghost out of the Deep. It was all but invisible in the darkness and whoever was flying it was good. Despite the turbulence that always rolled off leeward docks, the ship stayed absolutely steady while the winch operator flew the kite back to catch the hook on the front of their landing skid. Once that was done, the pilot then lifted, backed away, and stowed the plow before signaling that they were ready to be towed in. Not only was it all remarkably precise, Dodi doubted if anyone more than a hundred meters in either direction down the docks could possibly have seen any part of the landing.

The cargomen made quick work of tenting and decontaminating the back of the ship, and in a few minutes Dodi and Lisa were greeting their mentor as she limped down the still descending cargo ramp. Az didn't bother to introduce the woman in the gown and fancy hairdo; she didn't have to.

"Well, I guess that explains how you survived." Dodi drew her pistol, but Az stepped into the line of fire. The others with Willamette, a familiar-looking young man, Em, Flint, and the girl they had been calling Kofi's Little Knife, quickly moved to do the same.

"Dodi, I will understand if you choose to walk away, but I cannot allow you to kill her," Az said.

"How could you?" Dodi shifted the pistol to aim at Az's face.

"For whatever brief moment I might survive after you pulled the trigger, I would understand that choice as well," Az said. "However, I would also hope you would respect the simple fact that I was convinced not only to let her live, but also to protect her and to arrange the opportunity for her to meet you and argue that the Blades should support her effort to quash this war before it begins."

"Our entire purpose was to cleanse the Drift of the disease that is the Lolofi family," Dodi hissed. "No matter what Colonel Kofi tried to make of us, or what he believed we were, you and I both know that every woman who has ever joined us was committed to the truth that every path to a better future started with the elimination of the Lolofis."

"She has sworn to respect that," Az said.

"And you would believe the word of a Lolofi?" Dodi sneered.

"No, I have no reason to trust a Lolofi's word on anything," Az said. "But Willamette has convinced me that she will respect our mission to eliminate the Lolofi name from the Drift. I also believe her when she says that her greatest desire is to save as many lives as she can by preventing this fighting from becoming an all-out war."

Dodi shook her head, disbelieving.

"Dodi, how many innocent people will never see any future at all if this chaos we have unleashed spirals into an all-out war over control of the Commonwealth?" Az asked. "How many will suffer fates so horrific that death would have been kinder? My faith in Willamette's intent may be misplaced, but right now, with the way this has unfolded, she is the only one offering us a chance to make a positive difference for the people we always meant to help."

"And if you are wrong about her?" Dodi asked.

"Then I will kill her," Az said. "Slowly and unpleasantly if possible."

"Agreed." Dodi nodded and holstered her pistol.

"I did not agree to that," Willamette muttered.

"Yes, you did," Az said. "It's in our contract, the second clause under contract termination."

"'Death of either party' does not mean you can end our contract by murdering me," Willamette said.

"Yes, it does," Az said.

"It is probably a moot point anyway." Willamette took a nervous moment before stepping out of her pack of protectors to face Dodi directly. "Being murdered by the woman I hired to protect me is probably the least of the dangers I face."

"Probably," Dodi agreed. "So, what is your plan, Your Highness?"

"She prefers to be called Little Princess," the young man who was standing possessively and protectively near Willamette quipped, getting a scowl and a glare from Willamette.

"Little Princess," Dodi said, smirking. "Your plan?"

"It depends on how many men we have available," Willamette said.

Dodi cast a critical glance at the men hovering protectively just behind Willamette, looking first at the young wiry one and then the heavy, old, disheveled captain of the Drunken Monkey. "Looks like one and a half."

"Or two and a half," Willamette gave Dodi a smirk as she nodded first at Flint and then the young wiry one. "If you measure by weight."

"That was unkind, Little Princess," Flint muttered.

"I don't know what you're complaining about," the young one said. "I'm the one she just described as half a man."

"That's what I meant was unkind," Flint said. "Everyone knows I'm four times the man you are, but to have your own wife come right out and say it …"

"Wife?" Dodi said, disbelieving.

"Yes," Az said. "Let me introduce you to Mrs. Willamette Persephone Lister."

Dodi considered that for a few seconds. "So, you erased the Lolofi name from the Drift ... with a technicality."

"Yes," Az said. "But as I said, Mrs. Lister swore to respect the spirit of my mission."

"Even if it was a technicality, it is reassuring to know you did not betray your oath entirely," Dodi said, then nodding to Willamette she asked, "What do you propose?"

"Let us start by unloading the food and transporting it to a secure location," Willamette said.

"Food?" Dodi was surprised.

"Yes, I presumed that after twelve days, whatever provisions you may have brought with you would be exhausted," Willamette said. "I also presumed it might create opportunities to resolve a few minor problems without fighting, so we brought some food."

"Twelve tons is more than some," Flint muttered. "Damn near sank my ship."

"Twelve tons," Dodi muttered, and nodded respectfully to Willamette, before nodding the responsibility for unloading the food over to Lisa. "Lisa, even though the cargomen are being well paid for unloading and cargo transport, I think it would be wise to give each of them enough food to feed a family for a few weeks."

"Fear buys obedience, but kindness buys loyalty and a desire to serve," Willamette quoted.

"One way to put it," Dodi said. "Though it is ... odd to hear those words from the mouth of a Lolofi."

"What is the situation on the streets?" Willamette asked.

"The tactical situation is ... confused," Dodi said. "It is only in the last few days that combatants have begun arriving in significant numbers, but there are now two of the Big 12 families, and three lesser families, who have deployed what I would call small armies to the city."

"Five?" Willamette sounded disappointed.

"Yes, the Auks, Morgans, Hitos, deGruens, and Knightlys have each landed at least two full transports of men."

"Have they taken any of the hardened Lolofi assets?" Willamette asked.

"No," Dodi said. "We destroyed the Marine barracks and the

Special Services Division in the initial attack, but the Signal Corps Headquarters, Central Bank, Government House, City Estate, and the rest of the high-security locations remain in the hands of Lolofi loyalists, and the armies on the streets have shown no inclination to even try taking any of them."

Willamette didn't react to any of that, but in refusing to react she all but screamed her disappointment.

"Then it hasn't become a war yet?" the husband asked, hopeful.

"No, it's more of a wary stalemate at the moment," Dodi said.

"Well, that's a bit of good news." The husband smiled, nodding, upbeat. "It's a lot easier to avoid something than it is to stop it once it's started."

"None of that is, by any stretch of the imagination, good news," Willamette corrected him.

He looked confused but Willamette showed no inclination to explain. She was just standing there, frowning slightly.

"Not only does the lack of fighting mean that there will be few options for playing them off against one another, it also means that they remain at or near full strength," Dodi stepped in to explain. "Further, this is nearly the worst possible combination of families for anything a Lolofi might wish to do. The Auks and Morgans have long been openly hostile to Lolofi rule. The Hitos and deGruens are basically just pirates who are always raiding the shipping of Lolofi allies. And the Knightlys ... well ... they're the Knightlys."

"So, anything involving diplomacy, subtlety, or finesse is off the table," the husband said.

"Worse, just the confirmation that she lives will probably be more than enough to convince the four sane families to join forces," Dodi said.

"What then?" the husband asked.

"We go straight at it," Willamette said, letting her displeasure with that option show. "It would have been far better if we could have taken a few days to play with some legal niceties, pull on some financial levers, and lay some political foundations. I would have also preferred to push some of the other families to take sides before I acted. However, resorting to a brute force approach and going straight to the trump cards was always a salient possibility."

"Brute force?" The husband looked around at the others that had arrived with Az. "I don't think any of us like the sound of that."

"Dodi, use that food now, and use it all." Willamette's tone sounded unpleasantly like an order. "There is no need to hold it, or anything else, in reserve."

"And that's not easing anyone's worries," the husband muttered.

Willamette gave her husband a look. Matronly, exasperated, but still prim and proper. It was impressive, and it shut him up.

Willamette turned back to Dodi. "What tactical assets do we have available?"

"We have a significant number of irregulars who are quite adept at spreading chaos and confusion. For anything other than that, they are pathetically ineffective," Dodi said. "In terms of reliable, trained troops, we have about eight hundred fully fit Blades, an additional three hundred who are wounded but still able to fight, and another two hundred who are too wounded to fight but are able to perform support tasks."

"Less than half," Willamette said. "I was hoping for more than that."

"We need more than that," Dodi said. "Even before troops began arriving in significant numbers, it was clear that we didn't have anything close to what we needed to effectively control the city. We fell back from most of the objectives we had secured on Regatta Day, and have concentrated on holding the central switchboard and the yacht club."

"The yacht club?"

"It's one of the more easily defended locations in the city, we already controlled it, and it provides ample space for storing the resources we secured during the first few days," Dodi said.

"By resources you mean the loot you confiscated from the irregulars before you shot them for stealing," Willamette said.

"That does make up a large portion of those resources, yes," Dodi admitted.

"Retaining control of the central switchboard was smart," Willamette said.

"It is a tremendous source of intelligence." Dodi sneered to make it clear she was unimpressed by Willamette's compliment.

"It also means we can use the city's civil defense communication system without taking the City Estate," Willamette said.

"If that's critical to your plan, you're lucky, because even with the Lolofi Homeguard still holding the City Estate, the deGruens have it effectively besieged, so it would be impossible to even get you close to it," Dodi said.

"The civil defense alert system is not critical, but it will be useful," Willamette said. "The only critical elements are securing the gasworks and—"

"Impossible," Dodi cut her off, tersely. "The Knightlys captured and hold the gasworks."

Willamette went pale. She quickly slipped back behind the mask of her expressionless refusal to show a reaction, but there was no way she could hide the way the rich tans and creamy olive colors in her complexion vanished from her face.

"Even if we had enough troops to confront the Knightlys, it would be foolish to try to take the gasworks from them," Dodi said. "The tunnels and passages down there may not have been intentionally designed to be easy to defend, but they're still pretty close to perfect for the task."

"Why would they take the gasworks?" Willamette asked, pleading, horrified, and bewildered.

"They're Knightlys." Dodi shrugged. "Do you expect them to have a reason?"

Willamette shook her head slightly and swallowed hard. Once more she tried to jump back behind her expressionless mask, but this time she failed. Her eyes looked haunted, and her hands were trembling.

"I take it the Knightlys have accidentally trumped your trump card?" Dodi asked.

"Yes … No, there are important things I still can do, and that …" Her whisper trailed off to nothing and it was several seconds before she finished the thought. "That I must do."

"Are you sure?" Dodi asked. "Because, if we added your ship to the ones we have on the docks, we could all just bugger off; regroup, rearm, recruit."

"No," she said, tears in the corners of her eyes. "That suggestion is more tempting than you can possibly imagine, but I cannot. We stand at a tipping point, a moment and circumstance where every act or omission will have an outsized effect. The situation could easily remain balanced on a knife's edge for days, or even weeks. However, it would certainly tumble into an all-out war before we could possibly return. So no matter how deeply I dread what I must do, if I were to forgo this chance, I could not live with myself."

The words may have been eloquent to the point of poetic, and the logic impeccable, but Willamette was utterly unconvincing. She was neither resolved nor determined, she was terrified and all but lost in despair, but somehow, she found the strength to push on.

"I won't lie to you," she said. "Without the gasworks, this is truly a worst-case scenario. Not only do I loathe the very thought of what I must do, I will only be able to remove one of the two most dangerous pieces I had hoped to take off the board. That slashes the odds of avoiding a war drastically, but I must try, nonetheless. I honestly could not live with myself if I did not. I will, however, understand if you and the women who fight with you choose to depart."

Dodi believed that. Willamette wanted so badly to just cut and run that she truly would understand if they buggered off, and that was what convinced Dodi that they needed to stay. "Well, I guess we're just going have to do the best we can with that worst-case scenario then, aren't we."

Willamette smiled and nodded slightly. She was thankful, but all Dodi could see was the dread in her eyes. Worse, that dread felt contagious. That was a problem.

"Unless maybe somebody's got a magical fairy key that opens one of those secret passages that will take us anywhere we want," Dodi quipped, sarcastically, glancing around at the other Blades and gesturing questioningly. "Magic fairy key? Did any of you murderous bitches remember to pack a magic fairy key?"

The Blades chuckled. That was better. They were unsettled, but it was better. Laughing at despair was always the first and best step toward defeating it.

"Son of a bitch!"

Dodi turned around, unable to believe that those words had just come out of Willamette's mouth, but they had.

Shaking her head as if she was trying to shake the stunned look from her face, Willamette looked at Dodi. It seemed as if she was silently pleading for help, and then she blinked, and the laughter started. Well, at first Dodi thought Willamette might be choking on her own tongue, but it turned out to be a gasping, choking snort of a laugh. After a second it became a rolling cackling laugh that was the dead ringer for the evil witch in a theatre production for children. It grew into a belly laugh, and then the tears started. It kept going and going and it must have hurt because she was grabbing her sides, and doubling over, and then she went silent. She was laughing so hard she couldn't breathe.

Everyone was looking around at each other, unsure, worried, but before anyone could decide on what to do, Willamette gasped, sucking in a big lungful of air. By the third gasp the overwhelming wave of laughter broke, and she was back to cackling. After two more gasps, she was chuckling through teary eyes, and finally she managed to speak.

"I brought a magic fairy with me." She gestured at Flint and Em.

"Hate to break it to you, Little Princess, but Flint's not the magical kind of fairy," Em said.

Willamette ignored Em, grinning at Dodi. "And she is indeed the key to a secret passage that will enable your Blades to take the gasworks."

Dodi looked to Az and got the slight frown and raised eyebrow that was her version of a shrug. Az didn't know what Willamette was talking about either. The slight nod that followed said Az thought they should trust Willamette, so Dodi nodded her agreement to Willamette before asking, "Are you sure? With the numbers it takes to hold the yacht club and the central switchboard, we can't commit many Blades to the effort."

"You will not need to continue holding the yacht club, so that should free up all the women you will need," Willamette said. "The other necessary objective will be reasonably easy to secure. We should almost be able to walk in, but I'm going to need to get Az and some of your Blades dressed in something other than those hideous blue outfits. I need the women who accompany me to look like they are a security detail I might have brought with me."

While Az had completely lost any desire to fight, and she knew that her injured leg would have made her a liability, she was uncomfortable hanging back amongst those who needed to be protected. It did, however, give her the chance to watch Willamette. The utility tunnels distorted the sounds of battle. The foam that provided the foundation of the city seemed to dampen the sharpness and impact of the reports from the rifles and pistols, but the shape of the tunnels seemed to then amplify the human noises. The Little Princess cringed noticeably with every shriek, scream, and wail of the wounded, and by the time the brief battle ended, she looked sick. If there was anything that would have steadied Az's wavering commitment to the girl's plan, that was it. No matter what her true intentions might be, they were underpinned by a genuine and unshakable empathy.

"Clear!" came the shout from well down the tunnel.

Willamette started forward but Az grabbed her arm and stopped her.

"Steady yourself, Little Princess," Az said. "Take the time you need to prepare for your performance."

Commander Evan Lisp knew that it was an extreme of hyperbole to say that the Signal Corps Headquarters smelled of death, though it did stink something wretched, and there was an overwhelming sense of despair that permeated the compound like a stench. Every single man under his command knew that even though it was nearly impossible for anyone to fight their way into the Commonwealth's central communication bunker, in the long run, that wasn't going to make much difference. They had the supplies they needed to hold out for another month, perhaps longer, but that was just delaying the inevitable. None of them were going to get out of there alive. The same prerequisite of unflinching loyalty that had gained each of those men a place under Lisp's command, also doomed him. No matter who won control of Lightcastle, it would be stupid for the victors to leave this facility in the hands of Morden Lolofi's most loyal men. Lisp tried to convince himself otherwise. He tried to believe that if they could just establish their neutrality in keeping the information flowing, then whoever won control of the Commonwealth might accept them, but that was ridiculous. Just like the Lolofis, the family who won would install loyalists in such a critical element of governing infrastructure.

"Commander, Lady Willamette ..."

"Don't!" Lisp barked. "I wish for a miracle as much as any of you, perhaps more so, but there is nothing good to be found in chasing the rumors of Lady Willamette in the messages we process. If she somehow survived, she is surely …"

"She just stepped through the outer door," the junior signal officer said.

"What?" Lisp had trouble wrapping his head around the idea that she could possibly be at the door.

"She had a valid emergency code. It opened the outer door, and it looks like her," the junior officer said. "I looked through the viewer myself, sir. I've seen her in person before and I swear that it is her. She is demanding to be let in, but you ordered a complete lockdown and …"

"Let her in!" Lisp heard the eager and hopeful tone, and he immediately tried to walk it back a step. "But carefully. Follow all the security procedures. Allow her through one section of the hall at a time, never allow two of the security doors to be open at the same time, and all the rest."

"Yes, sir." The junior officer raced off.

Ten minutes later, accompanied by a young man and backed by a small, inconspicuously dressed entourage of a dozen security personnel, all women, Willamette Lolofi entered the fortified bunker's foyer.

The watch officer, Major Kirkpatrick, stepped up to Willamette with striking assertiveness, and just as Lisp was about to scold him for demonstrating such familiarity, Kirkpatrick drew his pistol and pressed it against the side of her head.

"Major!" Lisp shouted. "What in the hell do you think you're doing?"

"I believe he is following protocol, Commander," Willamette said, coolly, as she gestured to her security team to relax. The quiet, calm authority in her otherwise girlish voice was both soothing and in an odd way, terrifying. "You did declare this coup attempt to be an existential threat to the Commonwealth, did you not?"

Lisp nodded.

"Good," Willamette said. "I am lavender."

"What?" Lisp's head was spinning.

"My identification verification package is lavender," she said, waiting a few seconds before adding. "Lavender is a pastel purple."

"Yes, of course, my apologies," Lisp said.

Lisp's security key hung on a cord around his neck. He handed it to a junior signal officer and in combination with Kirkpatrick's key, they were able to open the code safe. Lisp retrieved the lavender envelope from the dozens of color-coded envelopes and opened it. Inside he found an unmarked card with five tiny fingerprints on it.

"My father picked lavender for me to help me remember that it was my left hand," she said, holding out her left hand.

Kirkpatrick's pistol never left Willamette's temple as her prints were taken and compared to the prints that had been taken when she was a very small child.

"Thumb ... match."

"Forefinger ... match."

It was only after five different officers verified five different prints, confirming beyond any possible doubt the young woman standing before them was indeed Willamette Lolofi that Kirkpatrick holstered his pistol. He gave Willamette a slight but sincere bow and stepped back to a proper distance to await her command.

"As a member of the designated line of succession, I hereby take command of this critical Commonwealth asset, and by doing so, I take command of all the resources and offices of the Commonwealth," Willamette said. "I confirm that I will immediately surrender my command should a more senior member of the designated line of succession be found alive and capable of taking command."

"Your identity has been verified. Your claim and pledge have been witnessed," Lisp said. "This facility, and the Commonwealth is yours, Grand Lady Willamette."

Willamette strode regally past Lisp, through the reception area, and into the command-and-control center. She cast a critical eye around the big, theatre-shaped control room, noting and considering several things before she spoke to Lisp. "I do understand that these have been trying times, but I must insist you clean this up, and I will need you to rearrange a few things so I may use this facility as my command center."

"Yes ma'am," Lisp said.

"I will also need some urgent records searches of recent telegraphs sent from the city, and I will require the services of all of the officers who are certified to record and transmit orders of law across the realm."

"Yes ma'am," Lisp said. "I will have every man we have ready to execute your commands within thirty minutes."

Em wasn't sure what you were supposed to call something one step beyond impossible but finding a hidden hangar door on the trailing edge of the starboard descending strut of Lightcastle's keel qualified. Hell, just wrapping her head around all the dimensions involved in the maneuver probably qualified as a step beyond impossible.

Em needed the pull of the plow to bring the nose of the Drunken Monkey up to the trailing edge of the descending portion of the keel, but everything about the design of habitats and their keels worked against flying a ship into that vicinity. That was precisely why the Lolofis had put their secret escape hatch there, but it was still a pain. The turbine array at the bottom of the keel meant she couldn't just drop the plow and creep her way up to that strut. The cables on the plow would hit the turbines well before she'd get anywhere near the secret hatch. Instead, she had to use the plow to fly in under the turbines, then rise up on the updrift side and back her way in over them. But even in doing that, the turbines were in the way. The front edge of the turbine assembly was where the plow rig would naturally sit with a standard angle for an updrift pull, so Flint had to fly the plow out at an extremely flat angle in front of them to keep it clear of the turbines. This not only put it at a difficult angle to control, it also extended the rig by hundreds of meters, further increasing the challenge of making gentle, precise, and delicate maneuvers. And if that wasn't enough of a challenge, the descending starboard strut was in the way. It was a vertical airfoil about forty meters wide at its thickest point, putting its trailing edge twenty meters in, behind the widest point on either side. That left little room to get the plow cables past it. Oh, and there was also the turbulence that the airfoil created. And it was dark outside. And there were no lights from the city that shone on the upright so all they had to work with was a handheld spotlight. And the person holding that spotlight had to stand outside on top of the wing, which was basically suicidal.

Given those challenges, the flying was going reasonably well.

Em and Flint had made so many unassisted landings that coordinating the plow and flight elements for something ridiculous had become second nature. He was giving her exactly what she needed to hold the leading edge of the Drunken Monkey's port wing just a couple meters off the trailing edge of the strut. Now all they had to do was find the damn hatch.

"Do you see anything?" Em said, glancing at the women who were standing on the port wing.

"No," Dodi, the woman who was holding the spotlight, said through the intercom. "But that doesn't mean that this isn't it."

"Great, now we just need to not rule out another hundred or so panels that could be hiding this damn secret launch bay," Em muttered, her voice dripping with sarcasm.

There was a click as Dodi cut the intercom feed and then, after what looked like a brief conversation out on the wing, one of the other women inched forward. She crawled as far down the curve of the leading edge of the Drunken Monkey's wing as she dared, and then she tried to poke at the trailing edge of the strut with the hooked pole they'd brought out with them.

"Can you pull us in a little closer?" Dodi asked.

"Yes, but poking at it with that stick isn't going to do any good," Em said. "Get back to the anchor point on top of the wing, all of you, clip in and hold on."

The women moved back to the safety harness anchor point, grabbed hold of it or the handholds, and crouched. Em gave them a second to make sure they were settled in, then she dropped the nose of the Drunken Monkey ever so slightly. The ship shifted forward and when it did, the wing bumped against the trailing edge of the vertical strut, sending a small jolt and a shudder through the ship.

"Em! What the hell?" Flint shouted. "You did that on purpose!"

"That felt pretty solid," Em said.

"Yeah, you think?" Flint shot back.

"Did it look solid from out there?" Em asked.

"Yeah," Dodi said.

"Okay, so we're agreed that it's probably got a solid, immobile framework underneath and it's not part of a giant hangar door?" Em asked.

"Yes, we agree. Let's try the next panel up," Dodi said.

"This is not cool," Flint said, as he worked the plow to allow Em to lift the ship past the seam that defined the next panel in the vertical strut cladding.

Em kept at it long after she was sure that they were never going to find the hatch, and then just kept at it after that, and it was fortunate that she refused to give up. They were well above where anyone could have possibly thought the hatch might be when they found it. Logically, she knew that it had to be above the zero-drift point, which was where the apparent movement of the atmosphere shifted from downdrift to updrift in relation to the city. It had to be up where airflow downdrift was strong enough to pull a small chute toward the rear of the city with enough force to pull the Lolofi's secret escape ship out of its hangar. However, logic said that it should have also been as close as possible to the zero-drift point in order to create the widest variety of options for a stealthy departure.

The easiest thing would be to just float downdrift until you were clear of the city, but that wasn't the best option. Not only would it risk letting someone working on the docks or port control spot you, but it would also put the ship in the line of fire of all the plows being used by ships approaching those docks. Em could imagine a few reasons for maybe wanting to depart downdrift, but not many and that made the hangar location damn stupid. If it had been closer to the zero point, a ship could make an updrift departure by using some negative buoyancy to glide forward or hold position as it dropped down below the zero-drift point, and once it was down there it could creep updrift and away, but this hangar was so far up that it would have been nearly impossible to do that. That seemed a bit daft, but no one had bothered to asked Em, and most people were stupid, so she probably should have expected stupid.

Having worked their way well above the seemingly ideal level, they had all become so certain that they weren't going to find the bay doors that they almost didn't notice when they did. They were well into the process of shifting to the next panel before they realized that the bump of the wing had shifted the one they had just hit.

Having found the door, their plan for opening it was simple. The Blades out on the wing had brought a small harpoon gun with them. All they needed to do was shoot a harpoon through the door and secure the cable to the Drunken Monkey. Then Em could use the ship to yank the door open. It worked. It didn't go as they had hoped or expected, but it worked. In fact, it worked so well that it almost killed them all.

The pull of the ship ripped the portside hangar door completely free of the framework of the descending strut and that door nearly killed the women out on the wing as it caught the flow of the Drift and flew over the wing of the Drunken Monkey. It missed them, thankfully, but in doing so it became a flailing, darting, weaving sail that was more than big enough to unsettle Em's delicate control of their position relative to the strut. She managed to hold the ship reasonably steady through the first three or four of the weaving gyrations caused by the door flapping around behind them. Then one of her corrections coincided with the direction of the door's next shift and that kicked off a self-amplifying oscillation. The ship was sent into bigger and bigger swings that were not only throwing them hard to the left and right, but also pulling them up and down.

As soon as Em's control of the ship became unsettled, Flint had begun slacking the pull from the plow. That shifted the Drunken Monkey backwards and away from the back edge of the upright, and it was those extra meters that gave Em just enough time to react when the plow rig hit the side of the upright. The shock that impact sent through the control cables turned the plow into a hard cut to port, which, because the rig was against the starboard side of the upright, pulled the Drunken Monkey hard and fast toward the back edge of the strut. Em pulled up hard on the flight controls. She had just enough space to kill most of the momentum that the plow had put into their rush forward. They still hit the upright hard enough to cause some damage to the portside wing, but the ship survived, and it remained flyable.

That was fortunate because they were basically out of control at that point. Flint steered the plow rig hard to starboard, carrying the cables off the upright. He then immediately gave Em some pull forward, which she used to steer the ship to starboard. Once the ship was well clear of the upright Flint put the plow into max pull. That was critical. Em set the ship hard against that combination, and the heavy drag she was putting into the aero-control surfaces on the ship overwhelmed the random inputs from the wildly flailing door. In seconds she had them flying steady enough for the women out on the wing to cut the door loose and dump it into the Deep.

"Thank god for safety harnesses," Dodi said. "As soon as we get another harpoon loaded in the gun, we'll be ready to go back in and send someone over."

"You'll have to give me a few minutes," Em said, wiping the sweat off her face and shuddering as the second kick from the adrenaline hit. "At least a few."

"Well, if there's one thing that all soldiers are good at, it's waiting," Dodi said, pleasantly. "So, you take all the damn time you need."

The rest of the maneuver was challenging, but for a pilot like Em, it was straightforward. The only element that threatened catastrophe was the turbulence from the missing door. It was bad as she brought the Drunken Monkey back into position with the wing in close behind the trailing edge of the strut. However, once Em mastered that and steadied the ride for the women out on the wing, the rest was almost easy. Another harpoon was fired, giving them a cable into the bay. Em drifted back to put a little tension on it and with that taut, a team of Blades slid across on it. They took the Drunken Monkey's nose winch cable across with them and secured it inside the hangar. Em used the pull from that instead of the plow to fly the ship while Flint went about the business of retrieving their plow.

Even if there wasn't already a ship in the docking bay, they wouldn't have fit in the hangar, but they could still secure themselves reasonably well. They wouldn't want to park for too long with their wings pressed against the door on one side and the frame where the door had been on the other, the damage from the rubbing and shifting would become worrisome, but for a few hours, or even a few days, it was going to be fine. Getting across to the inside of the hangar involved going out through the topside air lock and crossing a makeshift gangway, so unloading the nearly three hundred Blades—and for some reason that the Little Princess refused to fully explain, Flint—was a tedious process, but it went well, and soon Em was alone on the ship.

She made a small pot of coffee, added a generous glug of whisky to the cup and sat on her favorite chair in the lounge. It was an ugly and overstuffed monstrosity that was perfect for staring out the narrow and tall window that looked out over the port side of the ship. Basking in the not quite silence of an empty ship, she savored every sip and every relaxing moment in her chair. It wasn't until she finished the coffee and wondered if she dared have another that she realized the ship was far too quiet.

"Ida?" Em called out. "Polly?"

There was no response.

"Ida! Where in the hell are you?"

Ida was over one hundred meters above the Drunken Monkey, inspecting the hole the Blades had cut in the wall of the secret stairwell connecting the City Estate to the emergency escape hangar. She could hear gunshots, but those noises were far away and hard to hear over the rumble of the big machines. She reached through the big hole in the wall and pointed Flint's gun around, just to be safe, but there was no one there.

Polly finally caught up. She was tired, and she sat on a step with a huff.

"These stairs go forever," Polly said. "This had better be worth it."

"Lady Willamette said the stairs go all the way up to the City Estate," Ida said. "There's lots of stuff up in the City Estate that's worth it, and I know where all the good stuff is. It's all locked in closets and cases, but that's not a big deal."

Polly looked at the pistol Ida had stolen from the safe in Flint's cabin and nodded. "Okay, but let's go slower or I'll never make it all the way up there."

"I think we should get mostly jewelry," Ida said. "I think we could get enough of it to buy a whole estate or something, and then my mum could come live with us and maybe Az would come live with us and help keep us safe. And my cuzzie. She's real smart and nice and she has a baby that's really cute."

"I want to open a dress shop," Polly said.

"We could have a dress shop on an estate," Ida said. "Or maybe we could buy a big townhouse, big enough for everyone and then you could have a fancy dress shop in a city or something."

"I'd like that," Polly said. "I've always wanted to live in a city and get a rich husband and things like that."

"You have to be a rich girl to get a rich husband," Ida said. "So, we'd better take some extra for you."

Even in ideal circumstances, moving between ships in flight was dangerous, and there was nothing ideal about boarding and inspecting transport ships flying into a combat zone. For some reason, it was even worse when the captains of those ships seemed perfectly happy to let you inspect their ships.

"It's empty, Lieutenant," Nick, the squad leader, reported.

"What do you mean empty?" Lieutenant Johnson asked.

"He means that this ship was chartered by Willamette Lolofi to fly to a location exactly five kilometers downdrift of Lightcastle and wait for up to five days for further instructions. Which is exactly what our bill of charter, tax invoice, and flight plan indicate," the captain of the ship said.

"You're a diversion," Lieutenant Johnson muttered. "You're all a bloody diversion."

"That would be my guess, yes," the ship's captain said, shrugging. "And I think she wanted everyone to figure that out. We have explicit instructions to accept any and all requests to board and inspect. And from what I have heard from the other captains holding station near here, it looks like they all have the exact same charter and instructions."

"Where in the hell did she send all of her troops?" Lieutenant Johnson asked, his guts sinking at the thought of what Lolofi troops, or their allies, could be doing back home.

"I honestly wouldn't know," the captain said, shrugging. "Which I think was the point."

CHAPTER 20

Reporting from a war zone was inherently treacherous. Some would say it was insanely dangerous. Even if no one was trying to kill you, explosions were indiscriminate, the territorial shifts of battle were unpredictable, and stray darts were just as deadly as the ones that flew true. On the professional side, no matter what you wrote, there was always the very real risk that it would provoke a retaliation from someone powerful enough to kill over a politically inconvenient fact or two. On top of that, Ariel faced all the additional concerns following from her habit of carrying her vagina around with her, and that was one hell of a big concern. The fear of simply being a woman in a war zone haunted her far more than she would ever admit, even to herself. Ever since she'd begun chasing unrest in the Commonwealth and reporting from the scene, the nightmare of waking to soldiers breaking into her room in the middle of the night had become so common that when it happened, it felt like she'd been through it before. She hadn't, but it felt like it.

A hood was yanked over her head and a cord bound her hands, but from there the nightmare went off script. She was tossed around, hit a couple times, and more generally handled with disregard for her comfort, but she was left unmolested. Dumped into what was probably a laundry cart, she was wheeled into an elevator and out through what was probably a service entrance of the hotel. She knew better than to discount the possibility that rape might still be in her immediate future, but by the time she was thrown ungently into the back of a vehicle, she was reasonably certain that rape wasn't the primary reason these men had abducted her.

She paid careful attention to the feel of every turn, listened to every noise, and tried to imagine the route, but it was winding, stop-start, and it wasn't long before she had no idea where she was, or even what direction they might be travelling. There was a brief skirmish along the way. It was just a quick exchange of fire between two sides that both seemed intent on avoiding a fight rather than winning one, but lying blind, bound, and helpless on the hard floor of a small truck made it terrifying in a way she'd never experienced before. After that, there was another half hour or so of a stop, start, and twisty ride; a descent into what she was pretty sure were the utility tunnels that ran beneath the city; more twists and turns and at least two more descents to ever-lower levels of the down below. They stopped and just sat in place for a surprisingly long time. Then she was pulled roughly out of the vehicle and marched down corridors and around corners, then down more corridors and around more corners. There was a long, drawn-out stop, start, wait, stop, start, and wait through what seemed like a ridiculously complex security cordon, and then finally she was shoved into a wheeled office chair. The chair rolled slowly across a hard floor until it gently bumped into something and came to a stop, and then nothing.

Ariel sat there for a while, how long she couldn't say, but eventually people returned. There was muttering and shuffling which suddenly stopped. Someone important had stepped into the room. There was a hushed exchange of whispers, some of which seemed angry, and then the hood was yanked off her head. The light in the room wasn't all that bright, but after so many hours in the hood it was bright enough to bring tears to her eyes so she couldn't see who it was who had ordered her kidnapping.

"Please accept my apologies for the bumps and bruises," a woman said, her tone leaving Ariel no doubt that the apology was sincere and also no doubt that acceptance of the apology was obligatory. "I should have been more specific. The necessity of your presence did not preclude giving you the option of being transported here in a respectful and comfortable manner."

The first shock was that it was a woman's voice. Ariel had expected her captor to be a gruff old general, or perhaps one of those borderline psychotic men that seemed to lead every special operations team she had ever encountered. The second shock was that the more her eyes cleared, the more the woman looked like Willamette Lolofi.

"So you're saying that if I would have just laid back and let it happen, I could have enjoyed my kidnapping?" Ariel shot back.

"That is a fantastic idea." Willamette replied to Ariel's sarcasm with a droll bit of her own. "I'll remember to have my thugs suggest that to the victim the next time I subject a woman to the involuntary loss of bodily sovereignty."

Willamette nodded at a grim-looking woman. The woman nodded back and drew a wicked-looking crystal-bladed knife. Ariel had just long enough time to wonder if her life should be flashing before her eyes before the knife cut the cord binding her wrists.

Something in Ariel's flinch at the blade amused Willamette. That seemed like a very Lolofi thing to find amusing, but there was also no cruelty in the look on Willamette's face. It was resignation and disappointment. She seemed to be sadly bemused by Ariel's fear for her life. Ariel wasn't sure what, if anything, she should take from that.

Ariel had never gone anywhere near anything anyone might call celebrity reporting. She didn't even read any of it. As a result, she knew almost nothing about Willamette Lolofi except for, perhaps, the occasional snippet of gossip that snuck its way into the real news. Most of that was propaganda anyway, so even what she had stumbled across couldn't be trusted. That meant the woman standing before her could have easily been anything from a raging hormone slave, who had slept with every man and beast she'd encountered since the age of twelve, to the pure little angel her parents wanted the world to see. Her appearance betrayed nothing. Petite, attractive in a cute rather than beautiful way, wearing a gown from the robust and utilitarian end of what a woman of her breeding might wear, she was perfectly poised, calm, and impossible to read. Even her droll sarcasm and the sadly bemused look were probably just a bit of theatre offered for effect. It was hard to tell.

Ariel guessed that a Lolofi was a Lolofi and took a stab in the dark.

"Look," Ariel said. "I don't know what kind of mind game you think you're playing by having me roughed up, kidnapped, and then playacting at nice, but I do know that it's not going to matter one damn bit. I am a reporter. That is my life. It is truly the only thing I care about and there is nothing you can do short of killing me that will shut me up."

"Ariel, I have no intention of silencing you or your reporting," Willamette said.

"Then why in the hell did you order your thugs to yank me out of my bed in the middle of the night and haul me halfway across the city?" Ariel demanded.

"It was three-quarters of the way across the city," Willamette said, giving Ariel another taste of that droll sarcasm. "And you were brought here to serve as a witness."

"A witness to what?"

Willamette thought about that for a few seconds before she said, "I suppose you could call it an execution."

"You expect me to watch an execution?" Ariel was stunned and horrified. "Whose execution?"

Willamette ignored the question, turned, and exited the small office. The grim woman limped after her, neither of them seeming to care if Ariel followed. That indifference was even more unsettling than being pushed around, and a glance around the office just made it all the more disturbing. Sitting on the desk next to a bag that had been hastily packed with what looked like all of the notes and other paperwork from Ariel's hotel room was a pile of government-issue office supplies: A package of pens, notepads, file folders, and file folder labels, everything. There was even a package of paper clips. Far from being silenced, it looked a hell of a lot like she'd been conscripted to report on what was sure to be Little Miss Lolofi's cruel and bloody spectacle.

Ariel wasn't sure if she wanted to play along, but like most conscripts, she probably didn't have any choice, so she decided to at least go through the motions. Grabbing a notepad and a pen she started by jotting down details, thoughts, and impressions. The hallway outside the office was lined with office doors, perhaps a dozen on either side, and at the end it opened into a huge, theatre-shaped room that was bustling with activity.

If there had been a big window looking out over the Drift, Ariel might have thought it was the helm of the most massive ship in the fleet, but instead the workstations and desks of the theatre looked down at a giant map of the Commonwealth. Ariel was at what was nearly the highest level of desks in the theatre. To her right and left, there were stations that would have been meant for officers if the room had indeed been the helm of some sort on a ship. It was impossible to guess the details. The arrangement of desks, the men manning them, the working groups and sub-command stations in the tiers below all made it confusing. However, there was no doubt it was indeed some kind of extensive and highly structured command-and-control center. And it was crowded. Most of the desks had two people working at them.

Uninvited, but also left unimpeded, Ariel climbed the stairs up to the topmost level where Willamette stood amongst what was obviously the senior command crew, or the admirals, or whatever the collection of officious and military-looking men were. While Willamette handled some detail or other, Ariel considered the activity of the room as well as the huge map, struggling to figure out where in the hell she was.

"The Signal Corps Headquarters." Willamette answered the unasked question, paused, and then answered the second. "The map charts the angles between all the Signal Corps' send and receive stations in order to precisely track the locations of all the habitats in the Commonwealth. The habitats in red have Signal Corps offices and the ones without Signal Corps stations are in blue. The blue ones are tracked through how the others report angles to their navigation beacons. It is remarkably precise. Every habitat can be located to within a few meters."

"So, we're in the bunker under the palace," Ariel said.

"Yes and no," Willamette said. "The Signal Corps' Headquarters is one of the most heavily fortified bunkers in the Drift. However, despite the common belief, it is nowhere near the City Estate. And, for the time being, it is also serving as my operations and command center."

"So, you've stepped up to take over the Commonwealth?" It was more of a statement than a question.

"Technically, yes, but the elements of the Commonwealth I am able to control are extremely limited," Willamette said, with surprising forthrightness.

"A situation you obviously intend to remedy with the execution you mentioned," Ariel concluded.

"That would indeed seem obvious." The look of bemused resignation returned to Willamette's face. "Tell me, Ariel, do you know anything about how an empire functions?"

"Are you admitting that the Commonwealth is an empire?" Ariel asked.

"Ariel, I do not have the time to waste on the trivially obvious," Willamette scolded her.

"I'll take that as a yes," Ariel said.

"You have been given an unprecedented opportunity here," Willamette said, still scolding. "You have unfettered access to the last surviving Lolofi while she navigates her way through a critical, possibly transformative moment in the history of the Commonwealth. I cannot believe someone who has earned your reputation would waste time pursuing gossipy stories about the disingenuous nature of political euphemisms and rhetoric."

"Then how about the story of how in the hell you survived the coup and so fortuitously came to be the sole surviving Lolofi?" Ariel asked, sarcastically. "I'm sure there are all kinds of dramatic twists and turns in whatever nasty things the fourth in line had to do in order to jump to the front of the queue."

"I was eleventh in line, after the sons of my brothers, and yes, the story of my survival is quite dramatic, although not in the way you so obviously presume." Willamette plucked a notebook off the cluttered desk in front of her and handed it to Ariel. It was filled with page after page of neat and precise handwriting. "My account. The details are all in there, but the basics are that we climbed over the wall to escape the yacht club, tried to hide in a hotel but were forced to flee by running across the top of the dome and to the docks. There, we had the good fortune to secure passage on a small ship that spirited us away from the city. We received some additional good fortune when a patrol ship engaged our pursuers. We believe our pursuers were destroyed, but we have no way of knowing because we took the opportunity to flee. We spent just over a week hiding on the estate of a loyalist, whose identity I have chosen to conceal to protect them from reprisals, and then we made a stealthy return to Lightcastle."

"Including a stop at Donovan?" Ariel asked.

Willamette nodded.

"That sounds like a story that you desperately want me to tell." Ariel flipped through the massive tome that was the notebook. "I am not your publicist."

"All stories are told with the voice of the teller." Willamette shrugged. "You know that, and I would expect a professional like yourself to take that into account as you interpret these notes and pursue whatever corroboration you might be able to find. However, if I can ask the favor, please do not discount my depiction of the young man who is now my husband. My father quite cruelly ambushed him with our betrothal. However, as displeased as Niven might have been to be coerced into joining the Lolofi family, he has still been everything that a foolishly romantic young woman could have possibly hoped to find in a man. He is remarkable, and regardless of its brevity, our marriage has been the joy of my life."

Willamette then gave a young man standing a short distance away a brief and very warm smile that he was too busy to notice. Her expression didn't look like theatre.

"You're married?"

"Yes, but like the rest of the story between the Regatta Day Murders and this moment, I would like to share the details through this notebook and ask you to focus on the story which needs to be told now."

"Then what is the story that needs to be told now?" Ariel asked.

"The story of empires and the reality of how they are ruled," Willamette said.

"Which you are about to demonstrate with this execution you want me to watch," Ariel said.

"In a roundabout way, yes," Willamette said.

The look on Willamette's face was indescribable. Despairing, resigned, brave, scared. Ariel started jotting down the words that came to mind, adding details like the slight waver in her voice and the tremble of her hands, which she was trying to hide. Ariel scribbled away, but she knew she would never be able to truly capture that moment in a description. There was something powerful and profound about to happen and it terrified the young woman who intended to unleash it. However, there was also a hint that none of it was what it seemed. There were a lot of pieces that just didn't seem to fit into the mosaic laid out before her.

"So, what do you know about the politics of empire?" Willamette asked.

"As much as anyone, I guess," Ariel said. "It's all about power."

"No, it is not about power," Willamette gently corrected her. "Power is necessary, obviously, but not sufficient. There are and have been countless military, economic, and political leaders who have amassed tremendous power, but only a handful of them have managed to create, sustain, or rule an empire. No, the rare few powerful men who become emperors are the ones who were given, created, or seized a fulcrum allowing them to leverage their power. Therein, if you will forgive the pun, is the crux of the unfolding events."

Ariel scribbled away, rushing to get every single word down.

Willamette noticed Ariel's rush and gave her a few extra seconds before she continued. "I know what those critical points of leverage are within the structure of the Commonwealth, and by an accident of birth and all the havoc wrought by the failed coup, I have been thrust into a place and a moment where I must claim control of them. However, what I can do with that leverage is limited by the fact that everyone knows I do not have the military or political resources it will take to physically secure Lightcastle and retain control of it or those fulcrums."

"And that means that this will indeed become an all-out war for control of these critical points of leverage," Ariel concluded.

"Not if I can help it," Willamette said. "There are over a million soldiers in the Commonwealth, and if this should spiral into an all-out war most if not all of them will find their way onto one side or the other. The death, destruction, and suffering of such a war would be indescribable. That is something I desperately wish to prevent."

"But if you can't even hold Lightcastle, how can you possibly stop a war?"

"By using the leverage provided by the same fulcrum of power that my ancestor used to turn the Commonwealth into an empire," Willamette said.

"Which was military might," Ariel said. "Which you just said you do not have."

"Ah, there you go again, thinking in terms of raw power, instead of the fulcrum," Willamette chided her. "For it was not the military might of the Lolofi family that allowed us to secure the Chairmanship of the Commonwealth in perpetuity."

"So, the stories about the Interfamily War are lies?"

"No," Willamette said. "Most of the historical details about the Interfamily War are well documented and can be confirmed through independent sources. However, even when history is not written by the victorious, the way those stories are told will always serve their political needs."

Ariel scribbled that down. Regardless of anything that might happen, those words, from the mouth of a Lolofi, were journalistic gold.

"Here is the reality; it was a simple and seemingly reasonable change in banking regulations that was the fulcrum, or the key to empire, if you will," Willamette said. "It is impossible to say when, precisely, the Commonwealth became an empire, but by the time the Interfamily War broke out, it had been at least a decade."

"Assuming I take that as true, why does it matter now?"

"Commander Lisp, shut down all banking communications." Willamette stared Ariel in the eye as she raised her voice to issue the order.

"Yes ma'am." The man who must have been Commander Lisp was quite obviously caught off guard by that order, but the way he quietly and calmly moved to execute it suggested that it was not a difficult command to obey. A few quiet words into an intercom microphone seemed to do it.

"Fractional reserve banking is one of the most flexible and powerful economic tools ever devised," Willamette said, her voice taking on the cadence and assured confidence of a university lecturer. "Throughout history, most economists have focused on the way it creates a dynamic money supply which can quickly grow and contract with fluctuations in the economy. This also gives the owners of the commercial banks, which in the case of the Commonwealth is the Big 12 families, the ability to leverage their wealth to an absolutely fantastic extent. At a 25 percent reserve rate, every coin the bank owners deposit allows them to lend four, and at a 10 percent reserve rate, one coin is leveraged into the loan of ten."

"Yes, I've heard it described as creating money out of thin air," Ariel said.

"In some ways, yes, but the dynamic of the reserve deposit is more like the way a seed allows an estate holder to create food out of dirt and water," Willamette said. "Politically, that fractional rate is the fulcrum upon which all wealth is leveraged and the most important element of the story needing to be told now. A slight increase or decrease in the reserve rate can cause a bust or a boom, or in some odd circumstances, both at the same time. A large increase in how much real wealth must be kept in deposit, or simply cutting access to those reserve deposits, can bankrupt the bankers in an instant."

"I think I see the power inherent in controlling that, but I'm not sure I follow how it creates an empire," Ariel said.

"It would not under normal circumstances," Willamette said. "What transformed it into the fulcrum of empire was the adoption of a seemingly insignificant regulation, requiring the reserve deposits to be held in the Central Reserve Bank in Lightcastle. Prior to that, what was then the Banking 15 deposited their reserve funds in their own central banks. What none of them, except for my family, seemed to realize back then was that letting the families hold their own reserve deposits essentially made their membership in the Commonwealth voluntary. Any of the banking families could, at any time, declare their commercial bank to be its own reserve bank and drift away. The loss of trade, market access, and all the rest would be costly, but the option of departing was the critical element constraining the power of any central authority, and it kept the Commonwealth a commonwealth."

Ariel saw exactly where that line of argument was going. "But once the reserve deposit was held in Lightcastle, the banking families were chained to the capital because if they left or attempted to revolt, they would lose all the wealth they had deposited as their reserve."

"Essentially, yes," Willamette said. "It is not clear how Lina Lolofi secured both the Chairmanship of the Commonwealth and control of the central bank at the same time, but he did, and he used the leverage offered by those fulcrums to great effect."

"So now that you've taken control of the banking mechanisms, you are going to use that leverage rather than military power to secure control of the Commonwealth and elevate yourself into your father's place," Ariel said.

"If that were possible, I might well be tempted, but as we have noted, the reality is that I cannot physically secure and defend Lightcastle either directly or through alliance. That in turn means that I cannot rule the Commonwealth," Willamette said. "It is a cliché to say the capital is the empire, but it is also close to the truth. The only effective way for a singular authoritarian leader to rule an immense, sprawling political and economic entity is to concentrate all the mechanisms of control in a central location where he or she can protect them. Further, as those mechanisms for leveraging power evolve into institutions and structures of rule, they are quite literally built into the city."

Willamette made a grand gesture at the room around them.

"And that's why there are five armies in this city and, if reports are to be believed, hundreds of thousands more troops lingering just downdrift," Ariel said. "The family that wins Lightcastle, wins the empire."

"Taking Lightcastle is not the only way to win control of the Commonwealth, and it does not guarantee success. However, it is one of the more straightforward paths to such an end," Willamette said, lowering her voice to make sure only Ariel could hear. "Which is why I intend to scuttle the city."

"What?" Ariel was certain that she must have misheard. "You can't be serious."

"It is an elegant solution," Willamette said. "Once Lightcastle and all of the mechanisms for ruling the empire that are built into it are gone, what is there to fight over?"

"Oh, I don't know, countless petty grievances and competing claims to thousands of towns, cities, and estates," Ariel shot back, throwing all the caustic sarcasm into it that she could.

"And how will any of the Big 12 families fund wars over any of those things when all of their reserve deposits have been thrown into the Deep?" Willamette asked. "It will not bankrupt them. They will still hold tremendous wealth, but almost all of it will need to be used to support their banks and the economies their banks enable."

"That'll just make it worse," Ariel shot back. "The Big 12 families have damn big armies and if they can't afford to pay their soldiers then it will be use'm or lose'm. That will make them even more willing to throw them into battle."

"You misunderstand why there are so many soldiers across the Commonwealth, whose troops they are, and how they are commanded," Willamette said. "The Big 12 families do not have armies, they have officer corps. And, with the exception of small home guards and expeditionary forces, those officers command aggregations of military units contributed by the second- and third-tier noble families."

"And again, this will just make it worse," Ariel said. "Bankrupting the Big 12 will destroy the leverage those families need to hold their militaries together and setting all those armies loose will unleash a thousand lesser wars between the smaller families."

"There will be at least a few horrific eruptions of violence, yes, but they will be far smaller in scale than an all-out war over Lightcastle and the Commonwealth. And, perhaps because of their incandescent fury, those smaller fights will also be brief," Willamette said. "However, if history is a reliable guide, most of the Big 12 will declare themselves to be kingdoms and focus their efforts on retaining the fealty of vassal families. To accomplish that, they will need to be extremely careful to avoid overextending their military or suffering foolish losses. And I am about to do a few things to both directly and indirectly encourage them all to focus their efforts on exactly that."

Ariel shook her head, refusing to believe in the fairy tale this little girl was spinning, but also desperately tempted to hope it might be real. "You seem like you care about the people who would be killed in a war. You can't imagine how refreshing it is to find a Lolofi who can even fake that, but the reality is that you are still a Lolofi. There is no way you will sacrifice Lightcastle and destroy the very thing that gives you power in return for a chance of averting a war."

Willamette raised her voice and ordered, "Commander Lisp, send the following order to the Lightcastle gasworks: Prepare to scuttle the city."

Silence fell in the highest level of the Command Centre, and it spread quickly until the whisper of the ventilation system was the only noise in the previously bustling room.

"I have obviously misheard," Commander Lisp said.

The commander's stunned disbelief was matched by everyone else, including the young man Willamette had claimed was her new husband. He was horrified, furious, aghast.

"We will be scuttling the city," Willamette said. "Tell the gasworks to stop sending fresh air into the dome and have them make preparations to execute my order."

"Grand Lady Willamette, the Knightly expeditionary force controls the gasworks," one of the other men in the room said, nervously. "They will never allow the engineers to follow your orders."

"I believe you will discover that there is a small force of elite soldiers I infiltrated into the below decks. They now control the gasworks as well as the defensive positions between the gasworks and where the Knightly forces are encamped." Willamette smirked, and in that moment the Little Princess looked like her father's daughter. She added a rather caustic, "Sometimes it is not about how big your military is, but how you use it."

"There are at least a quarter of a million innocent civilians still in the city," Ariel hissed. "What kind of monster would kill a quarter of a million people just to chase some fantasy of keeping the peace?"

"Do you honestly believe I would allow them to die?" Willamette smiled sadly at Ariel, looking profoundly disappointed with her. Then she raised her voice again to issue a command. "Commander Lisp, please make certain the engineers formulating and executing the scuttling adhere to the plan I sent with the engineer accompanying the expeditionary force to the gasworks. I wish to give everyone in the city, including all of the invading military forces, ample opportunity to leave. They'll need breathable air and at least three hours to evacuate before we hit the Deep."

"Three hours or three minutes isn't going to make one damn bit of difference," Commander Lisp shouted.

"Yes, it will, Commander," Willamette said, with threatening calm. "It will make all the difference in the world."

"Confirmation from the gasworks. They are ready to cease the provision of air and begin venting auxiliary lift bladders on a three-hour schedule, awaiting confirmation of your command," a nervous functionary reported.

"Before I confirm, please contact the central switchboard and tell them to activate the civil defense broadcast system," Willamette said. "I would like to add a message to the breach alarm."

"But the central switchboard …"

"The central switchboard is controlled by a small band of elite troops who are now working on my behalf," Willamette said, again smirking like a Lolofi.

Polly was sure they were well and truly done for. Em was sitting there waiting for them to climb down the ladder from the upper air lock, and she looked mad. Em always looked mad, but right then she was frowning, and she was really good at it. They were in for a beating, for sure.

"You know, it'd be one thing if we crashed and died on the way in here," Em said. "Willamette would have never forgiven me for getting you killed, but I'd be dead too, so who cares, right? But if you two chicken-brained numbskulls fell off that gangway, or got shot when you were up there, or something else stupid killed you, then I would have to listen to Willamette forever giving me grief about it. That is unacceptable. I expect better from you two."

"We're sorry, Captain Em," Ida said.

"So what did you steal?" Em said.

"Captain Em, we wouldn't never steal things," Ida protested.

"First," Em said, "wouldn't never is a double negative so that's basically you saying that you did go up there to steal stuff. Second, you're both wearing loads of stupidly fancy jewelry."

Ida looked at the necklace she was wearing, stomped her feet and huffed. "Oh, that was dumb."

"Yes, wearing some of what you stole is seriously dumb," Em said. "Now spill it."

"I've gotta buy an estate so my mum can come live with me. Polly is going to open a dress shop and she needs to be rich so she can have a rich husband, so we might buy a big townhouse that we can all live in, and …"

"No, spill the bags," Em said. "I want to see what you stole. And it damn well better be worth you two risking your lives."

Polly and Ida dumped their bags on the floor.

"Hmnn." Em crouched and inspected the jewels. "First, see these, these are diamonds. They're pretty but they're worthless. Big factories make 'em out of air from the Drift and you can buy them by the bucket. This is glass, it's worth more because it's made out of stuff that has to come up with the whales, but it's also not worth all that much. What you want is metal. Solid metal like this."

Em handed Ida and Polly bracelets that were a reddish color.

"Feel how heavy those are?" Em asked. "Plastic made to look shiny like metal, or a thin layer of metal on plastic, isn't heavy, but real metal is heavy like that. That's how you tell the real stuff that women like Willamette wear from the cheap stuff that the women pretending to be rich and fancy wear. Understand?"

Ida and Polly nodded.

"Good," Em said. "So, this time get as much real metal as you can."

"This time?" Polly asked.

"Well, yeah, if we're going to be partners and share it fair and equal, you're going to need to go get another load," Em said. "And make sure you get the right stuff this time."

"Splitting evens three ways ain't fair," Polly protested. "We're the ones getting it and it's a really, really long ways up to the City Estate."

"Who do you think you're going to sell this stuff to?" Em asked. "You take it to a shop, and they'll call the police. If you try to sell it to someone who doesn't have a shop, they're probably just going to kill you and take it."

"That would be bad." Ida was scandalized.

"Yes, it would, but I know how to find the people who will buy it fair and square and not call the police," Em said. "And I can hide things on this ship so Flint and the others won't find them. I can also make it so we can get all the money from selling this stuff into a bank so that you two can buy things like houses. That's totally worth evens. Besides, if I didn't want to be fair about it, I could just beat your little asses 'til they burn and take it all for myself, couldn't I?"

Polly and Ida both nodded.

"So, we can split what you have here, or we can split this and one more load of the good stuff," Em said. "And I bet that if you steal the right stuff this time, you'll both end up with way more than you have now."

"Okay," Ida said. "Evens is a deal, right, Polly?"

Polly nodded. The idea of walking all the way back up there annoyed her but getting more sounded like a good idea.

"So, this time get metal and just metal," Em said. "The Lolofis have got to have lots of stupid things made out of metal for no good reason; like in those stories about using silver forks, spoons, and knives at fancy palace dinners. If those were real, they'd be worth a lot."

"They are real," Ida said. "And I know where they are."

"Perfect," Em said. "Now hurry and don't get yourselves killed."

There was nothing more terrifying than a breach alarm. No matter who you were, no matter what kinds of evils lurked in your waking or sleeping hours, those torments were nothing compared to the horror of a breach.

The drills they taught children involved getting in a line and marching calmly to evacuation stations; however, even the youngest child had some inkling of the pointlessness of that exercise. Even in the busiest ports of the busiest merchant towns, the capacity of the ships available was never more than the tiniest fraction needed to evacuate the population. The wealthy would escape, as would a portion of the dockworkers and a few other lucky souls. But for nearly everyone else, if the habitat you counted on for your survival was ripped open in an attack, or otherwise failed, you died. Worse, all of those unfortunate souls who knew that they had no hope of escape also knew that they would probably have hours to sit and wonder which horrific death awaited them: suffocation, acid, or madness. If they were unlucky, it would be a little of all three.

The fear of a breach was even more salient for soldiers. Even though breeching attacks were extremely rare, they did happen, and when soldiers were on the streets, they were in exactly the places at the exact times when that kind of attack might occur. So, it was unsurprising that the breach alarm ended the skirmish. Both the soldiers of the Knightly Expeditionary Force and the strange women who had somehow found a way to surprise them with an attack from below, stopped fighting. No one retreated or withdrew, they just stopped firing their weapons.

"Fall back!" Hamish shouted, but only a handful of his men responded. "I said fall back, you insufferable horsefuckers!"

A few more men responded and that shook the rest into action.

"Real or a ploy?" Actus asked Hamish as soon as they retreated to cover.

"Ploy?" Hamish asked.

"Set off the alarm to get the forces on the streets to retreat to their transports," Actus said.

"Piss-ass nobles like you would pull that kind of stunt, wouldn't they?" Hamish asked.

"If it gave me or my men an advantage, hell yeah I would," Actus said.

Hamish nodded, approvingly. There was nothing a soldier hated more than a noble who would choose propriety or property over the lives of his men.

"We should get someone up to the streets," Actus said. "Get eyes on the dome."

"No need," Hamish said. "Give it a few minutes and your ears will tell you the truth of it. They start poppin' and that's a sure sign we're going down."

The alarm stopped, and a woman spoke from the loudspeakers.

"This is Willamette Lolofi, Acting Chairman of the Commonwealth, Commander of the Commonwealth's Combined Armies, and Executive Director of the Lightcastle Governing Board. I regret to inform you that this is not a drill. The city is being scuttled."

"Scuttled?" Actus muttered, aghast.

"This unfortunate but necessary action is being executed in a manner that will allow all persons in the city, both civilian and military, ample time and opportunity to evacuate. I have chartered over sixty large transport vessels which are being sent instructions to land upon the Lightcastle docks. Transports will be accessible from all of the passenger and cargo terminals along the entire length of docks, so you may walk directly to the nearest one and board the first ship you find."

"Is that really the little Lolofi bitch?" Hamish asked.

"I think so."

"I thought they were all dead," Hamish muttered.

Actus shrugged.

"While there is no rush, you should also avoid delay," Willamette continued. "The city's auxiliary lift cells are now being vented to initiate our descent into the Deep, but we will delay the venting of the dome for two hours to allow ample time for everyone to reach the docks. When those two hours have elapsed, we will not interrupt the air supply to the passenger and cargo loading areas of the dock, the subway system, or the utility tunnels, but we will begin pumping carbon dioxide into the city. At that point, the air will become unbreathable. So, again, please do not delay in making your way to the docks. Move quickly, take care to stay with your loved ones, and take no more than what you can easily carry."

Hamish's ears popped, and from the way Actus worked his jaws, his had just confirmed the truth as well.

"Unbelievable, a Lolofi sinking the city," Actus said. "Why in the hell would she destroy the capital of her own empire?"

"A tactical move, spite, stupidity, some kind of dumbass foolishness?" Hamish shrugged. "Why doesn't matter. What matters is that if she's doing it on purpose, that gives us a second option."

"And that is?"

"We could take back the gas works and keep this bastard afloat."

"I think it's smarter to run for the transport," Actus said.

"But ..." Hamish said. "I know I heard a but in that tone."

"Taking the gas works to stop the scuttle, and then having that in hand when it comes time to negotiate our way through the end game could be incredibly valuable," Actus said. "And can you imagine how the fat old buggers around the table would react if we had a real chance to accomplish something with a dumbass headlong charge into a fight and we didn't take it?"

"Chargin' in is what we're good at, but how about we make sure the men know we ain't just going to go down with the city," Hamish said.

"Pass the word that if we don't break through within the hour, we retreat to the transport," Actus said. "We hold nothing in reserve, but if we fall short, we will cut and run the very instant that hour is up, no matter how close we are."

The soldier rolled off Kala and jumped to his feet. Naked from the waist down but still wearing his socks, he looked particularly vulnerable as he pointlessly glanced around and then looked at Kala. The sight of her lying on the bed with her legs still spread, mortified him. He looked away, embarrassed and apologetic, as if he had somehow just violated her modesty.

Kala decided that she should feel empathy for him.

She pulled her skirt down to avoid causing the young man any further embarrassment and considered how she should offer him empathy. He had not only paid his fair price, he had also been kind and gentle, albeit in an awkward and clumsy way. Her rules said that he was good, twice over, which meant he deserved as much empathy as Kala could offer. Perhaps she should slit his throat. Her knife was sharp. It would be painless and quick. It would be a mercy compared to the death waiting for him in the Deep. Or perhaps she should encourage him to evacuate. By a small margin, encouraging him to evacuate won out.

"You must take advantage of the chance to evacuate," Kala said, returning her half-drawn knife to its sheath.

"Evacuate to what?" the young man asked, distraught. "My father's shop is here. My job is here. The home I would someday inherit is here. That evil bitch is throwing any hope I might have of a future into the Deep."

"You should put on your pants, gather whatever valuable things you can carry, and head for the docks," Kala said.

"Yes, I know. I will," the young man said. "Come back to the shop with me and I'll show you what's worth taking. You can have what you want, and you can walk to the docks with me. I'll make sure no one robs you."

"Thank you, but no." Kala pulled her purse from amongst the severed genitalia in her shoulder bag. The purse was heavy with coins, so she doubted if he would mind that it was covered with blood. "Please take the money I have earned from pleasuring good soldiers."

"What are you going to do?"

"As you said, the little Lolofi bitch is evil," Kala said. "To scuttle a city and destroy so much is unforgivable. Now will you please take this money."

Dodi's first instinct was to grab her fallen sister, but the thinking part of her brain kicked in before she acted. The splintering dart had torn the guts out of the girl, and even though she was somehow crawling back toward the line, she was dead. There was no saving her and anyone who tried would be risking her own life for nothing.

"Back," Dodi yelled. "Fall back and make them pay for every step!"

Her sisters followed orders, and they knew how to make the Knightlys pay, but in the end, that was not going to matter. They were still going to lose because there was always a point where numbers would win. The Drunken Monkey could only carry about three hundred Blades down to the secret hangar, and she had already lost a quarter of them. A few dozen more casualties would break them, and the Knightlys had more than enough men to make that happen.

When they surrendered the second to last stretch of tunnel between the Knightlys and the gasworks, Dodi had estimated they could still hold out for another hour, but a sudden shift in the Knightlys' tactics threatened to cut that to minutes. The Knightlys had decided to start using their shoulder-fired missiles as covering weapons. The high-explosive munitions weren't very accurate; they were meant to be used for piercing cover, not antipersonnel fire. Dodi couldn't imagine how they had convinced any of their men to run down a passage while the damn things were being fired past them from behind, but they had, and it was working. Not only did those rounds take out a few of the women covering the long passageway with rifles, the concussions set off the mines and other traps they were setting up in preparation for the next tactical retreat.

Her Blades fought the charging men back, killing twenty, maybe more, but the damage had been done. They would break with the next attack. A suicide stand might buy another twenty minutes, but that was not something she would even contemplate doing for a Lolofi, no matter how genuine the Little Princess might seem. Fortunately, she was reasonably certain that the Knightlys would accept their surrender. All she had to do was find a way to make the offer.

"We're going to execute a full retreat, all the way back to the gasworks," she said to Sal, the rookie who had somehow become her lieutenant. "We throw a big volley down the hall to drive them back, then we drop all of our weapons and run back there."

Sal shook her head, indicating confusion rather than a rejection of the orders.

"If we quickly retreat all of the way back to the big space just outside the entrance to the gasworks, we can probably set up something there so that the first of the Knightlys to rush in will see that we want to surrender," she explained.

"Surrender?"

The word echoed into an unexpected silence. Almost as if it was on cue, the Knightlys had stopped fighting.

Panic was Dodi's first reaction. She wasn't sure why that would be her first reaction, but it was. The second was disbelief, and the third was stupidity. She stepped around the corner and into the hall. The lull was real. She wasn't shot and there was nothing at the other end to shoot at. She was smart enough not to trust that, but all was quiet, and it stayed that way. It was twenty minutes before they dared send a scouting team down the hall, and it was another twenty before their careful advance through those passages ended with the discovery that the Knightlys had abandoned the utility tunnels.

"Call the Little Princess and let her know that we have repelled the attack and it looks like we can hold the gasworks for as long as needed," Dodi reported to the injured Blade manning what had been the reception desk of administration area. She then spoke to Flint. "And I want you to find out exactly how long she expects us to stay and how the hell she expects us to get all of these engineers and laborers out to the docks for evacuation."

"I think she expects us to stay until the end," Flint said.

"I did not sign my girls up for a suicide mission, and even if I did, I would not let them suffer the cruel, slow death of the Deep!" Dodi screamed as she pointed her pistol at Flint's face. She was so angry that she damn near pulled the trigger. "I followed you into the Deep once and I will not let anyone under my command ever again suffer that horror."

"Wait, wait, I can guarantee that the Little Princess wouldn't ask anyone to agree to a suicide mission!" Flint pleaded.

"It's Willamette on the line," the Blade at the desk said, surprised.

Dodi reached out, expecting to be handed the phone, but the woman at the desk shook her head and said, "She wants to talk to Flint."

Flint made a point of moving very slowly and holding his hands well away from his body, as if he somehow thought he had to make it clear to Dodi that he wasn't going to reach for a weapon when he took the phone.

"Well, hello, Little Princess." Flint listened and nodded. "Yes, our new blue friends seem rather anxious to depart."

Flint chuckled, and then spoke to Dodi.

"Willamette says she has a small transport being paid a princely sum to wait until just after we enter the Deep before they depart. The captain will follow your orders, and she says the ship should have more than enough room for all the Blades, engineers, and workers that are down here."

Dodi lowered her gun.

"She would like you to stay and protect this position for as long as you feel is safe, then escort the engineers and workers to the transport."

Dodi considered that for a few seconds and then nodded her agreement, "The Bluehawk is parked in M23, and our transport in M24. If her transport can land near there, we'd be glad to escort the engineers to the transport."

"Can that transport land near …" Flint chuckled.

Dodi holstered her pistol. "She knew we were in M23, didn't she?"

Flint nodded, listening intently for a few seconds to what he was being told on the phone before he muttered, "Yeah, it makes sense that the City Estate would have a separate and secure air supply. What I don't see is why you want me personally to handle that. I'm sure the engineers would be much more qualified to make sure the air flowing into there …" Flint realized something and shook his head, chuckling. "Oh, wait, now that I said it, I see exactly what you want me to do. You want that air to be set up 'properly,' for the dive into the Deep. That's the whole reason you wanted me down here in the first place, isn't it?"

Willamette handed the phone back to the communications technician and smiled. Ariel thought that looked relieved.

"Commander Lisp, do you have the legal documents I asked the certified officers to draw up?"

"Yes ma'am, one for every habitat in the Commonwealth, grouped and organized exactly as you requested."

"And you are ready to transmit them?"

"Yes ma'am, on your order."

"The order is given, use as many frequencies as you need, transmit them as quickly as you can, but instead of filing the official copies, please give them to Ariel so that she may deposit them with whatever authority she deems appropriate."

"As you wish, ma'am," Lisp said and handed Ariel a thick satchel full of paperwork.

Ariel opened the satchel and read one of the orders aloud. "I, Willamette Persephone Lolofi, as the Chair of The Commonwealth so on and so forth, hereby bequeath sovereignty over the city of Skyborn, along with all associated rights and responsibilities attendant thereof, to the Noble House of Tetley."

"And with a whimper, the Commonwealth ends," Willamette muttered.

Ariel checked the next few orders in the satchel before she said, in disbelief, "You're disbanding the Commonwealth?"

"I know it would be far more dramatic to end this with a fierce battle where the plucky heroine manages to snatch victory from the jaws of certain defeat. And I apologize for being unable to offer you such a story, but we both know those heroic tales are nothing more than fantasies," Willamette said. "The only way to prevent a war over the Commonwealth is to disband it, and the conditions I have placed upon the legal transfer of sovereignty is the only way I can exert any influence over what happens going forward."

"Acceptance of this endowment of sovereignty includes a pledge to faithfully execute all the terms and conditions specified below." Ariel fell silent as she skimmed the conditions and then started shaking her head. "An end to inherited service, a minimum stipend for servants, rights of the impoverished … you can't possibly think any of the families will do any of this."

"After you report that I placed those conditions on the transfer of sovereignty, the intelligent ones will," Willamette said. "Sovereignty is all about people accepting the legitimacy of rule. So, for those who wish to rule the kingdoms and principalities that will spin out of the Commonwealth's ashes, enacting those laws and guaranteeing those rights will provide their citizens with a concrete demonstration of good faith. That will reinforce the symbolic and political value they can derive from the legal transfer of sovereignty, and it should help them fend off challenges to their rule. Refusing to meet those conditions will do the opposite."

"And in the longer term?"

"Hopefully …"

"Hopefully? Hopefully?" Ariel couldn't help but yell. "I'll be the first to admit that I know almost nothing about you, but you just spent half an hour explaining to me how destroying Lightcastle destroys all the tangible sources of influence you might be able to wield. Now, with these orders you are surrendering whatever value there is to be found in your legal and moral authority to rule. That leaves you with zero, absolutely nothing. You will not have the slightest ability whatsoever to influence how this plays out and that's just stupid! What comes next, little girl? Tell me that! What are you going to do after today, after tomorrow?"

Ariel's outburst rattled Willamette, and briefly, her composure faltered.

"For Willamette Lolofi, there is no 'after today,'" she said.

"What in the hell do you mean by that?"

"Lightcastle is only one of the two most obvious fulcrums that someone might use to seize control of the Commonwealth. In fact, conquering the city is the more difficult of the two obvious paths toward that end, and as such scuttling the city has always been my second priority, not my first." Willamette took a deep breath, and Ariel was surprised to see that there were tears in her eyes. "In many ways, capturing me and using my place in the line of succession would be a far simpler means of pursuing control of the Commonwealth which makes me, by far, the most dangerous piece left on the board. I am pleased to have removed Lightcastle from the game. Of the two fulcrums of power that I wished to eliminate, it was by far the more difficult. However, the simple task of removing myself was always the one thing that I absolutely had to do."

"So, the execution you asked me to witness is … yours?" Ariel said that far too loudly. Everyone heard her and the bustle around them vanished.

"Yes, I had you brought here to witness and report the death of Willamette Lolofi." Though Willamette spoke softly, her trembling voice rang out through the cavernous room, hitting everyone like a physical force. The silence that followed broke when her husband dropped the stack of papers in his hands, and the look on his face was yet another part of the tumble down the rabbit hole that Ariel knew she would never quite be able to describe with mere words. Shocked, horrified, hurt, confused, angry, there was neither a word nor a combination of words that could ever hope to capture it. Willamette had hidden that part of her plans from everyone, even from him. Perhaps, especially from him.

"I do hope everyone will forgive me for being relieved that I will be able to extinguish the Lolofi name with some dignity," Willamette said, recovering the air of calm and confidence she had sustained through most of their conversation. "If I had not been able to arrange the scuttling of Lightcastle, I would have been forced to throw myself out of a window or find some other bloody, public, and spectacular way to kill myself. For a brief time, I believed that would be necessary, and I will admit, the horror nearly broke me. Thankfully, however, I can instead descend into the Deep with Lightcastle and in a single act, eliminate both of the fulcrums that could have been used to reforge my family's empire. There is also some symbolic value in the last Lolofi going down with her sinking capital."

"And all these people serving at your side?" Ariel asked. "Here, down at the gasworks, guarding the estate, holding the switchboard for you?"

"You just heard what I said to my delegate in the gasworks, did you not? How could you think that I would not make similar arrangements for the others?" She was offended. "I will need a few to stay until we are well into the Deep, and I hope you will stay with me until that very last group leaves, but please rest assured, I have made the appropriate arrangements so that every single person who wishes to depart, may do so."

"And your husband?"

"I do not know what he will choose to do." She turned to face him, speaking to him. "He may wish to leave. He may wish to reclaim the life stolen from him with our betrothal, but he has once already stood by my side as we descended into the depths of hell, and I could not have found my way back without him. I will understand if this is too much, but the selfish, foolishly romantic girl inside me desperately hopes he will choose to stay by my side again."

The husband nodded. The dumb son of a bitch looked relieved that she was letting him commit suicide with her. There could be no greater testament to the insanity of being ruled by nobles than that pathetically insane pantomime of nobility.

"I have taken extreme care in crafting those orders ceding sovereignty, particularly in terms of what each family will receive." Turning back to speak to Ariel, Willamette returned to her little miss professor voice. "I left the heart of each of the Big 12 family's holdings intact, and I made sure the minor nobles with strong ties to a particular Big 12 family were granted holdings naturally aligning them with those families. However, I did play politics with the way I distributed estates, towns, and cities among the many families who are less than fervent in their loyalties. In doing so, I tried to create a situation which would encourage the Big 12 families to coalesce into three reasonably balanced alliances. The history of Earth, as well as extensive theoretical and mathematical arguments, provide compelling evidence that a triad of competing, self-interested powerbases creates a dynamic of stability that will constrain any wars or fighting that might arise in the near future."

"But how can you be sure it will work?"

"I cannot. However, I am certain this is the best chance there is of preventing the war that Colonel Kofi's failed coup would have unleashed."

Ariel nodded.

"Now, shall we move on to the story you wish to tell?" Willamette asked. "I believe we will have roughly an hour or so before the last of the Signal Corps Officers, and presumably you, will depart for the docks. That hour is yours. However, before we begin, may I ask one last favor of you?"

"Anything," Ariel said, and to her surprise, she sounded like she meant it.

"I know this is vain, but I hope you can find it in your heart to write your story in a way that is kind to the memory of Willamette Lolofi," Willamette said.

"I think that the truth will accomplish that far more effectively than any flattery I might add." Ariel was certain she meant that.

CHAPTER 21

Niven wasn't sure what he expected to find on their journey from the Signal Corps bunker to the City Estate, but it certainly wasn't a scene straight out of a horror story. Like the prototypical tale, it was approaching the dawn of the darkest day. That lonely and quiet time before the first waking hours of the day that started during the forty-eight hours of darkness in the cycle of the Drift was always just a bit eerie, but like in the stories, there was something peculiarly ominous about it that morning. Somehow, just knowing they had dropped below the clouds and were in the Deep made it just a tiny bit more unsettling. Also like the stories, there was an unnatural, haunted feel to the dark and quiet city. None of the typical denizens of the wee hours were about. There were still people to be seen in apartments, and even in a few shops, but there were no police on patrol, no waitresses on their way to work the breakfast shift, no bakers making their way home from their night's work, no young men or women furtively sneaking home from a lover's bed. The streets were abandoned. Of course, the only reason that he, Az, and Willamette were on those streets was precisely because they expected the streets to be abandoned, but still, it was creepy.

Flooding the dome with CO_2 had not only displaced most of the air that served as a lifting gas, it had also made the air in the dome unbreathable, and that eliminated almost any worry they might have about their safety. While breathers were common pieces of kit in the Drift, especially on ships and around docks, they weren't the sort of thing everyone had access to, or that most people knew how to use. They were also far less useful than the comic books and stories might suggest. Tanks were heavy, which made it difficult to carry more than a few hours' worth of air around. That made it nearly impossible to engage in anything other than brief, well-planned and well-coordinated actions, and even then, you had to be wary of accidents and equipment failures. It simply wasn't smart to stray more than a few hundred meters from a reliable resupply depot or a stash of extra tanks. So even the people who could get to them and knew how to use them, such as the soldiers, were unlikely to be on the streets.

Niven also hadn't expected Willamette to be so upset about the zoo, but once she made that first little exclamation of dismay, he was unsurprised by it. Perhaps he was starting to get to know her. Despite all his worries over her coded orders and secrets, he had never lost his belief in her, and she had validated his faith.

"Oh, those poor, precious animals," Willamette said.

"It's too late to do anything about it," Niven said, his voice echoing back at him from inside the breather.

"I know, but I should have thought of them," she said. "I thought about how flooding the city with carbon dioxide would drive the armies out. I even thought about how it would help preserve the art in the museums and the books in the libraries, but it never occurred to me to worry about what it would do to the animals in the zoo."

"The animals would not have suffered unduly," Az said. "They would have fallen asleep well before the worst of the effects."

"And what about all the people still in the city?" Willamette asked, bitterly. "They will suffer horrendously. The air in many of those buildings will last for several hours, if not days, which means it will be the madness that kills them."

"So, you've noticed them," Az said, disappointed and worried.

"Yes, I have," Willamette snapped. "And given how many I have seen staring out windows, any reasonable guess would suggest there are thousands of people still in the city. Also, what about the woman with the breather who is following us?"

"I am impressed that you noticed her," Az said. "She has been doing a pretty good job of hiding."

"What kind of fate have I imposed upon her?" Willamette asked. "How will she die?"

"If she gets any closer, she will be killed by a dart from my rifle," Az said.

"Willamette, you did everything you possibly could," Niven said.

"Did I?" Willamette asked. "Have I truly done everything I possibly could for them?"

"Oh god, I don't like that tone," Niven said.

"Hey!" Willamette stopped, turned, and shouted, "You, the woman who is following us. Please join us and walk with us. We will protect you."

"This is not a good idea," Niven said.

"I agree," Az said. "This is foolish and dangerous."

Niven kept his pistol at the ready as the woman with the breather stepped out of the shadows and slowly, warily approached them. At first, Niven thought he was just being overprotective of Willamette, but the moment he got a good look at the woman, he was certain he hadn't been worried enough. Something about her bothered him.

She was obviously a prostitute. She wore a short-skirted sequined dress that had seen some rough times, as had the torn fishnet gartered stockings. She also wore tons of gaudy plastic jewelry, and she was carrying the big shoulder bag they all seemed to carry around with them. What she was, however, wasn't what bothered him. Prostitutes were a normal part of nearly every port district in the Drift, and if you didn't learn to accept that you would be seeing and occasionally talking to them, you simply weren't going to make it in any business related to cutting the Drift. Still, there was something about this woman that felt wrong. Women who had to sell themselves to survive always had a toughness to them, but it was the sort of toughness a person earned by enduring the cruelties of a rough life. The tough edge to this woman felt menacing, her movements aggressive, predatory. Willamette didn't seem to notice any of that, but Az did, and she made sure the prostitute knew it.

"Drop the bag." Az gestured threateningly with her rifle. "Now."

The woman looked dismayed and shook her head.

"Az," Willamette scolded.

"Not negotiable, Little Princess," Az shot back. "If she wants to walk anywhere near you, the bag goes."

Willamette and Az exchanged cold glares, but not even Willamette was going to outstubborn Az and she knew it.

"Fine," Willamette huffed.

"Ditch the bag or bugger off." Az again gestured with the rifle.

The woman dropped the bag and it hit the ground with a disconcertingly heavy, soft thump.

"Now lift the skirt and show me that you don't have a little gut-cutter hidden in those garters."

Niven looked away as the woman lifted her skirt. She must have been carrying a small knife because he heard the snap of elastic against skin and then the clatter of the knife landing on the street.

"Okay, we're walking to the City Estate," Az said. "You lead the way. Five paces out front."

They resumed their walk. It wasn't much farther. The zoo was on the edge of the park that surrounded the City Estate.

"I think we need to invite everyone who remains in the city to join us at the City Estate," Willamette said.

"That is a really bad idea," Niven and Az said in unison.

"I can't just let them die," Willamette shot back, stubbornly.

"You gave them every possible chance you could," Niven said. "You brought in all those transport ships, and you gave them over two hours before you flooded the dome, and there's still good air flowing to the docks, subways and utility tunnels."

"But so many still didn't make it," Willamette said.

"And you should ask why they chose not to take advantage of what you provided," Az said.

"Perhaps they were unable," Willamette said, bitchy.

"It's too late to save the people who were physically unable to evacuate when given a clear and open route to the docks," Az said, sharply. "They will be unable to make it across the city now that the air has gone toxic. Which means the only people who might respond to an offer to join you at the City Estate will be the ones who chose not to evacuate when given the chance."

"I cannot just let them die," Willamette said, with a finality that left no doubt the conversation was over.

Az gestured at Niven, a plea for him to stop his stubborn wife from doing something so foolish.

"Do you honestly think she'd listen to me any more than she's listening to you?" Niven asked, sarcastic.

Willamette seemed to think that was funny.

"I think we'd better up our pace and get ourselves into some good air," Niven said. "That sounded a lot like a giggle."

"Agreed, I'm starting to feel the madness myself," Az said.

Willamette was also starting to worry about the madness. When they reached the side entrance to the ancient mansion that was the City Estate, there was a delay while Az orchestrated their entry and that irritated Willamette immeasurably. She knew that her irritation was unreasonable, but just like the giggle, it was undeniable.

The City Estate did not have any air locks, but it did maintain a slightly positive pressure to prevent gas infiltration when people entered and exited, so there was a gentle and cool rush of air as Willamette stepped in through the small door that served as the working entrance for government officials. She took several deep breaths of the neon and oxygen air that Flint had arranged for the estate. It was probably just an illusion, but it felt like that cleared her head immeasurably.

She would not say that it felt like she was returning home. The wide-open spaces, intricately manicured gardens, and magnificent buildings of the Lolofi Estate had always been her home, but she had spent a lot of time living in the City Estate, so there was a certain hominess to be found. As a young child she had played under the feet of kings and diplomats in its halls. She had dropped things down the center of the big spiral staircase just to watch them fall. She had explored every nook and cranny, including all the forbidden, secret, and secure places. She had been allowed to be a child in the building and that meant something to her, but those memories were also tarnished by the way her whims had shifted as she grew older. She had imposed upon even the highest-ranking officials to ask pestering questions about how things worked. She had shadowed her father as he tried to work. She had behaved as if she was being trained to rule. It had still been quite childish, but somehow playing at working in the building had made it feel less like a home. By the time she had been given some modest but notable diplomatic responsibilities, and a small office on the second floor, everything about the City Estate had become about work, duty, and responsibilities, and the feeling of hominess had faded to little more than a memory.

"I believe I have worked this out," Willamette said. "As you said, the subway and utility tunnels still have good air, and even though the City Estate is not connected to any of them, the Council Hall is, and the Council Hall is less than fifty meters from that door over there."

"Little Princess ..." Az tried to interrupt.

"I have to believe anyone who can get to the Council Hall through the subway or utility tunnels can cross fifty meters of paved walkway while holding their breath," Willamette said. "All we will have to do is unlock the door and let people know how to get here."

"And how do you intend to let people know?" Az asked. "The Blades abandoned the central switchboard over an hour ago."

"The City Estate's security office can send alarms and messages through the civil defense system." Willamette was prepared for that question. "It will not reach every intercom and phone in the city like the messages I sent through the central switchboard, but most people will be able to hear it."

"I beg you to reconsider this foolishness," Az said as she began opening doors off the hall to check for threats.

"Those people will die if I do nothing," Willamette said.

"And we will die if you persist with this!" Az shot back. "Ask yourself why a person who was otherwise capable of evacuating would choose not to and then think! Some will have stayed because they are suicidal or otherwise mentally deranged and that will make them dangerous. Others will have stayed because they were unable to bear the thought of leaving homes, businesses, or other assets that define their lives or their livelihoods. They will be furious with you for destroying that, and that will make them dangerous. Others would rather die than suffer the misery of life as a refugee, and again, they will be angry at you for destroying Lightcastle and again, that will make them dangerous. Pick any reason for staying and it will lead to people who wish you dead. This is a secure compound, meant to serve as a refuge, but if you throw open the doors to those people, we will be killed."

Willamette considered what Az had said. She was not stupid, and she knew that there was a tremendous difference between persistence and just being stubborn.

"It tortures me to admit I cannot save those people, but you are right, Az." Willamette felt physically ill as she spoke. "We will stick to the plan."

Az nodded.

Willamette turned to the prostitute and said, "The main kitchen is through the dining room, just down the hall on the right. Beyond that there are the servants' locker rooms, the laundry and all the rest. Why don't you grab yourself a uniform or something else clean to wear and a shower?"

The woman hesitated, oddly, reluctantly.

"That life is over now." Willamette gestured at the woman's dress. "I do not expect you to be my servant. The uniform is nothing more than a way to offer you some clean clothes. Combined with a shower, I believe that will be an excellent first step toward whatever you will choose to make of your new life; do you not agree?"

Without any hint of thankfulness, the woman turned and strode down the hall.

"I'm glad you reconsidered," Az said to Willamette.

"I suspect I will be thankful you convinced me, but please forgive me if I find it troubling," Willamette said. "Although, I have to admit I am relieved to know those doors will remain locked, and that I can just feel safe for however long we stay down here."

"You should heed your own advice," Az said. "Nothing is urgent at this point. I would think a shower and change of clothes signifying your first step into a new life would be an appropriate indulgence."

Willamette had several far more urgent things to which she needed to attend, but Az did not give her the chance to object.

"And I believe that the first time a husband and wife enter their bedroom together, it is traditional to allow him to carry you through the doorway," Az said pointedly, giving Willamette just the tiniest hint of a smirk.

Regardless of Kala's deranged state of mind, she was perfectly suited to the task of punishing Willamette Lolofi. As a Blade, she had been trained to carry out exactly this kind of covert operation. It also helped that she was looking forward to dying, which she was just then realizing had always been the end point of her quest for atonement.

Once she was in the kitchen and out of sight, she broke into a run. Willamette had foolishly given her ample time and space to act, but there was a tremendous amount she had to accomplish in however long Az would allow for a shower and change of clothes. Inflicting pain and suffering on those who had sinned was important, but first and foremost, she had to ensure that Willamette was killed. The odds were that Kala would accomplish that directly by torturing her, but Az had stupidly offered her former trainee the perfect way to create a backup up plan out of nothing.

Regardless of who designed a security system, the purposes that all security systems had to serve led them to converge on one of a few variations. For a government installation such as the City Estate, it would include a central command-and-control center which would be housed in a securable and hardened location inside of the building. It wouldn't be the on the ground floor, which was dominated by the formal and ceremonial parts of the complex. Instead, it would make sense to put it up or down a floor, and next to a stairway. Up made the most sense. That would allow security personnel to stay between the public areas below and the private areas above.

There was nothing at the top of the first flight of steps other than a small kitchen and a staging area for the servants who attended the people working in the offices, but just off the stairs on the next floor up there was an armored door with a combination lock. That had to be it.

It both irritated and pleased Az that Willamette was so easily manipulated into hauling Niven off to bed. The girl's utter failure to care that she was being manipulated was a worry, and it irritated Az to think she would have to correct that, but she was pleased it had been so quick and easy. Locking the Little Princess away in a secure room for an hour or two was the most efficient way to make sure she stayed safe while Az checked to ensure that the City Estate was indeed clear of threats. Just because the Homeguard had been ordered to secure the facility before departing, that did not necessarily mean the compound was empty or safe.

Having surreptitiously trailed behind Willamette and Niven as they fondled, giggled, and teased their way up to what was now their apartment, Az had already worked her way back down through the two residential floors at the top of the West Wing and was on her way down to the private offices situated on the next floor down. She had spotted some evidence of opportunistic thievery, but for the most part the estate was in perfect order. It would not be too long before she could indulge in a shower of her own.

It was in that hopeful moment that the distinctive wail of a civil defense siren hit Az like a kick in the gut. Even before the message that followed, the obvious piece fell into place: the prostitute. She had all but forgotten about the prostitute.

"Willamette Lolofi must be punished for her crimes." A woman's voice resonated with the strange echo of something broadcast loudly through countless speakers spread across a huge area. "She is in the City Estate. The doors are now unlocked, and she is unguarded."

The alert and message repeated as Az ran down two flights of stairs. With her injured leg, just walking down stairs had been difficult; running was reckless, painful, and dangerous. She felt the stitches tear apart, again, and the strength of the leg was consumed by pain. Fortunately, when her leg gave way she was just two steps up from a landing. She crashed hard onto the landing and into the wall, but she didn't tumble down any stairs and she was back up and moving in a moment, though she was moving much slower. On the ground floor she pushed her limping run as fast as she could down the hall and through the kitchen, but when she burst into the servants' area beyond the kitchen, it was not the prostitute she found.

"Ida, Polly, what in the hell are you two doing here?" Az demanded, swinging the aim of her rifle away from the two girls.

Ida jumped back and then looked guilty and scared, but she thought through her response carefully. She thought it through too carefully, and too slowly.

"Ida!"

"We're stealing stuff." Ida opened her rucksack and showed the contents to Az. It looked like tableware. "It's okay, Em said we could steal as long as we did it properly this time."

"We will talk about that later, young lady," Az said. "There is a time and a place for stealing and this is neither."

Ida bowed her head.

"Did either of you see a woman in a sequined dress?"

Both girls shook their heads.

"Run away if you do. She's extremely dangerous."

Both girls nodded.

"Now get back down to the Drunken Monkey!" Az shouted. Not bothering to make sure they obeyed, she turned and ran back into the kitchen and up the servants' staircase. Up was far easier on her wounded leg than down. She found the security office and the moment she saw the combination lock on the outer door another piece fell into place. She had let the prostitute stand where she could watch Willamette use her emergency code to open the door locks when they entered the building.

"Son of a bitch I should have thought of that," she shouted at the door.

Az considered trying to get into the office to shut down the alert or relock all the doors to the building, but she dismissed those thoughts almost as soon as they arose. She had a much more significant and much more immediate concern. Up more stairs, she reached the top floor of the building and there, just as she had feared, she found the woman in the sequined dress.

Unfortunately, Az had arrived just a few seconds too late. The woman already had a fistful of Willamette's hair and was dragging her away from a bloody-nosed Niven.

"Niven, stay in there!" Az shouted, raising her rifle and taking aim. "Last thing I need is you getting in my way."

"Hello Az," the woman said, putting the muzzle of her pistol to Willamette's temple as she pulled the disheveled and nearly naked Little Princess another step down the hall.

"God damn it, Little Princess! You couldn't just stay in the goddamn locked room for a couple of hours?"

"I have the code to relock the doors!" Willamette shouted, adding a gesture and using that movement to disguise the shifting of her feet. She gave Az a pointed look and Az knew what she was thinking. It was a very bad idea, but before Az could say or do anything, the woman in the sequined dress angrily yanked Willamette's head back and forth, getting a wince from Willamette.

"Don't even try it, little bitch," the woman hissed.

"You were a Blade, weren't you?" Az aimed the rifle. The rifle would constrain what the woman could do, but it would do little more than that. She was positioning Willamette perfectly to use her as a shield.

"Some would say I still am," the woman said. "Unlike you, I have stayed true to my sisters."

"Willamette pledged to help us," Az said. "Our sisters chose to fight and die to help her, and with their assistance, she has accomplished more than we could have ever hoped. She ended the Commonwealth. She erased the Lolofi name from the Drift, and she gave us a damn good chance of limiting or even avoiding a war."

"She may have fooled you, but I see her for what she is." The woman's voice rang with evangelical fervor. "She is a crime against humanity. To kill so many, to steal the pasts and the futures of so many people by scuttling this city, that is nothing less than evil. If I am to be redeemed, I must make her suffer a punishment that equals her crime."

Az wracked her brain, trying desperately to remember the woman's name or any other personal detail she might be able to use for leverage. It was hopeless. Even if she had been good with names, and even if she had trained the girl, there had been so many, and she so rarely worked directly with them. She remembered only a fraction of them.

"Yeah, you know what she's in for, don't you, Az?" The former Blade's eyes were wide with a hideously twisted kind of glee as she kept backing down the hall. "I'll start with a little pain to get her attention and then I'll add something to get her mind running, because like you taught me, torture is all in the mind, isn't it, Az?"

That rang a bell. There weren't that many of the younger Blades who had been trained in interrogation techniques.

"I think disfigurement is the best way to get into the head of Morden Lolofi's precious little princess, don't you?" the former Blade asked, more to taunt Willamette than anything else. "That has to be the nightmare of someone who was born and bred to prance around in fancy gowns, but I can't overdo that first cut, can I? If I ruin her too quickly, she might shut down, so it has to be something she can almost hide, like a finger. No, an ear."

Az was at a loss for what to do. She could probably keep her former pupil talking for a while, but that wouldn't shift the course of events. It wasn't all that far to the door of the next apartment; a door Az had left open after inspecting it. Once the woman got Willamette in there and got the door locked, it would be hours before Az would be able to cut, chop, or bust her way in. They all knew that, just like they all knew that Az would have to try the rifle before she let that happen.

The rifle was designed to prioritize rate of fire over accuracy, so at best Az figured there was only a 10 percent chance of killing the woman without killing Willamette, but even if the dart went through Willamette first, dying quickly would be a mercy compared to the cruelties that waited for her behind a locked door.

"What do you think, Az? Should I cut the ear off bit by bit, or should I crush and mangle it?" the woman asked, cackling as she flicked at Willamette's ear with the muzzle of the pistol. "I think I should mangle it. If I cut it off, it's gone but if I mangle it, I can come back to it and burn it, and then cut it off. That's how Kofi liked to do it. Isn't it? Smash, burn, cut. Smash, burn, cut."

"No!" a little girl shrieked as a pistol fired.

The eyes of the woman in the sequined dress went wide and Willamette lurched like she had been kicked in the back. They both fell, and the former Blade landed heavily on Willamette. The woman pushed herself up to her knees and raised her pistol, but didn't point it at anything. Instead, she looked down at the arterial blood surging out of the little exit wound below her ribs. She was falling to the side, but she seemed completely unaware of it. She didn't react in any way, she just hit the floor.

Ida and Polly stood behind the fallen woman, both of them wide-eyed and trembling. Flint's pistol was in Ida's hands. She looked pleadingly at Az and shrieked, "She was going to hurt Lady Willamette!"

"I know, Ida," Az said softly, gesturing for the girl to calm down.

The woman in the sequined dress shuddered as she died. Ida shrieked again and shot her again.

"Ida, drop the pistol and you and Polly get back to the ship," Az said, softly but commandingly. "Go, fast, but don't run."

Ida nodded but didn't move. She was staring at Willamette's bloody back, horrified.

"Ida, you did nothing wrong, but you need to get safe," Az said, and when Ida still hesitated, she shouted, "Ida! Drop that pistol and go!"

Ida didn't drop the pistol, but she did pick up her rucksack and run toward Az. Az thought she was running toward her for comfort, but she ran past and down the hall. It took a glare from Az before Polly rushed to follow her. The route to the escape hangar must have been down that direction, which made sense. You would want to be able to get to it from the family's private residences.

"Niven, my love," Willamette whimpered, gasping and sobbing as she reached out to Niven.

Niven rushed to her, dropping to his knees as he took her hand.

Az rushed over as well, even though she knew there was nothing she could do. Unless you happened to be near a surgeon, shots to the torso were usually either fatal or they weren't. It all depended on what the dart hit.

"We almost made it through," Willamette whispered, teary.

"Almost," Niven whispered back.

Az inspected Willamette's back. There was a tremendous amount of blood. None of it was Willamette's, but there was still a lot of blood.

"Please, do not let the future we lost harden your heart," Willamette said, breathy, whimpering, and dramatic. "Treasure the moments we stole from our cruel and unkind destiny and carry on. You can find the way to escape the tragedy which will consume the world, I know you can."

Willamette gasped as Az yanked the dart out of her back. Now she was bleeding a little, but the emphasis had to be on how little. At worst, the dart had penetrated far enough to poke at the cartilage between her ribs.

"I feel cold," Willamette said. "Hold me. I want to die in your arms."

"You know, the whole Little Princess thing is unpleasantly tolerable, but I draw the damn line at drama queen." Az shoved the pistol dart in front of Willamette's nose.

Willamette shook her head, confused.

"Little darts from little pistols don't pack much of a punch to begin with, and after you shoot one clean through someone's aorta, they aren't going to do much more than bruise and scratch," Az said. "You'll need a bandage, maybe a stitch."

Willamette looked confused, incredulous, embarrassed, stunned, and hopeful all at once.

"Get up, woman," Az huffed. "I'm hurt worse than you are."

"It felt like I had been struck by a harpoon fired from a cannon." Willamette gingerly sat up and paused to make sure she was going to live before shaking her head. She was angry and embarrassed. "The impact was tremendous, and the pain overwhelming. The pain is still quite substantial."

"Pain is usually a sign that a wound's not too bad," Az said, pointing at her own leg. "The bad ones send you straight into shock. You hardly feel a thing until later. If it hurts when it happens, it's seldom all that traumatic."

"I feel quite stupid," Willamette said.

"Good," Az said, drolly. "Perhaps that means you will prepare a better speech for the next time you die."

"It is not a good sign when the woman I hired to protect me tells me I should prepare my last words, is it?" Willamette asked Niven with exaggerated concern.

Az smiled and lifted Willamette to her feet. The girl winced again but that was it. Despite the melodrama, she was a tough one.

"Now run, get yourself cleaned up, and both of you get dressed," Az said. "I want you on your way down to the Drunken Monkey in five minutes."

"No. We shall stick to the plan. All we have to do is relock the doors," Willamette protested.

Az nodded at the woman in the sequined dress. "I trained her, so I'm certain she would have sabotaged whatever system there is that might allow us to easily return this compound to a state of lockdown."

"We should try," Willamette insisted.

"You two get dressed. I'll go see if it can be done."

Willamette accepted that and strode into her apartment with as much dignity and nobility as a nearly naked woman could have possibly managed.

Az never discovered the extent of the sabotage. As soon as she reached the spiral stairway at the center of the estate, she heard angry, belligerent voices echoing up from below. It didn't sound like many, but it would only take a few to be more than she could fight off and who knew how many more might enter before she could get things locked down again. The building was already lost. All she could do was bar the doors to the family's apartments to ensure that they had ample time to make their escape.

For the most part, the escape was uneventful. Willamette and Niven were dressed and ready well before five minutes had passed. The only delay was a brief wait for Willamette to pack a suitcase, which turned into three, but she still accomplished that with tolerable haste. The secret door was hidden at the end of the hall, behind a floor-to-ceiling mirror. It was thick and heavily reinforced, as was the door to the bunker under the City Estate. On the lowest level of the bunker, another hidden and hefty door opened to the stairway leading down to the secret hanger. Once all three of those doors were behind them, closed and bolted, Az believed it was safe to relax. She sent Willamette and Niven on ahead so she could take her time and favor her injured leg as she worked her way down the seemingly endless staircase. The only surprise she came across on the way down was the little girl who was heading back up.

Az made some noise just to make sure Ida knew she was coming. There was no way of telling if Ida still had a pistol, and if she did, the last thing Az wanted to do was startle her. Curiously, alerting Ida to her presence sent the girl scurrying down a flight of stairs to hide under a table at one of the many rest and refreshment stations set up along the way down to the emergency escape hangar.

Az stopped at the rest station, took a bottle of water, and sat on one of the benches. The water was warm, and it tasted like the bottle, but like stopping to sit on that bench, it was something she needed more than she had expected. Ida was also far more patient than expected. She seemed determined to hide for as long as it took.

"Well, Ida, I believe that this is where the two of us are supposed have some kind of heartfelt conversation," Az said.

"Do we have to?" Ida asked.

"No, we don't have to," Az said. "I could tell you to haul your little butt back down to the Drunken Monkey and you could just do that."

"I can't," Ida said. "I'm dangerous. Em said so."

"Well, you are indeed dangerous," Az said. "But that doesn't have to be a bad thing."

"Yes, it does." Ida crawled out from under the table, her eyes down, her shoulders hunched. "'Cause I'm bad."

"You are not bad, Ida," Az said sternly.

"It wasn't like before," Ida said. "No one made me kill that sparkly lady."

"That's not true," Az said. "That woman made you kill her."

Ida frowned, unconvinced.

"Sit." Az patted the bench.

Ida shook her head.

"I said sit!" Az barked.

Ida scrambled to sit.

"Ida, there is no such thing as good or bad. There is only better or worse," Az said. "The woman in the sequined dress gave you a choice between shooting her or letting her torture Willamette to death. No matter how annoying the Little Princess might be, I think we can both agree that you shooting the woman was better than letting her hurt Willamette like she threatened, right?"

Ida nodded.

"So, you were forced to make a hard choice between two bad things, and you chose the better one, and you know what, that is what life is, trying to make the better choice."

"This is starting to sound a whole lot like a heartfelt conversation," Ida said, annoyed.

"Well, that's your own damn fault, isn't it? You could have just made the better choice of hauling your little butt back down to the Drunken Monkey when I told you to."

"Maybe this is better." Ida leaned against Az. "I needed to sit down for a rest anyway. I've gone all the way up and down these stairs twice already and my feet hurt something horrible."

Az put her arm around the girl, and they rested while they debated what exactly constituted a heartfelt conversation.

EPILOGUE

Standing at the back of the helm, holding a little hand that Ida had somehow managed to make both sticky and slimy, Az watched Em and Flint work their way through a standard assisted launch as the sunrise brought light to the Drift.

"You two really should be strapped in," Flint said, again.

"We're practicing balance," Ida said. "Balance is the foundation of control. Control is the foundation of choice. Choice is the foundation of life."

"Well, that karate voodoo is all well and good, but when you two fall down and break your heads, you just remember that it was your own damn fault for not strapping in," Flint said.

Flint spun a couple of dinner plate–sized control wheels, and somewhere below and behind where Az stood, valves opened. She could hear the rush of high-pressure gas being unleashed as nitrogen flowed to the lift cells in the wings.

A few seconds later a tiny wiggle under her feet was followed by an upward push as Em pulled back on the control yoke. Em was using the aero lift from the flow of the Drift over the town to quickly fly them up and through the zone where a twist of turbulence could smash them back down into the dock. Em held them at about thirty meters above the dock for several seconds while Flint fiddled with knobs and control wheels.

"Float's good," Flint said. "Let me know how the balance feels once we're underway. Not sure about having all the lift cells repaired properly like this. It's kind of strange."

"It's unnatural," Em said. She gave the ship a tiny side-to-side test of the controls before she said, "Cut the cord."

"Cutting the cord." Flint pulled a lever, releasing the clamp that held the cable from the dock's landing winch.

The Drunken Monkey surged upward and backward. Ida clenched Az's hand tighter, but she didn't make a noise and she didn't lean on that grip for balance.

"I'm going to miss Polly," Ida said.

"She's gone to a better place," Az said.

"She's gone to a better place?" Flint muttered. "Uh … Az, what exactly did you mean when you said we needed to 'put Polly down' on Faust's Reward?"

"She has been enrolled in their small business academy," Az said. "Willamette assures me that it will be the perfect place for a girl with a light head and a heavy purse."

"Speaking of Willamette, where did the Little Princess go?" Em asked.

"Where do you think she went?" Flint muttered.

"Those two …" Em huffed. "They just got out of bed a half hour ago."

"Those two are acting exactly like newlyweds should," Flint said. "And you damn well know that you're just as bad when you get your hands on someone new."

"Yeah," Em admitted. "But it's her turn to cook."

"About that," Flint said. "I know you mean well with this cooking rotation thing, but I think we should put some serious thought into teaching Willamette to cook before we let her cook anything."

"But …"

"Do you honestly think that the Little Princess has ever cooked anything in her entire life?" Flint asked. "Anything at all?"

"Probably not," Em admitted.

"And may I presume that you will not be making the argument that a woman is born with an innate ability to cook," Flint teased.

"Fine, you can teach her how to cook first, but you're on the hook for her meals until you get that sorted," Em said.

"Hey little one, how about we cook some breakfast?" Flint turned and asked Ida.

"Cookies?" Ida asked, pleading.

"You made cookies for breakfast yesterday," Flint said. "Which reminds me, we also need to teach you how to cook something other than cookies."

Az gave Flint a smile as he stepped past her to climb up into the main cabin. He looked surprised, but he returned the smile and gave her a wink before he chased Ida up the ladder and made a racket helping her cook breakfast.

Az took a slow, deep breath, closed her eyes, and invited the sensations of the world to fill her.

"You know, that whole serene, 'I'm one with the world' thing of yours makes me want to just smack you upside the head," Em grumbled, snarky.

"I would advise against that," Az said.

"I would advise against that," Em mocked her, childishly.

"You are welcome to join Ida and me in the exercises," Az said.

"I might," Em said. "You know, just to help Ida feel like it's a good thing to do."

"I'm sure she'd appreciate that," Az said.

Em shifted the rising ship into a gentle gliding turn to starboard.

"Us helping Willamette turned out to be a good thing, right?" Em asked. She sounded distressed. "I mean the scale of it, sinking Lightcastle and all of that; it gives me nightmares."

"I'm sure that when Willamette decides to crawl out of bed long enough to read the newspapers we retrieved for her, she will be upset by how badly she overestimated the intelligence and rationality of the nobles," Az said. "There is a lot of fighting, and some of it is extreme, but for the most part, her effort to manipulate the broader political context appears to have had the desired effect. It doesn't look like any of those irrational nobles have been stupid enough to make any real effort to seize control of the Commonwealth, or even try to hold it together. So, she appears to have prevented a massive and protracted war, and in that accomplishment, I believe we should all be pleased."

Em levelled the ship, ending the slow turn. "Take Flint's seat and I'll teach you how to pop and set the kite."

"I could fetch Flint for you."

"No, I asked you," Em said. "Flint and I decided that everyone on this crew needs to learn all the basics. You know, for when one of the Little Princess's crazy-as-hell schemes ends up getting a bunch of us killed."

"That seems prudent." Az sat in the rigger's seat, secured the lap belt, and smiled. The idea of being a part of a shambolic menagerie felt good, very good, and Az let the moment flow through her. The moment filled her even as it slid into the past to make way for the next, which was how it should be. Moments were not meant to be isolated. They were not meant to be captured. They were not even meant to be defined. They were meant to be experienced. They were meant to be lived.

"And there's that damn 'I'm one with the world' smug little smile again," Em huffed, teasing.

ACKNOWLEDGMENTS

Despite the lack of any solid ground in the Drift, this is a story with some very deep roots. It began with the research of Geoffrey A. Landis and his commentary about colonizing the Venusian atmosphere, which transformed what had seemed like an outlandish idea into what became the Drift. Comments that Peter Thompson and Steven Barnes offered on martial arts might have seemed like innocent conversations, but they helped me bring critical aspects of key characters, particularly Az, to life. Geoff Husson read the screenplay that was first version of the story, and like a good friend-producer-director, he sent me back to the drawing board to rethink pretty much everything.

David M. Potter and Jean-Sébastien Rioux generously agreed to give the typo-laden monstrosity that I called a first draft a read, and Art Protin added several valuable comments before Bob Mecoy read it and insisted that I needed more. Liz McLay's editing helped bring that bigger story together and Art returned for an encore reading, not only confirming that more was indeed the right way to go, but also tracking down several typos. Iain Morrison hunted down a few more typos, and Lee Murray went above and beyond the call of duty, helping me with one last edit before I handed it off to the publisher. It is impossible to express just how thankful I am to have so many friends who are so eager to help.

And none of that would matter without a family that puts up with the thousands of hours that go into writing a novel like this, Wendy, Tabitha, Jensen, Samantha. They long ago learned that I never mean it when I say, "I'm almost done," and they still put up with me.

ABOUT THE AUTHOR

Douglas A. Van Belle is an author and screenwriter, and winner of New Zealand's prestigious Sir Julius Vogel Award. His recent work includes science fiction novels *The Barking Death Squirrels*, *The Care and Feeding of Your Lunatic Mage*, and the YA title *The Kahutahuta*.

He spends his days as a Senior Lecturer at Victoria University of Wellington, New Zealand, where his research includes the politics of crises and the role of science fiction in society, which are related in surprising ways. Also an artisan bladesmith, he is a passionate advocate for the therapeutic value of playing with fire and pounding the living daylights out of white-hot steel.

Email: doug.vanbelle@outlook.com

IF YOU LIKED ...

IF YOU LIKED A WORLD ADRIFT, YOU MIGHT ALSO ENJOY:

Whistling Past the Graveyard by Kevin J. Anderson
Dr. Alien by Rajnar Vajra
Today I Remember by Martin L. Shoemaker

Our list of other WordFire Press authors and titles is always growing. To find out more and shop our selection of titles, visit us at:
wordfirepress.com

www.ingramcontent.com/pod-product-compliance
Lightning Source LLC
Chambersburg PA
CBHW030228120726
47903CB00005B/1410